THE
UNIVERSE
IS A SMALL PLACE

THE
UNIVERSE
IS A SMALL PLACE

RJ AMOS

Chapter One

The captain stood in front of the large IGP logo, the symbol of the intergalactic police, and looked over the bridge of his stellar cruiser with satisfaction. The atmosphere was quiet and alert. It was a small ship, just a crew of fifty. They had a job to do, but right now, the job required a lot of waiting. The captain had heard of crews like his losing their discipline, lazing around, eating junk and playing games as they waited for the signal and forgetting they had been trained to work like a well-oiled machine. He was not about to let that happen to his crew.

He clasped his hands behind his back and nodded approvingly. This was a work ship. There was no question. The grey walls were sparkling clean. Not a hint of corrosion. Not a piece of rubbish in any corner. The lights and dials on the consoles were all in good working order. All ready for action.

Not a crease was out of place on the grey uniforms of the five officers under his command on the bridge. Each was at their station, alert and waiting. There was no playing children's games on the ship's computer. No mucking about. No extraneous conversation.

They had criminals to apprehend. Each offender on the list had somehow escaped capture or broken bond and was hiding somewhere in this vast universe. They told him that some were just missing persons, but really, who would go to such great effort to hide if they hadn't done something wrong? No, he knew he was tracking miscreants, no matter what his superiors said, and he was going to treat them as such when he got them. And he would get them.

In the past, as a junior officer he'd had to follow the orders of his superiors and, to his mind, stupidly criss-cross the universe to find these criminals. So much effort had been wasted, especially since he wasn't allowed to give them the clip around the ear that they needed. If he'd just been allowed to … anyway, things had improved. These probes had cut down on the travel at least. He was no longer heading to the last planet the miscreant was seen to find that they had moved away ten star rotations ago. No more talking to dirty informants who reeked of the low-grade alcohol they used to prop up their self esteem. No more rewards given to ingrates who really didn't deserve anything.

He remembered with disgust having to give a smelly, slimy rat enough credits to kill himself on drink so that he would give up the information, 'I'm sure it was him,' he slurred. 'In the back corner of the hangar, taking a pod. They say he's gone in the direction of Centuri Zeta.'

And when you got to Zeta, you would lose even more credits to find out that the criminal had now disappeared in the opposite direction. It had all been such a stupid waste of time. In the captain's opinion the informing rat should have been arrested too. Once he was in the cells he would have told them what they needed to know. The universe was much better without those idiots in it. They should all be locked up. Zero tolerance was the way to go. He just wished he could convince the powers that be, but they wouldn't listen. Trying to get his superiors to see sense had been a waste of time. Too gentle they were, too merciful. He just didn't understand it.

But now, now things were better. Now he'd graduated from lieutenant, to major, to captain of his own ship. Now he made the decisions and didn't have to tolerate the crazies anymore. And these probes helped too, when they finally–

'Sir?'

His musings were interrupted.

'Sir, the probe for criminal 13-L-67-CG has activated.'

He blinked a few times, bringing himself back to the present. He straightened his shoulders, and went to look at the screen where a small blue pixel had now turned to a flashing red.

'Very good. Which sector?'

'Sector 378, one of the smaller suns. He's really gone to the back-blocks to hide.' There was a snigger in the officer's voice. This was the attitude that started the rebellion in the ranks. The captain would not stand for useless chatter on the bridge. What those under his command did in their own time, well, he didn't want to know. But in his presence …

'I don't require your opinion. Just state the facts,' he barked directly into the underling's face.

Discipline. That was what was needed.

'Sorry, Sir. Sector 378, Region H92, Sir,' the officer shouted in reply.

This was it. Technology had come through. The time of waiting was over.

'Set coordinates. Sector 378, region H92,' he called to the pilot.

'Coordinates set, Sir.'

'Launch.'

'Set for launch, Sir.'

The ship's crew leaped into action. Announcements rang around the corridors. The tension eased as each of the police officers attended to their tasks. There was a tightly restrained sense of rejoicing. The time of waiting for the probe signal had been almost unbearable. But now, now they could do something. The waiting was over.

Under his breath, the captain gloated.

'Let's get 'im.'

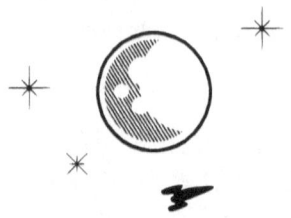

Chapter Two

Henry sat at his desk and glared at the two teenage girls who were standing by the back bookshelf pulling down books and leafing through them. He was sure they weren't going to buy anything. Kids these days didn't appreciate real books, they were all about screens. No, these girls were just going to paw his books to death, break the spines, probably put something sticky all over them, and then once they'd finished their little chatty conversation about their clothes, or their boyfriends, or their computer game, they'd leave the books sitting all anyhow and leave the shop.

And who'd go and pick everything up and clean it all? Why, Henry, of course.

The girls were so involved in what they were saying to each other that they didn't even notice Henry's thousand watt glare. He wished they'd leave.

What's the point of having people in your bookshop if they are not going to buy anything? Did they think he was a library? There was one of those just up the hill. They were welcome to go and hang out there.

Granted, for a place filled with books, the library had no personality at all. A square box of a room built by the government to meet some legislative requirement. Tom, the young librarian, he did his best, but what can you do if a place has no personality?

Henry's shop, Swansong, had personality. From the front door, which was so cleverly painted to resemble a bookshelf that it was difficult to even see that it was a door, customers walked into Henry's front room with its two picture windows looking out onto the street. The walls of this room were lined with bookshelves and there were a couple of love seats in the centre upholstered in fading forest green. This room contained fiction. Classics of course, and science fiction, fantasy and romance, crime and children's books, new and second-hand. Henry had it all.

Near the hallway was Henry's desk. The rare and valuable books were locked into a cabinet behind him, and from his desk he could see out to the street, and in to the rest of the shop. He liked to sit there and keep an eye on everything. This was where the bookshop cat liked to sleep too. The beautiful white longhaired cat. Like something from a cat food commercial, she was. She sat up on his desk, in his inbox, on top of the bills and papers. Maybe if the library had a cat it would give the place more personality. He wouldn't say that she was his cat. Like most cats, she was definitely her own person. But she had chosen the bookstore as her home, and he enjoyed the company.

The nonfiction books were kept in a room further back that connected to this one through an arched doorway. History, philosophy, science. The back room had small windows looking out to the fields beyond. The bookshop lay on the main street of the hamlet of Cygnet, sandwiched between the real estate agent and the butcher's shop. But despite being on the main road, the town was so small that the back of the shop looked over empty paddocks.

That wasn't really fair on Cygnet, it wasn't quite that small. From the other side of the road, houses reached all the way up the hill. And new houses were being built all the time. But on this side of the main street, there was a line of shops, and then the fields, reaching back to the fence line of the orchard that Henry had had to sell.

And that was another gripe. Henry should be still living out there, in that gracious old farm house. Not here, in the poky rooms up on the second floor above the bookshop. His daughter Vivienne should have married a farmer. A Cygnet lad, or someone from Huonville. There was enough choice here, certainly. She and her husband should have taken over the orchard and made a go of it.

But no. She chose not to. And Henry had to sell the land and house to that family from Japan, wasn't it? Or South Korea? Somewhere in Asia anyway. A nice enough family, but definitely strangers to the town, not locals. And that still rankled.

But Henry couldn't keep going with the orchard by himself. When Dorothy was alive, she'd kept the house going, and Henry had employed local lads for the busy times. Together they'd made it work. He smiled to himself, thinking not of the long days out on the land, but of the dark winter evenings spent reading with Dorothy in front of the fire, eating her amazing Rubigold apple loaf, and sharing interesting facts or well-written phrases. She was more into poetry, especially near the end. The poems spoke for her the words she could not find for herself.

He shook his head. If he was honest, the orchard had been too much for the two of them; it was definitely too much for him on his own. And with no family in town to help out …

Speaking of family, Henry would have to kick these girls out if they didn't leave soon. It was time to close up, pack up, and get up to town to visit Vivienne, and that man who took her away. And Bekka. In spite of himself, he smiled. It was always good to see Bekka. Grandkids did that to you. Even at those times when they brought a frown to their parents' faces.

They didn't like the fact that she wore only black to go with her glossy black hair, that she carried everything in her black bag. But Henry knew it was only a season. It wasn't a sign of things to come. It was just a small teenage rebellion.

He knew that the black season would pass. She'd get over it. Vivienne had, in time.

Time. It really was time to go. He would have to go and say something to the girls in the back.

He patted the cat and pulled himself out of the chair, but just as he did, the girls put the books down and, still chatting and not giving a glance in his direction, wandered out of the shop.

He locked the door behind them and gave a sigh. Bekka wasn't like them, he was sure. She had much more sense.

'Time to go,' he said to the cat. 'I'll make sure there's food in your bowl, don't worry. And I'll be back before ten.'

Why he talked to the cat he was never sure. He tried not to do it when there were customers in the shop, but things being how they were, that gave him a fair bit of time to chat to the animal. And she seemed to understand him. She was a clever cat, more than the norm.

Or maybe he was just biased about the cat like he was about Bekka. Who knew?

'Are you more intelligent, do you think?' he asked the cat.

The cat purred and butted her head against the old man's hand.

'I guess you were smart enough to find me and move in here. You could tell a sucker when you saw one.'

Henry thought back to that night, five years or so ago.

It had been a dark night, moonless, with clouds scudding across the sky. Stinging winter sleet was blowing sideways. Henry had awakened about midnight to a thumping noise and a howling wind. He had tossed and turned, and had gradually become aware that the noise was coming from his shed out the back. The door must have somehow become unlatched and was banging in the wind. With that realisation came the worry that the rain would get into the shed and damage the books stored out there. He had to get up and deal with it.

He got out of his warm and toasty bed, put his slippers on, and wrapped a dressing gown around his flannel pyjamas. He fought with the wind for control of the back door and struggled down the short path to the shed. Latching the shed door securely, he turned back to the house and nearly tripped over a bedraggled ball of fur that was wrapping itself around his ankles.

'What are you doing out on a night like this?' he asked.

The cat purred so loudly he could hear it above the screaming wind.

The two of them rushed through the rain back to the shop. The cat walked in with Henry and immediately made herself at home. She cleaned herself carefully, sitting on the back doormat. And then she inspected the shop thoroughly before curling up and falling asleep on one of the love seats.

Henry had tried to find the cat's owner. She was obviously not a wild cat. Even if she did look a bit scrawny when she turned up, she had done all the domestic cat things and was happy to be around people. No, she wasn't feral, but maybe she'd been through a bit of a hard time.

He had used the local grapevine gossip line but no one had come forward. He had put an ad in the little local rag. He had made a poster for the tiny Cygnet supermarket, and the new fruit and veg place.

But after weeks of looking, it seemed that no one wanted her. After a while he gave up. The cat had made herself his, and he, well, to be honest, he liked the company. Someone to grumble to about the day.

Sometimes she slept upstairs on the foot of his bed. But mostly she was a bookstore cat. Making friends, keeping the bills warm, accepting the admiring comments.

She was a good looking cat. That was for sure. Long silky white fur, grey tips to her ears. Some sort of purebred. Henry wasn't sure what.

He'd never named her. It felt like that would have been an impertinence. She knew who she was, and Henry always called her, 'the cat' or just 'Cat'. 'Cats don't come when you call anyway,' he'd say to people who asked him.

He enjoyed her company, but he didn't think she'd like the travel. Cats didn't generally enjoy car trips. He'd always left her in the shop. Sometimes she tried to get out, but he was careful not to allow nocturnal wanderings. Cats did dreadful things to Australian wildlife. She had chosen his shop and that's where she'd have to stay. He was careful to keep her safe at home.

And he was doing the same tonight.

'You're in charge. Wish me luck with the offspring. See you later.'

He grabbed his keys and wallet and locked the door behind him.

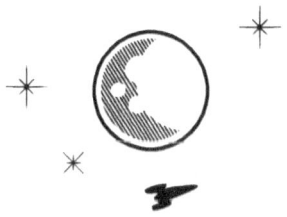

Chapter Three

Cat waited until she heard Henry's ute drive down the main road towards Huonville. Then she let her frustration out, tearing furiously around the bookstore up the stairs into the kitchen and dining room, over Henry's bed in his bedroom and back down to the front desk again. After three or four laps of the house, she had exhausted herself sufficiently to sit and think seriously again.

At first, after she'd arrived on Earth, setting off that major thunderstorm as her ship disintegrated in the atmosphere, Henry's bookstore had been the retreat she had longed for. She had needed to lick her physical, mental and emotional wounds and pull herself together. She had been desperate for a safe space to rest.

She'd been drawn to Henry's house by some beneficent chance. She'd unlatched the shed door, hoping that someone would come out to investigate the banging. When she'd seen the short plump old man, with his white hair plastered to his scalp by the rain, him pulling his tartan dressing gown tighter around himself and securing it with the tie with the tassels on the end – what Kadwa can resist a good tassel, really? – and slopping through the puddles in his matching tartan slippers, she was immediately, in a way, in love with the man.

This was the safety and security she needed. The bookstore and the unit upstairs became like a rest home for her, a place to recover. She could sleep whenever she liked, eat regularly, and run up and down stairs for exercise when she felt like it. No one was asking her for anything, or sending her constant communications through the day and night. No one was talking about her behind her back – no one even knew where she was. There was no working through the night, day after day. No collating the research for another legal battle that would be thrown out before it even began, making all her work worth nothing. Karthur and Julis, the Vyynx, the court system and all the issues were far behind her.

She was tired when she came to Earth. Burnt out. Bone weary. Her fur was falling out and she was stick thin. She thought that this little planet in the back blocks of Sector 378 would be just the place to live out her final days. She'd done a little research and knew that Kadwa looked just like the domestic cats that humans loved to have as companions. All she wanted to do was sleep and eat, and that's all that domestic cats seemed to do. She didn't think she'd ever recover her energy or her joy, and living as a companion of a human sounded like paradise.

Henry gave her what she needed. And she would always be grateful to him. Though she could never tell him, of course. It was forbidden by intergalactic law to let these humans know they weren't alone in the universe. Their technology wasn't nearly advanced enough. They needed to be left in sweet ignorance.

But there was the frustration. Right there. Because Cat had recovered her joy and her energy. After the years of nursing that Henry didn't even know he was doing, she was feeling bright and chirpy, fully refreshed and ready to do something. But she was not allowed even to leave the small confines of the shop.

And she knew why. She'd let him know, without words, just how anxious she was to take a step outside. And he'd told her, in words, that cats were very bad for Australian wildlife. Terrific hunters, amazingly good at killing, and therefore expert killers of the possums, the Tasmanian devils, the gorgeous little spotted quolls, all the nocturnal animals. And during the day, killing the parrots and other bird life. He wouldn't allow it.

How could she convey to him that she wasn't at all interested in hunting down live animals and … ugh … killing them and eating them … raw. Her whole body bristled with revulsion at the thought.

The salmon treats in their nice little tin can, they were the thing. Hunting down criminals and prosecuting them, yes, that she would do. But killing and eating her own food … just disgusting.

But without using words it was just too hard. And there would have to be a lot more at stake before she'd go breaking IG law like that. So she was stuck in this place. The nursing home that had become a prison.

She could escape, of course. Slip out the door as a customer came in. Or run out between Henry's legs when he came in with groceries. It would be easy. But it would be letting him down and she couldn't do that to the sweet man. He had been so good to her; she didn't want to disappoint him.

If only he would take her with him in the ute. Or take her out on a leash. Would she allow a leash? Yes, she was really that desperate. She'd do anything to escape these confines.

But it wasn't to be.

The frustration somewhat abated by the mad run around the house, Cat pulled a book off the shelf and read for a while, learning more about this planet that had become her home. Then she once more settled herself in the in-tray, curled herself into a ball, and waited for Henry's return.

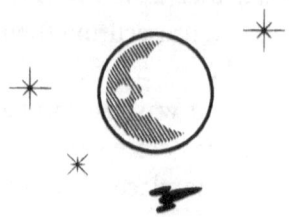

Chapter Four

Henry enjoyed the drive up to Hobart, through Huonville and up over Vincents Pass. They were always on at him about it. 'You live so far out. It's a dangerous stretch of road. Are you sure you don't want to get a nice little unit closer to us?' And it was true, the road did get covered with snow in the late winter, and you did have to look out for frost as you drove over the Pass, but Cygnet wasn't that far away from town, only forty minutes.

And his life was in Cygnet anyway. Always had been. It was Vivienne who had the need to explore, who wanted to see more of the world. Henry had never felt that compulsion. Cygnet was beautiful, peaceful, full of friends. He had everything he needed there. People were giving up high-paying jobs in big cities to move to his little town. And yet, his own daughter had wanted to leave. It didn't make sense, but there it was.

He was lucky, really, that she'd moved back to Tasmania after all that time in America. He was sure he'd lost her for good when she moved over there to study, and then met Paulo. But they had decided to move back to Australia when Bekka was on the way, and by some miracle they had both found jobs in Hobart.

As he parked outside their West Hobart house he gave silent thanks. How dreadful it would be to face old age without some family around.

He saw Bekka watching from the bedroom window, looking out through the winter dark for the arrival of his ute. As soon as he parked, she danced out the front door, and threw her arms around him.

'Grandad, you're here!'

'Well, and I am.'

Henry smiled at his granddaughter. Her outfit might be black as midnight, but her mood certainly wasn't.

'Come inside. Mum and Dad have some exciting news to tell you.'

'Really?' Henry made his slow way up the front steps and through the heavy wooden door. The old house felt like home, it had so much in common with the old farmhouse that stood on the hill above his orchard. Maybe that's why Vivienne and Paulo had bought it, because it reminded Vivienne of her family home. Although, she wasn't that sentimental. To be honest, they probably had chosen this house because it was old and run down, and therefore affordable. They were slowly doing it up, but the carpet was still threadbare in places, most of the walls needed a coat of paint, and the bathrooms were still that horrible yellow and green with dated fixtures. But all of that made Henry feel at home. Would he still like it when it became new and shiny?

Bekka danced her way downstairs to the dining room. It was like she didn't even touch the stairs. Henry followed at a more sedate pace.

'He's here!'

'Welcome Dad,' Vivienne gave him a kiss on the cheek. Paulo came out of the kitchen wiping his hands on a towel and kissed him too. That was something Henry had come to terms with over the last 15 years. A handshake was still what he thought would be more appropriate. But he managed not to stiffen now when the kiss was offered.

'Want a drink? Have a seat. We'll be out with dinner in a minute.' They both disappeared back into the kitchen.

Henry took the glass of wine and turned to Bekka.

'And how's school going?'

'Ugh. Midyear exams. They don't give us any time off to study, we just have to go in and do them. It's a pain Grandad. They just don't understand.'

'But you're going OK?'

'Oh sure, Mum's helping me with the bio, and Dad's pretty good with the chemistry and physics. And I love the books we're doing in English. *The Happiest Refugee* – do you have that one in the shop Grandad? It's brilliant.'

Henry thought through the shelves.

'Fiction, is it?'

'No, it's about Ahn Do, he came over on a boat from Vietnam. You should have it, really, if you don't.'

Now Henry pictured the shelves in the back room and remembered the slim orange volume.

'Oh yes, I have that one. I'm going to have to read it now.'

'You really should. It's brilliant. And it really makes you think, you know?'

'What else are you studying in English?' Henry took a seat at the table and relaxed.

'Poetry. Not so much a fan of that.' Bekka shrugged and sat down too.

'But there's some beautiful poetry. I love Wordsworth and Robert Frost.'

'I think it's the way the teacher is teaching it. She keeps saying, "what do you think he's using alliteration to express here?" or "what is this a metaphor for?" And I think, you know, that if he's writing about the beautiful daffodils, maybe that means that he thinks the daffodils are beautiful.'

'You could be right there.' Henry gave a wry grin.

'Alright, here we are, dinner time.' Paulo carried in a bubbling lasagne and placed it on the rough wooden table. Vivienne followed with a salad in one hand and garlic bread in the other.

Conversation ceased for a time as they enjoyed the delicious food, but eventually Henry took a sip of wine and asked, 'Bekka says you have some good news?'

'Well yes, it's pretty good news. A bit difficult though,' Paulo said.

'It's not difficult. I'll be fine,' Bekka pouted.

'No. We're not leaving you on your own for that length of time, and that's final.' Vivienne laid down the law.

Henry looked from one face to another. 'What's going on? Who is leaving? Tell me, what's the news?'

Vivienne sighed.

'Do you remember Dad, that Paulo and I both applied to research in Antarctica for the summer?'

'Yes, you want to do something with the plankton or something. And Paulo – ice cores, wasn't it?'

'Yes, that's it. It would be so good to be on the scene looking at how they are taken and what's in them. Did you know that about 400 metres down there is evidence of ...'

'Paulo, he knows.' Vivienne laid her fork down on her plate and put her hand on Paulo's arm. 'This is why you should go. You're so excited you can't stop talking about it.'

Paulo covered her hand with his. 'But you're excited too. You do incredible research. You should go. I can wait. The ice is brought back here after all. I can work on it next year. You need to work with the plankton on site.'

'I don't know. I don't want to stop you from going.'

'Hold on, hold on,' Henry interrupted. 'What's the problem here?'

'It's me,' said Bekka sitting up straight in her chair. 'They've both been accepted by the Antarctic Division. They both want to go. And they both can. But I'm the problem. They don't want to leave me. But it's fine, I keep telling them. I'll stay here. I'll be fine. I can walk to school, I can cook, I can look after myself.'

'For four whole months? I don't think so.' Vivienne shook her head firmly. 'You're just too young. I know you're a very responsible girl, but really, anything could happen. I just wouldn't be able to sleep.'

'*M...u...u...m...*,' Bekka whined, making the single syllable do the work of four.

'No, your mother is right. You are just too young. You don't know what's involved in looking after a place like this.' Paulo put his hand on Bekka's back and she shrugged it off.

'You two are going to have to let go sometime.'

'Bekka, you are only 16. You are not old enough, and that's final. Dad will go down, and you and I will stay here.'

'No indeed. You will go down and Bekka and I will have fun back here for the summer.'

Henry watched as the three of them started talking at once, their arms flying about as they tried to make their points. He wondered how often this conversation, this fight, had happened.

'I have an idea.' He spoke quietly but somehow it cut through the noise and the three of them stopped talking and turned to look at him.

'Bekka can come and stay with me. And you both can go down.'

'Oh no, Dad, I'm sure that's too much fuss for you.'

'To Cygnet? But it's a long way from the school. It would be a lot of travel.'

'Me, come to you? Well …' The parents were both against the idea, but Henry could see Bekka thinking it over.

He wasn't sure what had made him make the suggestion. Having a teenager living with him wasn't something that had ever been in his plans. And she'd probably find life with her grandad truly boring. But there she was, thinking it over, not immediately saying no. Maybe it was a good idea. Wherever it had come from.

Bekka met his gaze and he winked at her. They could have fun together. He was sure they could.

'So that's settled then,' he said. 'You two can make the trek to Antarctica, though why you should even want to, I don't know. It's going to be cold and uncomfortable. But Bekka and I will make ourselves comfortable in Cygnet and laugh at you from there.'

Vivienne and Paulo looked at each other. Then Vivienne shrugged.

'Well, Dad, if that's what you want. I suggest you take a couple of days to think it over. It's not a small ask, that's why I didn't ask you. She'll have exams, you know, and she'll have to get to school somehow. And it's been a while since you've had a child in the house.'

'She's not really a child. As she says, she's pretty much grown up. And there are busses into town. And she can help me with the shop on the weekends and through the summer. We'll be fine. I just hope it won't be too boring for you, Bekka.'

'It's not exactly the same as being at home by myself …'

'Which is not going to happen.' Vivienne was strong again.

'But it will be an adventure. It should be fun. Let's do it.'

'I'm going to give Grandad a few days to think about it. But if you still want to after that … Well, it would be wonderful to be able to go down with Paulo, that's for sure.'

Vivienne and Paulo smiled at each other excitedly and Henry knew that he couldn't back out now. It was going to be quite the summer adventure. He wondered what the cat would think of it all.

* * *

The intervening months disappeared quickly as they tend to do. The winter passed and spring arrived, and Henry realised it was time to clear out his spare room so that Bekka had somewhere to stay.

He hoped this would be the hardest part of the whole visit because it really was painful. There was stuff everywhere in this room. This was where he pursued his hobby – electronics. There were bits and pieces all over the place. Soldering irons, wire, boards, chemicals to etch the boards, boxes of this and that. An old stereo with the back taken off, even that very old record player that he'd been meaning to fix. He'd always felt it was a room of possibility, but now that he was looking at it through Bekka's eyes it looked more like a room of rubbish. He hadn't had to clean this stuff up since Dorothy was alive.

He hadn't had to do much cleaning at all since Dorothy passed away, come to think of it. He'd kept the shop nice and tidy for the customers, but upstairs was a different story. What was it going to be like living with a female in the house again?

If it came to that, what was it going to be like having another person in the house? He had been alone for so long.

He dumped a roll of solder into a box and picked up some scraps of the plastic insulation to put in the bin. He had to get the amount of stuff down to a minimum so that he could store it in the back shed with the boxes of books. He sat on the edge of the desk that had been his workbench and now would be (he guessed) Bekka's study area. He sighed at the enormity of the sorting that he needed to do, then turned to the cat who had appeared in the doorway.

'I guess I haven't been truly alone. I have had you to keep me company.'

The cat wound around his legs.

'But you're not the most talkative. I have to do all the work myself.'

Henry bent to give her a pat but she nipped at his hand and turned her back.

'No need to take offence. It's just that you're not a human, that's all.' The cat sat with her back to him. 'Still, it's like you understand every word I say. Living with a teenager though, that's going to be different. At least you don't require me to clean out this room.'

The cat slowly unbent and started to wind around his ankles again. Then she hopped up on the desk he had been using for a workbench, and as she sat there, the packing seemed to go more smoothly. Maybe it was just the company, but she also swatted things towards him at the right time, or walked over and placed her paw on a speaker or a box of screws, seeming to know which items would fit into each box. And gradually, the room started to take shape as a bedroom.

Sometimes Henry was sure that Cat had more intelligence than the average feline. But then he convinced himself that he was imagining things. He was lonely, that was all, and without a human companion he was making Cat into something more than she was. That had to be it.

He almost ignored her as she pointed out another roll of solder that could fit neatly into the corner of the box he was packing. How could she know anything? She was just playing with the stuff and enjoying the new activity, that was all. But … that roll would fit very neatly. He picked it up and packed it and hoped he wasn't becoming senile.

Bekka was bringing her own linen, there wasn't much that Henry could do to make the room beautiful, but he went downstairs and picked some books for the bedside table. The cat helped with that too. Then he placed a glass and a carafe of water on the bedside table, and even went so far as to pick some flowers from the garden, giving thanks that it was spring and everything was bursting with colour.

'I hope she'll like it here,' he said to the ever-listening Cat. 'I hope she doesn't find it too boring. I'm not the most exciting person, as you well know. Ah well, what's done is done. She'll be here tomorrow and I've done all I can to make space for her.'

The cat curled up in the centre of the single bed and fell asleep. If Bekka felt as comfortable as the cat, things would be fine, Henry thought.

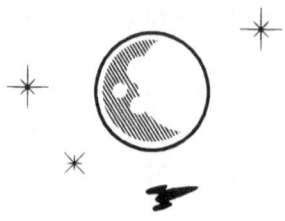

Chapter Five

Friday morning dawned bright and clear. The warm weather had finally begun. Spring was definitely here and summer was just around the corner.

Henry left the closed sign on the door of the bookshop, asked the cat to wish him luck, and jumped into his ute. It was time to bring Bekka back to Cygnet.

Bekka met him at the door of the West Hobart house, but it wasn't the dancing, bubbly Bekka that he usually saw. Instead she was quiet and subdued.

The house had been packed up (tenants were renting while the family were away) and all that remained were Bekka's belongings and the sleeping bags that Vivienne and Paulo were taking on the ship. They had spent the last week packing the ship to get ready to go down to the southernmost continent. Most of the researchers had been sleeping on board already but Vivienne and Paulo were spending as much time as possible with Bekka before they left. They were almost vibrating with excitement. Bekka not so much.

Henry packed Bekka's bedding and suitcase and the two sleeping bags into the tray of his ute, filling the back seat with her bits and pieces. Somehow the four of them squeezed in and Henry drove them down to the wharf.

There was the large orange ship, the *Aurora Australis,* in dock, dwarfing the Institute of Marine and Antarctic Studies building beside it. Even though the hour was still early, there was a lot of activity around it. As they arrived, Vivienne was immediately called over to a camera and TV reporter to give a quick prècis of her research. Paulo took their belongings on board, he'd have his own interview later.

Henry looked at the ship with distaste. Why would anyone want to put themselves through so much discomfort? What was the point of it? Why not stay in this beautiful place, where you could be comfortable, know where you were, not stuck in the middle of the ocean on such an ugly vehicle? He was sure there were plenty of things that you could research right here in Tasmania. There had to be little creatures in the pools on the tops of mountains just a few hours' drive away that could be just as interesting to research as Antarctic plankton. What was wrong with his daughter? It had to be the influence of that Paulo. Why couldn't she have married a nice Huon Valley man and stayed in Cygnet with him? Right now she was risking her life for no good reason. And leaving her daughter behind.

Oh yes, Bekka. That interrupted Henry's gloomy thoughts. She was standing right next to him, staring at the ship too. Goodness knows what her thoughts were doing.

'Let's go and get a cuppa, hey?' he said, putting his arm around her shoulders. 'They'll be busy for a while, we'll make sure we get back in time to give them a hug and watch the ship pull out.'

She nodded, and they turned away, crossing the street to Salamanca to find an open café.

* * *

'The scientific research vessel, the *Aurora Australis*, left today on its final voyage to Antarctica.' The news reader spoke calmly, talking of the significance of the ship and the research performed on it.

Henry turned the volume up and Bekka put down her fork and studied the footage on his tiny TV, trying to spot herself in the farewelling crowd, or at least to see footage of Vivienne and Paulo. Despite both of them doing an interview, the reporters must have thought their work wasn't exciting enough, choosing instead to focus on the leader of the expedition and the skipper of the ship.

Bekka was sure she saw her parents waving from the ship as it pulled away, Henry wasn't so sure, but he went along with it anyway. Bekka hadn't been her normal bubbly self through any of the day. Reality had hit hard.

'Well, love. There they go. Off on their big adventure.'

'Just like they wanted.' Her voice was quiet. The cat wandered into the kitchen and jumped on Bekka's lap, and Bekka gave her a hug, leaning over to hide her quivering lip.

'Now then, they'll have a great time. And we can always Skype.'

Bekka nodded and Henry thought he heard her sniff. He got out of his own chair and awkwardly patted Bekka on the shoulder.

'Last voyage, hey. It was good of you to agree to come here and let them take part in that. I wonder what the new ship will look like?'

Bekka nodded again, and wiped her nose with the back of her hand. 'Probably just as big and just as orange,' she said with a small quaver in her voice.

'Ha. I reckon so. Well. Are you ready for some ice cream?'

'Sounds good.' Bekka's voice grew stronger, and the cat jumped off her lap and onto the next chair over.

'Was dinner alright? I mean, it wasn't your dad's cooking or anything …'

'Yeah, it was great. I'll have a go tomorrow night, if you like?'

'Sure, if you want to, you go right ahead. My kitchen, such as it is, is all yours.'

'Thanks, Grandad.' Bekka brushed her hair out of her eyes, and pushed her shoulders back. 'This could be fun, you know?'

'I know you're not having the adventure of living by yourself, but still, we'll have a good time together, won't we?'

'Oh, I'm glad I'm not in that old house by myself tonight. I thought I could do it, but now I'm not so sure.'

Henry nodded to himself as he scooped out the ice cream. He was glad she could see it so clearly. She wasn't quite old enough to be at home alone for four months. She was better off with him.

Chapter Six

Henry opened the shop at 9 a.m. on Saturday as he usually did. He had got up, bustled around, made himself breakfast, done all the usual things. He hadn't really tried to be any quieter than usual either – to be honest, at first he'd forgotten about Bekka sleeping soundly in the second bedroom. But she hadn't stirred at all. Not with any of the noise he'd made.

He wondered just how he was going to get her out of bed to catch the bus on Monday morning. Ah well, sufficient unto the day are the evils thereof. And she deserved a sleep in after the drama of Friday. Not that there was a lot of hardship, but there was a lot of waiting around. And that's always tiring.

Late in the morning, so late that Henry was already thinking about lunch, she appeared, dressed in the t-shirt and long track pants that she slept in, hair all tousled, eyes sleepy.

'Morning Grandad.'

'Good morning Bekka.' Henry was glad that she'd chosen a moment between customers, though she didn't seem worried by the chance that people would see her like this. 'There's cereal and bread and things in the kitchen. Go ahead and make yourself breakfast. Whatever you like. I need to stay down here in case customers turn up.'

'Sure.' She turned back to the stairs. Then she looked back over her shoulder. 'Would you like a cup of tea?'

'That would be lovely, thanks. Bring it down when you're dressed.'

He hoped she'd got the hint. What would people think of his shop if she treated it like her own lounge room? She needed to have at least a little bit of respect. But he did like the idea of someone bringing him a cup of tea without having to go upstairs and make it himself.

When Bekka appeared again, she was dressed in her usual black jeans and black T-shirt. She walked carefully down the stairs to the shop holding a cup of tea in one hand, and a bowl of cereal in the other. The tea she delivered to Henry, then she sat in the green love-seat and ate her cereal.

Henry wasn't sure what to say. Was this the behaviour he wanted? He didn't want to banish her to the kitchen when she was so obviously in need of company. But did he want to allow food into his precious bookshop? What if she spilled it on a book?

He decided to let it go for the day. Then he'd think hard about it and maybe set some rules later.

The cat gave a leisurely stretch from her position in the in-box, then to Henry's surprise she got up and curled herself next to Bekka on the couch.

'You've made yourself a friend there.'

'She's so lovely. Aren't you a beautiful cat?' Bekka pulled out her phone to take a selfie with the cat but the cat would have none of it. She turned her back on the phone and then curled herself into a tight ball. Nothing that Bekka could do would make the cat face the camera and eventually Bekka chuckled and gave up.

'What are your plans for today, Bekka?'

'I don't know, I was just going to hang here, I guess. I mean, I don't suppose you can take me up to town?'

'I don't suppose I can, no. I have a shop to look after. You're going to have to get up much earlier to go into town if you want to catch a bus.'

Bekka pulled a face. He could see that she really was not a morning person. She didn't have any of the dancing vibrations that he usually saw when he visited the family for dinner and he didn't think it was just because she was missing her parents.

'So I guess I'll just ...' she gestured at the shop vaguely.

'Why don't you go for a walk around the town? You haven't spent much time in Cygnet, have you? There are things to see.'

'Mmmm...' Bekka wasn't convinced, but then the door bell jangled and Henry stopped the conversation to say hello to the older couple who walked into the shop for a browse.

'Looking for anything in particular?' he asked.

'Just browsing, thanks,' was the response. When Henry turned back to his granddaughter she had turned to her phone and was typing furiously. Probably telling her friends that she couldn't make it out of the small town she was stuck in. He left her to it.

Eventually, when nothing much had happened beyond a few more customers in the shop, Bekka put her phone in her back pocket, patted the cat, gave a big stretch, and stood up.

'I might just go and have a look around then,' she said.

'Right,' said Henry, hardly looking up from where he was updating shop records. 'Have a good time. See you when you get back.'

The bookshop felt empty when Bekka left. She had a presence that had made the place warm and friendly. Now there was just a dirty cereal bowl sitting on the arm of the couch.

Henry picked that up and ran it upstairs to the kitchen. That would get old very quickly. He'd have to train her not to leave stuff around the bookstore. She might feel like it was her lounge room but it really wasn't.

A couple of hours later, Bekka danced her way through the front door, causing a rioting jangle of the bell.

'Here it is,' she said to the guy following her. 'Drop in here anytime.'

The guy following her was not as enthusiastic. He looked around the same age as Bekka, maybe a couple of years older. His hands were pushed into the pockets of his old blue jeans and his green t-shirt was crumpled and had a couple of holes in it. His messy black hair needed a cut. Bekka wasn't going to get any hints on fashion from this guy, Henry could see that. Or perhaps she was – would it be worse to have holes in her black jeans? He missed the neat suits and skirts of yesteryear. His Dorothy had looked so sweet when she dressed up, even back in their school days. Of course, she wasn't averse to getting holes in things when she was climbing a tree or some such thing.

This kid looked a little disreputable, but at least he had manners. He put his hand out to shake Henry's.

'Hello Mr ... um.' He obviously hadn't thought this through. Bekka had probably just told him to come and meet Grandad.

'Just call me Henry.'

'OK ... Henry.' The kid was obviously unsure, but Henry liked that. Showed he was brought up correctly. But still, times had changed and all this Mr and Mrs business was unnecessary.

'I'm Davian, pleased to meet you.'

'Come on Davian, come and have a look around.' Bekka was keen to show off the shop and soon they were in the back corner of the back room looking through books on, of all things, space and the planets. Henry would never understand Bekka, he was sure.

'Have you read this one Grandad?' Bekka was showing him *Enders Game*. They'd moved on from nonfiction to fiction now. 'Davian says it's very real.'

'Not for a while, but yes, it's excellent. Very real. A very clever ending. I prefer *The Hitchhikers Guide to the Galaxy* though, just for a bit of fun. Have you read that?'

'Of course!' said Bekka but Davian shook his head.

Henry went through the shelves to find a second-hand copy.

'Can he borrow it Grandad?' Bekka asked but Davian was too fast for her.

'No, I'll buy it. Don't even think about it, sir ... Henry.'

'Well thank you. It's only $7.'

'Oh Grandad.' Bekka was disgusted, but Henry was firm and Davian was happy to pay. This was a shop, after all. Not a library.

Bekka wanted to show Davian everything.

'Where's Cat?' she asked.

'She's upstairs,' Henry replied.

'Can I take Davian up to see her?'

'I think ... not just now.' Henry shook his head. He was having enough trouble with his privacy being disturbed by Bekka. Having a complete stranger in his little space? That was a bit too much.

Bekka seemed to understand, and the two kids settled into the green couches to read.

After a while, Cat made her majestic way down the stairs, her sights set on the inbox at the front desk. Bekka didn't notice her, but Davian did. He looked at her, his eyes widened and he stood immediately and turned his back to her, moving as quickly as he could to the front door.

'Bekka, I ... um ... I have to go.' He hunched his shoulders and stumbled out the door without any further goodbye.

As he spoke, Cat's ears pricked up, her hair stood on end and her tail bristled. She ran to the door as Davian slipped out, trying to catch it before it closed. Henry was taken by surprise. She hadn't done that for months, she had seemed perfectly content to be in the shop. He caught her with both hands, picked her up, and firmly told her 'no!' And she responded with a quick swipe of his arm with her claws.

'What's got into you?' he asked, dropping her to the floor. And then more worried, he asked, 'Are you hurt?' But of course the cat didn't reply.

'I'll take her up to my room for a while, Grandad,' Bekka said. 'It might calm her down.' She picked up the still-bristling cat, held her in her arms like a she was a baby and disappeared upstairs.

Maybe it was having Bekka in the shop that had encouraged the cat to try to get outside. Henry had no idea why her behaviour had changed. But if she kept this up, he might have to take her to the vet to find out what was wrong.

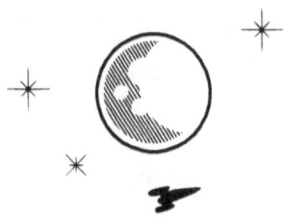

Chapter Seven

Davian ran down the main road, putting the bookstore as far behind him as possible. His heart rate soared and his legs felt weak. That Kadwa … he was sure he'd seen her before.

It couldn't be, could it? What would one of the premier lawyers of Karthur be doing in Cygnet? Maybe she was just a domestic cat.

But out of the corner of his eye, he had seen her run towards him. Like she recognised him too. And he couldn't have that. Recognition, that was the worst thing that could happen.

He ducked around the corner of the pub and leant on the wall, rubbing his sweating palms on his legs. This was the middle of nowhere, he really thought he'd be safe here.

That was the worst thing about this kind of life. You just had to keep running. Everywhere you thought you would be safe, you would see someone, or you'd think you had seen someone, and it was best not to take chances. It was best not to relax at all.

But honestly, Sector 378, who would come here? He'd thought he was going to be able to stay this time. There were a few visitors, but they were all here for a quiet life, for a restart. Jones, he was alright, he'd given Davian work. But he didn't expect anyone high powered to be here. It was really so far off the main track, so far away from any of the big places. So far away from Karthur.

He looked back down the main street, then with a nonchalance he didn't feel, he strolled towards the yacht club, his brain churning at a hundred miles an hour.

He'd have to fix up his ship and find another place to hide. Though there weren't many safe planets left. Not many where he wouldn't have to check in and be bio-tagged and set off the whole security shebang immediately. That's why he'd chosen this one.

But if he'd been found by that Kadwa, of all people, then they must be on to him. They must be.

So it was time to repair the ship and go. He'd see if he could borrow the welder from Jones, and then, well, he just had to hope that the ship's power supply was up to the job. It wasn't ideal, he had been hoping he'd have a bit more time.

As his pulse slowed and he put his plan together, Davian began to feel more normal. There was nothing like having a plan. He turned up the hill towards his ship's hiding place. He'd start by making a list of all the things that needed doing before he could get out of here.

The walk was good. He felt the sun and the gentle breeze and a smile came to his face again. He shook his head. He was probably imagining that he'd seen that cat before. She just brought it all back to his mind, that's all. What would a Kadwa be doing here in the middle of nowhere? There were plenty of cats and dogs in Cygnet and he just had the bad luck to find one that looked familiar and triggered his panic attack.

He picked up a fallen branch and swiped at the tree trunks and scrub as he walked through the bush. His thoughts turned to Bekka and Henry. They must have thought he was an idiot. He'd have to come up with some excuse for running away like that.

He had just panicked, that was all. And could you blame him with his background? But looking down the gully at his little spaceship he decided that it wouldn't be a bad idea to work on it anyway. To get that welder from Jones. And, while he wouldn't avoid Bekka as such, he would not go back near that bookstore if he could help it. Just in case.

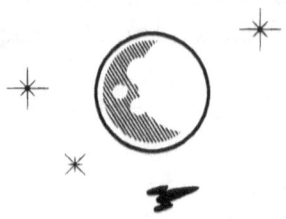

Chapter Eight

Meanwhile, Cat was still cursing below her breath, her tail bristling like a bottle brush. Was that the kid from Karthur? And how could she find out? The bookstore was feeling less like a nursing home and more like a prison each day.

She struggled and twisted in Bekka's arms, trying to get down so that she could at least go for a mad run to remove her frustration. Bekka held her tightly, patted her fur and murmured sweet nothings.

'If my colleagues could see me now,' Cat thought, and the thought made her almost laugh out loud. This was so ridiculous. So undignified. But, if she was honest, quite nice. Bekka was just being kind. Cat relaxed and allowed her bristling feelings to be soothed.

When Bekka was satisfied that Cat had calmed down, she allowed her on to her bed to sleep. Cat curled into a croissant of fur but she didn't sleep. She thought deeply.

Did she want to know who that kid was? Did she really want to get involved in all that again? If she remembered rightly, the kid was part of the whole Vyynx situation. He and his ilk, they were the reason she had become burnt out.

The investigation had gone badly. Witness after witness had chosen to change their tune. And while they'd got some evidence, there hadn't been enough to bring the Vyynx down. Cat had been discouraged, but Julis, the detective, had told her that she had an ace up her sleeve. There was one gang member that Julis had been depending on to be the final nail in the gang-leader Xedrog's coffin.

A final witness that would bring the whole thing to a close. An untarnished witness. The witness was a young kid, and Julis hadn't approached him yet, but she'd looked into his background and she was sure he was perfect. All communication about him had been top secret and classified and kept in code. She had even kept his role in the deal secret from the kid himself. Just kept tabs on him so she could bring him in when the time was right.

And then he'd disappeared. And everything had fallen apart. It didn't matter how many times Julis had reassured Cat that this kid would be safe. Apparently no one from the gang had known they were looking at him as a witness, Julis had said that. But the kid disappeared.

And his disappearance had led to Cat's big argument with Julis. Cat was sure the gang had found out, that there must be a leak, even in Julis' own team, as well as the leaks they knew of in the other legal departments. Julis was convinced that she could trust her team, but Cat was sure the kid was dead. They had both been running on fumes for so many months, and this was the breaking point. They screamed at each other. Said things no one should say.

After that, Cat had continued with the court case half-heartedly but she knew that without their star witness they could not win. They lost the case, Xedrog went free, and she lost Julis' friendship as well.

Life couldn't have got much worse. Cat was exhausted.

She was so desperate to get away and find a place to rest. And she'd found it.

She stood up, stretched, and curled up the other way on Bekka's bed, trying to become more comfortable. But the discomfort was in her mind, not her body. She covered her face with her paws and tried to go to sleep.

It was no good. She did want to know if that was the kid. Wasn't his name Davian? Yes, she was sure that was the name. And, for crying out loud, if the kid was Davian, she did want to get back into it. For starters, if her Bekka was hanging out with a criminal on the run, she wanted that to stop, quick smart.

Secondly, if he wasn't dead, what had happened to him? How had he disappeared so completely?

And on top of that, what was a criminal from Karthur doing on Earth? Were the Vyynx starting a new 'franchise'? Because that needed to be stopped too.

And, dammit, now that she'd made a fool of herself by trying to escape out of the shop, she was sure that Henry would be keeping a closer eye on her. How was she going to get out and find out more?

Chapter Nine

Monday dawned bright and clear, and it was just as well. It was going to be hard enough to wake Bekka at 6 a.m. as it was. Goodness knows what Henry was going to do on a rainy day. But Bekka had to get to the bus at 6.50 a.m. and he did not want to have to drive her into town.

Henry pulled himself out of his own warm bed and knocked on Bekka's door. He heard a few grunts from inside and made a mental note to come and check again in five minutes if she hadn't surfaced.

He put two mugs on the bench, and a spoon of loose-leaf tea into the preheated teapot. Then stood at the kitchen bench and stared out over the valley towards his old orchard as he usually did while he waited for the kettle to boil.

Eventually Bekka made it out of her bedroom. She cupped her tea in both hands and sipped it slowly, staring blankly at the dining table.

'Breakfast?' Henry asked.

She looked up at him and shook her head.

'I couldn't face it this early. You know, Grandad, in West Hobart I would only have to get out of bed at eight to make it to school on time. This is torture.'

For us both, Henry thought, but he chose not to say it out loud. Instead he made sure he put plenty of snacks in her lunchbox.

She drained her tea, picked up her backpack and checked through it, and then the race began.

'Where's my phone? Grandad, have you seen my phone?'

'It's probably in your bag, isn't it?'

'No, it's not here.'

'In your room?'

Bekka was scrambling around checking under her bed and beside the mattress.

'Should I call it?'

'It's on silent, it's always on silent.'

'I'll go down and check in the bookshop. But if we don't find it in two minutes you'll have to go without it, or you'll miss the bus.'

Henry had just made it to the bottom of the stairs when Bekka came flying down behind him.

'It's OK, I found it.'

'Where was it?'

'In the bathroom. I must have left it there when I cleaned my teeth.'

The bathroom, why didn't he think of that?

'Right. You're ready to go then?'

'Yep.' All her panic had disappeared and she was completely cheerful again. 'See you tonight Grandad.' She landed a kiss on his cheek and swept out the door.

Henry locked the door behind her, making sure the sign still said 'closed' and trudged back up the stairs. He considered going back to bed, but there wasn't really enough time to sleep before it would be time to start his day. He made a second cup of tea and a piece of toast and sat in the kitchen to enjoy the peace that had descended as his whirlwind granddaughter left.

And it was lovely to sit in peace again, and to have those tranquil hours in the bookshop when Bekka was at school. But as time went by Henry had to admit that he found himself looking forward to the chaos of her arrival at the end of each day.

He started making special dishes for dinner, and counting down the minutes until the bus arrived. Holding himself back from walking to the bus stop to be there as she stepped off. He was sure she wouldn't like that – it would have felt like he was treating her like a child and she was so keen to be an adult.

She brought life into his quiet existence. She was messy, yes, and totally disorganised. So many times they had to look for the phone, or for a vital textbook. So many times he picked up bobby pins after she left. He found them in the bathroom, in the kitchen, even down on the shelves of the bookstore. They seemed to grow and proliferate. They were taking over. And the kitchen was devoid of clean glasses now, they had all been used by Bekka and left beside her bed, and on the bannister, and on the bookshelves, and on the front counter.

But despite this, or maybe because of it, Henry felt his mood lifting day by day. What a joy she was to have around. Vivienne and Paulo thought that he was doing them a favour, but he could see that the favour was all the other way.

On Friday night they Skyped the ship.

'How are you going?' Vivienne asked. 'Not making Grandad's life too hard?'

'I'm loving having her,' said Henry with real warmth. 'We're really enjoying ourselves.'

'I hope you're washing up and helping out, Bekka?'

'Yes, Mum.' Well, what other answer was she going to give?

'How's the travel going?'

'Your mother was a bit ill there for a while,' Paulo gloated. 'But we've both acclimatised now.'

Vivienne shot him a dirty look. 'He didn't get sick at all. You'd think he was born on the water. But yes, I'm used to it. It's getting colder. And it stays light for ages.'

Henry left the three of them to chat. He felt like an outsider again. Like a babysitter. Well, he just had to make the most of having Bekka over to stay. The four months would go like the wind. Just like Vivienne's childhood had.

He could give in to feeling sad, but it was more worthwhile to be grateful for what he had. And the weekend was here, Bekka would be around all day for the next two days. He'd make the most of it.

Chapter Ten

Bekka didn't spend much of her weekend sitting in the shop with Henry. After a late breakfast, she took off again to explore the small country town, getting to know all the residents, finding activities to do. On Saturday, she decided to take an inventory of all the stores in Cygnet, and to plan her Christmas shopping. In the afternoon, she brought a new friend to meet Henry.

Rose had dark skin and a wealth of deep red hair, arranged in a loose bun so that it sat like a halo around her face. She wore bright clothes, in many different shades of green. And she had the greenest eyes Henry had ever seen. He wondered if they looked such a intense green because of the reflection from her clothes.

'Grandad, this is Rose.'

'Henry. I'm pleased to meet you,' Henry said, as he shook her hand.

'And I you,' said Rose in what he thought must be an accent from somewhere in the UK or maybe a Nordic nation. It was a very hard-to-place accent, anyway. Where did Bekka find her, he wondered?

'Rose said I could come over and see her drones and her model planes.'

'Drones? Like some kind of robot?'

Rose laughed. 'Well, sort of. More like some kind of helicopter. I've been making them from scratch and Bekka told me she was interested.'

'She's interested in everything,' Henry admitted. 'Do you live far from here?'

'My house is up the highway a bit, but I have a small workshop just a couple of blocks north, just near the big art shed. Bekka wanted to make sure you knew where she was.'

'She's a good girl,' Henry said, then he patted Bekka on the back. 'Off you go then.'

And off they went. Bekka came back a couple of hours later, but once again she wasn't alone. She brought two children into the shop. They looked to Henry to be about four or five years old; tall and willowy children with white blond hair. They looked otherworldly. Henry couldn't think of how Bekka could have picked them up.

'This is Amber and Grecco. I met them at Rose's place. Their parents said they could come here and pick out a couple of books and they'll be in soon to buy them.'

Henry couldn't complain about that. Bekka took both children to the shelves of picture books and all three were soon fully occupied, Bekka reading story after story, and the children making piles of their favourites.

Eventually the parents came in. Henry had no problem recognising them. They were both over six feet tall and both had the same pale skin and blonde hair as their children. Henry could remember now seeing them around town. They weren't easy to forget. He wondered if they were Dutch. Surely they were. Though again, the accent wasn't so easy to pick. They introduced themselves as Evi and Marc, then went to see what their children had found.

Evi and Marc helped their children choose a single book each from the piles that had accumulated.

'This is a wonderful place. I wonder why we haven't been here before?' Evi asked.

'Grandad, you should make a kids play area here,' Bekka directed. 'We could have a table with crayons and paper. Then the parents could browse the bookshop for longer.'

Marc laughed. 'You'd want to put a play pen around it or something. They'd write on the books otherwise. If you put a pen in a child's hand, they're not going to just limit themselves to a nice sheet of paper.'

Henry nodded and bagged up the books. 'I'll think about it,' he said. But looking at Bekka's disappointed face, he thought he wouldn't be able to hold out for long. Maybe he'd get her to do some woodwork to make the playpen over the summer. That might keep her occupied for a while.

'This is a lovely store though,' Evi said. 'We might make this a regular place for pocket money spending. It's better than buying lollies.'

The children cheered and bounced up and down, cradling their books as though they were precious jewels. Evi instructed the kids to say goodbye and thank you to Bekka and Henry, then shepherded them out of the store.

'Whew,' Bekka threw herself into a couch. 'What a day!'

'Time for a break?'

'Well, just for an hour or so, then Davian and I are going to go on that nature walk down near the playground.'

Henry was exhausted by her enthusiasm.

'You stay here and mind the place for a minute and I'll go and make us a cuppa.'

'Sounds good.'

But the restful cup of tea was not what he had hoped. He came down to find a frantic Bekka checking all the shelves of children's books, looking under the cushions of the couch and even on the front desk.

'What's up?'

'I've lost my phone.' Her voice was panicky.

'Again?' Henry's tried to suppress the rolling of his eyes.

Bekka looked at him, her tears threatening to fall.

'Think about where you've been today. Maybe you put it down at Rose's house.' He put his arm around her shoulder.

Bekka thought about it, one finger playing with her top lip.

'Yeah, I think I did. When we took the drones out into the back paddock.' And she was off. Out the door like a shot.

Henry sank down on the couch with a sigh and patted the cat.

'She'll be the death of me. I'm not sure how much more of this emotional rollercoaster I can handle.' The cat purred comfortingly.

He was nearly at the bottom of his cup of tea and wondering whether he should throw Bekka's out or just drink it himself when she turned up again, all smiles.

'Found it?'

'Sure did. And Rose put this thing on it so that I'll never lose it again.'

'Thing?'

'An app. She made it. She's a genius at these things. It's like "Find my phone" only better, she says.' Bekka sat herself down in front of Henry's computer and started tapping.

'If you look here, on this website, you can see where it is. I'll never lose it again. Stoked.'

Henry had a look over her shoulder. There, sure enough, was a map of Cygnet, and a blinking red spot right on the bookshop where Bekka's phone now was.

'What if I lose the webpage thingy?'

'I'll bookmark it for you.' Bekka clicked the mouse. 'There you go. All done. She says she'll do my laptop too if I need it.'

'It looks like Rose is a very handy friend to have around.'

'She's pretty cool. One day you're going to have to go and see her collection of drones.'

Henry nodded. One day he would be dragged there by Bekka, he was sure.

Then she saw her cup of tea.

'This mine? Thanks.' She downed it in nearly one gulp. Henry winced.

'Did you even taste that? Wasn't it cold and disgusting?'

She smacked her lips. 'Nope, just right. Easy to drink. Which is good because I need to go and meet Davian now. I just need to pop up to the loo.'

And she disappeared upstairs.

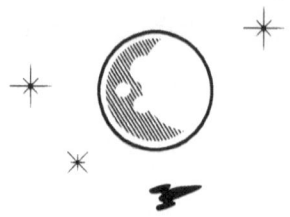

Chapter Eleven

Davian put the welding wand down and checked his watch. He'd better pack up and get going. Bekka would be waiting for him at the nature walk.

It was sad, really, that he was avoiding the bookstore. Henry seemed like such a nice guy and Davian was missing having a family.

Everything changed when his Dad got so sick and his Mum so busy being a nurse. He'd felt lonely and bored and that was why (he supposed) he fell in with the Vyynx. Oh it sounded so cool, and it was so good to be a part of a group. He'd had no idea.

The day it all blew apart would be seared on his memory forever.

He'd already spent a few weeks on the periphery of the gang, but they didn't seem to want to let him in.

He had seen the looks between the older gang members. Heard their comments.

'Do I have to babysit today?'

'He's just a runt, not worth looking after.'

All with additional curses of course. They didn't bother to hide their disdain for him, but somehow Xedrog, the leader, and Zimmin, the second-in-command, had thought he was worth investing in. And Davian himself? He just wanted to be part of the action. Part of the adventure. But they wouldn't let him come along. Not yet.

'He's still in school. Still attending classes like a good little baby.' He'd heard that one just the week before. And that had been an accusation he could do something about.

He hadn't told anyone. He'd just decided to skip school and deal with the consequences later. What would the school do to him? Kick him out? All the better. And Mum and Dad? They didn't have time to care about that. Had they cared about his homework? About his slipping grades? Not that he could see. It was all about the sick room, all the time. That was important, of course, but Davian wanted to be important too.

He remembered the mixture of nerves and anticipation in his belly as he walked the familiar back alleys looking for someone to hang out with. He'd hung about the town, turning up to the usual gang hangouts, but no one had been there to see him. It felt babyish to go straight to headquarters and say, 'See? I can skip school, just like you guys.' He was at a loose end.

And then he became hungry as well as bored, so he decided to go home, sneak into his own kitchen and get food. But when he got there, opening the door quietly and cautiously, he found his mother in the kitchen, sitting at the table, and crying. His stomach screwed itself into a ball just remembering.

She hadn't noticed that he should have been at school. Her mind was on other things. Between her tears she had shown him a communication she'd just received. The medication they'd been waiting for that would make such a difference to his dad had been stolen from the delivery ship. It was gone. Unless she could find something on the black market, and it was almost definite that they wouldn't be able to afford that, there was no chance of Davian's dad getting what he needed. Death was now probable.

At that moment, Davian realised the truth. He knew where the medicines were. They were in the stores of the Vyynx. There had been a heist just last week and Davian had so wanted to go, to be part of the adventure, but Zimmin hadn't let him. And what had they stolen? The medicines that would save Davian's father's life.

He felt ill. He was the reason his father was dying. Part of the reason, anyway. He cried for a bit and then he pulled himself together. He'd have to do something about it. Surely Xedrog would be willing to give him some of the pills. He was part of the gang, after all.

At the headquarters he grasped his courage with both hands.

'I need to speak to Xedrog,' he said, his voice wavering with the fear he was feeling.

'Now is not a good time,' Zimmin, the lizard man, the second in command, answered. But Davian pressed him and eventually he was let into the main office.

He laid out his need. 'My Dad's dying,' he finished. 'And we have the medicine to save him. I only want a dose to get him through the next month or so.'

Xedrog laughed, a sinister gurgling laugh. 'Give you the medicine? Give it to you? What? Do you think we're a charity? I'm running a business here.' He leaned forward over the desk. 'No. I'm not doing something as stupid as that.'

'But … my family,' Davian managed to stutter.

'We're your family now,' was the stern reply. 'Get used to it.'

'No.' Davian had thrown his shoulders back in defiance. 'No, I'm never coming back. I'm done with you.'

'Oh, done with us are you?' Xedrog leaned back in his chair. 'No. I don't think so. Zimmin, let's show this little turd what happens when members are "done with us".'

Zimmin had smiled, and Xedrog had laughed his horrible gurgling laugh. They'd grabbed hold of Davian and taken him into the next room. And then – Davian's blood ran cold at the memory – then they'd killed Kasp. Right there. Right in front of him. Just picked up a blaster and shot him.

Zimmin had held Davian's arm so tightly that it hurt. And after the shot was fired he turned to face him.

'You're not leaving,' he said with finality. 'And if you so much as whisper about what you've just seen, I'm happy to let the police know that you were involved. Yes, we have our people there and they will happily arrest you at just one word from me. I can give them fingerprints, DNA, everything they need to put you away for life. Or would you rather we dealt with you like we dealt with Kasp?'

Davian lifted his eyes to meet Zimmin's, terrified by the ice he saw there.

He backed out of the office, Xedrog's horrible laugh following him. 'Well done on watching that,' he'd called after him, as if Davian had been given a choice. 'You're wanted for murder now. You're an accomplice. You're one of us for good. See you tomorrow, runt.'

That was that. He'd found a berth on a transporter at the docking station. They didn't ask any questions and he didn't mind where he was going, as long as it was away from Karthur. He couldn't face his parents, and he wanted to get as much distance between himself and Xedrog as possible. He didn't know how much distance would be enough, he'd just kept running.

Since that day he hadn't stolen a cent, he'd worked for every penny, every scrap of food. He'd kept himself anonymous, hadn't even contacted his parents past a small note sent from a borrowed communicator to say that he was OK. He knew he had to stay out of touch, just disappear. He had got so tired of the continual moving through the universe and had truly hoped that here, Cygnet, Tasmania, Sector 378, Region H92, would have been a safe place for him to settle.

Oh well, seems it wasn't. And it wasn't a great place to try to fix a spaceship either. He'd never been to a place with such rudimentary technology. Still, he had to keep trying, because he had to keep running.

And he had to keep all of this from Bekka. He wasn't even sure why he was still meeting up with her. He told himself that he was just trying to forestall unwanted curiosity. He knew that he could fake an argument, of course, and stop all communication that way. But he didn't want to ruin another friendship, and he had some feeling that Bekka wouldn't let an argument stop her trying to be friends. There was something stubborn in that girl.

Of course, this would make the leaving so much harder in the end. He hated this life.

Chapter Twelve

For Henry and Bekka, the weeks fell into a routine. Early to rise so Bekka could catch the bus, then at the end of the day, dinner and a bit of homework before bed. Henry had the bookshop to himself during the weekdays, and a reasonable number of customers were coming in as the days got warmer and more tourists visited the little town.

One Thursday he heard the front door bell jangle and looked up to see Rose walking down the hallway.

'Hello,' he said, 'Welcome back.'

'Hi,' she said with a smile. 'I was passing and thought I'd have a little look around. Not that I have much time to read, but Bekka was a very good advertisement for your shop.'

'Feel free,' Henry said. 'No obligation. Anything you like particularly?'

'Something short and sweet, I think.'

As Henry catalogued the books in his head, trying to think of the best one to recommend, the cat came alive. She hopped off the desk and wound around Rose's ankles and then strode in the direction of the classics. Lightly hopping up the shelves, she came to rest in front of Jane Austen.

Or maybe she had put herself at just the right height for Rose to pat her more effectively. Henry couldn't make his mind up. She was an intelligent cat, sure, but rubbing her face on a particular book couldn't mean that she was choosing something for Rose, could it?

Whatever Henry thought, Rose decided to choose that book.

'Interesting choice, *Pride and Prejudice*,' Henry commented. 'Not necessarily short and sweet, but it's good. It's a classic. Have you read it before?'

'I'm ashamed to say that I haven't.'

'I'm sure you'll love it. Everyone does.'

'Well,' Rose smiled. 'The cat seems to think it's right for me.'

Henry looked at the cat sitting smugly on the shelf. She did seem totally pleased with herself.

'Oh, and I'd like to invite the two of you to a barbecue at my place Saturday fortnight. Are you free?'

'Let me think. Bekka's exams should be over then, and I'll be free after I've closed this place. We could be there anytime after 3 p.m.'

'Excellent. Make your way to mine when you're ready on Saturday afternoon then. I'll have a few friends over and Bekka can meet some more locals.'

Henry packed up the book and said goodbye. He was happy that Rose was giving Bekka a social occasion to look forward to. But he was sure that they wouldn't meet locals. Not real locals. Rose had obviously come here from somewhere else, as had Evi and Marc. None of them were from here. All were sea changers. Or tree changers or whatever. The point was, they were new. Not local. Not his kind of people.

He was also a little concerned about the amount of time that Bekka was spending in the company of that boy, Davian. She managed to meet with him on the way home from the bus most nights; he saw them chatting outside the shop before she came in, but he never came inside. And she spent time with him on the weekends too. Henry tried to bring him up casually in conversation a few times but the outcome was always the same.

'That boy, Davian, where's he from?'

'I don't know. I guess he's from here. I never asked.'

'And what does he do?'

'Do?' Bekka shrugged. 'Dunno.'

'Well, what do you talk about?'

'Oh, you know, books. Tech. Stuff. Just whatever comes to mind. Why the third degree, Grandad? He's just Davian. You've met him.'

Henry couldn't explain his concern. Maybe he was just worried that she'd end up with a steady boyfriend before her parents came home; how would he explain that? But he felt like there was something Davian was hiding. There was something in the way he met with Bekka but didn't come into the shop. There was something in his overwhelming politeness. He was sure there was something there. But he couldn't explain what.

He'd be able to keep a closer eye on her over the next week though. She had a week off school to study for exams and therefore, no bus, no loitering around the village. Henry would be making sure she prepared properly. These end of year exams were important, and Vivienne and Paulo had given him the responsibility.

* * *

A few days later, Henry put the kettle on, leaned against the kitchen bench as he waited for it to boil, and watched Bekka study at the dining table. She didn't use the study nook in her bedroom after all. That desk was covered with bits and pieces that she had thrown there over time. She was much happier at the dining table where she could take the opportunity for a break and some conversation whenever Henry came up for a cuppa.

'I thought this exam period would be easy peasy lemon-squeezey, but it's not. It's difficult, difficult lemon difficult.'

'It's what?' Henry laughed.

'Difficult, difficult –'

'Right, got it. Are you sure it's not ... um ... hang on ... not stressed, depressed, lemon zest?'

'Thanks. That makes me feel much better.' Bekka gave a mock frown.

'We've all done it, you know. I remember how stressed your mum was by exams. But she got through, and so will you.'

Bekka sighed.

'I know. I just wish I didn't have to do them.'

The kettle boiled and Henry filled the teapot. Bekka stretched and brought her empty cup to him for a refill.

'When's your first one again?'

'I have Monday, Tuesday and Friday. That's all. Then I can be a person again.'

'Be a person?'

'You know, talk to people, have fun, go out.'

Henry thought that by Bekka's estimation he wasn't a person at all. He wished that he had an excuse to sit at the kitchen table and read. Maybe he should do that, shut down the shop, go and do a degree or something. No, what was he thinking? He was still a farmer at heart and reading the books in the shop was enough for him. Just as serving the customers in the shop, and the occasional beer with his mates at the pub was enough interaction. Enough 'being a person' as Bekka would say.

He was missing the cat though. She seemed to feel like she needed to be upstairs helping Bekka study, rather than downstairs helping him run the store. That was an unexpected outcome of having Bekka to stay. Though most of the outcomes of having Bekka to stay were unexpected.

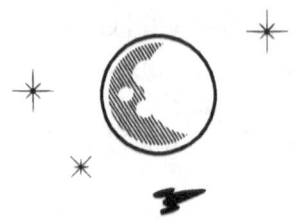

Chapter Thirteen

The exams passed as exams do. Henry was quite impressed by the way his granddaughter dealt with them. She had her mother's brains, and her father's too, so he shouldn't have been too surprised. But he had been expecting a week of intense stress, and despite her 'lemon' comments, she really managed it all quite well. Even to the point of catching the bus in the mornings. Though he did have to run up to the bus stop more than once with a calculator or notebook that she had forgotten. It was a pity that Rose couldn't figure out some sort of app that connected all of Bekka's important things to her so she didn't leave them behind.

Fortunately, most of the town was asleep when Bekka was catching the bus so they didn't see him trying to run in his slippers with his dressing gown flying behind him.

Henry was thrilled when the school year was over and they could both relax into a more decent rising time. He wondered if Bekka would get bored with Cygnet over the long summer break. Whether he would have to make decisions about which friends she could stay with in Hobart, or whether she'd start rising early to catch the bus again just to get out of the little town. But for now she seemed to like the new routine of a lazy sleep-in and then time with her new friends and exploration of the countryside. He hoped it would stay like that for a good while.

Sunday morning Bekka left the house to see what adventures she could find, but she was back in five minutes.

'Grandad! It's a market. You have to come and see.'

Henry had seen the market before, enough times that he wasn't excited by it anymore. But he couldn't bear to disappoint his granddaughter so he left his paperwork behind and, checking his pockets for keys and wallet, he followed her.

'Look, there's some Turkish food there. We'll have to come back here for lunch. And the books, do you want to check them? And look at that steelwork! Isn't it amazing?' Bekka was impressed by everything.

The steelwork was pretty good. If Henry's garden had been more than just a square of grass he would have bought one of the fire pits. He was impressed by the workmanship. He stayed and chatted to the steelworker for a while. The guy had an American accent and sat in his camp chair waving his hands at the different pieces as he talked.

'I make the designs using autoCAD and then send them to Mona to be cut. It takes them no time, it would take me forever. And then these leaves I just bend myself – the machine crunches at about a centimetre a minute, just crunch, crunch, crunch and you get this nice design.'

All this technical talk made Henry realise that he was missing his own hobby. He wanted to go back home and set up his electronics somewhere. Maybe he could unpack more books and move them to the shelves in the shop and make himself a workbench in the back shed. Or maybe he'd just have to wait until Bekka went back home.

He didn't have time to think about that now, Bekka was on to the next thing. She'd tried on a red felt hat and wrapped a red scarf around her neck. She was posing and laughing at him. The look was a nice relief from her usual 'black on black' and Henry was tempted to buy them for her but Bekka wouldn't hear of it.

'I look like an idiot,' she said.

'I think you look very nice. That colour really suits you.'

'Now you're starting to sound like Mum. "Wear some colour Bekka." No, not for me.'

She hung the hat and scarf back up and they moved on.

The next stall was a woodcraft stall. The wares included hat stands, turned pieces of fruit and tiny goblets made from all sorts of native woods. There was a gorgeous coffee table made from Huon Pine. Bekka was very taken with it.

'Grandad, we could use this for our kids area in the shop.'

'I don't think so,' Henry said, trying to keep his voice low so the stall holder wouldn't hear. 'You don't want three-year-olds scribbling all over a beautiful table like that.'

'We could use his help to make our own though. I'm going to talk to him.'

The wood turner was a fit and active-looking man, with wispy white hair and a wispy white beard. He wore an Akubra hat with a bit of possum pelt around the brim. He looked like he'd seen it all and done it all. And he was happy to talk about it.

'I love wood turning,' he said. 'I told all my kids, find the thing you love and do that. Don't work some job just to make money.'

Henry thought about it. That was the advice he'd given Vivienne too, and look where it had taken her. Away. That's where she'd gone. Overseas, and now down in Antarctica. And here was this fellow giving the same advice to Bekka.

'When I was in central Australia, you know, Uluru, there were some Americans, and it was obvious that they were from the army base. I had so much fun with them.'

'Fun, how?' Bekka asked.

'Oh well,' he said, warming to his subject. 'I'd ask them, "Are you locals? You look like locals. Where do you work?"'

Henry nodded. 'And they couldn't tell you.'

Bekka was confused. She looked from one man to the other, the question all over her face. Henry took pity on her.

'They couldn't say where they worked. The army base shouldn't exist there.'

'It was great. They just didn't know what to say. They'd stutter something at me.'

'Did you do woodwork there too?' Bekka asked.

'Everywhere. Everywhere I go I work with wood. But the wood here is the best. I think I'll stay here now, this beautiful place. This beautiful Huon Pine.'

'Do you think you could teach me some of this stuff? Grandad says we can't buy your beautiful table, but we need one for a kids spot in the bookstore – you know us? Swansong, just up the road.'

'Well, sure.' The man turned to Henry. 'If you're happy for her to come up to the farm? Maybe you could bring her along? We can teach her some wood skills. I'm Jones, by the way.'

'Henry. And this is Bekka.'

Handshakes were given all around and Henry learned first-hand how Bekka made her new best friends.

'I'll think about it,' said Henry. Was he supposed to fit woodworking classes in as well as run a bookstore? He didn't know this man from Adam and he was supposed to entrust his granddaughter to him? With woodworking tools? No, he didn't think so.

When Bekka could drag herself away from the wood turner and his many anecdotes, the two of them moved from the outside market to inside the town hall where there were even more stalls.

On the more sheltered stalls inside were more delicate items: clock stands and bowls turned from Huon Pine with resin filling in the knots and carvings, blown-glass bowls and plates, and ceramic jewellery. And one table that was just full to overflowing with random bits and bobs. Bekka was fascinated. She took her time, looking at everything.

'What's this Grandad?'

Bekka had picked up a dark metal ball, about the size of a baseball. It looked like it was made of wrought iron. It was heavy and had strange patterns worked into the surface. Henry thought it might open up to form a vase or a bowl. Bekka wondered if it might work as a lamp if you squeezed or touched a hidden switch. But no matter how much they pushed and prodded, the ball did nothing.

'Excuse me, what is this?' Bekka asked the stall holder. She was wearing a long shapeless skirt over shapeless trousers, a baby blue jacket over a loose blouse, and she had a oyster grey scarf tying back her greying frizzy hair.

'To tell you the truth, I don't know. I was out walking down by the yacht club and saw it nestled up against a tree trunk. I asked at the club if anyone was missing it, but they said no. I've tried asking around to find the owner, but no one has missed it. I ended up putting it with all my collectables, and I've brought it here in case anyone is interested in it. Are you interested?'

'I am. I'm really interested.' Bekka brought her purse out to pay for it. 'I mean, Grandad, you could look at this and figure it out. You're a whizz with electronics.'

'I don't know,' Henry said cautiously. 'I've never seen anything like it before. And we can't get it open.'

'I'm not sure if it's supposed to open,' said the woman. 'I've tried to force it with a screwdriver but I didn't get anywhere. I couldn't even scratch it. Not that I was trying that hard. I didn't want to damage it. Maybe it needs to be plugged in somehow, though I can't see where a power cord goes.'

'Well, it's pretty cool anyway,' said Bekka. 'Look at the patterns on it. I like it. I'll buy it. How much?'

'Seeing as I didn't buy it anywhere, I'll give it to you,' said the woman. 'My name's Fran by the way.'

'Bekka, and this is Henry. Nice to meet you.'

'You obviously live here?'

'Yes, I moved from Sydney four years ago. I love this community. They've made me feel so welcome. Are you from around here?'

Henry bristled. He was the community here. He was a local, so much more local than this woman. But before he could growl his response, Bekka answered for him.

'Grandad's been here forever, haven't you Grandad? He had an orchard down over that way, and now he runs the Swansong bookstore. Have you been in it?'

'Oh, sure I have. But not for a while I confess. But I wondered why you looked so familiar. I'll have to come in and have another look sometime. I'm needing some new books. I keep thinking I'll buy online, but it would be so much nicer to buy in person.'

Henry twisted his grump into a smile. It would not do to alienate potential customers. But he was ready to stop this awkward conversation.

'Shall we have some of that Turkish food now?' He said to Bekka.

'Oh you should,' Fran responded. 'It's so delicious. It's wonderful to have so many choices in this little place, isn't it?'

Was every stall holder in this market a newcomer to Cygnet?

As they pushed through the crowd to get out of the hall, Henry felt the need to be surrounded by the things he knew and not forced into making any more 'new friends'.

'Bekka, I'm going back to the shop. Here's some money for your lunch, but I really need to do some more pricing and sorting and I'm not going to get it done hanging around here. You keep having fun.'

'Can you take the ball back so I don't have to carry it around?'

'Yes, I can do that. You enjoy yourself. But let me know if you're going to head further afield.'

'Sure, I'll do that. Where's my phone?'

Henry groaned to himself, but for once her phone was safely in her bag where it should be. He waved to her and took the strangely heavy ball back to the shop. He sat it on his desk next to the register to use as a paperweight. He was ready for a cuppa and to put his feet up.

He would have forgotten about the ball over the next few days, but the cat kept drawing his attention to it. She seemed intensely interested in it. She sat by it. Watching it and watching everyone who came into the shop. She wouldn't even leave the ball to eat, and Henry found himself bringing her biscuits to the front desk. He worried about her, was she sick? Would he have to take her to a vet? But she didn't seem unwell. Just intensely interested in that black ball.

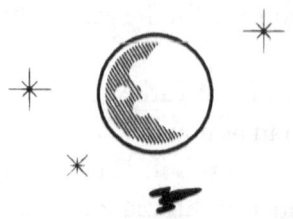

Chapter Fourteen

Saturday morning dawned beautifully clear and calm. Henry watched Bekka dance around the bookstore.

'Are you looking forward to going to Rose's, Bekka?' he asked with a smile.

'The weather is perfect! I knew it would be. Rose's barbecue is going to be fantastic.'

She was looking forward to the event much more than Henry, but even he thought that it might be a bit of fun. The weather was, after all, perfect.

'What are you going to do today before the barbecue?' Henry asked.

Bekka stopped dancing for a minute. 'I don't know. There's such a long time to wait. Are you sure you can't close the shop early so we can go earlier?'

'Very sure.'

'Oh. Well then, I might go hang out with Davian.'

Henry needed to put a stop to this, or at least keep an eye on it. He didn't mean for his commitment to his business to promote this concerning relationship.

'How about you bring Davian here?'

'What would we do here?'

Henry gestured vaguely.

'Hang out? Read books? He liked that last time.'

'I don't feel like I can ask him to buy a new book every time we get together.'

Henry nodded; that was fair.

Then he had a brainwave.

'You could help me out. You and Davian could sort out some of the books I have in the shed. The back room shelves are looking a bit bare in places. I'll bring some boxes in and you can organise them. I'll pay you in books.'

Bekka thought about it while she scrolled on her phone. Then she flashed Henry one of her friendly smiles.

'Alright, I'll go find him.'

It felt like Bekka was gone a long time, but eventually Henry saw her walk up the street, literally dragging Davian behind her. His head was down and he looked completely unenthusiastic, but Bekka was holding his arm and pulling him along, chattering happily as she did so.

* * *

Henry moved to the doorway to greet them and the cat opened her eyes and looked up from her bed in the inbox. And that's how they all saw the ball come alive.

The black ball that Bekka had been given at the market opened up, short projections stuck out and the ball rolled itself until it stood about a foot high on three legs. As Henry watched, astonished, a hatch opened in the top and a small antenna and dish shot out. Blue and green lights lit up all over it and flashed in rapid time.

Henry blinked and shook his head. Bekka clapped her hands in excitement. The cat arched her back. But Davian's reaction was the most extreme.

The colour drained from his face. His legs buckled under him, but he was able to pull himself to the gutter outside before he threw up. Henry and Bekka were by his side in an instant. The cat was more interested in the flashing blue ball. She looked it over, checking it with her whiskers, her hair on end and her tail fluffed up. She hissed menacingly.

Davian wiped his mouth and held weakly on to the wall of the building. 'I've got to go, I have to go now,' he moaned.

'What? What's wrong?' Bekka looked at him with wide eyes.

He shook his head. 'I can't explain, I just have to go.'

'Can we get anyone to help? What's going on?' Henry was all compassion.

'No. No one can help. I just need to go.'

'You can't go like that,' Henry said. 'You look like you're about to faint. Come on upstairs and have a cuppa first.'

But Davian would have none of it. He shook his head, shot Bekka a regretful glance and then ran up the street as fast as his weak legs would take him.

'Oi! Come back! What's wrong?' Henry shouted after him. But Bekka didn't shout. Bekka just ran. She caught up with him and grabbed at his arm, but he shook her off and kept going. And she kept going too.

'Bekka! Come back,' called Henry but there was no stopping her either. They rounded the corner and were gone.

Henry stood in the street looking after them. Where were they going? What had just happened?

It had something to do with that blasted blinking ball. And it was a blinking ball now. Blinking blue and green. Henry turned back inside to look at it.

'Well so much for that idea,' he sighed. 'I'm not going to get the books stacked now. I hope they get back in time for the barbecue.'

'Bekka meeyight,' came a voice. 'But I don't think you'll see any meeeooore of Davian.'

Henry froze. Then he slowly turned and looked at the cat.

'No, you didn't. I'm ... going crazy.' That process had happened more quickly than he thought it would. Wasn't dementia supposed to be a slow and gradual affair? Had he missed all the previous signs? Was it just the stress of having a granddaughter to stay?

'No, you're not crazy. I'm sorry to shock you like this but we need to talk.' The cat's voice was a little croaky, but she was definitely speaking.

'You can talk!'

'MmYes. Though I'm a little out of practice.'

'You are a cat.'

'MmNoo. Not a cat. A Kadwa. We need to talk. Maybe you could close the shop so we don't get interrupted.'

'Not a cat.' Henry did as he was told, moving like a zombie, changing the door sign to 'closed' and turning the lock.

The cat sniffed at the flashing ball one last time, then jumped off the desk and led the way upstairs.

'Whiskey, I think,' she said jumping lightly onto the dining table.

'You ... you want a whiskey?'

'No. You want a whiskey. I will just have one of those salmon snacks.'

Henry pulled out the box of snacks, and poured himself a large whiskey. He must be dreaming, he thought. He had thought he was awake, but he was just dreaming. Though the whiskey tasted strong enough. He sat at the table and drank with a trembling hand.

'Are you alright?' the cat asked.

'Me? Sure.'

'Have another sip.'

Henry did as he was commanded and as his pulse calmed he tried to make sense of what had just happened.

'Bekka is gone,' he said. 'But you said she'd be back.'

'Well, she might. That's not determined yet.' The cat delicately licked the remains of the salmon snack off her whiskers.

'But Davian, you think he's gone.'

'Mm... Yes. He needs to leave as soon as possible.' Her voice was calm and in control. Like she was talking about the weather. But she was talking about, what?

'He needs to leave Cygnet?'

'No, he needs to leave this galaxy.'

Henry tried to take it in.

'He needs to leave this galaxy. Right.' Henry's voice was flat. 'Maybe you need to tell me what's going on.'

I'm listening to a cat, he told himself. I really am crazy. But his brain was starting to come to terms with the situation. Even as he thought about how strange it was, he decided to relax and just let things happen. The whiskey was working. He would listen to the cat. And she wasn't a cat. She was a, what was it again?

'What are you again?' he asked. 'And what should I call you if you're not a cat?'

'I'm a Kadwa,' the cat said pleasantly. 'But you can call me Cat. MmYes, Cat will be fine. It's the name you know me by, and we have been friends now for five years. Let's stick with that. How about I tell you my story first, and then we can talk about Davian.'

'That sounds sensible,' said Henry and he settled back into his chair and took another sip of his whiskey.

'You need to know that many of the people here are newcomers.' Cat began.

'I know they are,' grumbled Henry getting into his regular groove. 'The locals are outnumbered. Every second person you meet is a sea-changer.'

'Mm... Yes, sea changer. That is a good term. I am a ... sea changer ... myself, a scene change was what I needed. I was born many light years away, you don't really need to know about my birth planet. I only lived there a few rotations. I chose to leave as soon as I could. I went into law like my parents before me, and like my 25 siblings. Many Kadwa are lawyers. Arguing is what we do best. Finding the way to open the closed door.'

Henry thought about how good Cat had been at getting her own way in the past years since she turned up on his doorstep. And that was when she was choosing not to speak. What was she like when she could use words as well?

'I had a successful career, many rotations, 34 different planets, I was head prosecutor for Jimlin and Family, but you won't know them.'

'Of course I don't know them,' Henry grumbled. He still felt somewhat dazed.

'I have the feeling that Davian knows them,' mused Cat licking her paw and wiping one ear.

'We'll get to Davian later,' growled Henry.

'Of course,' said Cat. Then speaking in the quiet and authoritative voice that had given her so much success in her career, she told Henry about her former life and the feeling of burnout that had overtaken her. She didn't give a lot of detail; the argument with Julis and the loss against the Vyynx was even now a bit of a raw nerve. She didn't need to bother Henry with endless stories in the present moment. It was clear that he wasn't taking much in. As he said, they'd get to Davian later. She just told him that a big case that had required lots of work had gone sour, and that her desire to work had gone sour right along with it.

'I did my research. I was looking for a place to heal. Somewhere that was away from everywhere. Somewhere I'd be anonymous. I looked all over the galaxy to find the most relaxing place I could go. Then I packed my little pod and prepared to move here. That's when things got a bit rocky.'

'They weren't already rocky?' Henry asked. Despite himself, he'd got sucked into her story. He was seeing her less and less as a cat, more and more as a person. She hadn't changed in essentials, she was still the cat that he'd got to know. But now she was communicating more freely and she had a lot to share, apparently.

'OK, they were already rocky, my health was bad, but my life hadn't been in danger. The travel to Earth though … well … I knew my pod wasn't good for multiple voyages, but I thought it would work a bit better than it did. Your atmosphere wasn't good for it, and the pod wasn't good for your atmosphere. It set off a bit of a storm, I'm afraid.'

'Five years ago, eh? I remember that storm. I wondered how it had blown up out of nothing.'

'Well, now you know. The landing was a disaster. The pod caught fire and I had to bail out. I was summarily deposited here with nothing. I had my savings of course, but no way to access them. I was stuck.

'And you took me in. Thank you, Henry. I hope I can repay the favour. You saved my life. You allowed me to recuperate. You gave me the rest I needed.'

Henry was stunned. He looked at his glass but it was empty. He got up and filled the kettle and put it on to boil. Cat remained quiet, watching him carefully, letting him process. Henry got out two mugs, and spooned some tea leaves into the teapot. Then, as the kettle came to the boil, the Kadwa intervened.

'No thanks, Henry. I still don't drink tea, even if I do talk.'

'Ah,' Henry looked at the mugs. 'I guess I'm working on automatic. Bekka would have …'

He dunked his tea bag and placed it on the sink, then he poured milk into his mug and sat down again.

'Bekka. And Davian. You said you have some idea of what's going on there?'

'I must say, you're coping with this really well,' said Cat with an approving purr.

'I won't be coping well if I lose my granddaughter,' Henry growled. 'And neither will her parents who left her in my safekeeping. What do you know about all this?'

'Well, I obviously don't know the whole story but I have to say I was surprised when you came into the shop and put that probe down on the front desk.'

'Probe?'

'That's what that blinking ball is. It's a … how will I explain this? Oh yes, it's an intergalactic police probe. They send them out to find criminals who have jumped bail, or escaped some other way. There are thousands of them out in the universe, hundreds of thousands. They are programmed with the biological signals of all the criminals on the loose and they are sent out randomly. When they come into close proximity of a criminal, they, well they do what you saw. They send a signal to the nearest police vessel, and the hunt is on.'

'So when Davian came into the shop …'

'Yes. I knew he wasn't from earth the moment I saw him. He knew the same about me. You noticed that he avoided the shop after that first visit. He was hiding something for sure.'

'Davian is a criminal?' Henry's voice rose.

'Well, yes. Sort of. He's a wanted man, anyway.' Cat remained calm, even licking her paw again to clean the other ear. But Henry was not calm. He slammed his mug on the table and rose to his feet.

'You have let my granddaughter run off into unknown danger with a godforsaken criminal who is wanted by the … the …'

'Intergalactic police. Yes. If you wanted me to stop her you're looking at the wrong Kadwa. The Sambiss are better at that. I'm sure I saw one walking past the other day.'

'I'm going to kill him. Right after I wring your neck. Right after I call the police.' Henry pulled his keys off the hook near the door and took off up the hall to find his coat.

'No you're not.' Cat sprung off the table and followed him to his room. 'You're going to calm down and sit down and we're going to work this out together. Where would you go to find them?'

'I … I have no idea.' Henry yanked open the cupboard door and snatched out a jacket. 'But the police should be able to help me there.'

'And what would you tell your police?' Cat almost purred.

Henry stopped. He sank down on the bed and put his head in his hands. What would he tell the police? That a talking cat had told him his granddaughter was in the hands of a dangerous criminal from another planet? At best they'd laugh him out of town. At worst, he'd lose Bekka to Child Protective Services. He really wasn't doing a great job of looking after his granddaughter.

'Exactly.' Cat jumped on the bed next to him. 'Now calm down. I have an idea of what to do.'

Henry looked at her helplessly.

'I don't think she's in any danger, by the way. He wasn't asking her to go with him, and they've spent hours together so far without him trying anything. No, my feeling is that he's not violent.'

Henry sighed heavily. He rubbed his hands on his trousers, then pulled himself together.

'You said you had an idea?' he asked Cat hoarsely.

'Yes. I think we should go to the barbecue.'

'What?' This really didn't compute. But Cat was patient and calm.

'Rose's barbecue. I think we'll find help there.'

'How are we going to find help at a local barbecue? Who there is going to believe us?' Henry ran his hands through his hair until it stood up around his head. This was not solving anything.

'Well, Rose for one. She's not from around here.'

'And by "from around here" you mean Earth, right?'

Cat purred. 'Good Henry, you're catching on. Yes, she's from, oh the name doesn't matter. But if I know anything about her barbecue, there will be others there as well.'

'Others! Aliens?'

'Yes, that's what you call us. Not foreigners. Aliens. There will be other aliens there. I'm sure we will be able to work together and find Bekka. Especially if that Sambiss is there. Ugh, I don't like them, so undignified they are. But helpful in this situation. For sure.'

'I guess all I can do is trust you.' Henry felt helpless.

'You can trust me, and you can drive the ute,' said Cat, ever practical.

'Do you want a cat box to travel in?' Henry managed a small smile.

'Not on your life!'

She climbed on his lap and rubbed her head on his chin. 'Don't worry Henry, we'll get Bekka back. And we might even make Davian's life better while we do it.'

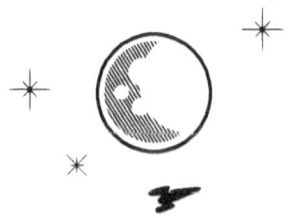

Chapter Fifteen

Cat sat on the front seat of the ute, looking intently at the scenery as it passed. Henry first thought that she was looking out for Bekka and Davian, but then he realised that he had kept this intelligent creature locked in a bookstore for years. She must have been so bored. This was a grand outing for her, seeing the scenery for almost the first time. No wonder she had cried when he had shut her in a cardboard box to take her to the vet.

'I'm sorry I didn't take you for a drive in all these years,' he said.

'You weren't to know,' said Cat. 'But I must say, I am enjoying the view.'

'I'm surprised you didn't try to escape.'

'I tried a couple of times, but you were very efficient with window screens and such.'

'Well, we're told to be, aren't we? The local cats kill the wildlife and in a beautiful country place like this … I didn't like to let a killer loose.'

'I am very much not a killer,' Cat said. 'But I understand what you were trying to do.'

The road dipped down to the ocean, and they drove past the little yachts floating in their safe harbour. Then it rose again through the bush, a quarry on one side showing the strata in the rock. At one point a beautiful orchard thick with leaves occupied the side of the hill, at another there were cattle in a rich green paddock. Cat took it all in with wide eyes.

Rose's house was a modern two-storey blue weatherboard mansion. It sat high on a hill, with spacious front steps leading up from a curved driveway. The driveway was full of all sorts of cars, from expensive Mercedes coupes to beat up Kombi vans. Henry couldn't figure out from looking at the cars what any of the guests at this barbecue would have in common. Had they all been invited off-the-cuff like he had?

He got out of the ute and opened the door for Cat. She looked at the jump down to the gravel driveway and then at Henry who was holding the door.

'Do you think you could carry me?' she asked. 'Would it be too much of an imposition?'

Henry moved closer to the seat and Cat climbed up his outstretched arm and sat on his shoulder, her tail wrapped around his neck.

'Yes, this will work,' she whispered into his ear. 'I can see everyone and talk to you like this. At least until I know for sure what is going on.'

Henry felt self-conscious, he wished that Bekka was there. She would have taken all the attention and allowed him to sink into the background where he preferred to be. But now, here he was, climbing the steps to a stranger's house, with a ruddy cat wrapped around his neck. He felt like an idiot.

But he'd be all kinds of an idiot to save Bekka. He needed to find Rose, and the Sambiss, whatever that was.

The front door of the blue house was wide open. The polished wood floorboards of the hallway made a path straight through to the back. There was no-one in sight and all the noise was coming from the back yard. Henry could hear clinks of cutlery, children laughing, a dog barking, and sounds of conversation mixed with some low-level pop music.

'Are you going to be alright with a dog?' he asked Cat through the side of his mouth.

'Don't worry about me, I can take care of myself.'

Henry's heart sank further as he imagined a massive cat and dog confrontation, filled with hissing and scratching and growling and barking and … ah well, it was too late now.

Rose stepped out of a side door carrying a large bowl of salad in one hand and a basket of bread in the other. Her dark skin was set off by her white sundress, which she had covered with a pink frilly apron to protect it from the beetroot in the salad, Henry surmised. She gave Henry and Cat a welcoming smile.

'Hello Henry, welcome. And hello to you too, Cat.'

Henry grimaced and nodded, and Cat purred. Rose didn't seem at all surprised to see Cat on Henry's shoulder, but she looked past them and asked, 'And Bekka? Is she out the back already?'

'Bekka is –' Henry didn't get very far. The two blonde children that Bekka had befriended raced past, followed by a couple of younger children happily yelling at high volume. They bumped into Henry and nearly caused Rose to drop the bowl.

'Now kids,' she called after them. 'Walk inside, running is for outside.'

The kids reached the bottom of the front stairs, turned around and raced back past them, paying Rose very little heed.

'Kids will be kids.' Rose shrugged elegantly, holding the bowl of salad out of bumping reach. 'Come outside and meet some others.'

She walked ahead of them to the back yard and put the salad on the table.

'Jones, do you know Henry?' she called. Henry looked in the direction that she was calling and beheld a familiar face.

'We met at the market,' answered Jones and sauntered over to say hi. He was wearing the same outfit – looking just like a Crocodile Dundee wannabe.

'Hello again.' Jones firmly shook Henry's hand. 'And hello to you.' He scratched Cat behind the ears, again showing no surprise at all to see a cat on Henry's shoulder. Henry waited for Cat to hiss or scratch, but she seemed to appreciate the attention. 'Now, you'll want a drink, Henry. Beer?'

Henry watched Rose head back into the house, presumably to deal with some more food. He had hoped to chat with her privately; he didn't want to draw attention to himself. He let himself be drawn along with Jones, to have a beer, to meet a few more people. He watched a golden retriever on the lawn jump to catch a frisbee the children threw for him. He smelled the sausages and hamburgers cooking on the barbecue. He wished he could just relax here, enjoy the atmosphere. But he was desperate to talk with Rose, to find Bekka.

He turned to go back to the house, but Cat stuck her claws into his shoulder. 'All in good time,' she whispered. 'Don't worry.'

Feeling frustrated, Henry gripped the stubbie Jones offered him. This delay was costing them valuable time. Bekka and Davian were who knows where? They could be long gone before he could even talk to his granddaughter. He wished he had asked Cat how long she thought they'd have before the police made it to Earth to find Davian. Did it take them minutes to travel through space? Or days? Or years? Was it like Dr Who? Or more like 2001 A Space Odyssey? But he didn't want to ask her that here, in public.

He shifted his feet and glanced again at the house.

'Just wait, just a little longer,' Cat whispered in his ear. He tried to force himself to relax.

Rose came out of the house with another plate of salad. She placed it carefully on the table looked everything over, ticking things off on her fingers, and then, apparently satisfied, she picked up a gong and struck it. The resonant, echoing sound got everyone's attention.

'Welcome everyone,' she yelled. 'Help yourself to food and drink. If anything is missing, or if you need other food, come and talk to me, I'm sure I can work something out. Make yourselves at home, and make friends. That's what this party is about.'

It didn't take much encouragement. Most of the crowd moved to the table and started serving themselves salad and meat. Henry stood back. He felt like he couldn't eat anything at all. Instead, he studied the odd collection of people who had gathered for this barbecue.

There were two mismatched women at the salad table, bonding over potato salad. One, the older woman, was dressed like a teenager. Dreadlocks that were dyed pink and purple and held in place with a tartan bandanna, a denim jacket with a frayed collar and cuffs, red tartan trousers and heavy black boots to complete the ensemble. She was talking to a much younger woman who was dressed like a millionaire from an old black and white movie. She wore a huge tent-like beige woollen cape and her hat looked like a cylinder covered in leopard skin. What would they have in common? Apart from an obvious love of potato salad.

The tall blonde couple were there, the woman was squeezing tomato sauce onto a couple of sausages in bread and calling to the kids who were racing around and playing with the dog. The kids didn't look like they were keen to stop playing and eat. Henry blinked and shook his head. It really looked for a moment there like the dog was rounding up the kids, pushing them over to the parents. Surely not. But he was being given his own sausage for his efforts.

From the far end of Rose's back yard a couple of familiar faces moved to the table and helped the younger children load their plates with food. Weren't they the people who had bought the orchard? He was very sure they were. What were they doing here?

Looking after the barbecue was a very short dumpy man whose fluffy white hair sat in a fringe just above his ears. He wore a suit, but it fitted him so badly that it looked like it was made for another species. He was cheerfully greeting everyone as they lined up to get their burgers and sausages.

His new friend Jones had gathered him into a group that included a young guy sporting the best curly-haired mullet that Henry had seen since the 80s. He wore a loose black t-shirt and working pants. On the chair next to him was a bright yellow chunky-knit jumper that he had obviously taken off as the weather had warmed up.

Rose moved off to the side, and patted the dog.

'Now's our chance,' said Cat.

Henry walked over to Rose, trying to look nonchalant.

'Rose, I must talk with you. I need your help.'

Rose gave him a beautiful smile.

'Cat told me to talk with you,' Henry started, then stuttered to a stop as he realised how stupid that sounded. But Rose didn't look at all put off. She smiled encouragingly.

'You see,' he started again. 'The thing is, Bekka has run off with Davian. Cat says he's running from the intergalactic police. And somehow we have to find them before I lose Bekka. And Cat said you could help.'

Now was the point where he found out whether he had actually gone mad, or whether Cat was right and Rose would help. He held his breath.

Rose looked concerned, but instead of calling a doctor, she nodded.

'Yes, I can help,' she said. 'In fact, everyone here can help you.' She moved towards the gong again.

'Oh no, I don't need everyone in Cygnet thinking that I believe in aliens.' Henry held her arm to stop her. 'Little green men and all that. They'd take Bekka away quick smart if they thought I was going insane.' He grimaced. 'Do you think I'm going insane? I'm talking to a cat and all.'

Rose laughed, a light and glittering sound.

'No, you're not insane. I know a Kadwa when I see one, and it's pleasant to be able to talk with you openly, Cat.'

'Thank you,' Cat nodded to Rose. 'I must say, I'm enjoying being free to speak again.'

'As for "little green men" well, there aren't any of those here. They find it too hard to disguise themselves. I've heard of a few visiting earth, but they leave again pretty quick smart.'

'Oh I didn't mean … I don't want to cause offence.' Henry felt his face warm. What a stupid thing to have said.

'Don't worry, Henry. I know this must be a bit for you to get used to. But you can see we're not that different to humans. Well, most of us aren't.' She spread her hands to indicate the crowd having fun in the back yard.

'Do you mean … ? Is everyone here … ?' Henry was stunned.

'Yes, we're all visitors, all from other planets, other galaxies. It's amazing that we all made it here, there's this whole planet to choose from, and of course, so many end up in the bigger cities. LA is full of us, and so is Mumbai. But there is quite a population of us in little Cygnet. It's just such a lovely place to live.'

'Well, I think so,' Henry was always pleased to hear someone praise Cygnet. 'But my daughter, she had to leave.' He started in on his usual complaint. Why did Vivienne have to leave? Look, people from all over the galaxy had decided to live here.

'Oh we're all individuals, aren't we? Anyway, we need to find Bekka. That's for sure.' Rose reached for the gong again.

'I thought the Sambiss could help,' said Cat.

'Oh, good idea.' Rose turned to the dog. 'Are you happy to help?'

The dog's tail wagged furiously and he jumped for joy.

'Yes! Help! I'm good at helping.'

'Not too smart, but a good nose,' Cat whispered in Henry's ear.

Even the dog! Thought Henry. Even the dog is an alien. The people who bought my orchard are aliens. All of them are aliens. I thought I knew this town. Obviously not.

'Give me a scent! I'll find her!' The dog was now turning in circles, his joy to help out too great to be concealed.

'Great, just wait a minute and we'll see if the others are willing to help too.'

Rose bashed the gong again and got everyone's attention.

'Folks, we have a situation. I'm afraid it might be serious. Can you all listen to Henry here and he'll tell us what's happened.'

Henry gulped. But then he thought of Bekka and he pulled himself together.

'There was a probe in my shop. Davian set it off this morning. He's run away, and my granddaughter Bekka has gone with him.'

Murmurs of concern spread through the crowd. Henry might not know these people, but they all knew Bekka. She had become a favourite of all of them in the short time she was in the town.

'I don't know where she is, but I want to find her before your police show up. I don't want her to be in any trouble. Will you help me find her?'

There was much nodding and calls of, 'yes' and 'of course'.

Rose took over.

'The Sambiss here is willing to help, but if any of you know where Davian kept his ship, or if you have any information, can you come and tell us now? The bush is a large place, I know you all know that. And there are numerous hiding places, so any direction would be great.'

The crowd surged towards them, all of them wanting to help whether they had any news or not. The woman in the denim jacket pulled a small notebook out of her pocket and a pen out of her hair.

'If they are not saying something that is relevant to right now, how about you send them to me, and I'll take notes,' she said. Rose nodded gratefully.

There was information about where Davian was seen when he turned up at town for the first time. The blonde kids had seen him traipsing into the bush to the south of the sailing club a few times. And Jones and the guy with fluffy hair both chimed in to say that he had originally came from the south.

Henry was eager to leave. As soon as the sailing club was mentioned he stood up to go. That looked like the place to start.

'Just hang on for a minute,' Rose said. 'You're not going by yourself.'

'Well I'm taking the dog.'

'Yes, and I'll just get changed and come with you. And Jones? Will you come?'

'Try and stop me,' Jones said. 'I'll just get some stuff out of the car.'

'Cat, are you coming?' Henry called.

'No, I want more information,' Cat said. She transferred herself from Henry's shoulders to sit on the veranda stairs.

'More information about what? We know where to go and find her.'

'I think there is much more information needed here,' Cat said firmly. 'You go find Bekka, I'm going to ask some questions.'

Henry shrugged and left her to it.

He and Rose took the front seats of the ute, the dog and Jones jumped into the back of the dual cab.

'Ready?' he asked. The Sambiss barked joyfully.

The ute spun the gravel up as they pulled out of the driveway. The children stood on the steps and waved them on their way. Jones waved back, but Henry didn't notice them at all. He was on a mission.

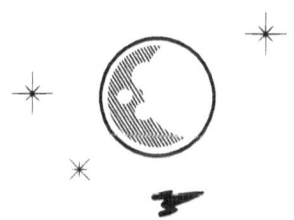

Chapter Sixteen

Henry rocketed back towards Cygnet at speed, cutting as many corners as possible as he raced along the winding road. He wasn't looking at the scenery now. Back past the orchard and the cows, back past the quarry and down the hill to the waterside. There were swans from which the town got its name sitting on the water, and over the other side of the bay sat the beautiful peaceful yachts. That's where Bekka and Davian had to be, where he would start searching.

He crossed the bridge over the little creek and pulled in to the Port Cygnet Sailing Club carpark at speed, slamming the ute into a parking space and throwing on the handbrake.

'Right. We're here,' he said.

'Let's do it,' barked the dog. Or the Sambiss. Henry knew it was a Sambiss, but the thing looked so much like a dog, like a golden retriever, that he knew he'd always call it a dog.

'Do you need something to get the scent from?' asked the ever practical Rose.

'Oh. Yes. Yes. Scent.'

Henry looked around from the driver's seat.

'There should be a black jacket back there somewhere. On the floor?'

Jones and the dog looked around.

'Yep, there it is. Found it,' said Jones. 'This is just like when I went with that tracker in Alice to find the deserter from the US Army.

They were good times. He was out there, stuck in the desert, if we'd been half a day longer he would have died from heat exhaustion.'

Henry didn't want to think about anyone dying.

'Got the scent?' Rose asked.

'Yep, yep. Got it.'

They piled out of the ute and the dog started sniffing all around the car park and the nearby paths.

While they waited, Henry took the opportunity to ask Rose, 'What's the dog's name?'

'That's a bit tricky. Here on Earth he's sometimes called Buddy. But the thing is Henry, it's more polite not to call him that. He hates it. The Sambiss takes his identity from his clan, his family group. He is a Sambiss. That's all.'

'It's going to be odd, not calling someone by his name,' Henry grumbled.

'You'll get used to it mate,' Jones said.

Henry thought that there was a lot for him to be getting used to, all at once. He crossed his arms and watched the Sambiss as he continued his investigation.

A couple of times the dog stopped and gave a second or third sniff to the same area. Henry wondered if it would be better to just send out several search parties. But eventually the dog barked.

The three of them rushed over to him.

'Yep, this good. This way. Your girl went this way with an arphaxad.'

So they set off, following the dog as he moved ahead of them, his nose to the ground, weaving side to side as he followed the scent.

They walked up Jetty Road. First past some houses near the water, then some fields with nicely ordered rows of green shoots just peeping up through the rich dark soil. Whatever vegetables they were, Henry guessed they would be sold at the market when they were grown. Then past a paddock, empty right now, but probably kept for sheep. One side of the road was lined with a rickety fence - wooden posts leaning all anyhow, and wires between them. They could climb it easily enough if they needed to, but Henry hoped they wouldn't have to. How would he explain his presence if the owner of the land asked what they were doing there? What could he say? We're looking for a crashed spaceship? That wouldn't go down so well.

Henry, Rose, and Jones were quiet as they walked. Each lost in their own thoughts, they kept trudging up the road, putting one foot after the other. But a bark from the dog brought them back to the present. He was behind them.

'Hey, here. They leave here.'

'Good boy!' Henry said. Then immediately regretted it. Did the dog like being called a good boy? Did Sambiss enjoy that kind of patronising praise?

The dog grinned at him, with his tongue hanging out.

'Yes. Good,' he said. Then he plunged off the road (fortunately, the side without a fence) and started to lead them through the paddock towards a line of trees.

It was slower going as they made their way through the bush. Henry hadn't gone for a walk like this for a long time. Probably not since Vivienne brought Paulo down for the first time and he had tried to show him the wonders of the Australian wilderness. He couldn't believe how dry the bush was today – tinder dry. He hoped that no spark would set it off this summer. He hoped that there would be rain soon.

The ground under the gum trees was littered with fallen bark. They walked through that for a while, the crunching and crackling of the dry bark under their feet the only sound. Then they passed on to a wetter area on the southern side of the hill. Ferns covered the ground now, a little creek wandered past, and the air filled with a sweet scent. And Henry noticed a humming sound. It started faint and grew stronger and stronger.

What was it? Henry looked up and around. Was it the police coming? Was it the sound of spacecraft engines? It was otherworldly, scary.

Then he realised that the sound wasn't anything otherworldly at all. It was insects, lots of them, making the most of the sweet smelling flowers in the tops of the trees. It was spring after all.

The Sambiss led them through the ferns and back up the hill to the sparse covering of gums and the dry-as-dust twigs, dirt, and bark on the ground. Henry's legs started to tire and he stumbled over rocks in the path. He stopped looking at the scenery and became more careful of where he trod. It wouldn't do him any good to sprain an ankle at this point. They all needed to be searching for Bekka, not providing first aid to an old man who was too stupid to watch where he was putting his feet.

Rose seemed to walk as lightly as a feather. She almost floated over the surface of the ground. Jones was solid and down to earth but he didn't make much noise in the bush either. He may have been an alien, but he knew the bushman's ways. He must have been learning since he got to earth, or maybe his planet was covered in something similar to the Australian bush. Henry would have to ask him (once he got his breath back) just how long he'd been on this planet.

He wasn't a fan of visitors, newcomers, but now he was stuck among them, dependent on them. And he was finding himself to be more and more curious about this new world that had opened up to him.

Another strange sound met Henry's ears. Was it a cricket or a cicada? It almost sounded like someone welding. How amazing it was that nature's sounds could sound like something so industrial.

The dog slowed down.

'Close now,' he growled.

The three of them looked down into the gully ahead. There they saw something Henry had never thought he'd see outside of a television.

In among the trees was a dark blue, metallic cylinder with a pointed nose and stubby wings. It looked a little like a space shuttle, but it was only just larger than a motor home. It was obviously a spaceship. It was also obviously being patched up.

The noise that Henry had heard was not a cicada, nor was it a cricket. It was, in fact, welding. Henry assumed the person he could see was Davian wearing a welding mask and fixing new panels to one wing of the ship. The panels had probably been torn away on landing.

There was no sign of Bekka.

'What if Bekka isn't here?' Henry whispered.

'She is. She is here,' the dog responded in a low growl.

Henry nodded. Then he wondered why they were whispering and hiding. Bekka hadn't run away from home. Davian hadn't kidnapped her. She had just come with him and was presumably now figuring out what Henry had discovered – that there were aliens in Cygnet and that Davian was one of them.

If he'd waited, she probably would have come home to him tonight, bursting with news, unsure of how he'd take it, but ready to take him on the ride. From the looks of the barbecue crowd, she had already made friends with most of the aliens around. He didn't think she'd be as shocked as he had been.

In any event, there was no need to sneak around. He stood up, and prepared to slither and slide his way down the rough gully to the spaceship.

He stretched out his legs, and brushed off his trousers. Then he stopped. The humming sound had started again. The insects sounded even closer than they had done before. And they were getting closer still. He looked around to see why the insects would have started to sing all together and where the swarm was. But there were no flowers in the tops of the gums this time. This humming sound wasn't insects.

The noise grew louder and louder. Jones pulled Henry back down to the ground. The dog whimpered and tried to hide his face under his paws. Rose whispered, 'Oh no.'

The humming materialised into a spaceship. An unbroken spaceship, that had no trouble settling into the gully and coming to rest next to Davian's clapped out wreck. A grey utilitarian spaceship with blue markings on it.

* * *

Bekka *had* enjoyed the unexpected adventure that the day had brought. Convincing Davian to come back to the bookshop had been harder than she'd expected, but she'd enjoyed the challenge. And she had been very concerned by his reaction to the probe activating. She'd followed him through Cygnet and ignored his repeated requests to leave him alone.

'I'm not going away,' she'd said. 'Not until you tell me what's going on.'

They'd slowed to a walk by then as Davian's path had taken him up hill. Though Davian's long legs and rapid stride had meant that Bekka still had to trot to keep up with him.

Eventually he'd given in to her repeated questions.

'Look, I'm really not supposed to tell you any of this. And you must not tell anyone, not even your grandad.'

'Oh come on, how bad can it be?' Bekka smiled but the smile left her face when she saw how serious Davian was.

'Bad,' he said. 'And if I didn't have to do this now, right this second, I wouldn't tell you. It's for your own protection. In fact, you'd make everything a lot easier if you'd go away.'

'I can look after myself,' Bekka bristled. But Davian just shook his head.

'I can't even look after myself,' he said. 'I can only run away. And I just hope ...'

He turned off the road to stride through the paddock, Bekka trotting alongside.

After a few false starts he said, 'Long story short: I'm an alien, I'm wanted by the police, and I need to fix my spaceship so I can get off this planet and try to find a safer place.'

'Right.' Bekka stopped and shook her head, then she ran to catch up with him again. 'Look, if you don't want to tell me, then don't. But I'm going to follow you anyway. I'm not the kind of friend that can just be put off like that.'

Davian sighed at that. A big long sigh. Then he shrugged and said, 'Come on then. I'll show you.'

They walked in silence through the bush until they got to the top of the gully. Then Davian pointed to his ship, sitting at the bottom.

'See?' he said. 'That's my little ship. I call her Vera.'

Bekka's eyes grew large and she stared at Davian.

'Really? You really are an alien? Where are you from? Which planet? Which system? How did you get here? Are there other aliens?' The questions tumbled from her mouth.

Davian laughed. Then his face grew sombre again. 'I'd love to tell you all about it, but I'm sorry, I can't. I'm not supposed to tell you by law, and now the probe has activated, I don't have time. My ship got damaged when I landed here and I need to fix her up and get off planet as soon as I can. It would have been better if I'd left yesterday. And Bekka, you shouldn't be here with me. It's not safe! I'm not safe!!'

Bekka snorted. 'As if I could leave now.' And she scrambled down the gully wall. This was the best thing she'd ever seen. Her excitement grew as Davian opened the ship door.

'I'm going to do some welding out here,' he said. 'You go inside the ship and check it out. You'll hurt your eyes if you watch me weld.'

'No problem!' Bekka said. 'This is the best!'

She looked around the ship with shining eyes. To the left of the door was the bridge. She sat in the captain's chair and studied the displays. They were dark, of course, the ship wasn't powered up yet, but she could imagine looking out the windows at all the stars and planets, she could imagine picking her path through an asteroid belt or landing on a brand new planet, untouched by human hands. Being the first there. The first human on a whole new world.

She swivelled the seat to face the back of the ship and then rose to explore it, opening cupboards and panels. She couldn't believe it. A real live spaceship. There were even places to sleep and eat. It was just beautiful.

Could she take photos? Well, no one would believe it was real, but she could pretend that she saw it in a museum somewhere, couldn't she? Or she could just take photos for her own memories. Maybe once Davian got the ship all fixed up he could even take her for a ride before he left Earth for good.

That thought stopped her in her tracks. If she wanted time to have a ride, and he was in such a panic to leave, she probably needed to help him with his repairs. She wondered if there was anything she could do.

The sound of welding stopped for a moment and she took the opportunity to step outside.

'Can I help you fix her up?' she asked.

He took his helmet off and wiped his sweaty fringe back from his eyes.

'I know I don't know much, or anything really about how to fix a spaceship,' Bekka said. 'But maybe there's something I can patch up for you? Or get ready for you to work on?'

'I guess you could open the console for me,' he said. 'I have to get in there and fix the wiring after I finish this. I mean, if you could find me a new power supply that would be better, but …'

Bekka grinned, 'Yeah, I know nothing. But show me the screwdriver. I'm sure I can do that.'

Davian led her back into the ship and opened a panel to a cupboard filled with tools. He took out something that had a handle like a screwdriver, but the end was neither Phillips nor flat head. It looked to Bekka more like a tiny stick blender.

Davian pressed a button on the handle a few times and the end attachment changed shape until it matched some small patterns in the console.

'You stick it against the pattern, and you press this button,' he explained showing her as he talked. 'There are about 20 places that need undoing.' He pointed a few out.

'Can do,' said Bekka. 'Glad to be able to help.' She thought about asking him if she could have a quick flight as payment, but looking at the frown that seemed permanently glued on to his face today she decided to give it a miss. She could ask him when the ship was ready to go.

It was fun to play with the new tool, and she was happy to feel like she was being helpful. The sound of welding kept her company and she sang to herself while she worked.

Then she heard a new sound. A humming sound that grew louder until it felt like it was filling her brain. She peeked out the door to see what Davian was doing, shielding her eyes in case it was something dangerous.

She saw the grey ship settle just behind Davian. Saw him drop his welding wand and stare, frozen to the ground.

'What's going on?' she asked.

Davian unfroze and gestured wildly at her. 'Get back inside. Hide. Hide!' But he was too late. The door to the new ship opened and six creatures filed out. They were all different shapes and sizes, but each wore a blue uniform with the letters IGP emblazoned on it. They lined up in formation. Bekka looked at their black helmets and a chill went through her.

A final figure stepped out of the ship and moved to the front of the group, the others making way and forming up again behind him. His helmet had a clear window and she could see his grim frown as he looked directly at her friend.

'Davian Jernoshef, also known as Stmille, Fornora, and Brentual, I arrest you in the name of the Intergalactic Law.'

Davian seemed frozen to the spot, and for a half second Bekka was frozen too, then she jumped into action.

'What? No!'

She threw herself at Davian holding his arm with two hands, trying to pull him into the ship. The officer moved towards Davian, his hand reaching for something on his belt. Was it a gun? Handcuffs?

Bekka gave up on pulling Davian, now she pushed herself in front of him, backing him into the small ship and waving her arms to keep the officers away. The alien now turned his attention to her.

'You don't want to do that, human,' he said. 'This arrest has to be made. And you should not try to stop it.'

'Of course I'm trying to stop the arrest,' Bekka said. 'You can't take Davian, he's done nothing.'

The alien's face changed from stern to angry.

'Are you obstructing me in the performance of my duty?'

'Yes! Yes I am,' Bekka yelled. 'You can't do this, you can't!'

'No Bekka, don't say that,' Davian cried out. But it was too late.

The captain turned to his officers. 'Make two arrests. The second for obstruction of justice.'

They looked at each other, just a slight hesitation, but the captain snapped, 'Do it!' And the officers made their move.

Two took hold of Bekka, one to each arm and pulled her out of the way so another two officers could get to Davian. The clasp of their hands felt like steel. Bekka kept kicking and struggling, but she couldn't get free. The guards holding Davian had an easier time. He walked slowly with them, his shoulders slumped in despair.

* * *

Henry had watched all this from the top of the gully. He couldn't hear what anyone was saying but when he saw the strange creatures take hold of Bekka he was done with hiding. He shook Jones off and scrambled down the side of the gully, scattering pebbles and twigs, holding on to tree trunks and branches to steady himself. He wanted to shout out to his granddaughter, tell her to hold on, but he couldn't seem to catch his breath.

Then his foot slipped on some rolling gum nuts and he fell. He looked up and saw Bekka being pulled into the new ship.

Davian walked behind her with his head bowed. His two guards were almost unneeded. The rest of the aliens followed behind, the captain last of all.

Henry pulled himself back to his feet just in time to see the door to the grey ship close with his granddaughter inside. The humming intensified again and the ship rose above the treetops, then winked out of existence, the humming lasting a few seconds after the ship was gone.

He stood and stared, holding on to a tree trunk to support himself.

They were gone, and there was nothing he could do.

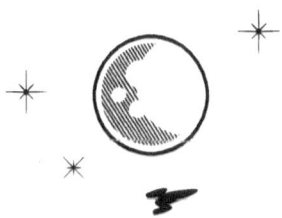

Chapter Seventeen

Rose, Jones and the dog made a much more cautious descent to the bottom of the gully. While the dog comfortingly leaned up against Henry, Rose and Jones had a good look around.

'It's a pretty neat ship,' Rose called from inside.

'Not much damage out here,' said Jones. 'I reckon he could have done the final patching in an afternoon or so.'

'Pretty much the same in here. There are a few loose connections. And he would have needed some parts from somewhere. But he was doing a good job.'

'A few more hours and he would have been out of here.'

Henry hardly heard them. The only thing he could concentrate on was that Bekka was gone. She was gone somewhere that made it impossible for him to follow. How could he face Vivienne? How could he face anyone?

Rose stepped out of the spaceship, brushed her hands on her olive-green pants and looked at Jones with a twinkle in her eye.

'Are you thinking what I'm thinking? Shall we do this?'

Jones grinned in reply. 'We can give it a good try.'

'Not without Cat though,' Rose mused. 'We might need a lawyer like her on our side. We should go back and see what she says.'

'Sure. You go talk to her, I'll stay here, I reckon. Maybe get started on this,' Jones waved at the welding gear. 'See if I can fix up some of his mistakes.'

'Me too,' said the Sambiss. 'Keep guard.'

'OK, good,' Rose said. 'Coming Henry?'

Henry looked up at her, his face covered with misery. The dog nudged his head under Henry's hand, but Henry shoved him aside.

'I don't care about the ship,' he said. 'You can drop me at home.' At least there he could be miserable in peace, without being surrounded by these aliens who didn't seem to understand in the least what he was going through.

'Henry,' Rose gently put her hand on his shoulder. 'How are we going to go and rescue Bekka and Davian without a spaceship? The Visser family live in theirs. Mine's been converted to a greenhouse. Jones, I don't suppose you have a working ship?'

'I do, but it's in Darwin. I started there, and made my way south.'

'Yes, and I'm pretty sure Devi and Sura are in the same position. Devi left his ship in India and Sura ... actually, you know, I think she found passage on a shuttle that dropped her off as it passed. They both made their way to Cygnet eventually and made their new lives here. This is a super community Henry, you should be proud of it.'

Henry pulled out a handkerchief and wiped his face. This was too much to take in.

'So ... you're saying ...?' He carefully folded the now grimy handkerchief and put it back into his pocket.

Rose continued. 'We need a ship to go and get them. And right here, we have a ship. We just need to get it going. Then we can go after them.'

'But ... the police. I mean, they are fully armed and we ... '

'We'll come to that bridge when we cross it,' Rose said.

'Cross that bridge when we come to it?' asked Jones.

'I always get that mixed up. But thinking of it, I reckon we'll cross it and come to it at pretty much the same time.' Rose smiled. 'Anyway, we need to get to work. We'll have to head back to my farm, there are some things I'll need to pick up. And, as I said, we need to talk to Cat.'

She looked back inside the ship, counting on her fingers.

'Do any of you know anyone with a working knowledge of electronics?' she asked.

'Just myself.' Henry felt a small tingle in his spine. Was this hope?

'You know someone?'

'No, I know about electronics. It's my hobby.'

'Do you have circuit boards and a soldering iron?'

Henry gave a wobbly smile. 'And components, resistors and such. But I don't know that anything I have is space age technology.'

Rose nodded. 'I'll supply the space age things. I stripped my ship out when I turned it into a greenhouse.'

'I've got all I need here,' said Jones. 'Hand me that mask and I'll get started. I can do an hour or so before we lose the light.'

Henry picked up the welding mask and passed it to Jones.

'Are you sure you want to stay here?' Rose asked the Sambiss.

The dog looked from Henry to Jones.

'Here. I stay here. Keep watch,' he barked.

'That's a good idea,' said Rose. 'Keep a look out.'

Henry looked at the dog, who was standing with his tail between his legs. Henry hadn't meant to hurt him. The dog had worked so hard to get them to Bekka and it wasn't his fault that they were two minutes too late.

'Thanks old mate,' he said. 'We wouldn't have known what had happened without you getting us here in time.' He gave the dog a pat on the head.

The dog barked joyfully and his tail wagged again. Rose patted him too, then she and Henry hauled themselves up the gully and started the long walk back to the ute.

'That dog, he's a fun one,' said Henry. 'Not too bright, but fun.'

'He's not so bad. Don't underestimate him. I mean, he's learned to speak English from scratch with a mouth that's not suited to the language at all. His sentences are short, but at least he knows the trade language. I guess you don't speak Sambiss.'

'Not Sambiss, nor French, nor Chinese. I only speak my mother tongue.'

Henry hadn't thought about that before. About just how clever people were to master a language not their own. About how stupid he would sound in another country, trying to get his point across.

He had a new appreciation for the dog, and for Cat. And for all the other aliens and human visitors in Cygnet when it came to that.

'What do you all speak in space?' he asked.

'We speak all different kinds of languages,' laughed Rose. 'Hundreds of them, millions of them. As many languages as there are different aliens, and more. In my planet, there are heaps of different groups and languages, just like there are here. But our trade language throughout the universe is a lot like English. That's the funniest thing about Earth, I think. The way you think all aliens on the one planet sound the same, talk the same language, think the same thoughts. I mean, they do in the mental dictatorship of Krazilec but that's due to that horrible mind forcing ability of the dictator.'

Hundreds, no millions of different kinds of aliens. Millions of different planets. Henry looked at the sky. The sun was getting low and the long Tasmanian twilight was beginning. He thought about all the stars you could see in the night sky out here in the country where there was no light pollution. So many stars, and so many planets around them, and so many different species on the planets. It made his head hurt.

'How are we going to find her?' he moaned to himself.

'Let's talk to Cat first,' Rose said. 'First things first, then we'll work out what's next.'

* * *

As they drew up to Rose's house, Henry could see the woman in the denim jacket standing at the top of the steps and Cat sitting at her feet. Light poured out into the evening dusk from the porch, welcoming them back. It was a homely look that made Henry ache for family dinners, and chats over a glass of wine around an open fire. He would never have that experience again if he didn't find Bekka.

The two of them climbed out of the ute.

'Did you find them?' Cat asked.

'Yes, and no,' said Rose.

'What does that mean?' asked the woman in the denim jacket.

'It means we were right there when the IGP dropped out of the sky and collected the two of them.'

Cat's fur rose and she arched her back.

'In broad daylight? On a Class D planet?' she asked.

'Yes. Just like that.'

'And took the two of them?' Cat's questions continued. 'Why did they take Bekka?'

'Well, we weren't close enough to hear. But it looked like Bekka did her best to get in the way, and that got on someone's nerves. Anyway, they took her.'

'That's just … all of that is against the law. There has to be a real reason to arrest someone. A daytime landing? Exposing themselves to a human, arresting a human? Ridiculous.'

'So, what do you think, Cat?' Rose asked. 'Shall we go and get them back?'

'It's a bit of a big deal, taking on the IGP,' murmured the woman in the denim jacket.

'Yes, but so is arresting a human. And for no good reason,' Rose said.

Cat settled again but the end of her tail twitched in frustration. 'Even Davian shouldn't be under arrest. Just collected. Not arrested.'

'Well, he was in handcuffs. So I think he was properly arrested. Cat, you seem very interested in that lad. You know more than you're saying.'

'Let's just say I have some unfinished business there.'

'What?' Henry had felt like he was following the conversation to this point, but now he was totally lost.

'It's an old case of mine,' Cat said. 'An unsatisfactory case.'

'She's been working on it all afternoon,' the woman said with a wry smile. 'If you can't get her to the kid, I reckon Cat is going to make her way there by herself. She may look cautious but I'm not all that sure she is.'

Cat declined to answer that, but she shot a sharp look at the woman and her tail waved even more.

'We can do it, I reckon,' said Rose. 'We have a ship – Davian's ship. It's in a state of disrepair, but it's almost ready to go. Davian was fixing it up when we saw him. We left Jones and the Sambiss there working on it tonight and we could head back at first light and do the electronics. I've just got a few things to do here in preparation.'

'Jones will come too?' asked Cat.

'He's keen,' said Henry. 'We're all keen.' He tried to keep the desperation out of his voice.

'It would be a worthy challenge. And I've missed the thrill of a good legal battle.' After a few more waves of her tail Cat wrapped it around her feet and looked up. 'Let's do it.'

Henry let out his breath in a big sigh. The decision was made.

'We've saved you some food. Come and eat,' said the woman in the denim jacket.

Henry didn't think he'd be able to force any food down, but once he sat at the large wooden kitchen table he found that he was ravenous.

'Thank you.' He stuck out his hand. 'Henry,' he introduced himself.

'Sura,' she said in return and shook his hand.

'How was the rest of the barbecue?' he asked around a mouthful of hamburger.

She laughed. 'You definitely changed the topic of conversation. Cat here was told many a story and given many a character reference for Davian. I nearly sprained my fingers writing it all down. It's been a while since I was a legal assistant, and never to someone so clever with the questions as this one.'

Cat looked modestly down her nose and purred. 'I think we have a very solid case,' she said. 'Davian is the witness I need. This is really satisfactory.'

Henry looked from one to the other. He was lost. Completely.

'I'll leave you with it then,' he said. He knew where he belonged. He ate as quickly as he could. He and Rose had work to do.

* * *

Rose and Henry stood at the door to Henry's back shed and

looked at the piles of boxes on the floor.

'It was all organised before Bekka came, then I had to chuck it all in boxes and squeeze it into the shed out here. I meant to come out and deal with it, but I haven't yet,' Henry explained.

Rose put her fingers to her temples.

'OK, let me think. What do I need? Resistors. Yeah?'

'Probably in this box here. I have them all in a folder, sorted by resistance.'

'Capacitors?'

'Should be in the same box, I think.'

'Right, and where are the boards?'

Henry stepped over the first pile and started rummaging around between the old radio, and the even older turntable.

'Make yourself at home,' he said. 'Anything you can find, take it. I don't care. I've never really used this stuff for anything important. But this, this is important. Take stuff apart if you need to.'

Rose pulled the nearest box towards herself and started sorting through it. Henry found some boards and a small box of capacitors. Then he emptied one of the larger boxes, dumping everything on the floor, and put all the necessary items into it.

'How are you going?' he asked after a few minutes. 'Got everything?'

Rose looked up, a vague smile on her face.

'Why didn't I know you had all this before? When we're done with this adventure, can I come back and have a play? I've missed this stuff, and you have some fascinating antique gear here.'

'Antique?' Henry's voice rose an octave.

'Oh come on Henry, this stuff is pretty out of date, even for Earth, I haven't seen anything like it on my planet. I can figure it out, well, most of it, you might have to help me with some. But it's so great! I love it.'

'Well, sure.' Henry couldn't stop the pride rising. 'Anytime.'

'When we've got Bekka and Davian back.'

The bubbles of joy went flat at the reminder. How were they going to get them back with this apparently antiquated technology?

'Anyway, yes, I think I've got all I need here. I'll put these resistors in your box. And, do we have the solder? And the iron? Then great. Let's go to my place and we'll put a few things together.'

Henry's electronics knowledge was pushed to the limit that night. He didn't know what half the components were that they were working with. But he could do the soldering, make the connections, and generally follow Rose's orders.

At around 3 a.m. she declared them finished. Inside they found Cat sleeping on an armchair. Sura had put out a pillow and blanket for Henry on the couch and he fell on the soft pillows with gratitude. Despite his exhaustion, it took him a few minutes to calm his brain enough to sleep, but eventually he dropped into an uneasy slumber.

Chapter Eighteen

He was gently shaken awake by Rose at about 6 a.m.

'Sorry Henry, but time is of the essence. Sura's made us some coffee. Let's get going.'

'Coffee,' said Henry groggily. 'Could I have a strong tea instead?'

Sura smiled and refilled the kettle.

The sky was light. Henry and Sura ate toast and Vegemite, Rose preferred peanut butter.

'I don't know how you can eat that horrible black grease. I only keep it in the house for guests,' she said.

Over breakfast they planned their day.

'Henry, you and I will pack the ute. Sura, if you can put together some sandwiches and leftovers from yesterday we'll take them to Jones and the Sambiss.'

'On it,' said Sura.

The delicate electronics that Henry and Rose had been working on were packed into boxes, and carried to the ute. Then Rose said, 'Now for the hard part.'

She called Sura to help, and took them both to the very back of the greenhouse. There, leaning against a shelf was a large cylindrical object, about the size of three microwaves, bolted to a larger rectangular metal sheet.

'This is the main thing. It's the power supply for the ship. I'm just not sure how we're going to get it there. It's very heavy.'

It didn't look too heavy but when Henry tried to shift it by himself he realised just how dense it was. He could get it to move, but it took all the strength of the three of them to pick it up and heft it out to the ute. They slid it onto the tray and Rose shook her hands.

'That hurt. It's so heavy. But it's absolutely necessary. I don't know how far Davian thought he was going to get with his tiny power supply.'

'Perhaps there's another one hidden in the ship? You only had a quick look around.'

'Perhaps.' Rose didn't sound too convinced.

'Well, we can drive further up this time. All the way to the paddock. Then we just have …' Henry's voice faded.

'Yes, the walk across the paddock, through the trees, past the ferny bit, and then down the gully to the ship.'

'You're sure it's absolutely necessary?'

Rose just sighed and shrugged. Henry's spirits sank.

Sura jogged back to the house, then came back carrying a cooler bag in one hand and a couple of grocery bags in the other.

'I'm ready? Are you two?'

'Sure.'

Henry pulled himself into the cab. He needed more sleep, he was running out of energy already. He could have done with another cup of strong tea. But he didn't want to waste time. They had a lot of work to do. Sura sat in the back of the dual cab ute, arranging the food around her.

'We're forgetting someone,' Rose said. She jogged back to the house. Next minute Cat calmly walked down the stairs and hopped lightly into the ute. Rose followed her, carrying a thermos, and locking the door behind her.

'I think we'll all need more coffee, and tea for you Henry, by the time this day is through,' she said. Henry flashed her a grateful smile.

Henry once more drove along the familiar road. But this time he drove further up the hill and parked by the paddock fence.

Each person loaded themselves up with boxes and bags. For the moment, they left the power supply in the ute. Henry covered it with a tarpaulin and prayed that no one would become curious enough to look underneath. They walked quickly and quietly towards the ship, Cat passing like a lion through the long grass.

Henry didn't want to say anything, but by the time they got to the gully his arms and knees were aching. He was very unused to this amount of exercise, and on so little sleep. He knew he wasn't going to be able to carry that power supply anywhere.

The Sambiss barked joyfully as they arrived.

'Here! They are here.'

Jones appeared from the other side of the ship.

'Welcome,' he said. 'Come on down.'

They scrambled down through the trees, their feet rolling on the gravel as they tried to make it down the gully wall without losing the gear they were carrying. By the time they got to the bottom Sura was looking considerably ruffled. She dumped the bags on the ground and put her hands up to arrange her hair and Henry stared in amazement. He could see two antennae poking out of her dreadlocks. She really was an alien. He had almost forgotten that these people he was working with weren't human. Obviously Cat wasn't human but he talked to cats all the time anyway, it was just that this one was good at talking back. But Rose, with her incredible knowledge of technology that was literally out of this world, and Sura with her antennae, and Jones, who knew what Jones could do? They were not human.

But they were people. And they seemed to be happily ready to help him find his granddaughter. He couldn't help but be grateful.

'We've got breakfast for you two,' said Rose to Jones and the dog.

The dog's tail wagged furiously and Jones grinned.

'I hoped you'd remember us. I've had a look all through the ship and there wasn't a smidge of food there. But the water refiner is working, so that was helpful.'

The cat and dog sniffed hello to each other, then Cat delicately stepped into the spaceship. Sura dug into the bags to find the food for Jones and the dog. Rose followed Cat into the ship, and Henry, boxes in his hands, stood in a sleep-deprived trance, wondering just what he was doing there.

'Henry,' he heard a call and he flicked out of his sleepy stare. 'Henry, can you come in, and bring the soldering iron?'

'We'll need to plug it into something,' he responded. He hadn't thought about that last night. They were out in the bush, no electricity here. And how was the welding being powered, when it came to that?

'Davian's little power supply can handle powering a soldering iron.' Rose poked her head out the door and laughed at him. 'I don't think it will push the ship very far through space, but a soldering iron should be fine.'

'What are we doing about that?' Jones asked through a mouthful of sandwich.

'I've got mine from my old ship. It's on the ute, we just need to figure out how to get it here.'

'Heavy?'

'Very,' Henry said with feeling. Jones nodded thoughtfully and went back to chewing. Henry dug through a box until he found his soldering iron. Then, for the first time, he stepped into the spaceship.

It was a very neat little craft. A bit dusty, perhaps, but every thing had its place. To the left was the bridge, which was looking a lot messier than he guessed it usually would be. Rose had pulled out a panel and there were wires spilling out everywhere as if she was performing some serious surgery on the ship's guts. Behind the bridge was the, well, it would be called the galley in a ship, a normal ship, a sea-going vessel. Small cupboards lined the walls. Below them were shelves but the shelves were not open. Meshed covers dropped from the top and hooked in under each shelf. Henry thought about it, the covers would stop the shelf contents from spilling out in zero gravity. There was a tap-like pipe sticking out of the wall – the water, Henry guessed. There were seats clipped to the other wall, one of them had been pulled out a bit and Henry could see how they could be arranged in a U-shape around a small table, or tucked back against the wall to make more space.

To his right was the sleeping chamber. Again, there were small cupboards tucked under the lower bunks, and drawers cut into the base of the upper bunks. Everything was designed for efficient storage. He could see that the ship was designed to hold about four people, though it would be pretty squashy. The sleeping chamber could be separated from the rest of the ship by a sliding panel. The colour scheme for the eating and sleeping chambers was blue and white while the bridge looked like it was made of something like stainless steel. The ship was designed for travel in space, but also for living in when docked in an environment like Earth that had gravity. Henry was impressed.

'Henry, you there?' called Rose, her head deep in the wiring of the control panel.

'Here,' he said. 'Where do I plug this in?'

'There's a power outlet just beside that seat.' Rose gestured behind her.

'Will the plug work?' Henry was suddenly worried. 'Won't it be a different design?'

Rose sat up and looked at him.

'Oh, right. In the box, one of the boxes, there are a couple of universal adaptors. They look like … white cylinders … Jones might know. I think you saw me pack them last night.'

Henry shook his head. There was so much strange stuff last night. He couldn't remember half of it.

'I'll go look,' he said, setting the soldering iron on the seat.

'Thanks,' said Rose and tucked her head back under the console.

Henry stepped outside, reorienting himself by looking at the gum trees around him. They were still there, still normal. He pulled himself together.

'Anyone here know what a universal adaptor looks like? There are apparently a couple of them in one of these boxes we've brought along.'

All of them got to work. Henry and Jones helped Rose inside the ship. Cat and Sura, on the other hand, sat a little to the side in deep conversation, Sura once again writing copious notes.

After a couple of hours, Rose stopped work.

'I'm sorry folks, I need to go out for a while. I need some sunshine.'

'Of course,' said Jones. 'Henry and I could do with a break too.'

'And another cup of tea,' said Henry.

Rose looked weak and pale. Even her hair looked pale. Henry felt so guilty.

'Have we been working you too hard, Rose?' he asked.

'Oh no,' she smiled. 'I just need the sunshine, that's all.'

She stepped outside, running her fingers through her hair. Then she stripped off her jacket to reveal a singlet top, hitched her cargo pants over her knees, found the sunniest patch of ground she could, and lay down.

Henry looked questioningly at Jones, but he didn't seem at all concerned by her behaviour. He just poured some hot drinks for himself and Henry and rooted through the grocery bags to see if there were any snacks. Sura looked up to see what he was doing, tucked her pen back into her dreadlocks, and got up to help.

Henry sidled over to Cat.

'What's going on?' he asked. 'I mean, what is Rose doing?'

'She told you,' said Cat. 'She needs sunshine.'

'Well, we all need sunshine, but I'm not lying down half-naked.'

Cat snorted. 'But you are not a plant. Rose needs sunshine to give herself energy. That's why she loves living here. Your sun here is much closer than hers in her home planet. There, they spend all day out in the sun. Here she can be energised in a few hours, half an hour in the strong sunshine of summer. Winter it takes her a bit longer and she tends to hibernate a bit. But give her just a little while and she'll be energised and working again.'

'She's a plant?'

'Why do you think she called herself Rose?'

'She's a plant.' said Henry flatly. 'A plant. Like, not an animal, a plant.' He tried to get his head around it.

'She's still a person.'

'A person, but also a plant.'

Henry tried to get it straight in his brain, but in the end he gave up and instead found himself a large flat rock to sit on while he sipped his tea. Sura brought him a piece of fruit. He sat and soaked the sunshine in, wishing that it could energise him like it energised Rose. Instead he found himself feeling more and more sleepy. He gave in, lay down on the warm sun-soaked rock, and drifted off.

* * *

Henry woke up, and stretched out his tired and stiff limbs. He couldn't tell how long he'd been asleep, but he was grateful that the sun had moved behind a tree and that he'd been in shade for a while. He didn't need a powerful sunburn on top of all the issues he had to deal with right now.

He looked around and found that the whole group of aliens were huddled together a little way off, chatting animatedly. He shook the blood back into his legs and walked over to join in.

'What's going on?' he asked.

'Welcome back, Henry,' said Rose. She looked totally refreshed, her hair back to it's glorious red, her skin a deep ebony. She really was a plant, he thought.

'We're just discussing how to get the power supply from the ute to the ship,' said Jones.

'It's the next thing we need to do. Other than that, the ship is pretty much ready.'

'If the four of us worked together,' Henry started.

'It's just too heavy, for that distance. I think we're kidding ourselves if we think we can do that.' Rose cut him off.

'We just use Davian's power to get the ship to the ute, then put in the new supply.' Jones suggested.

Cat shook her head and her tail fluffed out.

'We can't do that. It will draw too much attention to ourselves. We would be sure to be noticed in the length of time it would take to install the supply and we can't let that happen, you all know that.'

'Why not?' Henry asked.

'It's fully against the law. We'd all be taken away by the IGP if we did that. It would change things on your world too much.'

'Maybe it's a risk we have to take,' Jones stated.

'As a very last resort,' Rose said. 'But only when we've exhausted all other options.'

Cat didn't look happy with that possibility; her twitching tail gave her thoughts away.

'We could get a shopping trolley and put it on that,' said Sura brightly. 'Then wheel it over here.'

'From Huonville?' Jones was not impressed. 'Getting the trolley here will be hard enough. What, do we put it into Henry's ute and hope no one sees us stealing it? Then drive the twenty minutes back here with no one seeing? Then push the trolley over the rocks, and down the gulley?'

'Maybe if we get everyone together again. If everyone from the barbecue came and helped to carry it, it would be hard, but we could do it,' Rose said.

'You guys don't have any of that anti-gravity stuff, like they do in the movies?' asked Henry. 'Or is that just fantasy?'

Rose looked at him and shook her head.

'What movies have you been watching?' asked Jones.

'So it doesn't exist then? I'm so disappointed.' Henry laughed a little at himself, but was brought short by the clear and factual voice of Cat.

'Oh it exists,' she said. 'But there are laws against bringing these things to early development planets.'

'Early development planets?' Henry was offended. Did she mean Earth? Earth was a developed planet. Not all countries, obviously. But Australia was a developed nation, with fast-growing technology. So fast he couldn't keep track of it. But it seemed that Cat was talking about Earth.

'Yes, undeveloped planets like this one. You have only made it as far as stepping on the moon a few times. You have so much further to go before you can handle things like an antigravity device. I've attended a few court sessions where people were seriously punished for playing with those things here.'

'So people have played with those things here?' Henry was amazed.

'Of course. Where do you think those tabloid stories come from? But they shouldn't. They get in heaps of trouble if they're caught at it.'

Through this conversation the dog had been behaving strangely. First he had put his head to one side, his ear flopping delightfully. Then his backside started to wriggle. Finally, his whole body exploded into action, tail wagging furiously.

'Yes! Yes!' he barked. 'Marc has.'

'Marc has? Been in the tabloids?' Cat was scornful.

'No, Marc has one that we want.'

'Marc has an antigravity device?' Rose asked.

'Yes! So much fun with kids. Chasing. Jumping.' The dog bounded around them to demonstrate.

'You and the kids have been playing with an anti-gravity device?' Cat's back arched and her tail flicked back and forth. She was obviously displeased.

'It's probably a fairly weak device,' mused Sura.

'Weak or not, Marc and Evi should know better. They shouldn't be letting their kids play with something like that,' said Cat. 'I'll have to pretend that I didn't hear about it.'

Jones chimed in. 'A weak one will be just what we want. It will help us get the power supply over the fields and rocks. We can all help to stabilise it, but the device will give us enough lift.'

Henry clapped his hands. 'Done. Let's go get it.'

'You go. The Sambiss and I will stay here with the ship. The Sambiss will help protect it,' said Cat and curled up on the warm flat rock to go back to sleep. The dog looked at her and sighed, a deep and mournful sigh. He tucked his tail between his legs.

'I have stayed a long time. I want to walk.'

The four others looked at each other, then Rose made the call.

'Sorry, but you need to stay here. You can protect the ship better than most of us. You can scare off or bite anyone who comes near. We don't even have a weapon that would help. I know you want to come with us, but you are much more useful here.'

'Useful is good,' the dog said and his tail lifted a bit. The others encouraged him, and patted him on the head. And then they scrambled back up the gully. Rose pulled her phone out of her pocket to call Marc and Evi and they set out through the bush back to the ute to wait.

Chapter Nineteen

Rose tucked her phone back into her pocket.

'Evi's looking for it now. The kids aren't home but she's pretty sure they didn't take it with them, wherever they went.'

'Imagine using antigravity as a kid's toy.' Jones was scornful. He had found himself a broken branch, stripped the bark off it and was using it as a walking stick.

'It does seem strange,' Sura said.

'Everything about this is strange,' said Henry with a laugh.

The others laughed with him.

'Steep learning curve, mate,' said Jones.

'Steeper than the gully wall, and I'm an old man. But I'll do anything to get Bekka back.'

'Well, we're nearly there now,' said Rose. 'We just need to get the power supply in, and do a full check, but I'm feeling confident I've fixed all the damage. Davian did well, he got the job half-done. I just had to finish it off.'

Henry looked around at the blue sky, and the gum trees, felt the gentle breeze and heard it whisper through the treetops, he smelt the gorgeous blossom and listened to the insects and felt the ground beneath his feet. He felt himself coming out of the strange fog that he'd been in, and settling back down to earth. Walking in the bush always centred him, strengthened him. And it was doing its job now, even though they were walking to get an alien power supply and an antigravity device. Was it any wonder that he was in a bit of a spin?

Everything he was doing and seeing was unfamiliar, unusual, even bizarre. It felt like he had fallen into a novel from his shop. It would be an exciting adventure if it wasn't for the fact that he had no idea where Bekka had been taken, and no idea how he'd get her back.

It occurred to him that the people walking with him were giving him a great gift.

'Thank you all for helping out with this. I know that it's very important for me to find Bekka, but I have no idea why you are all putting yourselves out so much. Working so hard. Staying up all night. I'll never be able to repay you.' His voice broke and Rose reached out to gently touch him on the shoulder.

'Hate to say it mate, but this isn't all about you,' said Jones. 'There are so many things here at stake for the rest of us.'

'Really? Like what?'

'We're a pretty tight-knit community here. You would have seen it if you'd been able to hang at Rose's barbecue for a while. We're like family. And even though Davian has been a bit of a quiet one, he's still part of us here.'

'A bit of a quiet one?' exclaimed Sura. 'He's been completely silent, I should say. I was happy that Bekka was taking him out of himself. That he'd found someone that he could relate to. But to think that he was running from the IGP. Well, he kept that to himself.'

'And wouldn't you?' asked Rose. 'But we would have been able to help him. I wish he'd said something.'

'Knowing the IGP it could be a wrongful arrest right from the get go. People told us some really interesting tales at the barbecue yesterday. I mean, we don't have the whole story, we need to talk with Davian. But the IGP have got it wrong many times before.' Sura said.

'Trigger happy. Look at how they arrested Bekka too. It's not like they had any cause to do that.' Jones swished his stick at an apparently offensive blade of grass.

'And there's another reason we're helping out too.' Sura said. 'We want this place to stay safe. To stay a refuge for people like us. If the IGP decides that we're all criminals on the run, they could come and do a blanket search. They've done that before too. Arrested everyone not born on a planet. Broken up families. Damaged communities.'

'Just think of all the damage they could do. Just think if all the non-natives in Cygnet just disappeared overnight.' Rose ran her hands through her beautiful hair.

Henry had thought of that. He had thought of it a few times in his grumpier moments. He'd imagined all the non-locals leaving, and Cygnet belonging to the people he felt really 'belonged' there. But he thought about it again. And this time his perspective changed.

What would the Cygnet market be like? It would have a third of the stalls, if that. And who would they sell their goods to? The health food place would go, and the Vegan Café that did such amazing cakes and slices, and they would lose at least one of the gift shops that came in so handy at Christmas time. And the antiques place. And with a reduced population there's no way they'd have funding for the library or the health care centre – they'd have to go to Huonville for those amenities.

And how about those open-mic nights that Bekka had been trying to convince him to go to? Or the winter celebration up at the cider place?

You can't keep things static. They either grow or they die. It works that way for plants, for businesses and for little country towns. When he thought about the Cygnet he had lived in as a child, he thought about it with fondness. But the same applied to the Cygnet he lived in now. It was a great little bustling active town. A town that provided enough customers to keep his bookstore going and keep him in his happy place. And it wouldn't be the same without the visitors, without the new residents. They were as much Cygnet as he was. He could see that now.

The little town of Cygnet was worth protecting. Not by kicking all the newcomers out. Not by keeping new people from coming in. But by welcoming people in, showing them the culture and helping them be a part of it.

And these aliens knew that. That's why they had adopted Davian as one of their own. Why they had adopted Bekka, come to that. And that's why they were working to rescue them both.

'Well, I'm still grateful,' he said gruffly.

The other three laughed. 'You're welcome,' said Rose on behalf of them all.

When they got to the ute, the four of them attempted to lift the power source but it was obvious that they couldn't carry it all the way to the ship without help. It was just too heavy.

'What's this thing made of?' asked Henry.

'Do you really want to know?'

'Is it radioactive? Is it going to give me cancer?'

'Oh it's so hard to explain. Do you know much about chemistry? Physics?'

Henry shook his head. He had finished high school, but that was all. Vivienne or Paulo might be able to learn from Rose, but he wouldn't.

'You'll just have to trust me. It's safe. As long as it stays in its metal shield. And it's a good long-lasting power source. It won't last forever, of course, but the restraints around it are pretty tough.'

Henry looked at Rose like she was from another planet. Then he laughed. She was from another planet. And she was a pretty bright spark as well.

'Don't you get bored living here?' he asked. Now it was Rose's turn to laugh.

'I keep myself occupied. I'm just happy to be out from under the pressure that I had in my job. I couldn't do more than just potter in the garden for the first three rotations – sorry, you say years – the first three years that I was here. But now I feel a little more active. I read the history of scientific discovery on this planet and it keeps me happy. And I do a little work now and then, write a paper myself and put it on the IG web. That sort of thing. A bit of editing. But I'm happy to take life a little slower now. Like you and the bookstore.'

He stared.

'You're retired? How old are you?'

Jones tutted. 'You never ask a lady that.'

Henry couldn't help himself. He continued to stare. Things would have got awkward if they weren't distracted by the little blue hatchback bumping up the dirt road towards them.

'Oh good, it's them,' Sura said.

Evi parked and got out of the car.

'Sorry,' she called. 'The kids are so messy. But I found it eventually.'

'Cat was a little put out that you have banned tech,' Sura informed her.

'Oh, I know we shouldn't.' Evi flicked her long white hair over her shoulders. 'But the kids are going back home to boarding school soon and I didn't want them to be totally behind in their knowledge of all the tech. Imagine how you'd suffer if you were a country bumpkin like the kids here. No offence, Henry.'

'None taken,' said Henry. 'Boarding school?'

'Yes, they are six and eight and they're going to want to head back to Handelivian at some stage. And we need them to go there soon before the gravity here totally stunts their growth. I mean, look at Marc and me. Getting shorter by the day.'

'It is a bit heavier here than Handelivian, isn't it?' Sura fluffed her dreadlocks as if the gravity of the earth was pushing them on to her head.

'They're already going to be shorter than most of the kids, but if we send them home soon … Anyway, that's what we're thinking. So we've smuggled in some tech and taught them some of the games that are played there. We're very careful. We've only told the Sambiss.'

'Well I, for one, am very grateful to you,' said Henry. 'I'm glad we've got something to get us over this roadblock we have. Is that it?'

Evi held a small green and yellow ball in her hand. It was about the same size as a juggling ball. She handed it to Henry and he studied it. It was squashy like a juggling ball, and had a single button on it. It looked far too simple to be any help in their situation.

'You press the button, like so, and then the button is also a dial so you can turn it to the strength you want. It's not too strong but it can float Marc to the ceiling with very little trouble. Want a ride?' Evi asked.

'No, no, no. No thanks. Not for me.' Henry quickly passed the ball to Rose.

'Well, thanks Evi, that's so helpful.' Rose said and turned to the ute again.

'Just one thing Henry,' Evi said. 'I know you probably haven't thought of this, but could Marc and I help you watch the store while you're busy? It looks so sad all locked up. The kids have been loving going there to visit you and Bekka. Would you mind if we babysat? Opened it for you?'

The store. Henry hadn't even thought about the bookshop for the last 24 hours. It had not figured on his radar at all. But ...

'Rose,' he called. 'How long are we going to be gone for? How long is this all going to take?'

Rose looked around. The power source was now floating a few inches above the flatbed of the ute. 'I don't know, Henry. It depends how far they've travelled and how much work we need to do to get them back. I hope it will only take a couple of days, but it might take a couple of weeks, maybe even longer. We're travelling into the unknown.'

Henry's heart sank. He had hoped that the part of the experience that they were just about to finish, the getting-the-spaceship-ready part, would be the long and difficult part. He had hoped that they'd jump on board, somehow materialise in the hold of a bigger ship, grab Bekka, (and Davian too, if they had to) and come back home. But Rose seemed to think that this was a much bigger adventure.

If they were gone a month and the bookshop remained closed that whole time with no explanation, well, he might find himself with no home to come back to. This time of year was the most important for book sales. The Christmas customers basically kept him in business for the rest of the year. And how would it look to Vivienne and Paulo if the shop had to shut? Yes, I looked after your child to keep her safe while you were away, and now you're back, here we are on the streets begging for food.

'But I'm sure you have things to do?'

'Well, sure. We make our little bits and pieces for the market here. But our business is mostly online. You know, it's kind of like a blog, but to people back home. So this will be a new venture, something we can write about, something that the people back home will love to hear about. We can combine the two.'

'Do you have books back home?'

Evi laughed. 'Sure, sure we do. They are pretty old-fashioned things but people still love to read them. Along with the other forms of media. And the 'paper' back home is ... well ... different to the stuff here. But –'

'Look, I'll be happy to give Henry a lesson in interplanetary differences on another day,' said Rose. 'We're all ready to go here, and we need to get back to the ship.'

Henry looked back to her. She was standing next to the ute, steadying the power supply with one hand. Jones was on the other side holding it up too.

'Uh, sorry,' he said and searched through his pockets. Removing the key to the ute, he passed the rest of the bundle to Evi. 'Here are the keys. Go ahead and open up. Do whatever you need to. I think you'll find it all fairly straightforward. I'm sure I'll be able to fix up anything when I get back. Just write down somewhere the details of what you sell. The prices are on the little stickers on the backs of the books. And thank you. Thank you very much.'

Henry and Sura took their places behind Rose and Jones to steady the power supply. Now that the anti-gravity device was tucked underneath it and was doing most of the work, the thing was quite easy to carry. They just had to get themselves into a nice rhythm, walking together. If they let go, the power supply would sink to a couple of inches above the earth, but together they could keep it at a good height and walk along easily.

They carried it between them across the paddock, threaded it through the trees and ferns, and manhandled it down the gully bank to the joyful barking of the Sambiss and the more sedate welcome from Cat.

Henry noticed that they'd gone back and forth from the ship to the ute so many times that a small track was forming. He hoped the wallabies would enjoy using it when they were gone.

Jones stepped into the spaceship and he and Rose pulled and pushed and squeezed the power supply inside. It belonged in a hatch in the floor of the galley. Removing the old power supply and installing the new one took a lot of messing around. For Henry it seemed like an age passed. He sat on the rock, unable to do anything but wait. It was alright for Rose to call this 'the last step and then we can go' but as steps went it was a big one, and Henry could barely conceal his impatience.

The dog showed his importance by running up to the top of the gully and back. Keeping an eye on everything. Keeping everything 'safe'. But Henry didn't have anything to do at all. And he was too keyed up to go back to sleep like Cat had, curled up on the flat rock. He sat, then stood, then sat again. He stuck his head into the spaceship to see what was happening. When he realised he didn't even understand the terms they were using to talk about the process he went and sat on the rock again.

'Are you alright, Henry?' Sura asked.

'Just a bit impatient, I guess. I'm doing a lot of waiting around. I'd like to be doing something.'

'I'm not feeling the most useful myself. But it's Rose's game right now. The rest of us will come in handy later.'

'I probably won't come in handy at all. This is so far out of my comfort zone.'

'Bekka will be happy to see you.' Sura smiled.

'That's true.' Henry smiled as well, then a frown came to his face. 'I'm trying not to think about the travel. What's it like? Space travel I mean.'

'It's not so bad. You get used to it. It's quite an adventure, really. So many new places to see. New things to do. I mean, I love it here, but there's a lot out there that I haven't seen yet.' Sura's voice faded out dreamily.

Henry was more interested in the nuts and bolts.

'I remember watching a movie about Gagarin, you know, our first man in space. Russian, he was. He was rattling around in that tube like a maraca. His teeth nearly shook out of his head. And he nearly burned up when he was coming back to earth.'

'Ah, well, no. No space travel isn't usually like that.'

'No?' Henry was hopeful.

'Well, I guess it depends on the ship really.'

'How did you get here?'

'Me? I can thank Marc and Evi for bringing me here. My life back home was pretty boring. I was stuck in an office. Just working. Working to pay the bills, buying stuff to make my life more fun, which gave me more bills, which I was working overtime to pay off. It was a total grind.'

'But you lived on another planet!' Henry said aghast. 'You had space travel and exotic places to visit and different suns and everything.'

'But I never visited other planets. I never even visited the beautiful places on my own planet. I just did the everyday normal things. And I had to wear sensible clothes to go to work. And stupid shoes that hurt my feet. And one day I thought: I'm done with this.'

Henry looked at her, his mouth hanging open.

'So I started looking around. Started really thinking about what I wanted. What could make life worthwhile. I thought if I lived somewhere where the cost of living was less, I could make a go of doing something more … creative.

'I started dragging my way through the IG web and I came across Evi and Marc's writings. They mentioned this amazing place. It was so different to home. Such a change. I couldn't resist. I cut down on all my spending. Cut my belongings by about 80 percent. Sold everything I could possibly sell. When I thought about it, all my life I'd wanted to have an adventure. To travel to different places. I'd watched all the travel videos, the holograms, I'd read books and articles. There were a couple of other planets that would have been similar, but this is the one I chose.

'My parents weren't thrilled, but I needed the change. I caught a shuttle that dropped me off here and here I've stayed.'

'You don't feel out of place?'

'Do I look out of place?'

'Well, no. Not if your antennae stay beneath your dreadlocks.'

'I admit I have to be a bit careful of that. I have to have them out when I'm talking to my parents, and tucked away all the rest of the time. It's a bit tiring, but I survive.'

'Don't you miss your parents?'

'I talk to them regularly. They are getting old. I'd love to go get them and bring them here but they wouldn't fit in. Not at all. And it would be hard for them to leave home.'

Henry nodded. He had been on the receiving end of that. Regular video chats with Vivienne as she roamed around the earth with Paulo – a year here, and two years there. He should count himself lucky that they came back when Bekka was born.

'Sometimes I wonder if I should be getting back, or maybe if I could visit somewhere else ...'

They were interrupted by a humming noise. Henry looked warily at the sky and then realised that the noise was coming from the ship right in front of them. It was alive. There was light flooding out the door and smaller lights flashing on the ship's nose-cone and the stubby wings and tail.

She was working.

It was time to go.

* * *

'Right, well. Who is coming then?' Rose asked, as everyone excitedly crowded around the ship door.

'Cat and I need to come, we've got the defence all ready to go,' said Sura.

'Henry should come as well,' said Cat. 'I'm sure that Bekka needs him.'

Henry hadn't even thought about not going. He was glad that Cat spoke for him.

'Well, that's four of us. And this thing fits four neatly, but I'm sure we could squeeze two more in.'

'Two more on the way there – four on the way back, all things going well.' Sura said.

The four of them looked at Jones and the Sambiss.

'You go,' the dog said. He looked crestfallen, and his tail had tucked itself between his legs. His eyes were large and limpid. 'I can stay.'

Jones looked similarly disappointed, but he nodded his head as well. 'There's no reason for us to come.'

Henry couldn't bear to disappoint them. 'Hang on, if it seats four and can squeeze six, and two of us are a cat and a dog, I'm sure we can make it work. You two don't take up too much room. Let's all go.'

The dog's tail wagged again and he butted up against Henry for a pat.

Then Henry looked at Rose. 'Unless it does something dreadful to the power-to-weight ratio or something?'

'You're in luck. The power supply is for a much larger ship. It's not going to have trouble shifting all of us, and should cope easily with Davian and Bekka on the way home. We'll make it work. How can we not all come when we've all worked so hard on this? Now, let's pack all that food inside and make this place look like we've never been here.'

'We're not leaving until dark, right?' Sura asked. Henry couldn't believe it. They'd taken so long to fix the damn ship, and now Sura was suggesting they wait another four or five hours until the long Tasmanian twilight ended and it was dark?

Rose, however, nodded. 'Of course. Dark with a quiet ship. No lights. That's the drill.'

'But the IGP ship came in the middle of the day,' Henry protested.

'That was a bit like the police speeding in with the lights going,' Jones said. 'You can do that if there's an urgent need and you're the authorities.'

'They still shouldn't have done it though,' Cat said. 'Davian's situation really wasn't that urgent. Not unless something has really changed.'

'It's just not safe to take off during the day,' Rose stated with finality. 'Besides, I could do with a shower and a change, and I'm pretty sure everyone else could too, well, all of us who wear clothes.

And it wouldn't be a bad idea to pack some spare clothes and quite a bit more food.'

That made a lot of sense. And when Henry thought about it, he was glad Sura had said something. Were they going to travel for days or weeks with only a few stale sandwiches between the six of them? There probably wasn't a take-away store on the dark side of the moon. Though for all he knew, there might be.

His legs felt like lead as he picked up the few cups and plates that they'd left around the place. He wearily brushed the ants off the crockery and put it in a bag. He didn't want to climb that gulley wall again, but hopefully this would be the last time.

Then Rose, who was also moving wearily, said, 'To hell with it.' She pulled out the antigravity ball and turned it on, using it to propel herself up the gully wall. The rest of them looked at her with astonishment.

'I'm tired,' she said in simple explanation. 'Anyone else want a ride?'

She threw the ball down, the Sambiss expertly caught it, and one by one they all used it to climb with very little effort.

There was a sense of excitement as the group made their way back to the ute. Henry's stomach was churning with nerves, but at the same time he shivered with excitement. He was about to go into space! He couldn't believe it.

The others talked nineteen to the dozen, stories about previous flights, stories about coming to earth, what the weather was like, what their first impressions were. Shared experience was bounced around them like a big beachball. They had all said they were happy here on Earth, but Henry could tell that they were just as excited as he was to get off-planet for a while.

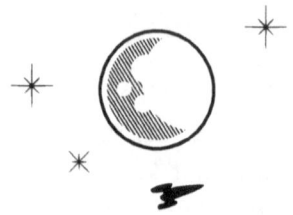

Chapter Twenty

Henry found the spare key under the back doormat and let himself and Cat into the house. The place felt so normal it was strange. There was the shop, all the books in place, and the black ball at the front desk that had started this whole process was no longer blinking but had tucked into itself once again and sat there quite innocently. Henry's world had taken a huge jump sideways, but the rest of the world, it seemed, had not.

He dragged himself up the stairs and relaxed into a long and very hot shower. Then, towel wrapped around him, he looked at his wardrobe and wondered what would be the most sensible thing to wear to space. He realised that he didn't have much choice. There was no space suit hanging in his closet. Not even right at the back. A shirt, a pair of pants, his boots, that was what he wore. He took a jumper just in case and threw a few bits and pieces into a backpack. On impulse, he added the book from his bedside table. He probably wouldn't have time to read, but you never knew when a book would come in handy.

Then he went into Bekka's room.

'Cat,' he called. 'Come and help me here. What should we take for Bekka?'

Cat padded up the stairs and sat on Bekka's bed.

'Just a change of clothes I think. And, does she have a journal? Or a favourite old toy?'

Bekka's well-loved teddy bear was sitting on the bed. Henry had given it to her for her second birthday. It was showing its age – its fur had been rubbed off all over the place. Bekka had grown out of it, then grown into it again, and now it took pride of place in her bedroom. Henry tucked it carefully into the bag with a black shirt, black jeans, and a jumper. He was sure Bekka would be glad to see some things from home. That was probably all she needed.

'Do you need anything?' he asked Cat.

'I wouldn't mind a supply of the salmon treats,' she replied. 'We have no idea how long we'll be away and I'm not sure that the IGP have decent food for my kind on board.'

'Will they have food for me?'

'Probably not Vegemite, but anything else you might need, yes.'

Henry laughed. Then he looked around at Bekka's room. The bed was unmade and clothes were strewn everywhere. Between the bedside table and the chest of drawers, he counted five half-filled glasses of water. The room reflected the girl living in it and he saw her clearly in his mind's eye. His stomach sank. What if they couldn't save her from the IGP? What if she didn't want to come back when they did find her? What if they didn't find her at all? She was somewhere in that vast universe out there. How were they even supposed to start looking? How would he face Vivienne if it all went wrong?

The light slowly drained from the sky, the clouds in the west became tinged with orange.

Henry sat at the dining table and penned a note:

December 2019
Dear Vivienne and Paulo,
If you read this, it means we didn't make it back. Were I to tell you the tale it wouldn't make sense, it would sound like pure gibberish, fantasy. But I want to let you know that this wasn't Bekka's fault, and that I did my best to save her. I'm with a great group of people and we are all trying very hard to find her and bring her back. She's a beautiful child, and her kind heart is the thing that has got her into this trouble.

I'm sorry for the weeks you were in Antarctica not hearing from us. I'm sorry that we disappeared from the face of the earth.

Now you are home, please don't waste time and energy looking for us. You will not find us. Just have a wonderful memorial service and say goodbye in a way that is meaningful to you.

And please, please forgive me.

All my love,

Dad

With tears in his eyes he sealed the envelope and set it behind the pot plant on the kitchen window. He hoped that Vivienne would never have to read it. He hoped that if she did, Paulo would take good care of her. He wished he could do more, say more, guarantee their safe return. But now he just had to take his courage in both hands and go.

The sky was almost dark as the six of them scrambled back down to the ship.

Henry was acutely aware of the special teddy in the backpack he carried. He felt like he was carrying the Queen's jewels. Jones was a lot less careful of his khaki duffle bag. It had seen a lot of life in his travels.

'Did you pick that up in Alice?' Henry asked with a chuckle.

'The US army has its uses,' Jones replied with a smile. Then he asked, 'Sura, do you need a hand with that?'

'No,' Sura replied shortly. 'I'm fine.'

'It's just that it looks pretty heavy.'

'She's never got the hang of packing light,' Rose laughed.

Sura replied brusquely: 'Some of us need more than light to live on.' And Rose did indeed have a tiny bag, but the sun wherever they were going, and the light box she'd set up on board the ship – those things were her essentials and she didn't need much more.

They packed their gear away in the neat cupboards that lined the ship then settled themselves into the seats. Jones and Rose in the cockpit, Sura and Henry behind them. Cat on Henry's lap, and the Sambiss sitting between them, his tail beating out a regular rhythm on the floor.

As the final shades of light fled the moonless sky, the door to the spaceship slid shut and sealed.

Sura clicked a harness into place around her, then reached down to strap the Sambiss in too. Henry, after a little searching, found his own harness and fastened it securely. This wasn't so different from being in a car or maybe an airplane.

Rose flicked switches and turned dials, and a humming started. 'Everyone ready?' she called. 'Ah, I've missed this feeling.'

Henry heard the chorus of agreement around the ship. He could understand. Here he was, going into the unknown, with people he hardly knew, to rescue his granddaughter who was in, for all he knew, grave danger, and yet he felt excited, thrilled. This was a true adventure.

Then he was pushed into his seat as the ship lifted off the ground.

It felt like three years ago that he was sitting comfortably in his shop, doing the paperwork, sorting the books, drinking a nice cup of tea and patting the cat. And yet only a couple of days had passed. And now, here he was, vertically rising above the trees, 'Fools and birds fly by day,' Henry thought, 'but only fools fly at night.' Rose weaved and dodged to avoid hitting the branches of the gums. They were going to space. It was surreal.

As they climbed, he saw the lights of Huonville through a gap in the clouds, and then the lights of Hobart. He decided not to think about how far up they were in this tiny craft that they had renovated themselves. It was alright to fly in a plane that was owned by Qantas or something but this tin box? Cat lightly nipped his arm and he realised that he had been squeezing her.

'Sorry,' he apologised and moved his hands to the seat rests where he clenched them so tightly that his knuckles whitened.

Rose kept the ship dark and quiet until they made it above the clouds. Henry started to see the curve of the earth, the outline of the island of Tasmania, the continent of Australia. In the dark sky were more stars than he had ever seen before. Brighter than he'd ever seen too. He was a country boy and he was used to looking at the sky with no light pollution but this was beyond anything he'd ever seen. Way beyond.

And they continued to climb until the stars now looked like they were below him around the curve of the earth. So beautiful, so terrifying. And they were going to keep climbing. They were going to go until …

'Rose, where are we going?' he asked.

'To get Bekka and Davian, of course,' was her shocked reply.

'Yes, but where are they? Forgive me, but this is a very big universe out here. Where do we even start to try to find them?'

She looked back at him. 'Didn't I tell you? Oh I'm so sorry.'

He gestured furiously that she should look where she was going. He was not feeling comfortable enough to ride in this ship if the person driving didn't have both hands on the steering wheel. But Rose was perfectly comfortable. She pointed out a blue flashing dot among the sets of lights on the dashboard.

'This is where they are. Or at least, that's where Bekka's phone is. You know how I installed the 'find my phone' thing for you when she kept losing it? I installed my own special version. It's good for pretty much the whole settled universe. It took me a little while to adapt it to the ship's navigation system but we're good. We're going there.'

Jones interrupted, 'Speaking of which, now might be a good time to jump.'

'OK.' Rose started flicking switches and turning dials. 'Everyone ready?'

Henry started to say, 'What?' and 'No!' and 'What's a jump?' But before he could, his voice was ripped from his throat, his arms and legs turned to jelly, and he was thrown back into his seat. Then everything went black.

Chapter Twenty-One

Davian shut his eyes and tried to block out the vision of the windowless grey walls that surrounded him. But that just made his internal vision of Bekka clearer. She was now, probably, shut into her own grey cell in the IGP ship.

He had spent so long running from the law, and he thought he'd always been imagining the worst that could happen. But to bring an innocent human into his problems, to have her arrested and taken off-planet? This was worse than anything he had even thought of. He'd opened a huge can of worms now. And there was no way he could make it right.

He was helpless, powerless.

That stupid IGP captain. The more that Bekka protested her innocence, the more that man had dug his heels in.

'Are you questioning my authority?'

'No, I just –'

'You be careful, young human, we can make your life very uncomfortable. You'll be lucky if you get to see Earth again.'

The fact was, as Davian well knew, the captain had broken the law himself by bringing a human onto the ship. And in daylight too. Once she'd seen the IGP, there weren't many choices open to him, and now he was trying to cover his backside.

And Davian hadn't been able to stop his own mouth from flapping.

'You shouldn't have her here. You know humans aren't supposed to be off-planet.'

'And who makes you the authority?' At least the stinging words had been deflected from Bekka. Davian had achieved that much.

It's not like the guy was imposing physically. He gave them their 'dressing down' looking up at their faces. And actually wagging his finger. Davian had thought that was only something they did in kids' programs on TV. Sometimes it was all he could do not to laugh. He would have laughed if the captain didn't have all the might of the IGP behind him.

And then, as if he had seen Davian's insolent thoughts, he'd decided to lock them in separate cells. And that was bad.

How on Earth was Bekka dealing with this solitary confinement? Her first experience of the wonders of space and all she gets to see is grey walls. She was a brave girl, but this was just wrong. And all because of covering up.

There was a knock on the door. A new officer he hadn't seen before entered, carrying some packets of food and drink.

'How are you going?' she asked.

'I'd be much better if I wasn't stuck in here. How is the human?'

'I haven't seen her yet. I'll take her food in next.'

Davian accepted the silver packets with thanks.

'Look, do you want me to try to contact someone for you? Your parents, perhaps?'

'Why are you being so kind?' Davian asked with suspicion. Was this some sort of ruse to get the prisoner to open up?

'Look, our captain, he's a bit … let's just say that not everyone takes his black and white view on things. I wish you hadn't stood up for yourselves when you were arrested. He hates that. And you both shouldn't be in solitary. There's no need to treat you this harshly. But I can't do anything, he rules the ship.'

'Are you going to get in trouble for this?'

'I can look after myself. But is there anything you'd like me to do for you?'

Well, now that he was arrested, now that he wasn't hiding any longer, there was one thing.

'Can you look up my parents for me? Hrahid and Vera Jernoshef, on Karthur. Can you tell me whether they are still there? Whether they are still …' His voice trailed away.

'Got it,' said the officer. 'I'll see what I can do.'

'And tell the human, Bekka, tell her … I don't know. Tell her I'm sorry.'

The officer nodded. Then she stepped back through the door which sealed shut behind her, and Davian was back to staring at grey walls again.

He wondered how his parents were and what they thought had happened to him. He'd send them a message, eventually. Once he knew what was going to happen to him. There was no point in doing anything right now though. He wasn't in a position to give them any hope.

'Hey, Mum, Dad. It's me, your long lost son. Arrested and awaiting trial for murder. Just thought I'd make contact!' Yeah, it didn't feel like the right tone for a family reunion.

But he'd like to know where they were. He couldn't bring himself to ask the really important question. A lump formed in his throat making it hard to swallow. The space goop he'd been given to eat wouldn't go down properly.

He gave up on eating and instead made a list of ways to get out of this situation. That didn't take long. He had no idea what to do.

Then, as he always did to calm himself, he took his mind back to his childhood in Karthur. All the fun things his family had done together before everything went wrong. He remembered his mum taking him to the Pelentra Forest and the special hollow tree that they would make their 'home' in for the day. He played the memories over in his mind until eventually he went to sleep.

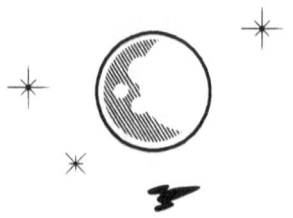

Chapter Twenty-Two

'He's back with us,' Henry heard Cat say.

'Great, I'll bring him a cuppa.' Sura was on the job.

Henry rubbed his eyes and looked around. He realised with a jolt that no one was driving the ship. No one was sitting in front of him at all.

Clutching the arms of his chair with both hands he frantically looked behind him to find a scene that crossed domestic bliss with something like one of his most surreal dreams.

Sura floated in the galley behind him, holding on with one hand and working on something with another. The Sambiss and Jones floated in mid-air towards the back of the ship. The Sambiss was stretched out – all four feet pointing up, Jones sat crosslegged on nothing and was reading a battered and dog-eared book. Rose was floating in a glass box that was glowing with light. And Cat was still curled up floating just slightly above Henry's lap, purring. She looked up at him.

'How are you feeling?' she asked.

Henry blinked, trying to take it all in. He remembered having his tonsils out when he was a kid, waking up after the anaesthetic. He felt the same sense of grogginess and unreality. His friends hanging out in the ship like they were on holidays at a shack somewhere, making themselves at home. No, in fact, it was like they were all together on a yacht. Only no one could go up on deck. They were all stuck inside together, just relaxing, chilling out. But it all felt wrong.

His mouth was dry. He tried to swallow.

'How long have I been out for?' he croaked.

'It's been a good ten minutes. Sura's been checking your vitals every now and then. I was pretty sure you'd come through. But it takes a while to get used to the jumps, even if you started when you were a kitten.'

Sura came over with a bag with a tube sticking out of it.

'Here you go,' she said.

'What's this?' he asked suspiciously.

'A nice hot drink of tea. It will do you good.'

'It doesn't look like a cup of tea to me.'

'We can't use a cup,' Cat explained. 'There's zero gravity here. I mean, it will probably be different when we get onto the big ship, but in this little one, we have to make do.'

Of course. Zero gravity. That's why it all felt like a dream. He realised that the reason he was still sitting in his chair was because of his harness. He made a move to take it off, then decided it would be better to leave it there. To stay there, in the chair where he felt safe.

'Why didn't you all warn me?' he grumped.

'You know, we all forgot. We were so used to working with you, we didn't think about the fact that you'd never been out here before.'

'Sorry Henry,' came Jones' voice from the back of the ship. 'Never occurred to me.'

'Right.' Henry looked suspiciously at the bag of 'tea' again, then decided to try it. What could go wrong? He was among friends, right?

The tea was only lukewarm, but it soothed his dry throat. It didn't taste any good. It tasted kind of like tea did back home when he had a cold. His nose felt all stuffed up. He'd have to get used to drinking like this, he supposed. This is how it would be when he ended up in a nursing home. Drinking from sippy cups while strapped into a seat for his own safety. He just didn't expect it to happen so soon.

'So we're in space, what happens now?'

Cat stretched and floated across the cockpit.

'Rose is just recharging, and we've all had a little to eat. We'll get you some, don't worry. And then we'll take another jump, a shorter one this time so it shouldn't affect you so badly. After that we should be close enough to the IGP ship to go in and get the kids.'

'It's all planned then.'

'We're doing the best we can.'

Sura brought him a muesli bar. 'Just try not to drop crumbs,' she said. 'They're a little difficult to clean up.'

Henry ate and drank and looked out at the wealth of stars that shone so brightly through the ship windows. While everything still felt strange, he relaxed a little. He was among friends. He was safe. And he thought he could gaze at this view forever. What did he do to be allowed this wealth of experience? Then as he looked at the huge expanse he wondered if their plans would work. Would the 'find my phone' app find Bekka? Was finding anyone even possible in a place this big?

He heard a click behind him and the light in the spaceship faded. Rose was out of the light box.

'Good to have you back with us Henry, ready to go again?'

Henry took the last bite of his muesli bar and washed it down with the last of the lukewarm tea.

'No,' he said cheerfully. 'But let's do it anyway.'

'Good to hear. Places everyone.'

Sura locked everything away in the galley. Jones packed up his book. Cat settled herself near Henry's lap again. The dog stayed where he was.

Rose once again flicked switches and turned dials and Henry's stomach dropped as they took another jump.

* * *

Henry roused to the sound of an argument.

'If I'd known you were going to try this I wouldn't have come. You're crazy to think it will work.'

'You really think they would just give up? That we could "rescue" them and get away with it?'

'You're just going to land all of us in prison this way. They don't listen. They don't care.'

'Your way would land us all in prison anyway, or running through the universe in fear of probes.'

'Not if they didn't know who the rescuers were.'

'They know, they already know. They scanned us in the millisecond we came within reach.'

Henry peered out of the cockpit window past the arguing Rose and Jones. There, looming in front of them was a huge spaceship. It looked nothing like the ship that had picked Bekka up. He wondered if they had even come to the right place.

'I thought you were installing shields.' Jones said accusingly.

'How much do you think I can do in two days? Do I look like superwoman to you?' Rose defended herself.

Well, it looked like Henry wasn't going to get a cup of tea this time around. Not even a lukewarm bag of tea. He stretched his arms while the battle raged around him.

'What did you think Cat and I were preparing to do? Of course we're going to do this lawfully.' That was Sura.

'What have you got in your huge great bag then? I thought you'd brought weapons.' Jones was almost spitting.

'That's my business.'

'Weapons?' Rose's voice was scornful. 'You've been watching too much TV down there. What makes you think we'd have any chance of outwitting a fully trained IGP squad?'

'Not trained. IGP not trained,' the Sambiss growled.

'I agree with the Sambiss. I've heard reports that they're losing their control over the outer squads. Squads going rogue and all that. If we try and go in there lawfully, all sweet and nice, they will just lock us up too. You guys are crazy even to try. We lose any chance we've got.'

The dog barked in agreement.

'It might have been better to talk this through before we all got in a ship together and came out.' That was Cat.

'Too right. I wouldn't have come. I thought it was bleeding obvious what we needed to do here.'

'And it is. We obviously need to make contact, and lawfully plead for their pardons.'

'We obviously need to break in and rescue them.'

'Why don't we do both?' Henry asked.

All five combatants stopped short and looked at him.

'What are you talking about?' Cat broke the shocked silence. 'How in the universe could we do both?'

Henry took a deep breath and hoped that his idea wasn't completely foolish.

'Well, it's like this. When I was a kid, we used to go scrumping. Stealing apples. There were plenty of orchards, I thought there was plenty of food and that it wouldn't matter if I took one or two, but strangely, the owners didn't agree. Funny, once I owned my own orchard I changed sides and was all against scrumping.' He gave a wry smile. 'But anyway, there were about four of us, used to go out and pick the fruit, and one day one of the farmers came out while we were helping ourselves. He caught Wes. And he knew there were more of us, but he didn't know how many.

'So there was Wes, locked in a shed, waiting for a whipping with the farmer's belt. We felt pretty bad, we were a close-knit group of kids, you know. So anyway, one of the girls, Dorothy, she went to the farmer's front door, all sweet-like with an apology. She was very good at being sweet.' Henry smiled at the reminiscence. His Dorothy was so lovely, and totally iron-strong at the core.

'While she buttered up the farmer with talk about how sorry she was, and how she and Wes wouldn't do it again, I crept around to the shed with Barry and we found a way to get Wes out. We'd prearranged a signal; if it was going badly she'd let out a cry and we would put our rescue plan into action. If it went well on her end, then we'd stay out of sight so that Wes could be released by the farmer and we'd keep our noses clean. In the end Dorothy was so good at her part that Wes only received a stern talking to. But the important thing was, we got him out.'

The Sambiss' head was cocked to one side. Jones nodded slowly. Cat's tail slowly waved back and forth. There were a few tense minutes of silence.

Then Cat said, 'It could work.'

The tension levels dropped slightly as everyone worked together to come up with a plan that incorporated the best of both worlds. In the end Rose summarised for all of them.

'So Cat, you and Sura, and Henry, you'll go in and make a big noise. Try to get a hearing. Do your best to get them out lawfully. I'll stay in this craft as the ship's captain. The Sambiss, and Jones will hide, and after you guys take all the attention they will work with me to figure out the IGP defences and find a way to rescue Davian and Bekka. We'll be backup. Are we all good with that?'

'It should work,' said Jones.

'We hide,' growled the dog.

'What's the signal then?' asked Henry. 'How are we going to let you know that things have gone badly?'

'Or well,' said Cat mildly. 'Things could go well.'

'Badly or well,' Henry corrected.

'Phones. Who's got them?' Rose asked.

'Oh, the good old mobile phone. Good for everything,' Henry said.

They found four mobile phones between them, and while the discussion continued, Rose pulled out some tools and started fiddling with the electronics.

Jones was still a little put out that he wouldn't be saving the day. If it all went well Henry knew that Jones and the Sambiss wouldn't have to do anything. But still, no one knew what they'd find and it was better to be safe than sorry.

Eventually, when they felt completely ready, Rose sent a 'permission to approach' signal to the larger ship and Jones and the Sambiss tucked themselves into the sleeping quarters to hide. Henry tried to prepare himself for what was to come. He prayed that Bekka was alright, that nothing awful had happened to her.

The magnetic field of the larger ship activated and drew them in to dock. Henry saw the side of the ship come closer and closer. The two ships were on a collision course. He screwed his eyes shut, then decided that he wanted to see just how this was going to work and forced himself to look. A large panel opened in the side of the ship, which swallowed their tiny craft whole. Then he felt and heard their ship clang as it hit the floor, and the panel swiftly closed behind them.

They were in a hold. Like a big black cave. The only light was coming from their own ship and by it Henry could see that they weren't the only ship in the cave. But he couldn't see quite how big the hold was. He jumped as a light flashed on, high above them. Then jumped again at a loud hissing sound.

Rose looked at the monitors on the dashboard. 'Give it a minute, they're just equalising pressure and oxygen. You'll be good to go shortly.'

She reached over and squeezed Henry's arm. 'Don't worry, we'll get you back home. We're all going to make it back just fine.'

He wished he could feel comforted by that, but honestly he knew that none of them knew what was going to happen. They would all try their best, both lawfully and unlawfully, and that was the most he could ask for.

Suddenly he noticed something.

'Hang on, that's the ship,' he said.

'What?' asked Cat.

'That ship, over there. That's the one they came out of and took Bekka in. We are in the right place after all.'

'Well, that's a relief,' said Rose.

'You weren't sure?' Henry was horrified. Then the whole crew burst into laughter around him.

'Of course I was sure. I put the link in Bekka's phone, remember?'

'Well, I'm glad to see that ship anyway.' Henry felt a bit grumpy but he couldn't blame them for laughing. He was just so outside his comfort zone. He tried to pull himself together. Soon he'd be seeing Bekka and he would have to be strong for her.

Red lights turned to green and Rose unlocked the door.

Chapter Twenty-Three

Henry heard the sound of marching feet coming towards the ship. He also heard the Sambiss' quiet growl. The marching sounded crisp. From the sound of it, this was not one of the rogue lazy IGP troops. This sounded more like a dedicated and disciplined army. Was that a good thing? He had no idea.

His hands felt clammy and his stomach roiled.

He unbuckled his harness and floated out of the seat. The movement completely took him by surprise. But there were Rose and Cat, floating around him, Cat using her claws like velcro to attach on to the side of the ship, and Rose holding on by cleverly placed handles that he had completely failed to notice before.

He bumped gently against the ceiling, then grabbed hold of his seat to steady himself. He looked out the window at the approaching crisply uniformed police marching in formation, and at the ships sitting firmly on the floor of the hold. He was so confused.

'How?' he asked. 'How come they are on the floor, and we are floating stupidly around our ship? Is there gravity out there and none in here?'

'No, that would be impossible. No, I reckon they are using magnets or something. I know that our ship is held to a magnetised dock,' Rose explained.

'So they are totally in control of whether we leave or not?'

Rose nodded. Henry could have panicked about that, but he had more immediate things to think about.

'What happens when we leave this ship? Do we just float around?'

'Hopefully they give us the same magnets, but at least for the beginning of this process, we hold on to our ship.'

'Great. Another thing to cope with.'

'Zero G is fun when you get used to it,' said Cat and there was a quiet bark of approval from the back.

'That dog needs to control himself,' Henry whispered. 'He'll give us all away.'

Rose and Cat nodded.

The police drew up to the ship with a final snap to attention.

'Come on then,' said Cat. 'It's time.' And the three chosen negotiators pulled themselves to the door to face the IGP.

They found themselves confronted by a group of twenty uniformed men. Were they men? Henry found his brain spinning. They were humanoid, that was for sure. They looked like any police officer back home. Crisp grey and black uniforms, helmets, and yes, some sort of gun or taser or something. They were prepared to fight if it was necessary.

The leader introduced himself as the captain of the ship, he told them that they were IGP and gave a troop and ship identifier. Then, in as officious way as possible, he asked the incomers to 'identify themselves and state their purpose'.

Cat was standing on Sura's shoulder. Having her sit there was probably quite comfortable for the two of them in zero G, as long as Cat didn't dig her claws in too deeply.

'We are here to plead the cause of the two defendants you picked up in Sector 378, region H92,' Cat said.

'You want to plead their cause, do you? The cause of a wanted criminal, and a human that obstructed the criminal's arrest?' was the reply. Not very encouraging. But Cat was not at all perturbed.

'That is to be decided in court. I am here to speak for them. I take it you haven't had a hearing yet.'

'No Ma'am, the hearing has not been scheduled. There has been no need to schedule it. The criminals can do no further damage now that we have them here.'

This guy really thought he'd saved the day. That he had caught two very dangerous criminals. Henry felt a nervous laugh bubbling inside him. There was no one less dangerous than his Bekka, and even Davian was as far from thug-like as you could get. What was this policeman on?

Cat was much more disciplined, though Henry could see her hair starting to bristle.

'I am here to schedule a hearing and perform the defence, according to intergalactic law.'

The policeman mulled that over and could not see a way to argue. He moved on.

'You have explained yourself, but who have you brought with you?'

'My legal secretary, and a family member of one of the defendants.' Cat was as haughty as she could be. Henry was impressed. He tried to pull his tired body into line. Between Cat's haughtiness and the crisp uniforms and upright stances of the officer and his men, Henry was feeling decrepit and scruffy.

'And her?' The officer waved towards Rose who was holding herself just inside the door of the ship.

'The captain of the ship. She has been our transport. That's all.'

'We will have to search the ship.' The captain started to wave his forces into action. But he was stopped short again by Cat.

'What for? There is no call for that under intergalactic law unless we come in threat. We are just here as a legal team. There are no weapons on us – you can scan all four of us.'

Henry held his breath. He hoped that Cat's reliance on the law would be enough to stop the captain. And he really hoped Sura hadn't been packing spare weapons like Jones thought she had.

The officer nodded and clicked his fingers. Nothing happened, so he cleared his throat and tried again, 'Scan them for weapons,' he barked. This time four of the police stepped forward and pulled scanners out of their belts.

'Move forward,' hissed Cat to Henry. 'Move out of the door, let Rose out.'

Henry floated out sideways, trying not to lose touch with the side of the spaceship. If he let go, who knew where he'd end up? The hold was huge and he didn't want to be floating around the ceiling somewhere.

Rose pulled herself out of the ship too, in apparent obedience and helpfulness, but Henry knew that she was trying to keep the scanner out of the ship. If they caught a whiff of the other two hiding up the back then there would be hell to pay.

The scanners didn't even touch them. They were like, well, if Henry was honest, it felt like being examined with Dr Who's sonic screwdriver. Truth is stranger than fiction, he thought. Or maybe some TV writers knew more than they were saying.

Suddenly one of the scanners let out a loud beep.

'Empty your pockets please sir,' commanded the man who had been scanning Henry. He froze. What did he have on him that would be a problem? He patted his pockets with one hand, then the other, keeping a firm hold on the ship. Then he found his flip phone. He pulled it out and handed it to the man, who looked at it closely, then handed it to the captain.

Henry saw Sura stiffen. The phone was essential. And he began to worry again himself. If they took his phone, would they have taken Bekka's too? They were following Bekka's phone, but there was no guarantee that Bekka was in the same place as her phone. Maybe she wasn't. Maybe she'd been moved elsewhere. Were they even in the right place? Henry tried to control his spiralling thoughts.

The captain gave the phone careful consideration.

'It's a communicator,' Cat stated blandly. 'Primitive, because it's from H92. You might not have seen anything quite so quaint for a while.'

'It is not like the communicator from the other human.'

'Ah,' Cat spoke quickly. 'The humans are going through a period of intense technological advancement. And this human is one of the elders. He is not interested in the change so much. The other human that you have arrested has more interest in new technology.'

This seemed to have an effect on the captain. He lifted one eyebrow, a move he had clearly been practising in a mirror. 'New technology, hey?' he said.

'Well, new to them. This is only H92. They have a long way to go.'

Henry bristled a bit at this. He was proud of where earth had got to with its technology. And wasn't he willing to Skype or Zoom to Vivienne down in Antarctica? And once Bekka had shown him how to do it a couple of times, he was able to set it up for himself just fine, thank you very much.

Then he thought about what he had just done. Travelled into space, into another complete galaxy. The 'jumping', whatever that was. The ability Rose had to make anything technical do just what she wanted, with a little bit of solder and a few new components.

Humankind had a long way to go. He was from a primitive race and he just had to accept it.

The captain, apparently satisfied, gave the phone back to Henry. Then gesturing to all of them he said,

'You will come with us now.'

Once again, Cat asserted her authority.

'Our captain needs to stay with her light box. She is a Fleurantil. She must recharge while we are here.'

Rose flashed them her gorgeous smile, and Henry was grateful for a Cat who had an answer for everything. It had been annoying back on earth, especially as she wasn't using English for her replies so they sometimes didn't make any sense to him. He remembered a few days where he had stood at the kitchen bench willing her to eat her food while she refused, or willing her to decide which room she was going to be in so that he could close a door. But now he could see how useful this ability to argue could really be. And come to think of it, her time on Earth must have been frustrating for her too. He had been pretty dense at times.

The captain gave Cat's reply a long consideration. But eventually he nodded. 'Very well,' he said. Henry let his breath out. Rose could stay in the ship. The first part of the plan was complete.

'We would like to see the defendants first, then I will need to make a time for the hearing with the court.'

'That is acceptable. Bring some shoes.'

Some shoes? Henry was confused. He was already wearing shoes. Why did they need more shoes? Was this a cultural thing? Then he realised that the captain wasn't talking to him.

One of the policemen opened a cupboard neatly contained in the wall next to an entrance door and brought out some grey overshoes. Sura neatly clasped them around her own shoes and within seconds was standing upright on the floor, Cat still holding on to her shoulder. Henry fumbled, turning himself around in circles. He was trying to work with one hand and hold on with the other. But he couldn't put the shoes on single-handedly. Letting go and using both hands sent him spinning slowly around. He panicked and reached out to grab whatever was near and his overshoes fell to the floor with a clang. The captain shook off Henry's clutching hand with annoyance and sent Henry spinning away again to hit against the wall of the ship.

Eventually Rose took pity on him and helped put the shoes on while he sat in the doorway of the ship holding on with both hands.

'Try that,' she said.

He put his feet down on the floor and stood up. He still felt strange. Just because his feet stayed put didn't mean that anything else was right. There wasn't the pull of gravity that there should have been. His arms felt strange. His clothes floated around him. Even his face felt odd without the familiar pull. But at the same time, he wasn't floating all over the place either. The magnetic shoes were better than nothing.

He took a few experimental steps, sharply pulling his foot up and then clanging it back down as the magnetic pull helped him.

The captain sneered at him. Then looked at Sura and Cat.

'Ready?' he asked.

'Thank you,' said Cat at her most dignified. 'We'll see the prisoners now.'

Chapter Twenty-Four

Henry clanged awkwardly along the brightly lit grey corridors. The colour reminded him of the navy boats he had taken Bekka to see in the Hobart harbour when she was about five years old. Like the navy ships, this ship had handles along the walls, but unlike the ships back home, this ship also had handles on the floor and ceiling (in case of not having your magnetic overshoes, Henry thought).

They came to an intersection and the captain brought everyone to an abrupt halt, before shouting some orders. Half of the officers marched to the left in strict formation, their magnetic shoes clicking in unison. From the sound of things, the formation dissolved as soon as they were out of sight. But Henry was glad that the captain didn't seem to think they needed to be controlled by such a large force.

The visitors were marched further down the corridor to the right. As they walked the captain asked, 'Which prisoner first?'

'Bekka!' blurted Henry.

'Yes, we'll see the human first, thanks,' Cat said in a much more measured tone. Henry thought he could hear a hint of reproof. Well, she'd just have to put up with him being human, because that's what he was.

They stopped outside a door.

'Here is the human. You may all go in. Call on the intercom to be let out.' He put his hand on a patch of wall that was a slightly darker shade of grey. An orange light flashed an outline of his hand, then the patch of wall turned to green and the door slid open to reveal Bekka curled up in a ball, floating in one back corner of the bare windowless room. Her face was hidden in her arms.

'Bekka,' Henry called softly.

She uncurled a bit.

'Grandad?'

Henry tried to run into the cell, clumsy and noisy in his magnetic overshoes. Bekka laughed in surprise as he enveloped her in a huge hug.

'Grandad, what on earth?'

'Not on earth at all,' he replied. Then the two of them were laughing and crying, holding each others' faces, then hugging again.

'It's going to be OK,' said Henry. And he truly felt it. It was going to be OK now the two of them were together again.

Eventually Cat gave a little meow. 'Sorry to interrupt,' she said.

Bekka looked away from Henry and saw Cat and Sura for the first time.

'Cat?' she gasped.

'Yes,' said Henry. 'Turns out, Cat is not ... not a cat.'

'Pleased to meet you properly, Bekka. And do you know Sura?'

'Sura.' Bekka smiled. 'Nice to see you again. Are you an alien too?'

'Sure am,' said Sura, pointing to the antennae sticking out of her hair.

'Wow, you guys hid yourselves well. Who else?'

'There's plenty of them,' said Henry. 'More than you would believe.'

'I dunno,' Bekka gave a shaky laugh. 'I'd believe quite a lot of things now. This has been a bit of a shake up.'

'Did you see the stars?' Henry asked. 'It's amazing how many there are, how bright they are. It's beautiful.'

'I haven't seen much, Grandad. They put me in this room almost straight away. No one has explained anything to me. I've just been waiting, hoping, for I don't know what. I thought, I thought this would be ...' She trailed off and tears welled in her eyes. 'There was no way I could even tell you where I was. They wouldn't let me talk to Davian. I just ...'

Henry hugged her close.

'It's OK, we're here now. And we're going to take you home.'

'Great,' she said letting out a shaky sigh. 'Let's go. What are we waiting for?'

'I'm sorry Bekka, we can't go straight away,' Cat said, curling herself up on Bekka's lap just like she had done to give her comfort in the kitchen at home.

'Why not? You're here, I'm here. We can go.'

'We're definitely going to take you home, one way or another. But you've been charged under intergalactic law. I need to get the charges dropped.'

'You?'

'I'm a lawyer,' Cat explained.

'She's a good one too,' said Sura.

'We're going to organise a hearing and we'll plead your defence. It shouldn't be hard to get you off. There's no question about it. Your arrest was an unlawful arrest. The captain totally overstepped the mark.'

'How long will it take?' Bekka looked from one face to another.

'It shouldn't take more than a day or two.'

'I have to stay here for another two days?' Bekka looked around at the grey walls. Her voice dropped to a whisper. 'I don't think I can.'

'You can. I'll stay here with you,' said Henry. 'I can do that, right?'

Cat and Sura shared a look.

'I'm sure you can,' Cat said, a little too quickly. 'We'll make sure you can.'

Henry held Bekka tightly to his side. Now he had found her, he wasn't going to let them be separated again.

'I'll talk to the captain. And all being well, we'll be able to leave you lovely people to chat while we sort things out. But just before I go, Bekka I need to ask you an important question. When you were arrested, did you kick or punch or fight at all?'

Bekka shrugged.

'It all happened so quickly. I remember grabbing hold of Davian, and pulling him. But then there were two of them pinning my arms down. They just …' Bekka started to cry again. 'They were too strong.'

'Yes, I saw it too,' said Henry. 'They had her bundled into the ship in no time flat. She didn't have time to fight.'

'Good, OK Bekka, that's good,' said Cat and Sura nodded. 'That's all we need.'

Henry could see the scene again in his mind's eye. He had been seeing almost nothing else whenever he took a break in the last few days. He remembered it all too well. He was no lawyer, but even he could see a problem with Bekka's defence.

'But they asked,' he said. 'They asked if she was trying to stop the arrest, and she said …'

'I said yes,' said Bekka in a small voice.

'Ah, but you didn't know the law,' said Sura.

'She still doesn't know the law.'

'And that will be our defence for you. You'll be fine.' Cat still sounded reassuring, but Henry wasn't so sure anymore. He pushed the thought away. What did he know? Cat was the expert here. She'd get Bekka back home. And if she didn't, well there was still Jones and the Sambiss. It would all be fine.

He hugged Bekka even more tightly.

Sura pushed a the intercom button on the wall near the door. A clear voice answered.

Cat used her persuasive powers to convince the guard that Henry should be left in the cell. It didn't take much, people apparently don't often ask to be locked in, usually they ask to be taken out.

Then Cat and Sura were gone, and Henry and Bekka were left to comfort each other and tell their stories.

* * *

Henry and Bekka sat, or rather floated, in the little cell. They had talked for a long time, eaten the rather bland food passed to them at the appropriate time by a uniformed officer, and had gradually fallen quiet.

'What I wouldn't give for a TV right now,' Bekka said eventually.

'Or a book. Or something to take our minds off things.' Henry agreed.

'I wonder how Davian is doing?'

'All we can hope for is that Cat can do her job.'

'It feels very weird to trust a cat to get us out of this situation.' Bekka shook her head.

'My life has never felt so strange.'

Bekka smiled. 'Well, at least you're here now. It feels weird, but not as scary as it did.'

'You poor thing.' Henry patted her knee. Then the two of them fell silent again.

It was completely silent in the cell. There was no noise beyond the faint whooshing of the air-conditioning system. There was no sound of birds, no traffic, no breeze shaking the leaves of a nearby tree. There was nothing. Their breathing sounded loud in the stillness. Henry's nerves wound tighter and tighter in the unnatural quiet.

A sniffing and scratching outside the door made him jump. 'Who's that? Who's there?' The noise stopped.

'Anyone there?' Henry called again. He looked at Bekka and she shrugged.

'Is this normal?'

'I've never heard that before.'

Then both of them flinched as a loud ringing filled the cell.

'What's that?'

'I don't know, I've never heard that before either.'

'Hang on.' Henry laughed shakily and pulled his vibrating phone out of his pocket. 'It's me.' He flipped the phone open. 'Hello?'

There was no answer. The two of them looked at each other, wide eyed. They held their breath for a minute, then slowly exhaled when nothing else happened.

'How is your phone working out here?' Bekka asked.

'Rose fixed it so it would. Just like she fixed yours. She's a bit of a wiz is Rose.' He looked back at his phone. 'But there's no one there.'

'What's the number?' Bekka asked.

But before Henry could work that out, the door to the cell slid open. Henry flipped his phone shut and slipped it into his pocket as an officer entered the room.

'Is everything alright here? We heard a noise.'

'Just hunky dory, if you're happy in a tiny windowless cell.' Henry said. 'Do we ever get exercise or anything here?'

'The prisoner has already had her exercise today.'

'Her name's Bekka.' Henry snapped. Bekka put her hand on his arm to calm him.

'We're fine, thanks,' she said. 'All good.'

'Good.' The officer left, and the door slid shut.

'The prisoner,' Henry said with scorn.

'There's no point in annoying them. They work to rule here. I gather that the guy who runs the ship is pretty firm and everything is done exactly by the book. Exercise at exercise time, food at food time, the lights go off at bed time. It's like clockwork. The same every day. When I was doing my exercise today I asked if things could be changed up a bit, they said there was no way. The captain wouldn't stand for it.'

'Well, I guess it could be worse. I prefer someone to follow the rules than to do whatever they like. Especially when that person is holding the gun.'

'I just hope that Cat knows the rule book really well.'

The phone rang again, and this time Henry answered it straight away.

'Hello?'

'Do you want to get out of here or not?'

'Jones?'

'You might want to turn your phone down. We had to beat a quick retreat when that racket sounded.'

'Sorry, I didn't think. Bekka, you'll have to help me turn this thing down.' Bekka nodded and Henry grinned at her.

'Anyway, the Sambiss found your cell. I just have to find a way to force the door. It might take me a while. Rose is staying with the ship and I'm bringing her the info so we can work together on it. Next time you hear us, don't say anything.'

So that's what the sniffing and scratching sound was. Henry realised that he needed to stop letting his wound up nerves run the show. If ever there was a situation that needed clear thinking, this was it.

'I won't next time. You scared us though. It sounded pretty strange from this side of the door you two scrabbling around.'

'Right. Well, now you know.'

'Thanks Jones. And pass on my thanks to the others.'

'Oh, and Cat says your hearing is scheduled for tomorrow.'

'That's fast!'

'Pretty normal. AI judges here. Can decide a case in milliseconds.'

Henry signed off and tried to keep his expression positive, but his heart sank within him. They weren't human judges? How were you supposed to pull the heartstrings of a computer to allow family reunion? They were never going to make it back.

'What was all that about?' Bekka asked. 'Jones is here too?'

'Sweetheart, it's probably best if you don't know all the details. But just know that we're doing our best to get you out of here. Oh, and best if you forget that you ever knew Jones was here.'

Bekka frowned and opened her mouth to ask more, but just then the lights dimmed.

'What's happening now?' Henry asked, a hint of panic showing in his voice.

'This is normal Grandad. They're just letting us know that it's time to sleep now.'

'Right, well, do we pull out bunk beds? Or what?' Henry tried to get control of himself. It really had been the strangest day of his life.

He had long since taken off his magnetic overshoes, and Bekka showed him how to unpack a sleeping bag from a small cupboard and hang it on the wall. Then he zipped himself into it and the two of them floated, each attached to the wall by their sleeping bag. Henry expected to feel awkward, sleeping standing up, but as the lights dimmed further and the room became totally dark he realised that in zero gravity it really didn't matter which way was up. He didn't need anything to support his head, he didn't need to find a nice comfy spot for his hip. He was supported, or rather didn't need support, and was the most comfortable he had ever been. He drifted easily off to sleep, happy that Bekka was doing the same thing right next to him.

Occasionally through the night he woke to the sounds of small scratches at the door or at the wall of the cell. But they didn't feel as frightening now. He smiled to himself and drifted back to sleep, happy that Cat and Sura, Rose and Jones, and the Sambiss were all working to get himself and Bekka back home. Surely with a team like that, they'd be fine.

Chapter Twenty-Five

Back in Davian's ship, things weren't quite so restful.

Electrical components were floating in the air all through the cabin of the ship. The soldering iron was held fast in the netting on the side and Rose was trying to thread a wire through a tiny hole, her tongue sticking out the side of her mouth as she concentrated.

The door slid open and she caught her breath.

'Only me,' said Jones.

'If I die from a heart attack tonight I will not be surprised.'

'Oh come on. You know that the IGP will always knock.'

'Yeah. You know, that doesn't actually help.' She turned back to her work. 'Now, where was I?'

She pulled a small disc closer to her, then twisted a wire from it around a resistor.

'This one is nearly done, I think. Have you found out about the airlock?'

'It looks like a regular MX35P.'

Rose hissed through her teeth.

'Looks like? Or is? No point in putting together an override for MX35P and finding out that it's actually the MX40. There's a big difference, you know.'

Jones yanked his phone out of his pocket and swiped the screen.

'Look. A photo of the registration stamp. MX35P.'

Rose caught his eye and smiled tightly. 'Say what you mean, Jones. We don't have time for miscommunication right now.'

Jones jammed his phone back into his pocket, shrugged and then, eventually, smiled back at her. 'Gotcha. Sorry. It's a definite MX35P. Can you work with that?'

'Thanks Jones. It will be next after this bio disc.'

The door slid open again, and this time it was Jones' turn to jump.

'Sura! What are you doing sneaking in like that?'

'See how it feels?' Rose turned back to the wires she was fiddling with.

'Where have you been anyway?'

'I've been chatting to the crew.' Sura nibbled at the end of one of her dreadlocks as she drifted around the cabin. 'Eating some yummy dlanca. Haven't had that in ages.'

She twirled a screwdriver in the air.

'Didn't bring any back for the rest of us I see.'

'Huh? Oh no. Sorry. Didn't think of it.'

Jones shot Rose a look that said, 'What's up with her?' And Rose shrugged in return.

'So did you learn anything useful?' Rose asked.

'Huh?' Sura nibbled some more on her dreadlock.

Jones had had enough. 'Wake up Sura, did you just stuff yourself with dlanca? Or do you have something helpful to tell us?'

Sura fiddled with a roll of wire, pulling it out and rewinding it back around the plastic holder.

'They're not a bad crew. The boss is a bit of a … let's just say he has "small man syndrome" and that might get worse. Did you notice that ship that came on board after us? Well, that was an old friend of Cat's and they are holed up discussing something. And Captain Brojiklan is a little put out that he's not in on the oh-so-secret conversation.'

Sura spun the roll of wire in the air.

'I'm not sure that I'm not put out at not being in that oh-so-secret conversation myself,' she mused.

'Great. So we have already put the boss off-side,' Jones grumped.

Sura nodded and started unrolling the wire again.

'The rest of the crew are are a little looser though. I got the impression (though no one said it in so many words) that they're a bit taken with our Davian and Bekka. If we were to make a move, I have the feeling that they won't pull out all the stops to get us back.'

Rose took the wire out of her hand.

'So if we manage to get out of the hold …'

'They will turn a blind eye until we jump.' Sura turned her attention to a little box of screws.

'But the captain, he's not going to let them do that?' Jones crossed his arms.

'Well, you know, he can give all the orders he likes, but it's up to the crew to carry them out. It's possible that we'll get away. Not that they'll give us the keys to the cells exactly, but they will probably decide to move slowly enough that we can escape.'

'Did you make any special friends that you could encourage to be on the bridge when we make our move?' Jones asked.

Sura looked up and grinned.

'I might have.'

'Well, every little bit helps.'

Rose pushed past Sura to get to the soldering iron. And then had to reach around her again to get back the disc that Sura had absentmindedly fiddled with and sent off in the other direction. She gave a puff of exasperation.

'Sura, if you're not going to be helpful then go put yourself into a sleep pod. I have quite enough on my plate already.'

'Oh sorry,' Sura apologised, and pulled her way up to the end of the ship.

'Something's going on there,' Jones whispered to Rose.

'Yes, but I don't have time to think about what,' Rose replied. 'Look, can you hold this for me? I just need to adjust it and then we'll be up to working on the airlock.'

'I just wish we could test things before we have to rely on them.'

'Me too, but there'd be no better way to give the game away than by having all the ships float because I turn the magnetism off, and then have them all clang back down again. Can you imagine? You're just going to have to trust me.'

'It's a risk. I hope Sura's right about the crew.'

'It was a risk from the time we left Earth. We just have to keep going now. No way out but through.'

Jones nodded and they went back to work.

Chapter Twenty-Six

Henry and Bekka, flanked by a couple of IGP officers, entered a large room. The room was grey, just like Bekka's cell, like the hallways, like the hold. But after the tiny cell it felt like there was more air in the larger space, and Henry took a deep breath.

Cat and Sura greeted him, Cat holding on to Sura's shoulder.

'When do we go into the courtroom?' Henry asked in a whisper.

'This is the room,' Sura said with a smile.

'Here?' Henry looked around. This was not the courtroom that he was expecting. There was no nice wooden bench, no dock, no people in black robes with wigs on their heads. This was just a big grey room. And somehow that made Henry even more nervous. Anything could happen here. But he tried not to let his nerves show. He needed to be strong for Bekka.

'Are you ready?' Cat asked Bekka.

Bekka just shrugged in response.

'OK, let's do this then.'

They stood at one end of the room. Henry stood holding his granddaughter's hand. Whatever happened now, he was facing it with her.

Cat and Sura took their places to one side of Henry, and on the other side, the captain stood, stiff as a ramrod. The whole room was waiting, at the ready. Henry wondered what would happen next, what this AI judge would be like. Was it going to be such a dreadful ordeal that Cat didn't want to warn them about it? He felt Bekka trembling.

With a discreet chime, a person appeared at the other end of the room. A woman with brown hair and deep brown eyes, wearing a long black robe.

'Is that a human judge?' Henry whispered to Sura.

'No Henry, it's a hologram. The AI adjusts to look like the accused,' she whispered back. 'It's supposed to make you feel more at ease.'

'It was working, until I knew the trick,' he said. 'Now I just feel manipulated.'

'Well, try not to look it. It's reading your body language, it's checking your emotional signals, looking for guilt.'

'Oh great. I feel worse now.'

'Don't be worried, they make accurate judgements in most cases. And Cat's good at what she does. You'll be fine.'

The captain saluted. 'Your Honour, I present to you the accused, the female human from Sector 378, region H92.'

'Bekka. Her name is Rebekah.' Henry growled. Sura put a calming hand on his arm and he swallowed and tried again to look calm and innocent.

The captain shot him a dirty look and went on speaking in a louder voice.

'The charge against the accused is that of obstructing the arrest of a known criminal. I submit that when the criminal 13-L-67-CG was arrested, the female human bodily obstructed access to the criminal, stated that she was trying to stop the arrest, and when asked if she was obstructing an officer in the performance of his duty, said, and I quote, "Yes, yes I am." Therefore, by her own admission, she is guilty as charged. Evidence from the recorder has been uploaded to your database. I rest my case.'

The colour faded from Bekka's face and her trembling increased. Henry tightened his grip on her. 'We'll be fine,' he whispered. 'It's going to be OK.'

Cat pushed herself from Sura's shoulder, floated to the table in front of them, and somehow anchoring herself with her tail while maintaining her dignity, began her defence.

'The captain, it seems, has not been to region H92 before and has no idea of its customs and practices. On earth it is quite reasonable to make a noise about being arrested, it is only once the police officers are in physical danger that any charge of obstruction, or even of resisting arrest would be laid. Our defendant had no intention of overstepping the mark or of causing any disrespect to the officers. She was throwing a tantrum, much as a small child would.

'As there is no malicious intent or intended disrespect, I apply that the charges be dropped. I would like to call my first character witness.'

Cat called Henry as a witness. He spoke to the hologram with passion, as if she was the woman that she appeared. Saying that Cat was quite correct in her summation of earth customs and that even when physical violence was threatened some officers would not make an arrest. He made a staunch defence of his granddaughter, focusing especially on her friendships with many people from other planets (he was careful not to use the word 'alien' just in case it was offensive).

Sura and Rose also made brief statements in Bekka's defence, talking about her care for the Visser children and her school-child status on earth.

As Cat summed up, Henry thought she had done an excellent job. Surely no one could be unmoved by the presentation. Bekka had done so little, her innocence was without question. The big job would be to get Davian off his charges, whatever they were. That's what Cat had been concentrating on, interviewing Davian and making sure she had the whole story straight.

'I rest my case, Your Honour,' Cat stated.

'How long until we know ...?' Henry whispered to Cat, but he didn't have time to finish the question. The judge was already speaking.

'I declare the defendant guilty,' it said. And the word 'Guilty' showed on the hologram in big red colours in case anyone had any question about it.

'Guilty? But ... but you haven't had time to think about it!' Henry shouted.

Sura leapt into action. 'Henry, quiet. You'll get in trouble yourself,' she hissed, holding his arm.

He shook her hand off, 'But she didn't take any time to consider. She just made a snap decision.'

'She's not human, remember. She's an AI. She had enough time there to consider millions of arguments. Millions of outcomes. To take into account millions of previous cases. I'm sorry, Henry.'

The AI had continued unemotionally during Henry's protest and he tuned back in to hear it say, '... ten standard months.'

Bekka turned to Cat.

'How long is a standard month?' she asked, her chin crumpling.

'Ten standard months is about an Earth year,' said Cat.

Tears ran down Bekka's face as she absorbed that information, and Henry found himself crying too. They hugged each other for as long as they could, but eventually the police officers prised them apart.

'I'll get you out, Bekka. I don't know how, but I'll do it,' he whispered to her. Then she was gone. Marched back down the corridor to her cell.

Sura and Cat encouraged the weeping Henry to walk to their small ship. There Sura made him a cup of tea, or at least a bag of lukewarm tea, and helped him to pull himself together.

'I can't leave her here,' he said. 'Not in that horrible cell. Did you see what she was like when we first got here? I can't leave her here like that. What are we going to do?'

'I'm so sorry,' said Cat.

'No, no. You tried your best. The judge was just so unreasonable. Holding her to words spoken in the heat of the moment. It's just so unfair. So cold.'

A voice came from the back of the ship.

'So we're going to put part two in action then?' It was Jones.

'Rescue?' asked the Sambiss.

'I guess we have to,' said Cat. 'We've tried the legal version, now we need to take other action.'

'When?' asked Henry. 'Can we get her out tonight?'

'Well … Davian's hearing is tomorrow. And after that, whether he gets off or not, we're going to have to get out of here. They won't be inviting us to stay.'

'I've noticed they're not very hospitable,' said Henry.

'Maybe if we'd come in other circumstances they would have been.' Henry shook his head.

'I think we should do a practice run tonight, then we will be faster tomorrow when we get both of them.' Jones was eager.

'I'm all for getting her out tonight. That will give her hope. But can we do it without being caught? If we don't get her out, then we'll all be stuck in here,' Sura said.

Jones shook his head.

'There's a risk, but I'm 98 percent sure we can do it. They might be strict and careful when they're around the captain, but you've told us, Sura, that the crew are more slack when they're not being watched. The Sambiss and I have been all over the ship after dark. And Rose has put together a very nice biometric amplifier that will make it look like Bekka is still in the cell, at least to the monitoring system. It won't fool anyone who actually looks, but still, for the night it should be fine. I think a dry run escape is a very good idea.'

The risk *was* huge. But Jones had answers for every one of the team's questions. And Rose was very sure of the success of her device. Cat didn't seem to be very invested in the outcome and Henry wondered if she had lost a bit of confidence from the day's events. Before they had even come to a decision, she had left the ship again, murmuring something about, 'Davian's case'. The others discussed the pros and cons for about an hour, but in the end they decided to go for it.

'But how do we get Rose's fantastic device to her?' Henry asked. 'How big is it?'

Rose showed him the little disc she had made. It was about the size of a jam jar lid, and about a centimetre thick. It didn't look that impressive, but Rose assured him it had some complex electronics inside.

'Where do we hide that?'

The Sambiss floated out from the back of the ship, with something in his mouth. It was Bekka's teddy bear.

'Good idea,' Sura said. 'Tell the captain that if Bekka is going to stay for a year, she needs some comforts from home, especially due to her age. Tell him you've brought her favourite toy. We can hide the device inside it.'

Rose approved. 'If they scan it, they shouldn't find anything amiss, and you can tell them that some toys have discs inside that make noise. I'm pretty sure they won't be interested in it at all. Once you've got it to her, press the disc to turn it on.'

Sura took the teddy and immediately began to unpick the seam on its back. Henry sat back with a sigh. He wished he could get through to Bekka that she would be OK, that they were coming to get her, but he knew he would just have to wait a little longer.

Chapter Twenty-Seven

His heart in his mouth, Henry took a bag containing Bekka's clothes, the teddy, her journal, and some scribbled notes of encouragement from the others, and went to see the captain.

'Sir,' he said at his most deferential. 'I'd like to give Bekka some belongings from home. She's a long way from Earth, and we didn't even realise this part of the universe existed. She's just a child, she's going to be away for a long time, and I won't be able to come and visit. Can I leave this with her?'

He tried to look as pathetic as possible, tried to channel the pain and grief he had felt during the sentencing earlier that day. And as it turned out, the captain wasn't totally heartless. He didn't even scan the bag, just nodded. Then, at his most condescending, he patted Henry on the arm.

'I'm sorry about how things turned out today. But the law is the law. The time will pass quickly and she'll be able to come back to you. If we don't uphold the law, then the universe will become chaos in very little time. I'm sure you understand.'

Henry nodded. He didn't allow himself to speak. He turned quickly and walked back to Bekka's cell. He stepped into the windowless room expecting to find Bekka curled up again, hopeless and full of grief. But she wasn't. She faced him bravely.

'Bekka, how are you?' he asked.

'I'm better.'

He looked her in the eyes, checking for any signs of despair.

'No, I really am,' she said. 'I can do this. It's only a year.' She pulled her shoulders back, affecting a brave stance, but her chin trembled.

'Well, I've brought some things to help. Here's your teddy,' he said, squeezing it as he passed it to her. 'And here's your journal, and a change of clothes.'

Bekka's eyes welled up again at the sight of things from home. Henry wanted to say more, but the officer was still near the door. He couldn't afford to let things slip. He couldn't mess up the plan. He gave her a hug. Then they sat in silence together until the lights dimmed.

'I'll see you again before we go. It's going to be OK,' he said as he put his magnetic shoes back on.

'Time to leave, Sir,' said the officer at the door.

'I'll be fine Grandad,' said the brave Bekka with trembling lips belying her words. 'I'll be OK.'

Henry wiped some stray tears from his eyes as he clanked back through the dim corridors to the ship.

'This had better work,' he grumped at Jones as soon as he stepped inside the smaller ship. 'It had just better work.'

The lights blinked off outside and the waiting game began. Jones and the Sambiss made some small preparations, but there wasn't that much more that they could do. Cat had returned from whatever she had been doing. She curled herself into a ball and went to sleep. Henry tried to sleep too, but he was much too antsy. They were taking a big risk tonight and he hoped it was worth it.

Rose worked silently on another disc. That was fair, Davian would need to escape too if things didn't go to plan tomorrow. And one hearing had gone badly already despite everyone thinking it would be a pushover.

Eventually Jones figured they had waited long enough. He pulled himself silently to the door of the small ship. Henry moved forwards too.

'Mate, what are you doing?'

'I'm coming with you.'

'No mate, you're not.'

Henry shook his head. 'No, I thought …'

'You're too noisy. Too clumsy. You've spent almost no time in zero G and I'm not taking those stupid overshoes with me. I can't afford any bumps or clangs tonight, we're going to have a hard enough time with Bekka as it is.'

Henry could see the sense of that, but it was with almost physical pain that he watched Jones and the Sambiss silently float out the door. What if things went wrong? What if this afternoon's visit had been the last time he would ever get to see Bekka? What if? What if?

He would have paced up and down the ship if that were possible, but floating back and forth didn't have quite the same effect.

He fiddled in the galley, pulling out a bag of 'tea' and then putting it away again, untouched. He moved to the back of the ship, pulled his book out of his bag and tried to read but the words swam and he couldn't concentrate.

He floated back to the front again, holding on tightly to the handles around the side of the ship. This weightless thing was strange, even with its benefits.

Cat had woken from her nap when Jones and the Sambiss left, and was now preparing for the next day's hearing with Sura, both of them doing a last minute check of their notes.

Henry floated over to them and interrupted.

'Shouldn't they be back now?'

'Give them time,' Cat said. 'They are being very careful.'

Henry tapped his fingers impatiently on the table. Then he moved back to the galley again.

No, he didn't want tea. At least, not the lukewarm space kind of tea. If a hot cup of tea had been offered he was sure it would have made a difference, but sucking from a bag of lukewarm liquid was just not the same thing.

'Where are they?' He muttered under is breath. 'What's taking so long.'

Rose squeezed his shoulder.

'Henry, they'll get here. You just need to be patient.'

Eventually, after what felt like years, there was a light tap on the door of the ship and Jones, the Sambiss, and yes, Bekka stepped in.

Henry crowed delightedly and wrapped his arms around his granddaughter. She laughed with joy.

'It worked then?' asked Rose.

'Was there any doubt?' asked Jones, a grin spreading wide on his face. The Sambiss's whole body was wagging – not just his tail, but the whole of him – and his tongue lolled out of his mouth.

'Well, yes.' Cat answered seriously. 'There were many things that could have gone wrong. You could have got caught, the Sambiss could have forgotten himself and barked, the biometric device may have broadcast on the wrong network. You yourself said that you were only 98 percent sure it would work.'

Henry stared at her for a bit. Then he decided to brush it off. Cat was enmeshed in facts and figures right now, getting the story straight for Davian's hearing. She had got it wrong once. He was sure she didn't want to fail again.

'The main thing is, we have Bekka here with us. It did work. And I'm eternally grateful to you.' Henry gave Bekka a squeeze and gave everyone else a huge smile. 'One more day, we'll get Davian out somehow, and then we'll all go home.'

'Oh no mate, you won't be going home.' Jones shook his head.

'What? Of course we'll go home. That's what we're doing this all for.'

'Don't you remember how you got stuck in this bind in the first place?'

'Sure, Davian ran off to the ship, Bekka here went with him (not that I blame you, it shows your beautiful heart) and got caught by the police when they came to pick him up.'

'No, he doesn't mean that,' said Cat. 'Think back further. The reason Davian ran away was because a probe had been sent out to find him. That's why I wanted to try the legal path first. When you and Bekka leave this place, you will go on the "wanted" list. You won't be able to go home, that's the first place they'll look. You will have probes sent out after you. You will be on the run for the rest of your lives.'

'It will be a life of adventure,' Sura chimed in. 'You'll see things that very few humans have ever seen. Endless travel. You'll just need to be a bit careful, that's all. Sounds OK to me.'

'Better than being stuck in that cell,' agreed Jones.

Henry looked at them all, aghast. Never go home? Never go back to his beloved Cygnet and see the rolling hills and the beautiful gums? Never see the Milky Way again? At least, not from the right direction.

He imagined his bookshop, the shelves, the view from the windows. The old worn out kitchen. Every part of it tugged at his heart strings. He gulped.

But Bekka saw even more.

'I'll never see Mum and Dad again,' she whispered.

'Well ... you could ... it would ...' Jones' voice trailed off.

Cat floated across the table to land on Bekka's shoulder. She rubbed her head against Bekka's cheek. Then she turned to the others with a firm voice.

'This is exactly why I didn't want to do this. I'm not convinced this is the best course of action.'

'Well, what is?' asked Jones. 'Sitting in a cell for a year?'

'Yes, it may be. After a year Bekka could come home without fear of reprisals. She will have done her time. It won't make her a criminal on earth, just an interesting missing person's case. And she'll be able to get back on with her life.'

'I guess it's up to Bekka to choose,' Rose suggested, lightly touching Bekka's hand. 'How about it, Bekka? What would you prefer? A life spent traveling the universe, or a year in a cell?'

Bekka leaned in to Henry and he squeezed her shoulder again. 'You do what you think best,' he said. 'I can't make this decision for you. If you choose freedom, I'll be right there with you every step of the way.'

She stared at the floor. It felt like everyone in the ship was holding their breath. Even the Sambiss was completely still, his eyes fixed on Bekka as she stared at the table. An age passed. Then Bekka looked up at them.

'Take me back to the cell,' she said to Jones. 'I'll do the year and come back home. It's going to be hard.' Her lip quivered again. 'But I want to see my parents again, and this is the only way it will happen. Take me back right now before they find out I'm gone and make my sentence longer.'

The shipload breathed out.

'Brave girl,' Henry muttered and kissed her forehead.

'You are doing the right thing,' Cat said. 'I'm very proud of you.'

'Remember that we'll all be thinking of you, all the time, all year. And we'll be back to pick you up as soon as it's over. I'll find a way to get messages to you too,' Rose said.

Sura squeezed Bekka's hand, and the Sambiss gave her a big lick on the cheek.

Then Henry gave her one last hug, and she and Jones carefully set out on their way back to the cell.

Henry sat with his head in his hands. What would he tell Vivienne? Would it be better for him to stay behind too? No, if Bekka had been as brave as she had, then he would be brave too. Brave enough to go home and face his daughter and son-in-law. Brave enough to face the music.

Cat landed on his shoulder, completely weightless but wrapping her tail around his neck for comfort.

'Henry, don't give up yet. I have one last trick up my sleeve. The fight's not over until it is over. But I have to get Davian safe first.'

Henry nodded, his head still in his hands. 'Don't give up hope.' What hope was there? But he didn't feel hopeless so much as helpless. And so, so tired.

* * *

When Rose looked around, she saw that Henry had nodded off to sleep, right where he was. She gently attached him to the wall so that he would not float into anyone and wake up. The poor man, this had all been a bit much for him.

Chapter Twenty-Eight

The lights in the hold flickered on and Henry roused. He blinked his eyes and looked around. He couldn't believe he had just dropped off to sleep, right in the middle of things, right In the way of everyone. But no one seemed particularly concerned. Rose was working at the console. The Sambiss and Jones were tucked away in the sleeping quarters again, Cat was eating a salmon treat, and Sura was preparing the bags of tea. She floated one across to him as she saw him wake up.

'Drink up, it's time for the last act. We're going to work on Davian's case today.' Her voice was bright and cheery. You'd think she was back at home, getting kids ready for school.

Henry took a swig of the tea. Sura had somehow managed to get it just a little warmer than lukewarm and the caffeine worked its wonders. He spruced himself up, running a brush through his white hair and putting on a new shirt. Cat finished the snack and gave herself a good clean. Sura tidied up her dreadlocks and made sure her antennae were upright and even.

'Ready?' Cat asked.

'As we'll ever be,' said Sura.

Sura and Henry put on their magnetic overshoes, Cat held on to Sura's shoulder, and the three of them clanged through the corridors to the hearing room.

This time it was Davian who stood in the dock, flanked by two officers. He didn't have Henry or anyone to stand with him. He stood bravely, head up, though he looked to Cat for reassurance as they walked in. One of the officers also gave Cat a nod of greeting.

Henry realised that he had no idea at all what Davian was under arrest for. He hadn't heard his story at all. He had been so concerned for Bekka that he didn't know what kind of criminal this kid was.

According to Bekka, Davian wasn't any kind of criminal at all. He was just a friend that she wanted to support and care for. But surely there had to be some reason that the intergalactic police were willing to hunt him down. Though if you judged by Bekka's experience, it might have been something as stupid as saying the wrong words and then running away. And he was a young kid, too. Henry looked at his pale face. Very young. What could he possibly have done to deserve any kind of a sentence?

Well, he was about to find out.

The hologram appeared again. This time as a tall man with white skin and black hair, dressed all in white. Almost human, but like Davian, a little too pale, and the hair a smidge too black. But obviously the same species as the creature in the dock.

The Captain spoke again.

'Your Honour, I present to you the accused, Davian Jernoshef, the arphaxad from Sector 28, Region V831; criminal 13-L-67-CG. The charge against the accused is the first degree murder of Kasp Rowivad that occurred in Region V831 on the 91st rotation during the time signature 8391.'

Henry felt his knees go weak. Murder? His granddaughter had been brought into all this mess by a murderer? He looked around in astonishment. How could Cat have kept this from him? Why didn't anyone tell him that this kid was wanted for murder?

The Captain didn't say any more, instead the AI took over and produced for itself the case for the prosecution.

Henry tried to take in the gory details of how the murdered creature was found with its chest blown away by a blaster, how the crime was part of gang violence of an obscene scale, how the creature who had been murdered was admittedly a drug dealer himself but that all life was valuable and no murder should go unpunished.

In addition to the voice, text appeared, laying out the case clearly and succinctly.

Cat and Sura seemed completely unperturbed by all of this. Henry, on the other hand, was grateful for the zero gravity that enabled him to stand through the shock. He was sure that if he had been on earth he would have been at least sitting down, if not fainting by now.

'How can the judge give the case for the prosecution?' he asked Sura in a whisper. 'Surely that shows bias?'

'It's not the judge giving the case,' Sura murmured back. 'This is just a computer reading out data from its memory bank. The prosecution case was uploaded when the original crime occurred. The AI is reading it out for our benefit.'

'For our benefit? It's not benefitting me at all. I don't want to hear all that.'

'Don't worry about it. Cat knows what she's doing, and she needs to hear the story from the other side. It's going to be fine.'

Cat threw them a look that clearly showed she was displeased with their chatter. Henry gave up trying to understand and just listened to the AI as it droned on. Eventually the case ground to a halt and it was Cat's turn to speak.

'Your Honour,' she said. 'It pleases me that the prosecution agrees that all life is precious. I wish to tell Davian's story in its fullness so that the preciousness of his life is on record. Is that permissible?'

The hologram nodded. If an artificial intelligence could have emotion at all, Henry guessed that the gift of information would be the thing to make it happy. He didn't know, maybe this AI was so advanced that it did feel emotion. Maybe all information was precious to it. At any rate, it let Cat talk.

'The accused, 13-L-67-CG, whom henceforth I shall refer to as Davian, was born in Karthur, in Region V831. He was born into a middle-class family. His father worked as a support to the theme park enterprise, working hard from early to late, and he was not at home much to help Davian's mother with his care. Davian's father needed to work long hours to afford the house they owned in the suburbs. It was a nice enough place, small but close to parks and nature. Davian would go for walks with his mother. He remembers fondly the purple trees, the green park.

'Of course, this kind of luxury doesn't come cheaply and Davian's mother had to return to work as soon as possible after his birth. She worked as a teacher. It gave her weekends and school holidays with her son.

'Davian's childhood could be seen as idyllic. But the good times didn't last. When Davian was still quite young, his father contracted an illness. I would like to tell you what that illness was, but Davian does not remember. He just remembers that the family moved from their lovely little house in the suburbs to a tiny, grimy flat in the city centre. Davian's mother still went to work for a while to try to support the family, but eventually she had to stop working to look after her dying husband. Davian remembers that his parents were now both too busy, ill and worried to concern themselves with him and that as long as he was keeping himself occupied and quiet they didn't pay him much attention.

'It's not a new story. This story has been repeated throughout the universe. Davian was quite young when the family moved, but he hated that he'd lost the old house, he hated his new school, he was worried about his parents, and he felt helpless and ignored.

'He began to skip school and spent time with other children who would congregate in the alleys and abandoned warehouses in the city. He was adopted by older hardened youths. He found his identity in a city gang calling themselves the Vyynx.

'Because of his extreme youth, the gang didn't ask him to do any crime. Not yet. He was still a very small fish in the pond. They were like big brothers to him. They would take him along with them as they broke into liquor stores or sold their awful drugs. He was being trained. But not being used, not yet.

'I want to be very clear that even though Davian was part of the gang, his activities and behaviour at this time were still lawful. If you look at the records for Karthur you will see that there are no previous allegations against Davian. And the prosecution case specifically states that this current accusation is Davian's first arrest.

'This brings us to the current accusation. I would like you to hear what happened in Davian's own words. I call Davian to speak and give an account of the proceedings as he remembers it.'

All eyes in the room turned to Davian who grew even more pale, if that was possible, and gulped audibly. Then he began to speak. His speech was quick and clipped, with very little emotion. Henry thought that Cat must have rehearsed this moment with Davian, got him to commit his speech to memory.

'One day I came home and found Mum very upset at the kitchen table. She was crying. I didn't normally see much of her because she was always looking after Dad, and she didn't normally let me see how worried she was. But this day, I had the sense to ask her what was happening, and she actually told me. She said that some gang had intercepted the ship that carried Dad's prescription medication, and that we were running out.

'I asked her, was there anything I could do? And she said, "Unless you know anyone on the black market who would be willing to give us the meds, then no." And she laughed a hopeless little laugh. Then she pulled me close and gave me a hug and said, "At least we'll still have the two of us."

'But I pulled away from her and ran out the door. I felt so hopeful. I thought that as a member of the Vyynx, as "family" to them (as Xedrog called it) that I could help out. I ran all the way to headquarters and demanded to speak to Xedrog.

'They told me it wasn't a good time, but I was determined and eventually Xedrog heard my voice and invited me in to his office. I laid out my story, told him that my dad was sick and would die without the medication that I knew they possessed. I pleaded with Xedrog to give me some.

'He laughed at me. Told me that he'd give me some, but only if my parents could pay the black market rates. That he was running a business.

'That made me so mad, and I told him I wanted nothing more to do with him. That we were through. And that's when they took me out and made me watch them shoot Kasp. Apparently, he was a police informant or something. Xedrog thought he was worthy of death anyway. They just shot him in cold blood.'

Davian shuddered and took a deep breath.

'They told me I was an accomplice, just as guilty of murder as they were. That they had my fingerprints and DNA and that they could prove I was there. That the police would now be after me.

'After that, I just ran. I ran to the docking station, got on board a ship, and left Karthur. It was the only option I had.'

Cat took over again.

'Now, an informant in the gang reported this murderous crime. The police made many arrests and Xedrog, to save his skin, gave lists of those present. Hence, the arrest warrant for Davian for a crime he did not commit.

'If you look at the case for the prosecution, you will see that Davian's fingerprints were not found on the blaster. That even his association with the gang was brought into question at the time. I present to you that his only crime was that of playing hookey, of skipping school. And that is punishable only by detention, not by life imprisonment.

'In Karthur, the law at that time was ridiculous, by the standards of intergalactic law. The Karthurians were concerned about the level of crime and were trying, by imprisonment, to remove any criminal element from their streets. We have seen over the rotations that instead of bringing calm to this city, all this did was to allow hardened criminals to educate young men like Davian in the traditions and morals that they shared, and to allow the culture of crime to expand. In fact, this law has allowed the gang, the Vyynx, to expand its numbers and it is now a greater force in the city.

'I put it to you that the law that Davian was imprisoned under, the Karthurian law, was and is illegal by the terms of the Intergalactic Legal Agreement. And that as such, all charges against Davian Jernoshef should be dropped.'

The AI nodded. Henry blinked. Did this mean what he thought it meant? Hang on, was Cat actually performing the impossible? How do you read the body language of a computer?

Then the AI spoke, 'Please report on the further history of criminal 13-L-67-CG.'

'The first ship that Davian boarded left him at the ports at Brenik and he worked there, doing hard manual labour for food.

'He then managed to get a job on a cargo ship as a cleaner. By continuing to labour with integrity, he found employment on various planets that paid him in credits (instead of only paying him in food) and eventually he saved enough to buy his own ship. He had never been given identifying papers and he was very aware of the lengths that the legal system would go to to find him. He didn't realise that he was essentially a refugee from Karthur. He thought that the whole universe was against him. And still, even though he did not have legal papers, he always made sure that he worked for his living. He did not perform any criminal acts, not even theft.

'If you examine your data banks you will find no other charges against Davian or any of his aliases. You will see that what I say is true.

'Once he could afford a decent ship, he looked for a planet where he could live for a while and lick his wounds. A calm planet. A planet that reminded him of the parks of his childhood. He found Earth, Sector 378, Region H92, and crash-landed there two earth-rotations ago.

'And now, with your honour's approval, I'd like Davian to tell you what his plans are for the future.'

The AI nodded again.

Davian looked at Cat, his face showing all sorts of doubt. She nodded at him and he swallowed hard, then said, 'I want to go back to Karthur.'

'Back to Karthur? Why on earth?' Henry broke in.

Davian's eyes filled with tears.

'I want to find my mum and dad. I don't know how they are. I don't even know if they're alive. But I have to try. I really have to try. I can't just leave them there when I could bring them to Earth. They would be so happy on Earth.'

Henry's eyes filled with tears too. He hoped the AI was moved. Though could it be moved? Did it have any emotions at all?

Cat was not finished. She had furnished herself with many character references for Davian from the time that he had spent on Earth. That's what she had spent the barbecue afternoon doing – collecting stories about Davian that she could present. Davian had been a quiet member of the community but he had been valued even so. Cat talked and talked, giving the AI all the information she could. Davian's care for the Visser children, the help he gave to Jones with his woodwork, the cleaning he did in the Cygnet streets, picking up rubbish even though he wasn't being paid, the way he worked hard at any job that came his way, the way he educated himself. In her summing up, she emphasised once again the vital point that the Karthurian law, under which Davian was charged, was fundamentally different to the Intergalactic Legal Agreement. That it was illegal for Davian to be charged with a murder that he did not commit or have anything to do with. That the only thing he was guilty of was being in the wrong place at the wrong time, an occurrence that was completely out of his control.

Once again the AI took what Henry considered not nearly enough time to make its decision. But this time the decision was in Davian's favour.

'NOT GUILTY' were the words in green, and the holographic man even smiled. Henry and Sura laughed and cheered and hugged each other. Davian stood perfectly still, his face a picture of shock and relief. Cat purred loudly.

Then she spoke again.

'While we're here, I'd like to lodge an appeal in the case of Rebekah, the human.'

'Appeal granted,' was the response from the AI. Again Henry was shocked, it would have taken months for a similar result on Earth. But here, the wait was milliseconds. The AI also morphed from arphaxad male to human female. Cat continued with her appeal.

'The human was arrested for obstructing the arrest of criminal 13-L-67-CG or Davian, is this agreed?'

'Agreed,' said the AI.

'And the arrest of Davian has now been ruled to be unlawful and unnecessary.'

'Agreed,' said the AI. Henry strained to hear some interest in the voice of the AI. He thought he could figure out where this was going, but he wanted to hear more. The AI, however, was not interested. The voice was as bland as any computer asking you to 'press 2 for more information'. There were drawbacks to this automated system, that was for sure.

'As Davian was not guilty of anything, his arrest should not have taken place. Bekka's statement was in agreement with the judgement that Davian should not have been arrested. Therefore, in her statement, Bekka agreed with Intergalactic Law.'

'Agreed.'

'As Rebekah's statement is in agreement with the law, she can not logically be found guilty of contravening Intergalactic Law. And therefore, she is not guilty of anything and should be released.'

Did Henry have to wait longer for this outcome? It felt like he did. It felt like he was holding his breath, like his heart had stopped beating, like everything had stopped to hear the AI's judgement.

But you couldn't fault the logic. And the AI was a computer and, therefore, logical.

'The appeal has been heard. The judgement is: not guilty. Rebekah the human shall be released to return to Earth.'

Henry breathed again. The green words were right there: Not Guilty. He whooped with delight.

Cat purred smugly as the hologram blinked off. 'I told you it wasn't over yet. But I just had to get Davian off first.'

'Congratulations, Davian,' Henry said and shook his hand. 'You're a free man now.'

Their rejoicing seemed to rub off on the police officers around them. Handshakes were given all around and drinks were even brought out for them. The door opened and in stepped Bekka, her backpack on her back and her teddy clutched to her chest.

'They told me I'm free,' she said. 'Is it true?'

'It's true.' Henry hugged her close, he never wanted to let go of her again. 'And you'll be glad to know that Davian is free too.'

'Really?' her tearstained smile turned to Davian.

'Yes, really. Cat has got me off. She did a fantastic job.'

The captain came over to shake hands with Davian and Henry.

'I'm sorry that all of this was such a waste of your time,' Henry said.

'No Sir, I don't consider it a waste at all. It is another longstanding case that is now closed, justice has been done, and that's what I care about. It makes me completely happy to have a not-guilty verdict.'

'I thought you were a good man when I saw you. Even if you had arrested my granddaughter.'

'Well, I'm very glad that's cleared up now.'

Sura touched the captain's arm.

'May I talk with you for a minute, Sir?'

Sura, the captain, and one of the other officers, moved over to a corner.

Henry could see Sura speaking urgently, but in a voice so low that he couldn't hear a word. The captain was shaking his head, crossing his arms. Then the other officer chimed in, she didn't speak as urgently but Henry could see the captain's shoulders slumping as he slowly nodded. He was so fascinated and almost moved closer to hear what was going on, then Bekka tugged at his arm and broke his concentration.

'How did this all happen?' Bekka asked. 'How did Cat manage to rescue me?'

'It's a long story,' said Henry. 'Maybe Cat can tell you when we're on our way home.'

'We're going home?'

'Yes. At least I hope so. Although, Davian, you wanted to go to … to Kar–?'

'To Karthur, yes. I want to go there. But I think you all need to go back to Earth first.'

'I'd be much obliged if we did. Bekka's parents are going to be wondering where we are and why they haven't heard from us lately. If we leave it too late, we'll have a lot of explaining to do.'

As they walked to the door, a prison guard ducked in and caught Davian's arm.

'I've had a look, Davian,' she said. 'For your parents. Like you asked me to do.'

He stared at her, his eyes wide.

'I'm sorry, your father has passed away,' she said gently. 'But your mother is still alive. As far as I could see she's still living somewhere on Karthur. I wish you luck in your journey to find her.'

Davian swallowed and nodded, then walked to the hold deep in thought.

Chapter Twenty-Nine

The happy company made their way back to Davian's little ship, pulling off their magnetic overshoes and returning them to the police officers as they tumbled through the door all laughing and talking at once.

Rose came to greet them. 'It all went well then?'

'Very well,' said Henry. 'Greet our two innocents.'

Rose closed the door and Jones and the Sambiss floated out from the back to join the celebrations. The Sambiss jumped from one to another giving large wet kisses to everyone. Jones was liberal with handshakes and congratulations.

Rose eventually called the party to a halt. 'Ready to head for home?'

'Yes, let's get going,' said Henry.

'I'm ready,' said Bekka. 'More than ready.'

'I'm not,' said Sura. And that caught everyone's attention.

'You're not?'

'No, I'm not ready to head for home, I'm not even ready to head for Earth.'

'You don't want to come home with us?' Bekka asked.

'I love you all dearly and I'm so glad I could help Cat with this. But part of the reason I came out in the first place was to get off planet. I've missed the travel, the new sights and sounds. I've missed spending time in zero G and I've so missed the stars. I think I've been ready to leave Earth for a couple of years but I didn't have a ship to do it in. Now I'm out here, I don't think I could go back.

The Captain says I can stay with them and he'll drop me off at the next planet.'

'That explains the huge bag then,' said Jones. 'You should've said something. Why didn't you tell us you were moving off planet? Why the big secret?'

'I had to wait and see how it all went. We really had no idea whether this would go well or not, did we? But I wanted to be prepared for the possibility.'

Henry's heart was so inclined towards home that he was feeling almost physically pulled back to earth. He couldn't really understand what Sura was saying. How could she bear to be of no fixed abode? How could she not want to make somewhere her home? But the other travellers felt differently. While Henry stood back, Rose and Jones gave Sura hugs and told her they would miss her but that they understood. Even Bekka had a look of wanderlust in her eyes.

She looked at Henry, 'Can you imagine? Just wandering through the universe, checking it all out, seeing new things every single day? Wouldn't that be awesome?'

Henry shook his head. 'Nope. Give me my comfortable bed, my little shop, and a good hot cup of tea any day. You're coming home with me, my lass.'

'But …'

'When you're grown, when you've left home and it's you telling your Mum what you're going to do, then you can take it into your head to go travelling. But not before. I'm not going to be the one to tell Mum and Dad that I've lost you somewhere and that it's not even somewhere on Earth.'

Bekka laughed, but she still looked with longing as Sura pulled out her big bag, made sure everything was packed, and said goodbye to everyone.

* * *

The door closed behind Sura. Rose (after some discussion with Davian about who should drive) started up the engines. The hold door opened and the magnetic field was turned off. The smaller ship drifted out into the large blackness of space and the larger ship winked out of existence. And Jones and the Sambiss came out of hiding for the last time.

'Good to be out! Good to be free. Good to be loud.' The Sambiss barked and frolicked around the small ship.

'You think it's good to be free,' said Davian stretching his arms out wide. 'I feel better than I have in years.'

Bekka just stared out the cockpit window. Henry realised that she hadn't seen the stars before. Not in this proliferation, or from this angle.

He called to Rose. 'Do we have to jump immediately? Bekka didn't get to see much of space in her travel. She could do with a bit of time staring at the stars.'

Rose smiled her beautiful smile. 'We'll take the scenic route home.'

'Could you tell me the story now?' Bekka asked. 'How did you manage to free us, Cat?'

'Yes, I want to hear the whole story too, now that we're free and away from the cops. Come on Cat, give us the whole thing, don't spare any details.'

Henry realised that for Bekka, Jones and the Sambiss the whole procedure was a mystery, a mystery with a good outcome, but still, a complete blank for them. They were happy to see everyone, but had no idea how it had all happened.

Henry took himself to the galley and fixed drinks for everyone, with a little help from Rose. The others found comfortable places to float in the ship and settled down to listen to the story. Cat told it just as masterfully as she had for the AI the first time.

'It was the logic of the thing,' Rose said approvingly as the story ended and was given applause. 'A good computer thrives on logic.'

'Clever, Cat.' The Sambiss approved.

'Nice job,' said Jones.

Cat purred and acknowledged their praise. Bekka didn't say much though. She had gone back to staring thoughtfully out the cockpit window.

'How far away is Karthur?' she asked.

'From here? I wouldn't do it in a single jump, but we could probably do it in two,' Rose said matter-of-factly.

'Well?' Bekka turned to Henry.

'Well what?' Henry smiled.

'Well, shall we go and get Davian's Mum?'

Henry's smile turned to a frown as he looked at her earnest pleading face.

'But we don't even know if she's there. What if something goes wrong? All sorts of things could go wrong. And all these lovely people don't want to go traipsing all over space do they? And we have to go home. Does Davian even want to bring his mother back to Cygnet?'

'Yes, I really do,' said Davian dreamily. 'She would love Cygnet. All the green, and the flowers, and the lovely countryside.'

'See?' Bekka was triumphant.

'But you can't just go and grab someone and bring them back, can you?' Henry looked at the others. 'Well, can you?'

'Karthur's really not that far out of our way,' said Rose. 'Davian's travels have taken him all around the universe and nearly back to where he wanted to be. It might take us another Earth-week to do it, but that would be all.'

'We'd need to hack into the database, see if we can find her. But I've had a go at that in my time, and I'm sure Cat could help me,' Jones said.

'Mother. Is very important,' was the Sambiss' response, his tail between his legs.

Henry felt outnumbered. He thought longingly of his little home in Cygnet. It was the teapot he missed most, he thought. His teapot and a proper hot cup of tea.

'The thing is, Sir,' Davian was deferential, but he had something to say. 'If this ship gets damaged on reentry, it will be months before I can go and get her. Karthur has a good docking system. We'll be able to get her and turn around and head for Earth in a matter of a few days.'

'If you can find her.' Henry said darkly. 'What if she's moved planets? We'll be stuck on a wild goose chase all over the universe and I'll never get home. And another thing, I know you're cleared by the Intergalactic Law now, but aren't you still a wanted man on Karthur? What if we take you there to get her, and instead lose both of you?'

'No, that's not a problem any more,' Cat said. 'All the databases will have been updated. I seriously don't expect us to have any issues with the law anymore, either the IGP or the local Karthur police. And if there is the possibility of trouble, that is a good reason for us to go along. If anyone tries to give Davian trouble, we'll be there to help. But the chance of that is very slim.'

Henry looked at the floor. He didn't want to go, and they were waiting on him. The vote was six to one, but for some reason they still wanted his approval before they'd go. He didn't know what to say. Why would he go on such a ridiculous errand? But then, why had they all helped him out in his hour of need? He wouldn't have Bekka with him now if this amazing team hadn't rallied around.

Cat curled her tail around her feet and tried again.

'How about this?' she asked. 'We'll enjoy the stars out here and let Bekka have some zero G time. And while that's happening, Jones and I will hack some Karthur databases. There has to be some record of Davian's mum somewhere in computational records. If we find her, find an address of some sort, then we'll go. If there's no sign of her, then we'll go straight to Earth.'

Cat was very good at arguing. Her plan was completely reasonable, and Henry had to agree to it.

'OK, fine. We'll do that,' he grumped. 'But if there's no record, we're going straight home.'

The rest of the crew cheered, making him smile despite himself.

'So what's her name, Davian?' Cat asked.

'Vera,' was the response. 'Her name is Vera. Vera Jernoshef.' He choked up.

'That's a lovely name,' said Rose. 'Let's go and get Vera, shall we?'

Cat and Jones huddled together in the cockpit using the ship's computer to search for evidence of Vera. Davian and Bekka sat at one of the wide windows, taking in the view.

Henry decided he would try to view this time as a holiday. He would try to relax. The big stress he'd been feeling for the past few days was over. They were no longer chasing after the police or after Bekka. They were just floating in space, an experience that not many men his age were able to have. And he had to admit that it was comfortable. His old knees were no longer aching, and sleeping in zero G was like sleeping in the most comfortable feather bed there was. He didn't have to arrange his arms and legs so that they didn't ache. He didn't have to squash his cheek on a pillow. He might look like a zombie with his arms floating out in front of him, but it really was comfortable.

Henry decided to take a nap, his hand on the Sambiss' head. It was all out of his control now. He'd have to wait and see what happened.

The search through the various databases of Karthur took a while. Cat, Jones, Rose and Davian spent a fair bit of time deep in conversation. Even the Sambiss went over and listened intently at times. Henry assumed they were talking about the search for Vera, though he wasn't really clear on why sometimes the talk got heated. But he didn't much mind, this wasn't his deal.

Henry got to know the galley quite well, though really what he was doing couldn't really be called cooking – he was just heating up or unwrapping foods. All the food tasted like he had a head cold. In other words, it didn't much matter what he was eating, he didn't taste much of it at all. But Rose had managed to scavenge some food off the IGP and along with what they had packed from Earth, there was enough for them. They weren't going hungry and that was a good thing.

He wasn't really getting used to floating around the little ship. Bekka, on the other hand, zipped back and forth from one end of the ship to the other like a natural.

'It's like flying Grandad, like those dreams I've had of flying. I love it. I don't want to go back to walking now.'

Henry smiled and nodded, but he couldn't agree. He did want to go back to walking. He wanted to walk up the Main Street of Cygnet and smell the roses and the eucalyptus. He wanted to walk up the stairs and into his kitchen and sit at the table and sip a cup of tea. But he had to admit, as adventures go, this part where they were just relaxing and enjoying themselves, this wasn't too bad.

He was just drifting off to another nap when a loud whoop made him jump and hit his nose on the roof.

'We've found her!' Jones yelled.

'Where is she?' asked Henry.

'Still on Karthur. Living pretty close to the docking station too. It all looks good.'

Cat and Rose exchanged a long look.

'OK, well, let's go get her then,' said Rose stretching her arms above her head. 'I must say, I'm in need of some regular sunshine.'

'Are you sure this is all right, Sir?' Davian asked Henry. 'You don't need to go back to Earth?'

'Let's do it,' said Henry gruffly. There was no way he could back out now. It would be murder to kill the hope in Davian's eyes.

Chapter Thirty

Henry was prepared for the jumps through space now. He knew they would knock him about. He hoped they weren't doing any major damage to him, or to Bekka for that matter. He wondered how many times you could black out before you got brain damage. He hoped that they'd get home OK. Oh boy, did he hope for that. He still couldn't really believe that he and Bekka had got themselves into this situation. What were they doing careening around space?

As he drew himself back into consciousness after the final jump, Bekka grabbed his arm, her eyes shining. 'We get to visit a different planet! Mum and Dad are only in Antarctica, but we'll be on a whole other planet! I can't wait to see what it's like.'

Henry looked out the window. There right in front of them a huge globe was slowly rotating. It looked … wrong. Strange. There were blue oceans, he was expecting that. But the land masses were all the wrong shapes. And colours. Some land masses were white, some purple, some green, some with what could be large cities, some possibly covered by vegetation, but all of them just … not right. Henry hadn't been expecting the planet to look like Earth of course. Only … on some level he obviously had been expecting another Earth. And this was, as Bekka had said, a whole other planet.

Henry looked doubtfully at Cat.

'Can we leave the ship? Will it be OK for us to do that?'

'What could be wrong with that? We're here now, we've come all the way to Karthur. What could be a problem with us just having a little look?' Bekka asked, looking anxiously from Henry to Cat and back again.

'What could be a problem?' Henry sighed. 'You know I don't want to deny you anything Bekka, but think about it. No one on Earth believes that aliens even exist. So I assume we won't be able to talk to anyone about anything we do here. And so many things could go wrong. You could get hurt in some alien way and not be able to heal properly. You could catch some strange alien disease. You could ... you could get captured by aliens and ...'

'Oh please Grandad, please, please.' Bekka grabbed Henry's hand and squeezed it until it hurt. 'I promise I'll be careful. I promise I will do whatever I'm told. I won't move an inch away from whoever's looking after me. Please?'

Cat exchanged a long look with Rose. Then, strangely, she also looked at Davian who gave a quick nod. Then she made her decision.

'I think it won't hurt for you to have a little look around. It would look a bit strange to the folks in charge here if you stayed on board the ship. Just make sure you stay with one of us at all times. No running off on your own.'

'Yippee!' Bekka bounced all around the ship, narrowly missing crashing into the flight desk.

'But won't we need a ... a visa or something? Passports or ... something?' Henry was clutching at straws now.

'Actually, you don't. Karthur is a tourist planet. People come here from everywhere.'

'A tourist planet?'

'Yeah, mate. They call it "The Jewel of the Universe."' Jones sounded only slightly sarcastic. 'Actually, it is one of the better planets to visit. The Falls of Gebria have to be seen to be believed. And then there is the natural forest of pelentra trees, when that's in bloom, well I've only seen pictures but it's something incredible.'

'And rides,' barked the Sambiss.

'Oh yes, the amusement park. "Best in the Galaxy" they say. I wouldn't know. Don't care much for those kinds of amusements, myself.'

'Fun! They are so much fun.'

Bekka laughed. 'We could go and visit that, Grandad.'

'I'm having enough of a ride as it is, thank you very much. If you need an amusement park after this, I'll take you to the Gold Coast.'

She laughed again. 'All good. I think I'm having enough of a mind-blowing experience.'

'So yes, as there are so many visitors, they have a system like your visa waiver system on Earth. You're definitely able to visit, at least for a short time.' Cat was ever interested in legalities.

Bekka squealed with joy.

'You won't be able to tell anyone at home about it,' Henry warned.

'Who cares! I'll talk with Davian, I'll talk with Rose, I'll ... I'll write a book. It doesn't matter, I'm just so excited.'

'You'd better calm down a bit right now,' Rose suggested. 'If you crash into the controls I'm not going to be able to land this thing and you won't get to Karthur at all. In fact, it's probably time for everyone to strap in for landing.'

Bekka sat next to Henry and put her seatbelt on, demure on the outside, but Henry could see her almost vibrating with excitement.

They dropped towards the planet's surface. Henry and Bekka craned to see the land through the windows. They flew over an ocean towards what looked like a huge built-up city. Spaceships of all sorts flew past them: round UFO-style ships, large tankers, small shuttles like theirs, long cylinders, ships in the shape of an X, any style of ship Henry could think of and more.

Great towers rose up to meet them. Each tower had several long arms stretching out from it. And at the end of each arm ... hands? Henry squinted and realised that each 'hand' was a ship, tethered to the tower by the arm. The setup was industrial and stark and he hoped that the whole planet wasn't similarly stark and built up. No, Henry reminded himself, airports and docks aren't the best advertisements for a city, especially not from the outside. He was sure things would be more aesthetically pleasing once they reached the surface.

Lights flashed on the ship's console. Rose spoke into the communicator, and slowly and carefully she manoeuvred the craft into a docking station.

The ship's engines powered down and Henry felt his body take on the familiar pull of gravity. He breathed out. This felt normal.

Rose opened the ship's door and bright daylight flooded in.

'Ah, sunlight. Real sunlight,' Rose breathed. 'If anyone needs me, I'll be sitting out on the stoop drinking in that beautiful sunshine.' She smiled beatifically.

'What's the plan?' Henry asked. 'Who's going where?'

'I think it might be best if I talk to Mum on my own first,' Davian suggested. 'She might be intimidated by all of you turning up on her doorstep.'

'And the rest of us?'

'We may as well all head out together. It might be easier if we go as a group of visitors attached to Davian's citizenship. Then we can separate and have a look around and meet up back at the ship later,' Cat said.

'Sounds like a plan,' Jones said. 'I'm good with that. Coming Rose?'

'No thanks, I'm happy here. This sunshine is glorious. Besides, someone should stay with the ship, refuel and talk to the dockers and such.'

'All good then.' Jones shrugged his backpack onto his back, picked up his hat and strode out just like he was going for a walk down the main street of Cygnet. The rest of them followed behind him, Cat riding on Henry's shoulder.

It didn't take long for Henry to lose the brief feeling of normality he had experienced when gravity kicked back in. This place was not like anywhere Henry had experienced.

Bekka looked around with wide eyes.

'It's all so big,' she said. 'And so strange.'

It was, too. For starters, the air was full of strange smells, and Henry could see Bekka wrinkling her nose in response. There were so many levels above their mooring that Henry couldn't see the top. And he couldn't see the bottom below them either. A maze of walkways led to other ships or into corridors to what he guessed was a city centre or a way of being transported into the planet proper. The noise of engines, the beeping of alarms, and the buzz of conversation assaulted Henry from every direction.

The landing stage where they had docked was a busy place. Ships were coming and going, people of all shapes and descriptions were walking in every direction; some in a quick, determined stride, some just wandering. Some of them looked like Davian, with pale skin and black hair. Some had the dark skin and red hair of Rose, some had antennae like Sura, and there were short, squat, hairless creatures with jet-black skin, and dog-like creatures like the Sambiss, and cats like Cat, and tall, pale people – taller than Marc and Evi – with long thin limbs. There were green four-legged people, and white lizard-like creatures, and red people with bulbous bodies and tiny little heads.

Henry held Bekka's hand and made sure they followed very closely behind Davian down a path, through an open archway and into the building proper. Then he nearly fell as the ground beneath him began to move. It took him a minute, then he realised they were walking on a travelator. 'Just like the airports back home,' he reassured himself. 'This is not too different at all. It makes sense to have the floor moving, especially when we have such a huge building to get through.'

The racket of the world outside hushed as they travelled the smooth white corridor. At the top of the corridor walls, scrolling words appeared in many languages. Henry wanted to ask Davian what they said, but Davian was striding ahead, looking up at the sign occasionally, but most of the time seemingly lost in his own thoughts.

Suddenly, with another glance at the scrolling sign, Davian moved from the middle of the corridor to the side. Henry nearly travelled right past him, but Bekka yanked on his arm to pull him to the side too, where the floor apparently wasn't moving.

'Are we all here?' Davian asked, then without waiting for an answer he placed his hand on the wall. The white wall disappeared and Davian gestured to them all to follow him into the new room that had appeared. Henry looked at the floor and ceiling and hesitantly reached his hand out and waved it in the air. The wall just wasn't there. Jones, the Sambiss, and even Bekka easily trooped into the new room but Henry had to wave his hands in the space a few times before he could be convinced to step over the threshold.

'How …' he began, but he was interrupted by a humanoid robot, all white and chrome who approached Davian in the manner of a butler and spoke deferentially.

'Welcome back to Karthur, Mr Jernoshef,' he said. 'Are these visitors all here with you?'

'Thank you, and yes,' Davian replied.

Well, that was that. If they were wanting to be anonymous, there was no chance now. But anonymity didn't seem to be the plan here. There had been no talk of rescues or hiding or anything. All vestiges of criminality had been dealt with in the court case with the AI and Davian had a clean slate. Henry couldn't see that it would ever be that way on Earth. Maybe the rest of the universe was just so much more evolved and civilised and an ex-convict could be treated with respect. It was confusing but it was good. Much better this way, arriving as a respected citizen rather than slinking in to Karthur as an ex-convict. Especially when the plan was to see your mother for the first time in years.

'Welcome to Karthur,' the robot addressed them all. 'Please present your preferred appendage for your waiver.' The robot held out his hand, the tip of his index finger opening to present a syringe-like tool.

Jones presented his hand to the robot like this was an every-day occurrence. There was a pneumatic hiss then Jones was done and the robot turned to the Sambiss and to Cat, who also meekly submitted to the process. Then the robot approached Henry.

Henry looked at the robot and then at the others.

'What does it want?' he asked.

'It needs to tag you,' said Cat. 'Just give him your hand.'

'Tag me with what? Why do I need a tag? What's going on?'

Cat sighed. 'Henry, don't panic. It's a bio-tag. Every visitor here gets one. We told you that people come here from everywhere and that everyone gets a three-week waiver, well this is your waiver and the bio-tag to make sure that you get back on board the ship when you should. Just give him your hand, it will all be over in an instant.'

Reluctantly, Henry proffered his hand to the robot. He heard the slight fizz, and felt a sharp sting where the bio-tag pierced the top layers of his skin.

'Ouch!' He rubbed his hand.

Bekka meekly held out her hand and also gave it a quick rub. The wall behind them solidified and the wall in front dissolved as soon as she did so. The robot moved out of the way and Davian led everyone out into a new white corridor.

'That really stung,' Henry grumbled.

'Don't be a baby, Henry,' Jones said dismissively.

'Will I have this under my skin forever?' Henry scratched at his hand.

'It will eventually dissolve. It's perfectly harmless.' Cat called over her shoulder.

'Well, I could have done with information about this beforehand.'

'It's the norm. Happens on every single planet,' Jones said.

'Not every planet. That's one of the things I liked about Earth,' Davian said. 'I mean, they found me anyway, but at least they had to take a little trouble. And I didn't have to break the law to try to hide.'

This corridor ended in another sheer white wall. But once again Davian placed his hand to the wall and it disappeared to show a small room.

'Can anyone do that? Or does Davian just have special powers?'

'No, we can all do that now that we've been tagged. It's just the door opening to the elevator.'

On all four walls of the cube-shaped room were bright and colourful pictures. On one wall, a beautiful sandy beach led into clear blue water. Another wall showed the tangled trunks of purple trees with pink leaves in a fairy forest wonderland. On another, pink and blue stalactites and stalagmites made striking patterns in a cave. And on the fourth, as the missing wall reappeared, were the rollercoasters and other rides of a theme park. That picture drew Bekka's attention.

'They're moving! Is it a video?'

'It's a live stream. Of all of them. You're looking at it all at real time.' Cat said.

'We told you this was a tourism planet. They will do everything they can to get you to see all the attractions.' Jones said. 'Every gimmick they possibly can use.'

'You seem a little put out by it,' said Henry.

'I just don't like being consistently manipulated,' said Jones. 'It is intensely annoying what they try on this planet. Incessant annoying advertising, everywhere.'

Henry's stomach lurched as the elevator dropped. There was no warning, no motor noise, no nothing, just that feeling that the floor was dropping under your feet.

'Welcome to Karthur,' a pleasant feminine voice interrupted their conversation. 'The planet where all your needs are met. Feeling stressed? Here you can truly relax.'

The four walls changed to surround them in a video of a day spa. Even the floor changed to look like purple-ish slate paving. On one wall, a cat lay stretched out in front of a roaring fire, and on another a human was receiving a massage from a creature that had six arms and was able to massage all the limbs and the back of the human at the same time.

'Can anyone else smell smoke?' Henry anxiously looked around.

'It's just part of the ad,' Jones grumbled. 'All part of the immersive experience.'

'Or are you bored? Adventure lies just around the corner.'

The restful day spa disappeared and instead they were surrounded by water. Seaweed and coral of rainbow colours floated around them and covered the floor. It looked beautiful. Henry began to relax. Suddenly, a red monster barrelled down at them, its huge sharp teeth snapping and its single eye focussed directly on Henry. Bekka let out a squeal.

Then just when he was sure he was going to be eaten, the disembodied voice continued: 'Maybe you just need to get away,' and the walls and the floor of the elevator changed so that Henry felt he was standing in the centre of a gully. A waterfall tumbled to the floor behind Jones' shoulder. And it looked just like Bekka was standing in the stream. She pulled her foot up, then put it down again, her eyes filling with wonder as the water appeared to splash around her foot.

The roar of falling water filled Henry's senses. The scene was beautiful, but somehow … wrong. Then he realised what it was. He had never seen plants like that before. The flowers were polka dotted, strange colours. The leaves were green, and the water was the same as it would have been on Earth. He supposed that water was water and it couldn't be anything else anywhere, but the plants were so strange. Even the rocks were wrong. Bright pink rocks were so wrong.

The scene was quickly whisked away again, and the voice went on: 'Or you can get your thrills at the best fun fair in the universe!'

Suddenly Henry was standing 150 metres in the air, a sheer drop below him. His legs felt weak as the ground rushed up to meet him.

He clutched Jones' shoulder to steady himself.

Jones chuckled and gently shook Henry's hand off his arm.

'See what I mean?' he grumbled. 'Super annoying.'

'Or totally chill out at the Solange Pools.'

The scene changed again. This restful scene of swimming pools and cocktails was much more to Henry's liking, but his brain was feeling whiplash at the constant changes. And was that … snow in the background?

'That's a pretty chilly place to have a swimming pool,' he said.

'No, hot. Very hot,' the Sambiss contradicted.

'But … the snow?'

'Desert, mate. Ochira is a white sand desert.'

'Right.' This planet was not good for Henry's brain. Bekka's young and pliable thought processes might be able to handle the changes, but everything was the wrong colour and Henry was feeling more and more confused.

As the disembodied voice continued her marketing speech and the scenes continued to flash and change around them, Henry tried to make sense of it all.

'How do the business people deal with this? Or the tradies who come to this planet? They must get sick of this advertising all the time.'

'They put up with it. Karthur is a tourism planet. Everyone here either works in the tourist industry or supports the tourist industry. There are a lot of tradesmen and business people who come, obviously, but they know that their income from here relies totally on the tourists,' Cat explained.

'What? A whole planet devoted to tourism? No manufacture? No other businesses?'

'Yep, that's what this place is. A hedonistic paradise.'

'But … you worked as a lawyer here.'

'Yes, the tourism brings a lot of legal work. People sue when things go wrong. When their expectations are not met by the reality. And the crime … well, we know enough about that now. I don't think we need to talk about it.'

Davian shot Cat a grateful glance.

'What about schools?' Bekka wanted to know.

Davian answered this one. 'There are a few schools, but you get sent away to boarding school mostly. I went to a school that was run for the few kids who stayed, but yeah, I was about to be sent off myself when everything went pear-shaped.'

The elevator slowed to a stop and the little company stepped out into the street.

'Right, I'm off,' Davian said.

'Take care of yourself.' Bekka reached out and touched his arm, then drew her hand back self-consciously. Davian brushed his hair off his face and strode away.

'What are we going to do?' Bekka asked.

'I think a cuppa and something to eat is a good place to start,' Jones said. Henry couldn't agree more.

'But there's so much we could do, can't we try some of those attractions?'

'All of them cost money,' Cat said gently. 'And we have some, but we don't know how long we're going to be here. And Bekka, your

Grandad looks like he needs a little time to acclimatise. Come on, you're on another planet and there will be plenty to look at. Let's go get a drink and something to eat.'

Henry gave her a grateful 'thank you' and the four of them made their way down the street.

Bekka was whirling around trying to look at everything at once. She bounced up and down on the pink and purple hexagon pavement, 'It's really soft and rubbery.' Then she was running her hand down the side of the building and on to the street. 'There's no seam between them, it's just like the building grew out of the ground.' She marvelled at the height of the trees, and pulled a purplish-green leaf off a smaller bush and stuck it in her pocket. She smelled the strange green flowers growing in a pretty garden in the middle of the street.

While Bekka was happy to point out the scenery, Henry was grateful that she was more circumspect when it came to the pointing or staring at the huge variety of creatures walking around them. People, Henry thought. These are not creatures, they are all people. But this was the craziest collection of people he had ever seen.

Occasionally Bekka would nudge Henry and nod in the direction of a particularly different alien, but the two of them knew that these people weren't here for their viewing pleasure, like displays in a museum. This huge variety of aliens were just here, like Henry and Bekka were, to enjoy the planet of Karthur. And in any case, Henry and Bekka were the outsiders here. They were the 'different' ones. Henry was so grateful that Davian's species looked so similar to human beings. And for the first time in his life, he was grateful for Bekka's fascination with black. Her black hair fitted right in with the Karthurians here. What if she'd dyed it purple instead? This way they were almost looking normal.

Suddenly Bekka grabbed Henry's arm and pointed up.

Up above them were vehicles zipping around everywhere. They were quiet, with no rumbling of engines and no noise pollution. It was like something out of the Jetsons.

'Flying cars?' Bekka breathed.

'Well, cars on wires here in the city.' Cat said sensibly. 'They are not quite free to fly anywhere that they want to. Free flight around cities is far too dangerous.'

'But surely the cars would have sensors and everything, reversing sensors and automatic braking and so on?' Henry asked. He really wanted to see one of these cars up close now.

'Yes,' said Cat wearily. 'They did. That worked for a while, then people cut corners, you know how it is. Companies wanted to make cheaper cars to increase their profit margin. And things started to go horribly wrong. In the end, the government had to put limits around vehicle use. So in cities, the vehicles have to run on the wires.'

'It's like the trams in Melbourne,' Jones explained. 'But in three dimensions. It works.'

'I'd love to drive a flying car,' said Bekka, echoing what Henry was feeling.

'You can't in the city,' said Cat. 'They are all driverless here. All automatic. If we went way out in the countryside you might find a car with controls, but you'd be unlikely to find one here, except for in a museum.'

Henry was disappointed, but then chided himself for being ridiculous. Of course he couldn't drive a car here. Not in the middle of all these buildings and crowds.

'If we can't drive one, can we at least have a ride in one?' Bekka asked.

'I think the budget can stretch to that,' Cat said with a smile.

'OK, great,' said Jones, and looking around, led them all up a moving staircase that was close by. Again, it felt more like climbing the trunk of a tree than walking into a building, and the platform that they ended up on was rounded like a large leaf. They waited for a few moments and then a vehicle arrived. It was a cross between a taxi and a cable car. There was no driver to be seen.

Jones, Cat and the Sambiss climbed in with no hesitation. Bekka and Henry looked at each other, then clambered in after them. Jones talked to a monitor on the side of the car wall and soon they were moving.

Now they didn't even have to concentrate on following Jones and avoiding bumping into all the strangers on the street, they could really drink in the sights of this strange planet.

The pinks and purples of the city buildings passed by, then the sky scrapers disappeared and the view around them opened up. It was a pretty town. You could tell that it was a tourist town by the effort that had gone into making it beautiful. The cars on wires helped, of course. But looking out and down they could see lots of little eating places, and lots of lovely parks, little knots of creatures chatting, or wandering around, or eating, or playing with some sort of throwing toy. It looked like a lovely place to live.

'How about down there?' Cat suggested, looking at a particularly pleasant courtyard of cafés, trees, and well-manicured purple lawns.

Jones spoke into the monitor and touched his tagged hand to the screen and the car came to a stop and set them down.

Cat, Henry and Bekka searched out a place to sit, and Jones and the Sambiss investigated the food options. Eventually they came back and Jones handed each of them a package.

'What's this?' Henry regarded the food with suspicion.

'Would you know what it was if I told you what it was called?'

'Will it make me sick? How do you know it's any good? What is it? Meat, veg, what?' Henry sniffed at the wrapped up parcel Jones had given him. He wanted a 100% guarantee. What if this food was fine for most species, but poisoned humans?

'Mate, just open it and have a taste. You're not going to recognise it. We're on a different planet, remember? But Davian can eat your food, so I reckon you can eat his.'

That was a good point. The two species must have somewhat compatible digestive systems. Henry reluctantly opened the wrapping.

A delectable scent rose towards him and Henry's mouth watered involuntarily. The food was wrapped in some kind of pastry or bread. He couldn't even see what kinds of things were inside. He looked sideways at Bekka, who was tucking in with great gusto, he envied her her sense of adventure.

He carefully nibbled a bit off the side of the bread. It tasted ... pretty good. Like real food, not like the bland astronaut food they'd been subsisting on in the last week. He took a larger bite and enjoyed the textures and tastes. That's all it took for him to forget about how strange this all was and to enjoy the feel of the hot food in his hungry stomach.

Chapter Thirty-One

Zimmin took one last look at the reports he had written, then sent them through to Xedrog. He knew that Xedrog was going to read every page. He was going to read slowly, and he preferred Zimmin to use words of one syllable, but he was going to read. He may be a little hard of thinking, but when it came to the business, Xedrog took the time to understand every sweet detail. And it drove Zimmin crazy. It made it that much harder to skim the money off the top to feather his own nest.

He had his property in the desert now. Not the ramshackle hideout at the oasis that Xedrog thought he visited regularly, but the other property, the one he had bought for himself that was a little closer to civilisation. It was still a beautifully hot place that made him feel alive and recharged. And it had a comfortable warm rock bed that he could just lie on and soak in the warmth while his ladies brought him the food and drinks. That refuge was a very nice result of Zimmin's hard work fudging the reports. And, so far, it was hidden from Xedrog. He would like to be there today, but instead he needed to explain these reports to his boss.

It was just so annoying that he had to pretend that Xedrog was in charge. One day he'd break out completely. But for now, he needed to put up with … ugh.

He tapped sharply on Xedrog's door and walked into his office. He moved silently, as expected from one of the lizard people. Silently, but quickly.

Xedrog was sitting, feet on the desk, drink in his hand. Zimmin groaned to himself. He'd got Xedrog off the painkillers, eventually, after years of fighting the addiction (yes, that same addiction that was now so profitable to the organisation) but now it looked like he was going to have to do the same thing with alcohol. Or he could let the arphaxad drink himself into an early grave. It was an idea.

But for now, business.

'Did you see the report, Xedrog?'

'I saw it. I'll get to it. I'm busy.'

Yeah, he didn't look too busy. But Zimmin had learned not to underestimate the man. Xedrog looked like an ageing wrestler. He was an ageing wrestler. All cauliflower ears and broken nose and muscle drooping into fat. But now that his muscles couldn't do the thinking for him he was slowly learning how to use his brain.

And it was incredibly irritating. Xedrog could just turn the whole business over to Zimmin, and Zimmin would make sure the thug was well looked after.

'A nice nursing home or something,' he said under his breath.

'You have something to say Z?'

'Of course not,' Zimmin said quickly. 'You're the boss. As always.'

Xedrog put his arm around Zimmin's shoulder. And squeezed, hard.

'A team, Z. Like always. A team.'

Zimmin winced and tried not to lick his lips. The stink of the man was awful.

Xedrog grinned.

'It's all going well then? Money rolling in? Drugs rolling out?'

'Well, yes. It's going OK. There are a few small problems.'

'Always a few problems,' Xedrog grumbled, turning on his screen and squinting at the report. 'You said that Karthur was unlimited. You said that the tourists would give us a continuous stream of new customers ready to take our wares. You said ...'

'Yes, yes,' said Zimmin. 'But nothing's ever totally smooth. We've been having a little trouble with the police.'

Xedrog cursed the police loudly and inventively. Zimmin wondered whether some of his suggestions were even physically possible. But on the whole, he agreed with the sentiment and let him get it out of his system.

'They are annoying. I agree. And we're running out of places to store and sell product. It's just a little. ... Expensive.'

Xedrog frowned. 'You know, sometimes I think ...'

Zimmin held his breath.

'... I'll read the report. Get out of here.'

Zimmin turned tail and closed the door behind him. Glancing out the window as he returned to his desk, he saw a familiar face. What was he doing here? He should be locked up in a prison somewhere, or at least hiding for his life on some godforsaken rock in the outer sectors.

Last he'd heard, that kid had been running like mad, trying to outrun the IGP and probably trying to get away from the gang. And now he was back here. Wandering along like he didn't have a care in the world.

That was a bit of a threat, really. For all his talk to Xedrog, lately he had been getting along quite well with the police. Some were nicely addicted to the product, and some were easily bribed. But here was a witness to that old mess, the mess he had worked for years to fix up, and he was just walking free. They couldn't bring the old stuff back up again, could they? Could they?

Davian was a threat. He was back then, and he still was now. Too young, too talkative, too easily influenced by the powers that be. They'd been quite happy when the kid had disappeared. They didn't care if he'd died or just run away. The fact that he wasn't around was the main thing. But here he was again. Zimmin had to get on top of this immediately.

All these thoughts flashed through his mind, and he acted immediately, calling a couple of gang members and racing to the door. He'd try the honey approach first, but he was always careful to make the honey look more appealing that the alternatives, and if worse came to worst, he had people to fix these kinds of situations. Whatever he did, this kid could not be left to his own devices.

* * *

Zimmin sent his burly six-armed henchmen ahead to block Davian's escape, then he called out, pleasantly, as if he were greeting a long lost friend.

'Hello Davian.'

Davian looked around at the sound of his name, and his eyes met Zimmin's. He turned to run but his way was blocked by the henchmen. Zimmin kept his voice casual as he covered the distance between them.

'Well, well,' he said. 'I never thought I'd see you again. Back on Karthur, hey? What are you doing here?'

The kid appeared flustered. He looked this way and that. But there was no escape. The police in this quarter were well trained (or well bribed anyway) to ignore the Vyynx and Zimmin was sure that Davian would remember from times long past how it was. He wouldn't bother with any stupid screaming or making a fuss.

Zimmin saw the kid swallow hard. How he loved this feeling of power.

'I … Just visiting,' the kid said.

'Visiting?' Zimmin let the word hang.

'Visiting Mum,' Davian said. 'I'm acquitted, see? I'm free. The charges have all been dropped. So I thought that I'd come back …'

'Oho, you're free? But you're never free from family, are you?' Suddenly Zimmin wrapped his tail around Davian's waist and drew him to his side. 'And who is your family? We are your family, aren't we? Weren't we always family? Did you intend to drop by and visit us too? Of course you did, otherwise why would you be here? It's so nice to see you.'

Flanked by the two brutes, Zimmin and Davian walked back to the headquarters in silence.

Zimmin kicked his office door shut with his foot, and pushed Davian into a chair.

'Have a seat, and tell Uncle Zimmin all you've been doing.'

'Nothing, nothing really. I've just been on Earth …'

'Earth? Where's that?'

'Oh it's a little undeveloped planet. Out past Sector 300. Not very interesting.'

No, Zimmin thought. This was very interesting. What if …?

'How can you say that?' Zimmin poured out a drink for himself and Davian and perched on the side of his desk. 'Anywhere you've been is interesting to me. Probably interesting to Xedrog too, come to think of it.' He pushed a button on his wrist. 'Hey Xedrog, want to come in here? Davian, remember him? He's here and he wants to tell us all about a little planet called …'

'Earth,' Davian said. He swirled the drink he'd been given, then carefully placed it on the floor next to his chair without taking a sip.

Xedrog trudged in to the room. Zimmin poured him a drink too. Then as Xedrog sat himself in Zimmin's desk chair and leaned back, Zimmin moved to stand over Davian.

'Earth. A little undeveloped planet. Where was it again?'

'Oh it's really not worth bothering about. Look, great to see you both again. But I'd better go visit Mum …' Davian tried to stand up, but Zimmin pushed him back down.

'So Earth, hey? Haven't heard much about that place.'

'Right. It's a new one to me too. Have they got many species there?'

'Um … I mean, apart from visitors. Well … the humans think they are the only sapient species. They call anyone else "aliens" and they don't think we exist.'

'Idiots,' snorted Xedrog.

'An undeveloped planet,' purred Zimmin. 'No technology to speak of. They would make ideal customers. Xedrog, have you ever thought of expanding the business?'

'Oh … I don't think …' Davian stammered.

'Like, getting new customers.' Zimmin all but winked at Xedrog.

'A whole new set of people we can sell our product to. Away from here. Away from the Karthur police.' Zimmin cursed to himself. It would be so much cooler if Xedrog could just get his hints.

The penny finally dropped for Xedrog and he rubbed his hands together and chuckled his sinister laugh.

'You going to help us then boy?' he asked.

'Um …' Davian gulped and looked longingly at the door.

'Of course he is,' Zimmin replied for him. 'He's family. And he knows what happens to family who betray each other. No, Davian is going to be helpful. Aren't you?'

'I was just going to see my mum and then I was going to go back to Earth. That's all.'

'Sure, sure. You can just stay a little while and visit with your mum. We have a shipment coming soon.' He shook his head and gave a small grin. 'That is to say, Karthur has a shipment coming soon that will be ours. And then when we have the gear you can show us where Earth is and introduce us to a few people. That's all. We're not asking for much.'

Davian looked from one to the other.

'How will you get the shipment off planet?' he asked. 'You're not intending to hijack the whole ship are you?'

'Why not?' Xedrog asked. 'That's not too hard.'

Zimmin nodded. 'It will leave less mess lying around too. We can make the whole thing just disappear.' He clapped his hands once, then spread them out. 'Gone.'

Davian's breath came faster. He rubbed his hands on his trousers.

'If I say no?' he asked.

'Then you never see your dear old mum.' Xedrog gurgled.

'But don't worry,' Zimmin added. 'We'll make sure she sees you. Well … parts of you anyway.'

Davian looked at the floor, his shoulders slumped.

'So it's agreed. Davian's going to help grow the business. New customers, that's great.'

'But Earth doesn't even have universal currency,' Davian protested.

'Oh I'm sure they'll have things we can use. Minerals, organics, all sorts of things. All very exotic and unspoiled. We can definitely make use of a new planet.'

'The people I'm travelling with, they'll be worried if I don't come back to them. They think I'm off to see Mum just for the day and that I'll be back with them tonight.'

'Oh you can do that,' Zimmin said.

'He can?' Xedrog asked.

'Sure, he's just going to wear the latest in fashion while he does it.' Zimmin sidled around to his desk drawer and pulled out a thin black strip of plastic. Then, before Davian could do anything, he slipped it onto his wrist. The plastic tightened twice and then adjusted perfectly to Davian's arm.

'It's a bio-tracer. I bet they don't have any of those on Earth.' Zimmin said. 'It will tell us your every move. Try to escape and we'll know about it. Tell anyone what we're up to, we'll know about it. You know we can bring a ship down. We don't just destroy the pharma transporters, we can bring yours down too if need be.'

Once again Xedrog laughed.

Davian stared at the band on his wrist. He tried to pull at it, to take it off. It started flashing red. He let go of it and the flashing stopped. This was going to make things difficult. He looked at the two thugs, then he stared at the floor for a while.

Zimmin gave him time to think. He frowned when Xedrog cracked his knuckles meaningfully. The idiot had no class. You had to do this properly.

'Well …' Davian started again.

'Mmmm?'

'You're not going to hurt anyone else are you?' Davian pushed his hair back and looked up at the two thugs.

'Oh that's our boy!' Zimmin crowed.

'You're in now, are you?' Xedrog asked. 'Knew you'd come around.'

'You're obviously not going to let me out. I just want to know that my friends are safe.'

'Why would we hurt them?' asked Zimmin. 'Just you make sure they don't get in the way.'

When he got to this new planet (what an odd name Earth was), he would get rid of Davian for sure, and all his friends. Or he'd let the crueller gang members have them to play with. And he'd send Xedrog back here to Karthur. And then, Earth would be his. Out the back of Sector 300 he could do whatever he liked. Xedrog would just have to lump it.

Davian nodded slowly and the deal was struck.

'Now where exactly is this ... Earth?'

'Sector 378, region H92.'

Zimmin nodded in satisfaction and Davian stood up.

'Right, then. I'll get back to my friends. Let me know when the shipment is happening, and I'll help you out.'

'Oh no, you'll see more of us than that,' Xedrog said.

'Yes, make sure you drop in every day. Come and see your family. Come and hear about the business. Don't be a stranger.' Zimmin's words were sweet but there was a sinister edge to his tone.

He watched Davian walk back out to the street, then turned to Xedrog.

'And that's how you find new customers.'

'Sounds like we won't have much trouble with police at the new place.'

'It could solve all our problems.'

'A bit odd him turning up though,' Xedrog's slow gears ground on.

'You know, I think he's missed his old gang and the excitement here. Trying to put on like he didn't want to get involved. Of course he wants to. Probably wants to run the whole Earth side of things for us.'

'We won't be doing that. I don't trust that kid. He ran away pretty quick last time.'

'This time we have him on a bio-tracer. I'd better put one of these on dear old mummy as well I think.' Zimmin took another black band from his desk. 'Better to be safe than sorry. She needs to be part of the family too. We can't lose, Xedrog. Whatever happens, we've already learned of a new planet, and whether Davian comes or not, we know where to go. He can come with us, or he can die. His choice.'

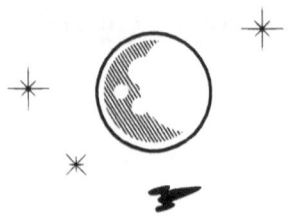

Chapter Thirty-Two

It had been a long and eventful day full of new experiences. Henry was quite surprised at how much he had packed into one day. He was sure he wouldn't have been able to walk that far on Earth. Cat had said something about there being slightly lighter gravity than he was used to. But even so, his feet were dragging as the little group of tourists walked the long white corridors back to the ship, and there was a twinge in his knee that he remembered from being on Earth and hadn't missed at all in zero gravity. Even Bekka was drooping. They needed some processing time.

Well, Henry thought, they could go home and process for the rest of the summer. It would be fine.

But when they got to the ship, the situation was not what Henry had expected.

'Where's your mum, Davian?' he asked. 'Didn't she want to come?'

'She wants to come,' he replied. 'But she needs a little time to put things in order before she leaves here. She wondered, actually, if you and Bekka would like to go and stay with her for a few days.'

Henry frowned. This was not the plan. They needed to get home. But, as he thought about it, it made sense. You can't just ask someone to up and leave their planet in an instant. It takes time to move house, even if you're not taking anything with you. It would take time to even make the decision to make such a large move, and a few days wasn't much to ask.

'Your parents are going to be wondering why they haven't heard from us,' he said to Bekka. 'I hope they're not getting too worried.'

'I've been thinking about that,' said Rose. 'It should be possible to connect Bekka's phone to Skype if I just tweak a few things. You could have a chat. You'd just have to be very careful not to tell them where you are.'

'I guess Marc and Evi are telling everyone that we've gone camping, or off to the west coast or something,' Bekka said. 'We could tell Mum and Dad the same thing.'

'Right, well let's do that,' Rose said. 'And then the two of you can go visit with Vera while she decides what to do.'

'What will the rest of you do?' Henry asked.

'Oh we'll keep busy,' said Jones. 'Don't stress about us, mate. We're going to be fine.'

Bekka handed over her phone and Rose opened the back to tinker with it. Henry sank down gratefully into one of the dining chairs and accepted a plate of food and a cuppa.

When the phone was ready, updated with new apps and a new receiver, Bekka and Henry found a spot with a background that didn't look too foreign and made the video call. Henry was a bit anxious about lying to his daughter, but when it came to it, they didn't have to talk much at all.

'Have you been missing us?' Vivienne asked. 'We're sorry we didn't get a chance to tell you, but we were given the opportunity to go travel inland a bit. We didn't realise we'd be out of contact until we'd been travelling for a day. Sorry if you've been worried.'

Henry opened his mouth to speak but was interrupted by Paulo.

'It was amazing, Bekka. You would have loved it. We got to abseil into a crevasse. The ice down inside it was so smooth and there was just this eerie blue-ness about it. It was so strange to not have the constant sound of the wind.'

'It's always windy here,' Vivienne took over again. 'there's a katabatic every morning. But if the wind drops in the afternoon, then you can actually get outside and walk. I miss walking. It's pretty cramped in these buildings in bad weather.'

'And the animals and birds, they are so friendly. They're not really worried by us at all. The penguins just wander over to say hello. And we went for a walk the other day, we heard this strange snorting sound and we looked around to see a seal pop its head out from the ice. Cool as you like.'

'Cool, hey? I'd say cold.' Vivienne looked at Paulo and they both laughed.

And on it went. Both of them tumbling over each other to share their new experience. Auroras, seals, penguins, the weather, the people, the housing, the vehicles. All of it came pouring out. And Henry and Bekka just let it pour.

Eventually, they paused and asked how Henry and Bekka were and what they'd been doing.

'Oh we're fine,' said Bekka. 'Just hanging about. Nothing special. Tell us more about Antarctica.'

It didn't take much persuasion, Vivienne and Paulo started telling their stories again and the small awkwardness was overcome. Then with lots of air kisses and promises of love they ended the video call.

Henry looked over at Bekka. Her face, that she'd kept animated and cheerful through the call, crumpled into a heap and she began to cry. He put his arm around her and let her tears fall on his shoulder. It was the end of a very long day.

* * *

The next morning, Henry and Bekka looked around with interest from the flying car. This part of town wasn't as clean and manicured as the tourist hubs that they had explored the day before. The car zipped crazily in between the large apartment buildings that rose all around them, looking like they had grown organically from the ground. Then, descending only slightly, the car stopped at a platform on the side of a building.

'Here we are,' said Davian. 'Home sweet home.'

Henry was a little anxious about stepping out of the car when they were so many stories above ground. What was wrong with doing things the normal way? They could go down to the ground floor, get out of the car and take the lift back up. But apparently that wasn't how you did things in Karthur. He just wished there was something to hold on to.

Gingerly he climbed out, following the other two who had no such concerns. As their feet hit the platform, the wall to the apartment building disappeared. Waiting for them in what looked like the hallway of the building was a tall woman with long grey-streaked black hair that was offset beautifully by her floor-length silvery grey dress. Everything about her gave an impression of elegance.

'Welcome,' she said in a deep gentle voice that matched her appearance. 'It's so lovely to meet the people who have helped my son so much and have brought him back to me.'

'It was our pleasure,' Henry said, warming to her instantly.

'It's my pleasure to offer you some hospitality. I hope you enjoy staying here. Come on in.'

Vera ran her hand over a sensor and the wall to her apartment opened, while the wall of the building closed behind them. The sitting room was small but comfortable, and the cleanest thing he'd seen since they left the touristy part of town. Everything was neatly in its place. It reminded him of Davian's ship. Everything tucked away, even though there was gravity here and the items didn't need to be tied down like they did in the ship. There was a vase of strange-looking square green and purple flowers on the small table. A tiny two-seater couch sat against the wall. The decor was neutral, with quiet blue and green accents. It was a restful place, an oasis.

Vera made some drinks and they sat and chatted for a while. She asked what Earth was like and Henry poured out his love for his planet, his country, his town. He talked of green fields, the blossom in the spring orchards, the babbling brooks, the tall gums. He talked of the tiny town, the community, the sharing, the number of aliens that were included. He talked of family, of blue skies, of the ever-changing weather.

'It sounds so lovely,' she said wistfully.

'Are you coming home with us?' Bekka asked.

'Oh, I …' Vera paused, uncertain. She looked to Davian for help, but it was Henry who came to her rescue.

'It's a big decision to make. We'll let you have a a bit of time to think about it. But you won't mind us acting like a constant Earth advertising machine while we're here will you?' he asked with a grin. 'You see, we really want you to come.'

Vera smiled in return. 'You do your best. It does sound beautiful and at the very least I won't mind hearing about it.'

Over the next few days, Henry tried to relax and enjoy the unexpected holiday he was having. But as the time wore on, he couldn't help feeling that something wasn't quite right. Part of it, he was sure, was that he and Bekka were not often in contact with the rest of the crew. He knew that the two of them had agreed to stay at Vera's house, but he still thought that all the visitors from Earth would be exploring together. Instead, the Sambiss, Jones, Rose and Cat were each doing their own thing. And even Davian was busy doing things that he seemed reluctant to tell Henry or Bekka about. Henry and Bekka were left to their own devices, with Vera to look after them.

There was plenty to do on this tourist planet. They used up many of Cat's credits visiting amazing natural wonders and less-than-natural theme parks. Henry gave in and let Bekka ride on the rollercoasters, but she couldn't convince him to join her. They visited museums and found out just how backward Earth technology was, compared to what the other planets had invented and used as a matter of course.

Occasionally Cat would come with them to something, or Jones would drop by to say hello. But mostly they were on their own.

One morning, Cat and Bekka visited a large shopping centre (Henry was much more enticed by the idea of a morning resting in the apartment), and afterwards Bekka came to Henry with a worried frown on her face.

'Grandad, do you think … could he be … '

'Bekka, I have no idea what you're saying. Start from the beginning.' Henry patted the couch next to him and she curled up against him like she used to when she was a kid.

'When I was out with Cat, she met up with a friend, another cat, that she knew from before. I think his name was Perkins.'

'Purrkins,' Henry said with a chuckle. 'Perfect for a cat.'

'Grandad,' Bekka admonished. 'Pay attention.'

'Sorry,' Henry said, but he continued to grin to himself. The grin soon faded.

'Perkins was asking what we were doing here. And Cat was being friendly and all, telling him about Earth and that. And then he started chatting about work stuff ('cause they used to work together) and she sort of shooed me away. I was happy not to be part of their boring legal conversation and I went to look at some shops. And then I wanted a drink, so I went back to ask Cat if we could buy one, and she ... she was saying something like, "He's in with the old gang, the Vyynx".'

'Are you sure?'

'Well, I didn't catch it all. But that's sure what it sounded like.' Bekka turned to face Henry. 'It got me thinking. Have you seen Davian much? He didn't hang around with us at dinner last night and he didn't want to come out with Cat and me this morning. And ... and what if he is trying to get back with the gang?'

'He hasn't had much time to do it.'

Bekka sat up and looked at him.

'Yeah. But if Vera doesn't want to come home, and it looks like she doesn't, and if he can't get a job because of his criminal record and all, maybe he just looked up some old friends or ...'

Henry patted her hand awkwardly.

'Let's not jump to conclusions.'

'But I'm sure that's what Cat said. And when we left Perkins said, "It's hard to go against your nature." And ... what are we going to do?'

Henry thought about it.

'Let's not panic,' he said. 'You need to talk to Davian. Ask him what he's thinking. And we both need to keep trying to get Vera to change her mind and come home with us. I had a good talk to her this morning about Earth and she seemed pretty interested. We just need to keep trying.'

Bekka slumped back against the couch.

'I guess so.' She gave a big sigh. 'Grandad, this is fun and all, but it's all so strange. I really want to go home now.'

'Me too Bekka, me too.' Henry wholeheartedly agreed.

Chapter Thirty-Three

Bekka didn't get the chance to talk with Davian at all that day. Nor the next. He was busy, he said. He did look busy. He was rushing around a lot. Leaving the house at all hours. When Bekka asked what he was 'busy' doing, he evaded the question, brushed it off and asked Bekka what she'd been up to. Bekka couldn't get through to him without showing her misgivings, and when she asked Vera, she looked vague (and worried) and said that she was sure he had a good reason to be doing whatever it was that he was doing.

'This is all going wrong,' Bekka said to Henry. 'What can we do to stop him? He won't even talk to me. Sometimes I feel like he won't even look at me.'

'Maybe we should talk with Cat,' Henry wondered. 'She's always known what's going on. She's given me wise advice throughout this whole trip.'

'Oh Grandad, you should have seen her face when she was talking to Perkins. She looked so angry. And her fur was all up on end, her tail all frizzy. She worked so hard on Davian's case to get him off the charges, and if he's just gone back to the gang as soon as he got back on planet, she must hate him. I wonder why she's not trying to get us all back to Earth?'

'Well, it's a bit difficult for her, isn't it? It's Davian's ship. We can't just take it and go. And then, she's hanging out with old friends more and more. She's with them again today. Maybe she's happy to be here too. Maybe she missed her old lawyer life more than she let on.'

Henry thought about their group of travel buddies. Who could they go to for help? He hadn't seen much of anyone since they moved in with Vera. It was like they were all avoiding him. Avoiding Bekka too. Jones and the Sambiss wouldn't be much good – he didn't think they could fly Davian's ship. Rose could, but would she be willing to steal the ship for them? None of their friends thought of Earth as their home planet. All of them might be just as happy as Sura to live somewhere different.

'Vera. She's the key,' he said. 'She's the one we came here for. If she will change her mind and come to Earth, then I'm sure we can convince all the others to come. Or leave them here if they want to stay. But I'm sure Davian would take Vera to Earth if she asked. And if he does that, we can get home too.'

Bekka stood up.

'You're right. And she'd be happy to get Davian away from any old friends that might lead him in the wrong direction, wouldn't she? We need to talk with her. Convince her. I've got photos on my phone I can show her. Let's see if she can talk right now. '

Henry smiled. Bekka was always about 'right now'. There was no waiting with her. But talking 'right now' sounded good to him too. The sooner Vera decided to leave, the sooner Davian could be taken away from the criminal elements on this planet, and the sooner Henry could get home. And then, when he got home, he wasn't letting Bekka out of his sight. No more hanging out with Davian on Earth. Goodness knows what kind of a kid he was. No. He was keeping her in the shop with him until her parents came back and he could hand her back over and get this responsibility off his back. She may not like it, but look where giving her freedom had lumped them.

When Vera came home, the two of them tackled her. She was happy to chat with them, happy to help with whatever she could, she said. They sat together in her neat apartment, and she waited, curious, faintly smiling.

Henry didn't know where to start. He began a couple of times.

'We wanted …'

'Vera, we thought …'

Then he decided to come straight out with it.

'Vera, we need you to come home to Earth with us.'

'Are you tired of being here?' Vera asked with a concerned frown. 'Do you lack credits? Are you bored? If you need more entertainment, I'm sure I can manage some mountain climbing for you. Or sailing. Whatever you want. I can make it happen.'

Henry held his breath at that. Maybe even Bekka would be sucked in to staying longer on Karthur if she could have all those adventurous experiences. But Bekka stayed true.

'No, no we're not bored. We love your planet. It's been a great visit. But, well, it looks like all our friends are relaxed about staying here, but my parents will figure out something's up soon. We need to go back to Earth. We shouldn't even be here. And the only way we can get home is if you agree to come too. That's what we came here for. To get you. Will you come with us? Please?'

'Earth is a beautiful place,' Henry added. 'I've tried to describe it, I probably did a bad job, but Bekka has some lovely photos she can show you. It's gorgeous. Especially our little town of Cygnet, though I may be biased. But you'll love it, I'm sure. And the people are really nice, totally accepting, friendly. We love having new people in our town. If you ask Rose, Cat, anyone, they'll tell you how easy it was to move there.'

Maybe he was pushing too hard. Henry thought about how grumpy he had been with all the newcomers to town. But he felt differently now. And there were lots of accepting people in Cygnet and surrounds. He'd help Vera make friends, he promised himself. He'd make sure she didn't feel out of place.

Bekka scrolled through the photos of Cygnet in her phone, showing photo after photo to Vera. Showing her all her new friends, the pretty park, the yacht club.

Vera didn't answer them. With every photo her frown deepened. Henry wondered if they were doing more harm than good. Eventually under the pressure of all the pleading Vera cracked.

'I can't come with you,' she said, tears in her eyes. 'I want to, I truly do. But I don't know how to tell you, I just can't come.'

'I'm sure you can. If you can't get work on Earth, I'll be happy to support you,' Henry said.

'No, no. It's not that ... I really want to come ... please believe me. I just can't.' Vera hid her face in her hands.

'Tell us about it. Maybe we can help.' Bekka put her arm around Vera's shoulders and felt the shake of a suppressed sob. She looked at her grandfather with wide eyes.

'I'm sure no one can help,' Vera mumbled through her hands.

'Tell us anyway. A trouble shared is a trouble halved,' Henry commanded.

Vera looked up, bracing her shoulders.

'Oh I might as well. I don't see how I can get into more trouble than I'm already in.'

She dried her eyes and began.

'It's like this. Just after Davian came back, I mean directly after I saw him again for the first time, some visitors, Xedrog and Zimmin, Davian's "friends", came to see me. Have you met them?'

'I'm not sure we've met them. We've seen some people come by to get Davian sometimes.'

'Yes, well. They probably don't want to talk to you. But they wanted to talk to me, and they sure want Davian. They are the leaders of the gang, the Vyynx. They are the source of all the trouble in the first place. And just when I got my boy back, back from the dead, there they were.'

'That's so bad,' Bekka said. 'What do you want with Davian?'

'They think there is something he can do for them. I don't know what it is, but they really wanted him. It was so awful. I never thought I'd see Davian again, but to see him again and then see him trapped by these horrible people. I think it's almost worse.'

'Do you think Davian chose to work for them?' Henry asked.

'Well, they told me that Davian had agreed to work for them again. But I can't believe he'd choose that. I'm sure he doesn't want to work for them, but I'm sure they haven't given him much choice. They are not weak. They would have threatened him with his death, or with my death, or both. I know you haven't seen much of him since you've been here. He probably doesn't even want to look you in the eye. He's a good kid, but he's got to do what they say. I know they won't hesitate to kill me. Their threats are not empty. Not at all.'

Henry and Bekka exchanged a long look. This all made perfect sense. But they couldn't leave it like this. They would never get back home. They had to do something.

'Vera, we have to get you away from here. This is crazy. You can't live like this. We can smuggle you back to our spaceship, to Davian's ship, then he can join us and we can leave here for good. I'm sure we can do it.'

'Bekka's right. Davian and the others aren't even here most of the day. What's stopping us just leaving?'

Vera shook her head. Then she pulled the sleeve back from her right arm to show the black band that encircled her wrist.

'They put this on me when they came. They know where I am every second of the day. If they saw me go anywhere near the docking station, anywhere near the ship, I'd be dead. I know they'd find us. There are gang members everywhere.'

Henry gently took her hand and had a look at the band.

'I'm sure I could get this off you. It would take a bit of doing, but we could send the band in a car going one way and we could go the other. It might give us the time we need to get away.'

'No,' Vera said, her voice catching. 'No, it's tuned to my bio. It measures my heart beat. If I take it off, they know. They just know. Please, don't ask me about this anymore. I just can't.'

She stood up and left the room, tears streaming down her face.

Bekka stood to follow her, then stopped and looked at Henry.

'What do we do now?' she asked.

'We'll think of something. Don't give up.'

She shook her head and slumped back down on the seat next to him.

'How horrible to have a tag keeping track of you. It's like being under house arrest.'

'I guess it is, yes.'

'Keeping track of her heart beat and stuff. It's invasive. It's …
it's rude.'

Henry laughed.

'I don't think those guys mind much about being rude. And
keeping track of heartbeats and stuff is pretty common out here. I
mean that's what they were doing with you on the IGP ship. We
had to trick them with that bio-disc that Rose made and stuffed
inside your teddy.'

Bekka looked up.

'That's it!'

'What? We need to give Vera a teddy?'

'No, we just need to get my bio-disc from the ship and use that
to trick the tracker. Rose will help us, I'm sure she will.'

'You could be right.' Henry nodded slowly. 'And even if she
doesn't want to help us, what's to stop you getting your teddy from
the ship, just for comfort?'

'What do you mean, if she doesn't want to help? This is Rose. Of
course she'll want to help us.'

'I don't know, Bekka, it feels like everyone's changed since we
got on this planet. Cat – now I thought she'd help us, but you say
she's not even worth asking for help. That she's given up on Davian
already. Jones and the Sambiss – I wasn't sure how much help they'd
be, but I thought that at least we'd have them around, but we never
see them. And Davian – who knows what he's thinking? So who's
to say that Rose will be on our side?'

He stood up slowly, stretching out his tired limbs.

'But I guess it's worth a try. Let's go and visit Rose.'

'But what if the gang find out what I'm doing? Won't they just
take Vera away somewhere else? She's in danger, Grandad.'

Henry thought that over. He didn't know how much danger Vera
was in, but if they lost track of her then their last hope was gone. Vera
was their ticket off the planet. Did they even know where she was now?
They needed to have eyes on her at all times. This needed some planning.

'OK, how about you go back to the ship and see if you can get
Rose onside. If not, at least bring back the bio-disc. It should still be

in your teddy bear. And try to get a screwdriver and a set of snippers. Do you think you could do that? And I'll stay here and keep an eye on Vera, make sure she's OK.'

It was a plan. Henry didn't like the thought of Bekka going off on her own, but if she had her phone then he knew that Rose could find her. He went back into the house to find Vera.

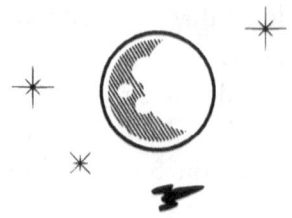

Chapter Thirty-Four

Rose was sitting in the sunshine just outside the door of the ship. Bekka ran up, slightly breathless and Rose opened her eyes and smiled.

'Hello, what are you doing here?' she asked. 'Sick of the new planet already?'

'It's a pretty amazing place.' Bekka smiled. 'Are you bored? Do you have to stay with the ship?'

'I'm fine,' Rose said with a smile. 'I'm just enjoying the sunshine and pottering away. I've never been a big fan of these touristy places. It's good of you to visit me, but you really didn't have to put yourself out.'

Bekka took a deep breath. It sounded like Rose was ready to go back to Earth too. She was their best hope.

'Rose, I am enjoying myself, but I think we really need to go home.'

'What? Already?'

'Rose, I'm cooked. I've had so many new experiences, I don't know that I can handle much more. And my parents ...'

'What about everyone else, are they ready to go home?'

Bekka shuffled her feet.

'No, they all look like they're quite happy to be here.'

'We might just have to be patient then. They'll be ready to go back to Earth soon.'

Bekka wasn't getting anywhere. She just had to come right out with it.

'Vera can't come to Earth with us. She's been kidnapped. She needs our help.'

Rose didn't seem at all perturbed. 'Kidnapped? But you're staying in her house.'

'Yes, but the old gang have tagged her. She can't get away.'

'I can't imagine a gang being interested in Davian's Mum. What can she do for them? Help in the office?' Rose had a gentle smile on her face.

'No, they're trying to get Davian back into their gang! And he's doing it!' Bekka was getting more and more frustrated.

'That's quite an accusation. Davian has just been acquitted, remember? He wouldn't go back to the gang that kept him away from his mother for all these years. Have you talked with Henry about this?'

'Grandad and I have both talked to Vera. Rose, it's true. We need to do something.'

'Listen Bekka,' Rose put her arm around the girl's shoulder. 'This is a different planet. It's like another country but it's even stranger. You might think you're seeing something like a kidnapping, but I'm sure it's nothing like it. And if Davian's hanging out with old friends, well, this may be the last time he gets to see them. Let's give him the chance to enjoy himself for a few days. I'm sure you and Henry have misinterpreted something. Don't panic about it. In a few days, maybe a week or so, everyone will have had their fill and be ready to come home. In the meantime, why don't you just enjoy the experience? Do you want me to organise a trip to the mountains for you? Or the ocean?'

Bekka shrugged Rose's hand off her shoulder. It was like there was a strange miasma on the planet that had changed the personalities of their friends. Rose was drunk on sunlight or something. She was going to be no help at all.

'No, I don't need to go to the mountains or the ocean,' Bekka said. 'I just need to go home. But if you're not going to help us get there, then I'm just going to take my teddy.'

'Sure, sweetheart,' Rose said. 'That's no problem. Anything else you need?'

'A gun,' Bekka muttered under her breath. But aloud she said, 'No. We're fine.'

Rose sat back against the hull of the ship, turned her face to the sun and closed her eyes again. Bekka made a face at her and climbed back inside the ship.

She pulled her teddy out of the cupboard where it had been stowed and lifted the raggedy toy to her face, breathing in the familiar smell. It brought tears to her eyes. Would they get home? There was no place that she'd rather be right now. This adventure had turned scary. How would her parents cope if they came back and she wasn't there?

There was no choice. She and Grandad would have to go ahead with their plan with no help from anyone else. And if that meant that the only people going back to Earth were Grandad, Vera, Davian and herself, then so be it. The others had made their choices.

She stuffed the teddy into her backpack and was about to leave when she remembered Henry's request for the tools he needed. Well, she wasn't about to ask Rose for those now. As she looked around the little ship she realised that she didn't need to. Rose had apparently been doing some work while she waited for the others. There was electronic equipment, wires and boards and tools of all sorts, strewn all over the table. Well, that was convenient. She quickly picked up a screwdriver and a pair of snippers and hid them in her backpack under the teddy.

Then, barely saying a word of goodbye to Rose, she marched back into the docking station, hoping that metal detectors would not be a problem when she passed through security.

Rose watched her go with half-closed eyes. When she was certain that Bekka was out of range, she pulled out a communicator and made a call.

'Cat? I just had a visit from Bekka. They're getting really worried. I feel so bad for them.'

'I know, it feels almost wicked to put them through this, but there's not long to go now, and I really can't see what we would gain from telling them the whole story. Henry would be sick with worry, and Bekka would want to help out. And she's too young to get involved in this. It's better that they know nothing. Then if it all goes belly up, they will just be deported to Earth, which is exactly where they should be.'

'Oh, I know all the facts. We talked this through. But to see them working themselves up …'

'Not long now. Not long at all. We just hold on.'

'Is the Sambiss clear with what he's doing?'

'Yes, he says he will "stay with Julis. Help find the leftovers." I like that – leftovers. He has a way with words, for a Sambiss. Do you think Jones is OK?'

'He seemed happy when he left yesterday. He's got all the necessary tech. He just needs to keep himself safe on that transporter until Davian arrives to use it.'

'And you, Rose?'

'I've done my bit. Now I'm just waiting. Like Henry and Bekka. How about you, Cat? How's your side of things going?'

'Better than I had thought. I think we'll get them all.'

Rose ran her hand through her hair. 'I feel like we're trapped in some sort of movie. Avengers or something. Who'd have thought this summer would bring an adventure like this?'

'Well, it's satisfying,' said Cat. 'Or it will be, if we pull it off.'

'It's risky.'

'That's why we just can't tell Henry and Bekka. They have family. They need to get home safe. If the worst happens, I'm hoping, like I said, that they'll be deported back to Earth. And the chance of that is higher if they are not entangled like we are.'

'You're right. But Cat, I could tell them tonight, right? After it's all gone down?'

Cat was silent for a while.

'Yes. I guess so. Tonight, if it all goes well, if "the leftovers" are taken care of and Jones and Davian are there to stop the ship, then I guess we can let them know. We'll have to explain why Davian's not around anyway, so, yes. Why not?'

'I know some sort of concert is being arranged for them tonight. I might go meet them at the end of it. I'll put their minds at ease as soon as I can.'

* * *

Bekka put her hand to the apartment sensor, already pulling her backpack off her shoulder to get the tools and the teddy out. It was time to rescue Vera from the gang of pirates and deliver her and Davian safely to Earth, taking herself and Henry back home at the same time. And then they could all live happily ever after.

She was about to call for her grandfather when she heard voices. There was a gruff low voice and a silky slightly higher tone that she didn't recognise, but Davian's voice stood out among the rest.

This wasn't good. Why was he here when they didn't want him? He'd been so busy with his 'friends' when she had wanted to see him and now ... it wasn't that she didn't want to see Davian, but she definitely didn't want to see his friends.

She stuffed her teddy back into the backpack and swung it back over her shoulder. She tried to arrange her features in a neutral expression as the wall opened and she looked in to see Davian standing in the living room with a couple of other people.

One was a short fat man (or humanoid, she thought) with black hair sticking up like a scrubbing brush off his head. His face looked all squashed up, like his nose had been broken at some stage, and maybe some other bones too. He looked like he preferred to settle any disputes with his fists, but that lately, the fist fighting hadn't been warranted and he'd got fat from waiting for the next fight.

The other was a lizard. A human-sized greyish-white lizard that stood up on his back feet. Bekka's blood ran cold just looking at him. It was the way his cool beady eyes focused on her, and how his tongue flickered in and out. She'd seen other lizard people on her way around the city, but they hadn't bothered her like this one. This one felt evil somehow.

She shivered. She was in trouble now, here in the same room with the bad guys. Bekka tightened her hand on her backpack.

'Hey Bekka, just the person I wanted to see.' Davian was all cheerful smiles, like nothing was wrong.

OK, maybe these weren't bad guys, if Davian wasn't worried it might all be OK. What did she know about aliens? These might be old school friends of Davian's. She shouldn't judge.

And then, on the other hand, the only 'friends' Vera had talked about were gang members.

'Yeah?' Bekka asked. But Davian didn't seem to notice her hesitancy. He just kept talking.

'I had this thought. There's a cultural display by the Engedot people at the colosseum tonight. It's pretty impressive. Thought you might like to see it?'

'Ah …' Bekka wasn't sure what to say. For one, she wished she could ask Henry how this would fit into their plans. And also, she had never seen Davian like this. At home he was much quieter. Maybe it was just because he was on his home planet that he was acting like some kind of flashy tour guide or salesman.

He barrelled on cheerfully, 'I won't be able to make it, unfortunately. But you should see at least some of the interesting things this planet can offer. You and Henry can go. It's honestly really impressive. Dancing, fireworks, an amazing light display.'

Of course he wouldn't be able to go. He didn't want to do anything with the crew from Earth. Bekka thought she'd call him on it.

'Why won't you be able to come with us?'

'Oh …' Davian looked at the ground for a moment, looking a little more like the friend she'd known back on Earth. 'I'm just … It's just been a bit busy. And anyway, I've seen it before.' He flashed her a smile. 'A few times, to be honest. I don't need to see it again, but you might enjoy it.' His eyes flickered from her to his other two friends, who were just standing there, silent, menacing.

Bekka wasn't thrilled with his excuses. But as she listened to him fumble his way through them she realised that this could be an excellent opportunity. Davian was setting them up to succeed. If only …

'Maybe your Mum can come with us?'

They could go to this thing, Henry could remove Vera's bio-tracer and stuff and they could get away without any of the security cameras in the apartment block seeing them. It could work in their favour.

'Mum?' Again, Davian's eyes flicked to the other two 'friends'. Bekka could see what was going on now. Who was making the decisions.

'Yeah, we've been spending a bit of time together and she's lovely. It would be really nice to have an evening out with her.'

'Uh ... what do you ...' Davian started, looking at the reptile. The lizard's tongue flicked out and in again. The other guy tightened his fist. Davian frowned and tried again. 'Well, you can ask her, of course. I don't know why you're asking me. I mean, she's her own person.'

Sure, thought Bekka, she's her own person. That's why you were thinking you'd just ask the big bosses of your gang who have her imprisoned here. Hopefully I've made it difficult for them to say no.

She gave Davian the friendliest smile she could, and answered, 'Well great. That sounds good. If your mum can come then I'd love to see something like that.'

'Great. That's settled then.' He smiled in return and Bekka felt like she was seeing the real Davian again.

But the feeling didn't last for long. As she started to move past them lizard spoke.

'Introduce us to your friend,' he said to Davian in a cold dead voice. Davian hesitated, then shrugged and performed the introductions.

'Zimmin, this is Bekka, from Earth. Bekka, my ... friend Zimmin. And this is my other ... friend ... Xedrog,' he said, but there was no smile on his face now.

'Pleased to meet you.' Zimmin reached out to shake Bekka's hand. She looked around wildly and could see no reason to refuse. She gave a quick grimace, hoping that this would be over soon.

'Yes ... hello Bekka.' The other man had a gravelly voice with an unpleasant gurgle in it. And Bekka hoped she would never see that predatory smile again.

'Davian, we have to get going. Things to do, people to see,' Zimmin said with a smile that went nowhere near his eyes.

'Yes, right.' Davian didn't smile at all, but he did follow Xedrog out of the room to do whatever it was they had to do, Zimmin following behind.

These guys were bad news, Bekka decided. Somehow they'd have to get Davian away from them. It was looking more urgent all the time.

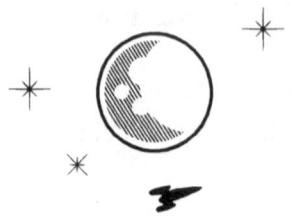

Chapter Thirty-Five

It all felt a little rushed.

Henry would have liked another three weeks to plan for a great escape like this. But he had to admit that Bekka had thought quickly when she arranged for Vera to come to the concert with them, and that getting rid of the bio-tracer and escaping for good would be a whole lot easier away from the apartment. They had no clue when anyone would be turning up – Cat or Jones (who would almost definitely disapprove of their plans) or worse, that Xedrog guy or the lizard-man Zimmin. They made Henry's skin crawl.

When the evening came, for a change, Davian ate with them at the apartment's little dining table. This rare occurrence filled the meal with tension. They couldn't talk through their plans with Davian there, and the three escapees found it hard to think about anything else.

The conversation was stilted. Henry, Bekka and Vera tried to pass off their nervous tension as excitement for the evening's entertainment. Henry noticed that Bekka was nervously jiggling her knee and, to distract Davian's attention, asked, 'What is Engedot?'

'You mean, who are the Engedot?' Davian corrected. 'They are the people group who come from the desert regions here on Karthur. They have really colourful traditions and great dancing. You'll never see anything like this on Earth. Zimmin, he's half Engedot. So you've already seen what the performers will look like.'

Vera spoke up, 'That reminds me, we'll have to layer up to go to the thing tonight. They usually keep the colosseum very warm to make the Engedot comfortable, but it will be cooler outside.' Vera hadn't really struck Henry as a mothering kind of person, she'd felt more like the queen of the elves – tall, serene, unemotional. But in this small comment he saw a resemblance between Vera and his Dorothy that made him feel much more comfortable.

'That's why you don't see many Engedot in this region. We find the weather here ideal for us, but an Engedot can't even move in the cooler mornings, and – '

A beep from outside interrupted Davian. The transport had arrived. Not too soon either, thought Henry. Let's get out of here, let's get this over with.

Henry and Bekka climbed into the car. Vera held back, and Henry could see tears forming in her eyes. This was the cut-off point, he realised. If their plan worked, Vera would be saying goodbye to the planet where she had spent the whole of her life. But hopefully she would not be saying goodbye to Davian. Still, she lingered and gave her son a motherly hug.

Henry breathed out as she climbed into the car with them.

'Thought you were going to change your mind,' he said.

'I was just letting him know where he could meet us afterwards,' she replied. 'I'm ready to leave this place.'

'Won't you miss all your friends and family?' Bekka asked.

Vera shook her head.

'You find out who your real friends are when your son is wanted by the police. The few friends who'd managed to stick around through the long years of Hrahid's illness evaporated into thin air after that. It's been a lonely life and I don't know why I didn't think to leave before now.'

'Where would you have gone?'

'That's true. I was waiting, always waiting for Davian to come back. If I'd left, I guess I thought I'd never see him again. But now he's here. And I'm ready to come with you. Earth sounds beautiful and you are already closer friends than any I'll be leaving behind.'

'OK then. Let's do this. I tell you what, this will make a great yarn later,' Henry said with a smile.

'A what?'

'A good story.' Bekka explained. 'You'll get used to the way we talk.'

The open-air auditorium was filled with all sorts of creatures. They'd been given excellent seats, right up the front. Henry wished they could have been a little further back, a little more hidden. He didn't think he'd be seeing much of the show at all. So when a tall couple, with the same shade of pale white hair as Evi and Marc sat in the two seats in front of them, Henry was more pleased that his activities would be shielded than upset that he'd miss vision of the stage.

As soon as the lights went down, they got to work, Bekka pulling at the seams of her teddy bear to get to the bio-disc inside and Henry using the snippers to cut the plastic of the bio-tracer from Vera's arm. He snipped the band very carefully, but he could still feel Vera trembling. He didn't think she was worried that he'd cut her. He thought it was more that the threat from Davian's 'friends' was very real. He had to get her away from these crooks. Away from this planet.

Once the plastic was cut, Vera held the tracer to her arm until intermission. Now Henry could breathe and watch a little bit of the show. The dancing, acrobatics, and fireworks were made more amazing by the fact that all of the performers were lizards. Very large, human-sized lizards with much more flexibility than the salt-water crocs back in Australia. Their hides changed colour over and over again, and they even managed to draw designs on the skin of their backs. They were climbing walls, jumping vast distances, making patterns by fitting their bodies together. It was truly crazy stuff.

As the intermission, and the time for their bold move approached, Henry felt his heartbeat speeding. This adventuring could not be good for his blood pressure. He was not made for this.

The big number at the end of the first half of the show was so spectacular that Henry was a little disappointed he was going to miss the finale. But they had a finale of their own to orchestrate. The applause began, the crowd roared their appreciation and he nodded to Bekka. She squeezed the disc to activate it and slipped it under the tracer on Vera's arm. They connected the two together, slid them down the back of the seat, packed the rest of their gear quickly into Bekka's backpack and rose to leave.

Squeezing through the crowd they made their way to the exit, careful not to lose track of each other. There were no cars lined up outside to pick the patrons up yet. This was only intermission. But Vera had suggested that walking would be their best bet if they didn't want to get traced. They could hail a car a few blocks away and not be so obvious to their pursuers.

All three of them were glancing around as they walked. Every shadow felt like a threat.

They slipped from street to street as quietly as they could. There weren't a whole lot of people around, just small groups here and there. Eventually, after they'd walked about five blocks, Vera said, 'I think we'll be safe to take a car now,' and led them up one of the stairways to a platform.

Henry trudged up the stairs and sat in the car with an audible sigh of relief. Bekka reached over and squeezed his arm.

'Doing OK Grandad?' she asked.

'I'll be fine luv,' he said. 'Just looking forward to a cuppa when all this is over.'

Vera put some coordinates into the car's computer and they flew away. Bekka leaned her head against the window taking in the sights of the city at night. The bright lights, the little knots of people wandering to and fro.

The silence in the car became oppressive. Henry decided to break it up with some conversation.

'Where are we headed tonight?'

'We're going to the Pelentra Forest,' Vera said. 'It was the only place that I thought that Davian would remember from when he was young.'

'I'm sure I've heard that mentioned before,' Henry said. 'What is so special about it?'

'It's very beautiful. It's a rainforest, and the trees grow beautiful flowers. Then, when the blooms are fully grown, they break free from the branches and fly around until they meet another flower. The two flowers do a little dance together, then they mate and bury themselves in the earth, where they grow to become another tree.'

Bekka's eyes were wide.

'Really? Flowers flying around? How cool!'

'I guess it would be a bit like butterflies,' Henry mused.

'I can't wait to see that!'

'They only fly during the day though,' Vera said apologetically. I don't think it will be quite that beautiful at night. But Davian and I had some great times there when he was little.'

'What's it like here in winter?' she asked Vera.

'Winter? What is winter?'

'Oh ... you know, when the weather changes and it's cold and raining?'

'The weather ... changes?'

'Doesn't the weather change here? Is it always like this?' Henry was taken aback.

'Yes, it's warm here. If you want cold and rainy you go north or south. The snow fields are especially fine once you get past forty degrees latitude.'

Now Bekka turned to Henry.

'Why does our planet have seasons and this one doesn't?'

This took a bit of thinking. Henry and Bekka threw a few ideas around and then Bekka remembered.

'I haven't thought about it for years. I guess we learned it in primary school. But our planet has seasons because it's tilted on its axis.'

'Oh yes. That's right. Our tilted planet, and the way the sun reaches us obliquely in the winter and so full on in the summer. That's the way it is. So I guess this planet isn't tilted?'

Vera shook her head.

'No, this planet has a straight axis. I've heard of tilted planets like yours but I've never been to one.'

'Well, that will be something to experience then.'

'If we get there,' Vera said.

'We'll get there,' said Bekka. 'We're halfway there already.'

Vera didn't answer and Henry found her pessimism a little scary. 'We'll get there,' he repeated. And he mightily hoped it was true.

Chapter Thirty-Six

Davian adjusted his ear piece. He remembered this feeling of anticipation. This knowledge that even the best-laid plans could go horribly wrong. From the nervous chatter coming through his earpiece, he knew other Vyynx were feeling the same thing.

Zimmin had planted someone on board the ship to hijack it. Someone who knew how to bring it to land in this desolate place. If things had gone well, and Davian was pretty sure they had, right now the pilot was flying with a gun to his head bringing the ship full of pharmaceuticals to land in this barren place. When it landed, the gang members would take over and take it to Earth where they would show a few intelligent people the effects of the drugs on board, and find themselves a whole new empire. There were, of course, some details to iron out on the Earth side of this mission, but Davian had convinced Xedrog and Zimmin that the problems would be small.

Xedrog's immense ego made it easy for him to swallow this story, but Zimmin was a little more difficult to satisfy. Davian sighed. He would have to stick close to Zimmin tonight. If anyone called this mission off, it would be Zimmin with his dangerous mix of intelligence and cynicism. Davian just needed to be there, feeding him information, showing him that he was on their side. That this new venture would transform the Vyynx to heights unimaginable as they gained easy access to the wealth of Earth. The minerals, the organics, and yes, even the human population.

Tonight's landing site was a rocky valley, out of sight of city lights. Nothing grew here but the most irritating of clingy vines that tended to stick up from the ground and trip you as you walked or ran. It was not good land for anything. One of the few places on Karthur that had been too difficult to capitalise on.

Once the action started, Davian knew he'd be fine. But right now, his stomach churned and his heart raced as he waited in the dark. He hoped Jones knew his job and had found a decent hiding place. He hoped that Rose's technology would work first time. He thought through all they had done to prepare. Had it been enough?

His thoughts turned to Bekka, and Henry and his mum, of course. He had eventually managed to get Xedrog and Zimmin to agree with him that having the earthlings occupied tonight was a better way to go. It was easy to find a 'special cultural celebration' on Karthur. There was one every night of the week. Allowing Vera to go with them was harder for the bosses to agree with. But Bekka had helped with that. It would have looked strange to everyone if Vera hadn't joined them, and they were all working so hard to avoid suspicion. Davian was sure that Henry was suspicious of his activity. Especially when he found out that Davian wasn't going to the Engedot concert. Davian could tell that there was something on Henry's mind by the way he was avoiding conversation and eye contact, but the fact that he'd not been around at all for the past few days helped his absence from the outing feel more natural. He wondered what Bekka thought of him now, whether she felt rejected and alone, and whether she'd ever talk to him again, especially if she found out what he was doing tonight.

His leg jiggled uncontrollably.

'Nervous are we?' Zimmin asked.

'It's my first time doing this in a while,' Davian responded. Xedrog and Zimmin had talked big talk to him about how the gang was just like a family and how they'd missed him. But Davian knew that this was all a front. If he stuffed this up, they had many and varied ways of making him suffer.

Tonight just had to go right. That was all. There was no second chance. It was tonight or bust.

A humming filled the air. They were on. This was the ship.

Looking up he could see a vast shadow descending onto the rocks. The ship was coming cloaked. That was risky. But it really didn't want to draw attention to itself.

All chatter in the earpiece stopped as the gang took their positions. Davian's stomach churned. He wished he could leave. Just walk out of there and keep walking. But there was Zimmin, right next to him. Why did he decide he had to keep an eye on the lizard again? Maybe Zimmin was keeping an eye right back on Davian.

This was too risky. Way too risky. Davian wanted to call the whole thing off. But it was too late. The sky lit up like a constant lightning flash as the landing lights below the ship were turned on. There was no going back now.

Then he heard Zimmin curse.

'What's up?' he asked. This was not right.

'What's up? Your mother and your friends. Did you know anything about this?' Zimmin pointed to a flashing alarm on his communicator.

'Oh no,' Davian breathed. 'What are they thinking?'

'Thinking they can get away, obviously. Thinking they can outsmart us. Did you put them up to this?'

'It's nothing to do with me,' Davian said. He didn't have to pretend his innocence, he had no idea they had been planning an escape. Why did his mother even think she could get away with this. Was she just crazy?

Zimmin cursed some more, his words almost turning the air blue, then he turned to his communicator.

'Call Xedrog,' he barked.

'Do we need Xedrog for this?' Davian hurriedly asked. 'Can't the two of us deal with it together?'

Zimmin cursed again.

'If you think I'm trusting you with anything, you've got another think coming.'

Davian froze as he felt the jab of a blaster in his gut. And Zimmin, now that he had Davian under control, took control of himself as well. His cursing stopped and his tone changed to the cool pleasantness that Davian knew led to truly horrible things.

'I'm sure that the team, our trusted team, can take care of the ship from here on. We are going to find your mother, and then you are going to find out what happens when you double-cross us.'

'But I had nothing to do with this! I swear.'

'Says the kid who begged us to make sure his friends and his mother were going out on the town tonight. No, it's all just a bit too neat, isn't it? I'm not that stupid. Get up. We're going.'

'What's going on?' The voice came from the communicator loudly enough for Davian to hear. Xedrog didn't really need a communicator, Davian thought, he always shouted so loudly that he could be heard light years away.

'Your golden boy has been playing tricks on us.' Zimmin motioned with his blaster that Davian should keep walking. Davian stepped carefully – one trip on those vines and he could be dead.

'My golden boy? I thought he was your project. What's he done?'

'He's trying to help his darling mother to leave our gentle care.' The sarcasm dripped from Zimmin's voice.

'Oh no he's not!'

'Xedrog, you're on your own here. Send me a Hunter. Davian and I are going to the colosseum to track down his mother.'

This was bad, very bad. Davian's brain worked at top speed trying desperately to find a way out of this situation.

'You can't leave things here. We're just about to take the ship.' Xedrog whined.

No, you can't leave things, thought Davian. Stay here. Please stay here.

Zimmin's eyes narrowed and he looked at Davian.

'You haven't messed up the heist, have you?'

'How could I?' Davian asked, his eyes wide. 'I've been with you all the time. I haven't been part of Mum's escape either. I swear I knew nothing about that. It must have been Henry or Bekka. Honest.'

'Honest, he says. Honest. If I wanted honest I wouldn't be a crook would I?' Zimmin turned back to the communicator. 'You've got enough people on the ground to take the ship. We need to find Vera if we're ever going to keep this rat under control. Davian and I will join you once we've got this sorted.' Then he gave Davian a chilling smile. 'On second thoughts, don't expect Davian. I will join you when I've dealt with him.'

There was a car waiting at the side of the valley. Zimmin waved Davian in, and put the coordinates of the colosseum into the computer.

'Listen kid,' he said, while they waited for the Hunter. 'I never trusted you. Not once. Xedrog may have, he's soft, but I never have. I know that the only way to keep you under control is through your darling mother.' Once again his mouth turned down and the words slid from his lips like black oil. 'There is no way we're going to let her leave the planet.

'The bio-tracer was our gentle method of keeping her here. But now, now that you've messed that up, from here on it's going to be either imprisonment or death. And you get to make that choice. Mess up one more time, and she's not just trapped, she's gone for good. Get that?'

Davian swallowed hard and nodded.

'And just to make sure you're not going to try anything stupid ...'

Zimmin reached for Davian's bio-tracer and with a signal from his communicator, separated the band into two and bound Davian's wrists together.

A large shadow detached itself from the dark. It was a black Sambiss, a Hunter, all muscle and sharp teeth. This Sambiss was nothing like Davian's friend from Earth in looks or in temperament. Davian shivered, knowing the Hunter could smell his fear. The Hunter looked at him and growled, then lay down in a corner of the car, his snarling mouth showing his sharp teeth. Davian shrunk away from it, trying to melt into the car wall as they took off.

The flying car set them down at the colosseum. Zimmin used the signal from the broken bio-tracer to direct the Hunter to the seats where the fugitives had been. He and Davian waited on the street outside.

Davian could hear the happy music coming from inside the building. He imagined the bright lights on the stage and the joy on the faces of the audience. It was like imagining another world. A world he was almost sure he wouldn't see again. That Hunter, going in there, was he scaring people? Would the theatre security throw him out? Or did he know how to stick to the shadows?

Zimmin's blaster was holstered, but Davian didn't feel any safer. Why had his mother done this? This was all wrong. Stupid. Why did they think they could trick a bio tracer? It had to have been Henry, getting all cocky from the success in the IGP ship, working with tech that he just didn't understand. This was going to destroy everything.

The Hunter padded out of the theatre, a black band held in his mouth. Zimmin took it from him delicately, and held it up to the light.

'Oh bless,' he said. 'They've put someone else's bio-disc against it. Like the tracer wouldn't be able to tell the difference between the heartbeats.' Then he turned to The Hunter. 'Let's get 'em.'

The Hunter growled in acknowledgement, put his nose to the ground, and the three of them began their pursuit.

Chapter Thirty-Seven

Jones took up his position, hidden in the storage closet just behind the back entry hatch of the pharmaceuticals transporter. Handy of the ship to have such a hiding place. It was an old beast, this ship. He tried not to think about the fact that the age of the ship meant that it was dispensable. And that maybe the team within could be dispensed with too, without too much angst.

The best case scenario was that no one would be hurt. But there was a fair risk of things going pear-shaped. He hadn't done a job like this for a long time. But working with Davian to sabotage the ship using Rose's tech, that was his kind of job. He was pretty excited, to be honest. Though you wouldn't know that to look at him. He slouched against the wall, fiddling with the gum tree branch he was still using as a walking stick. He'd become attached to that stick now. It reminded him of Earth. He didn't go anywhere without it.

He hefted his bag. The heaviness of it made him feel a little more secure, filled as it was with Rose's contraptions. He just had to get them to Davian when he came on board with the gang. Then Davian would be able to work from the inside to sabotage the ship before it got anywhere near Earth. It was a pretty nifty plan if he did say so himself.

He felt the reverse thrusters kick in as the ship slowed its descent toward Karthur, and took a firmer grip on his gum tree branch. Things were about to get interesting.

The golden Sambiss waited patiently in the police car. He waited very patiently. Oh how he wanted to stop the ship being taken by the gang. It was wrong to let them get away with this. Wrong! But Cat and Rose had told him why it was better this way. They had introduced him to Julis. Julis was the police. She was the good guy. She was helping them out.

He remembered Julis from that first IGP ship. The ship where he and Jones had made the plan to rescue Bekka and Davian. He remembered her scent from on the ship as he had snuck around. And her scent coming back on Cat, after she had met with Davian. He hadn't seen her then, though they told her she had been there for the "trial". Henry and Cat would have recognised her slim build and the bob-cut black hair. But that wasn't a problem for the Sambiss – he knew the scent, and Cat told him that Julis was good.

Cat and Julis had planned all this back then. Back on that first big ship. Cat had told the Sambiss on the way to Karthur. Davian couldn't be free unless they did this big job. This was the way to fix it all. The bad guys would be stopped and Davian and Vera could come home. If they didn't do this job, there was no way Davian could come home. He'd have to go to prison instead.

It was a good plan. Jones would get on board the transporter when it was loading the goods and he'd hide there. Davian would join him, posing as one of the gang. Then Davian and Jones would use Rose's tricks to stop them landing on Earth. The Sambiss and Julis would mop up on the ground. The bad guys would be caught in the act. Cat would help at the trial. All the Earth visitors could go home after. Job done.

It was hard to wait for his turn to work. But soon the Sambiss would be able to find all the hiding bad guys. He would show them to Julis. Commander Julis.

She was waiting patiently beside him, her hand on his back.

He growled quietly.

'Yes, but we need a crime before we can arrest,' Julis said.

'You police, you arrest. I Sambiss, I bite.'

'If you bite, I arrest you,' Julis said with a smile. And the Sambiss smiled in return, his tail gently thudding on the floor.

'Not long now.'

The plain flooded with light as the ship's landing lights came on. The Sambiss tensed, sure they would be found out, but Julis reminded him, 'We are cloaked. They can't see our vehicles.'

They watched the brightly lit scene as the Vyynx attacked, running in through the ship's open door, throwing crew to the side as they entered the ship's belly.

Julis gave a command into her communicator and a small band of police moved, uncloaked towards the ship. Julis had explained to the Sambiss that this was to allay suspicion.

'They won't believe if they have no response at all. Normally we would try to stop them. Normally there would be someone here. So we will send this crew to stop them.'

'Risky?' The Sambiss asked.

'Yes.' Julis smiled. 'But we send the androids. They will not see the difference.'

And it was good that the police were androids. The gang attacked with blasters. Several androids fell and the others fell back. The ship's door closed, engines started, and the ship took to the sky.

'Now!' Julis commanded, and the police cars surrounding the scene uncloaked their vehicles and became visible. The team poured out and began to arrest any Vyynx that were left behind. There was some hand-to-hand combat. The Sambiss, tail wagging furiously, ran from rock to rock and made sure no one was hiding.

Then he stopped. He smelt something familiar. There was a trail here of Davian's scent and it didn't lead towards the ship.

He could smell Davian's fear. And the anger coming from someone that smelled like a lizard man. He barked loudly to get Julis' attention. She stopped what she was doing, and came over.

'Here is Davian, going the wrong way,' he said.

'He should be on board the ship.'

'He is not. He has gone the wrong way.'

Julis was not convinced.

'I couldn't say that I saw him go on board, I couldn't recognise anyone from the distance, but I don't think the gang would let him get away, would they?'

'He is with a lizard man.'

Julis looked around at her busy troops. There were people everywhere now. Arrests and gathering of evidence was in full swing. She sighed.

'Just go and check. Go up to where the ship landed. Check that Davian's scent doesn't resurface there.'

'I will check, but he has gone.'

The Sambiss was unhappy. He knew they were wasting time. But he did as Julis asked. And as he knew it would be, there was no trace of Davian near the ship's landing. He couldn't find him anywhere. Davian had gone the other way. Away from the ship. The Sambiss might not be good with words but he knew a scent when he smelled it and he knew he was right.

Eventually Julis gave in. The two of them followed the scent through the rocky countryside.

'Uh oh,' the Sambiss said as they rounded a particularly large boulder. 'Here is a Hunter.'

'They were joined by a Hunter?'

'Yes, and he is … scary.'

'How did we miss this?' Julis asked. 'We should have kept a closer watch on him.'

The Sambiss agreed with a low growl, and the two of them continued to search. The Sambiss following the scent, and Julis looking for visual clues. And then, abruptly, the Sambiss stopped. He retraced his steps, then traced a wide circle, then he looked up at Julis, his tail tucked between his legs.

'Gone,' he said.

'Are you sure?'

'Gone.' The Sambiss spoke with finality.

'They must have taken a car from here,' Julis said.

'What now?'

Julis thought for a few minutes. Then she said slowly, 'I think we need to go to Rose, that's a starting point. We'll make sure Bekka and Henry are kept safe, and see if Rose has any way of tracing Davian. I'll put a call out for a vehicle check. Can you tell me anything else? Anything the patrols can look out for?'

'Davian, Engedot, big Hunter Sambiss.'

'Right, party of three. In a car. Unregistered, I'm guessing. Definitely not wired.' Julis passed the details on to Central as they walked back to her car. Then she entered the colosseum coordinates into the computer and the two of them travelled on in dejected silence.

* * *

Rose stood at the gates to the colosseum, carefully watching the audience as they dawdled out. They filed past her, laughing, singing snatches of the music from the show, and even sometimes breaking out a dance step or two. There were couples with linked arms, there were young children, sleepy eyed now but trying hard to stay awake as they were carried along by their parents, there were groups of teens giggling and sharing data on their communicators. But there was no Henry, no Vera, and no Bekka. She couldn't understand. Where could they be?

Of course, looking at a crowd like this it would be easy to miss someone. Even someone so positively human and Earth-like as Henry. This would have been so much easier if the Sambiss had been here.

Well, she could always go back to Vera's house. Maybe she should have waited there instead of here at the concert. It was just that she didn't want Vera to worry when Davian wasn't there. She wanted to get to them first. But where were they?

Her communicator buzzed. Julis. What did she want?

'We have bad news, I'm afraid. Davian is missing.'

'No,' Rose shook her head. 'No, Davian is on board the ship. That's where he's supposed to be. He's helping Jones.'

'No, he didn't get on the ship. An Engedot and a Hunter have gone somewhere with Davian, but they've taken a car. We have no idea where they are.'

Rose ran her hands through her hair.

'But that means … we're in big trouble now.'

'Have you told Henry anything? Or Vera?'

'I couldn't see them leave the theatre. I must have missed them. I can go back to Vera's if you like?'

'I'll come and get you. We can talk about what's best to do next.'

'Right.' Rose signed off. While she waited for Julis to turn up, she did one more pass by all the entry points of the colosseum. But there was no sign of any audience members now. The staff were cleaning and locking up. The place was quiet. She asked the door staff if they'd seen any of the three, but no-one remembered seeing them leave.

When Julis turned up, Rose asked her for a more detailed run down of the situation. While they talked, Sambiss nosed his way around the area, taking in the confusing scents of audience, sorting and sifting until he got the whole story. The scents led him to one small piece of plastic, discarded on the side of the street. He picked it up and brought it to Rose.

She pulled it out of his mouth and stared at it.

'We are in so much trouble,' she said and handed the bio-tracer and bio-disc to Julis.

'What's this?' Julis asked.

'Well, part of it is my own workmanship, and part is not.'

'Are you sure?'

'Definitely. I recognise my own work, hasty as it was on board the IGP ship.'

'But what is it doing here?'

'Davian was here too,' the Sambiss said. 'Davian, lizard, Hunter, all of them.'

'Here with the others? Or separately?'

'Everyone has touched the tracer,' the Sambiss said slowly. 'But, it's very hard. So many scents. I know they were all here.'

The three of them stared at each other.

'Do you think…?' Rose started.

'I hope not,' Julis replied.

'It looks like Henry thought he could trick Vera's tracer.' Rose turned the plastic over and over in her hands.

'That will have brought the Vyynx here. The tracer would have made an alarm.'

'Then the hunter grabs all of them.' The Sambiss' tail was firmly tucked between his legs.

'Zimmin would capture Vera, with Davian. Henry and Bekka are collateral damage.'

'And so is our plan for the ship. Jones is on there, alone, with no Davian to set up the technology.'

'All the plan has gone bad.' The Sambiss lay on the pavement, his chin on his front paws. 'Cat will be so mad.'

Chapter Thirty-Eight

Zimmin dragged Davian along the street at speed, following the black Hunter. But after just a few blocks the Hunter stopped with a snarl. 'They took a car. They are gone.'

'It's OK,' Zimmin said pleasantly. 'Davian knows where they are, don't you?' He sneered at Davian. 'And he's going to tell us.'

'How would I know?' Davian squeaked. 'You were with me all day, you know Mum didn't tell me anything. How would I know where she is?'

Zimmin pulled out his blaster again, but he didn't need to say or do anything – the Hunter snuffled at Davian's pocket and growled low and menacing.

Zimmin reached into the pocket and pulled out the note that Vera had tucked in there when she had hugged him goodbye.

'What have we here?' he asked. He unfolded the note. '"We meet where we meet." What does that mean? "Where we meet?"'

Davian hadn't looked at the note at all. He had known it was there, but there had been no time to check it out. But even hearing the words in Zimmin's sibilance brought back sweet memories of his mother. Memories from when he was young, just a tiny kid. From before his dad was sick. Before his mum became so overworked and overtired. He and his mother would pack a picnic and go to that special tree. There was a hollow in the trunk, about the size of a kid's play house. It was shady and pleasant and his mother had made up a silly song to go with it:

We meet where we meet
When it's sweet in the heat
We meet where we meet
And we eat

His throat thickened and he swallowed hard. He knew exactly where she was, and he wasn't willing to give that away.

'I don't know,' he stammered. 'I don't know what that means.'

Now the blaster waved in his face again.

'We don't need your hands, you know,' Zimmin threatened. 'Or your feet. And we don't even need to have you around to find your mum. I can easily hack the system, find out where their car took them. We'll find her eventually. And wouldn't she prefer to see you with all your parts intact? Or do you think she'll enjoy spending the rest of her life nursing an invalid? An invalid who is still working for us, by the way. Whatever way you look at this, you're not getting away. But you can make it much easier on yourself.'

There was no way out. None at all. Zimmin called his car, the three of them got in, and Davian reluctantly entered the coordinates. The car sped through the city streets, staying low unless it detected pedestrians. Keeping out of sight of other traffic. But all the time heading to the last place Davian wanted to go.

Zimmin's communicator buzzed and he opened up the conversation.

'How are things down there?' Xedrog croaked.

'We're still in pursuit,' Zimmin said. 'All going well.' And for fun he poked Davian in the gut with his blaster. 'Is all good in the skies?'

'All secure. But I haven't heard from Cthatch about the ground work.'

'Let me pull up the satellite images. Should be fine. You're all good and we're all good.'

But the Hunter and Davian were caught off-guard at the stream of cursing that came from Zimmin as he checked the footage. The names he called Davian were inventive and the curses called down upon him were cruel.

Davian felt a sense of victory and couldn't hold back his smile. The video clearly showed the flashing lights and uniforms of the police. The gang members being handcuffed and led away. The cars being examined. The wreckage of an ambush being cleaned up. The plan came off. It actually worked. But then he remembered where he was.

Xedrog was a little slow on the uptake.

'What's happened? What's your problem?' he asked.

'This little ...' the curses started again. 'This traitor. He's turned us in. Look at the satellite footage for yourself!'

There was a few seconds of silence while Xedrog brought up his own footage. Then his curses joined with Zimmin's.

Davian's stomach screwed itself up into a leaden ball.

He had thought things couldn't get worse, but now he realised that they had. And that it was his fault. He thought he'd looked into every possibility, he and Cat and Rose and Jones. They had talked it through. But they hadn't taken Henry and Bekka into account and now everything had fallen apart.

He was supposed to be on that ship to help Jones with the takeover. If he'd been there he could have stopped anyone from looking at the satellite images. Now Xedrog would be prepared for any attack within the ship.

It would be a disaster if that ship made it to Earth. But there was nothing Davian could do. He couldn't even save his own mother.

* * *

Henry, Bekka and Vera shivered in the cramped tree trunk. It was dark and damp.

'So this is where you used to bring Davian when he was a kid?' Henry tried to make polite conversation.

'It's a lot nicer in the day time. We used to bring a picnic and he would play, trying to catch the flowers. I ... I couldn't think of anywhere else that he might remember. He was so young when he went away.'

'I'm sure it would be fun in the day time with a little kid,' Bekka said. 'Things are so different with little kids.'

'I'm sure it would be a lot nicer if we weren't hiding out here too,' Henry admitted. 'It feels very different when you're trying to escape from … everything.'

'I just hope he remembers.' Vera wrapped her arms around herself and rubbed her arms to try to keep warm.

'How long will we wait?' Bekka asked.

'I guess at most a day or so,' Henry suggested. 'I would have thought that if he was coming, he'd come tonight. But it might take a while.'

'We'd better figure out how we're going to sleep then.'

How would they sleep, sitting upright in this cold cave of a tree trunk? Henry looked around and realised just how completely ridiculous this was. How underprepared they were. He was not an adventurer. Not even when he was back at home. And here he was literally light years away from his comfort zone. But even Vera looked light years away from her comfort zone.

'Maybe …' he began.

Bekka and Vera looked at him expectantly.

'Look, what are we doing here? Should we just give it up and go home.'

'No!' Bekka exclaimed. 'We just have to wait for him. He'll turn up.'

More slowly, Vera replied, 'We can't leave now. We have shown our hand. Xedrog and Zimmin are not people you mess around with. They are dangerous.'

Henry's chest suddenly felt tight and he swallowed hard. He had bitten off more than he could chew. And he had made his inabilities plain now. What did he know about adventuring? About protecting people? He thought back to his childhood. He had done a little adventuring then. Scrumping and so on. Camping out in the bush. He tried to remember the Biggles books he'd read. He used to love reading about these kinds of situations. It was definitely different when you were sitting in the middle of one.

'OK, well, we need to keep warm,' he said in a more authoritative tone. 'We will need to huddle together. And we should have one of us awake and keeping watch at all times.'

That sounded better, yes. Though their eyes were still wary, Bekka and Vera moved closer together, away from the damp trunk of the tree.

'I'll take first watch, shall I?' Henry asked, and the other two nodded in agreement.

'Fake it until you make it,' he muttered to himself, then turned his head to look out the opening of the tree.

It really was gloomy in the rainforest. Apparently, during the day, the place was filled with colourful flying flowers. Probably it was also filled with weird insects with springs on their legs, or birds that gave birth to live young instead of eggs, or other strange and alien things. But right now, in the dark, it was just damp and unpleasant. Trees loomed out of the darkness. Weird sounds came to Henry's ears.

He tried to remember camping as a kid. How excited he had been. And there hadn't been nifty electric torches or nice downy sleeping bags back then. But the sounds of the Australian bush were different from what he was hearing here. There were no comforting crickets tonight. The occasional bird call sounded like a scream and put his neves on edge every time.

He pulled his jacket tighter around him and crossed his arms. He moved from foot to foot, trying to keep warm, trying to stay awake. But probably, if it was his turn to sleep, he'd be struggling to do that too. Bekka and Vera were struggling, judging by the sounds of them changing position over and over behind him.

Now it sounded like one of them was crying or something. There was a sniffling sound. Or was that behind him? Maybe it was in front.

He peered out of the tree trunk into the dark shadows. Then froze as a darker shadow detached itself and moved towards him. It was a large black dog. Did they have wolves here in this forest? He should have asked Vera.

The dog looked up and met Henry's eyes. It barked, then shouted, 'Zimmin. Here.'

Henry blinked. Was he dreaming? Then he realised, no. This was a Sambiss. Like their own Sambiss and yet so unlike. Huge and black and terribly frightening.

But he had no time to think. He stretched himself across the tree opening. Bekka looked over his shoulder, saw the huge dog and screamed. Henry may have screamed himself.

The dog moved closer, snarling and growling. Henry waited for it to attack, steeling himself for the horrible warmth of the breath, the sharpness of the teeth.

Instead, he was greeted by an urbane voice.

'Well done. Thank you Hunter.'

A light shone in Henry's face and as he squinted past it he saw the lizard man, and he saw what looked like a gun pointed straight at him.

'You're not going to take us,' he said.

'Oh yes, I really think I am,' Zimmin answered politely. Then he gestured to the Hunter and the dog flew at Henry, knocking him flat.

Bekka huddled in the back of the tree hollow, Vera holding her protectively. The Hunter stood over Henry's prostrate body and growled at them. A squeak escaped Bekka; she was past screaming.

Zimmin roughly yanked Henry's hands together and tied them with a plastic loop that seemed to tighten of its own accord. Then he pushed Henry out of the way and moved to the back of the tree. He grabbed Vera's arm and pulled her roughly towards him.

'Thought you could get away?' he asked, pushing the blaster into her side. 'I should kill you right now. I warned you at the beginning.'

Vera had tears running down her cheeks but she stood tall and refused to comment. Zimmin tied her hands together, then did the same to Bekka.

'Right,' Zimmin said. 'Come with me. There's someone I'm sure you want to see.'

With the big black dog bringing up the rear, there was no option but to follow. The escape was a failure.

Chapter Thirty-Nine

Jones listened carefully through the door of the storage closet. He couldn't hear a sound. Probably meant there was no one in the hold then. That was something.

He checked his phone one more time. No messages from Davian. No sign of anyone getting in touch.

So. Something had gone wrong. What exactly, he didn't know yet. But it was to be expected that some part of this carefully crafted plan would fall apart, and if that part was the communication – the part he was dependent on – well, that made sense really. That was how the rest of his life had gone.

He was on his own, making his own decisions, solving his own problems. And that suited him just fine.

He pushed his hat on more firmly, adjusted his hold on his walking stick and quietly opened the door.

It was good that he'd had all that practice sneaking around the IGP ship. But then, he was good at sneaking anyway. The fun he'd had at the US military base. Oh good times, good times.

What he really needed to do was find Davian. That was the first thing. Then he could deliver the tech and get the plan back on the rails.

He decided to walk the corridors of the ship and accost some minor weakling. There had to be some of those on board, didn't there? A gang can't be made of just alphas. There have to be some dweebs as well.

With a bit of judicious hiding and sneaking, eventually he saw just such a weakling as he had in mind. He grabbed him by the collar and pulled him to a side corridor.

'Where's Davian?' Jones made his voice as gruff and angry as possible. He'd decided that attack was the best form of defence.

'W… who?' The weakling asked.

'You know, Davian. The bosses' golden boy. The one from Earth.'

'Oh, he … he didn't come.'

Now it was Jones' turn to be nonplussed.

'He what?'

'Weren't you there when we took off? It was just Xedrog.'

Jones gave him a good shake.

'I … I could be wrong,' the weakling said. 'But I haven't seen him, or Zimmin either. And I just came off the bridge.'

Jones threw him hard against the side of the corridor, then left before the dweeb could collect himself or see where Jones was going.

Jones didn't know where he was going either. Yes he had expected the plan to go wrong, but not this wrong. He truly was on this ship by himself. No weapons. No nothing. What on earth was he supposed to do?

What on earth. Earth. That was the bottom line, wasn't it? This ship had to be stopped before it got to Earth.

And just as that thought entered his head, he felt the lurch of his stomach that meant that they were jumping. He held on to the anchor point on the corridor and waited for the sensation to pass.

Now to remember the layout of the ship, and make his way to the bridge. That was the problem with these ships, not too many back roads. Especially when it came to the control space. But that was where he had to be. There was no question.

Fortunately, the gang wasn't as organised as the IGP. There was no regular patrol, and the few people he saw didn't seem to worry about someone they didn't truly recognise. Maybe they'd locked the remaining crew away somewhere. Definitely someone had brought grog on board and several of the gang were feeling pretty happy. A few looked like they'd been getting into the cargo and he was sure that … Xedrog was it? Yeah, Xedrog wouldn't be too happy about that.

Either way, he managed to get by most people even without question, and the few boisterous ones he met he blustered his way past, the big gum tree branch helping him along.

There wasn't even a guard on the door to the bridge. But he was sure that there'd be a fight when he got through it.

Would he just barge his way in? Or was this a case where he could maybe slip in unnoticed?

He listened at the door. The crew were making plans.

'Without Davian we don't even know the best place to start.'

'Without Davian.' The gravelly voiced speaker spat in disdain. 'Who needs him? I'm your leader and I am here. He gave us the information we needed. And we've used it. This is a completely undeveloped planet. We could start anywhere. I say, pick a big city and go there.'

'But they might think we're hostile, they don't know anything about trade signals. They are savages.'

The gravelly voice swore roundly.

'This is what happens when I listen to Zimmin with all his talk of business. Trade signals.' He swore again. 'Hostile? Of course we are hostile. We are Vyynx. Aren't we? If you're not, I can lock you in with the rest of the stupid crew of this ship. We are Vyynx.'

There was a fair bit of, 'Yes Xedrog. Vyynx Xedrog.' Which Jones thought would be accompanied by some bowing and scraping. But the gravel-voiced speaker interrupted again.

'Prisorg what communication have you found? Anything about big cities?'

Another voice spoke now, so there were at least three in the room.

'All I get is "we are peaceful, we welcome you" and some trash about what being human is, like we don't know.'

'Well, then, they welcome us. Let's go and be welcomed.'

The first, and most worried voice spoke again.

'But nothing about trade. Nothing about … What if they attack us?'

'They won't attack us. One shot from this blaster and they'll be ready to listen. If they want to trade, we'll trade. We know how quickly we can get the important people addicted to this stuff. If they don't want to trade, well, they are so backward that we could probably take over the whole planet with the weapons we have. Come to think of it, that sounds like a better plan.' Xedrog's gurgling mirthless laugh made Jones groan quietly to himself.

The humans will either listen, or they'll get out the nuclear missiles, Jones thought. Best case scenario, this ship lands quietly somewhere out of the way, gets humans addicted to the drugs, and then builds a business. Which would be pretty bad, really.

Or, alternatively, this whole plan of ours gets taken the wrong way by the IGP and everyone involved from Xedrog right through to Bekka gets banished from Earth for damaging the natural evolution of the human race. Maybe Julis could stop that from happening, but so much of Cat's plan was built on this ship never making it to Earth.

Worst case, the nuclear governments on Earth closest to where the ship lands get scared and start bombing the ship. And that could lead to nuclear war and the end of life on Earth altogether.

There was no good scenario if this vehicle got through Earth's atmosphere. Not one.

Jones opened the door a crack. He could just see through the large windows that surrounded the bridge. There it was, the blue planet. Right there in all her beauty. Well, he couldn't let her be destroyed.

He'd have to stop Xedrog, or die in the attempt.

Chapter Forty

Henry, Bekka and Vera joined Davian in Zimmin's car. They huddled together as much as they could, pulling back from the sharp teeth of the Hunter, and trying to give each other comfort.

There were no other cars. Nothing that they could see or hear. There were no buildings. There was no way to get a signal to anyone that could maybe help them escape. In the silver moonlight they could at first see the thick leaves of the rainforest, then the landscape gradually changed and became drier, and the vegetation became smaller. Fewer trees, more little bushes on the ground. Then it changed again, this time the bare ground was dotted with little spiky bushes. And then just sand, white sand, glittering in the moonlight. They had come to the desert.

If the situation had been different, Henry would have enjoyed seeing a bit more of the planet. But right now he could feel Bekka trembling as she huddled next to him and he could see the tears rolling quietly down Vera's cheeks and the miserable face of Davian who stared at the floor and didn't attempt to make eye contact. Hope drained out of the soles of his feet.

Eventually, in the middle of nowhere, the car stopped. Surrounding them was desert as far as the eye could see. But the place where they stopped was a small oasis. Water, palm trees, and a few small buildings.

'What do we do here?' the Hunter growled. The first words since they had got into the car.

'We lie low,' said Zimmin. 'We wait for all this to blow over. We get our legal team working like we did before and it should all be fine. Or else we wait for Xedrog to come get us and take us out of here. Either way, we wait.'

'And what do we do with these?' The Hunter looked at the miserable captives. 'We should have just killed them and dropped them out of the car on the way.'

'We don't want anything that leads directly to us. No, storing them here is a much better idea. The desert air will desiccate them, they'll be harder for a police Sambiss to sniff out. Eventually we'll be able to deal with the remains. Or, if you get too hungry, they can be food.'

'Ugh, they don't smell like good food,' the Hunter growled as the four captives shivered hearing their fate. 'You are too soft, you don't want to see blood.'

'Blood stains, blood leaves tracks. No, there are cleaner methods. Maybe, one day I'll curb your bloodthirsty ways.'

Zimmin pulled his blaster out and waved it in the direction of the captives.

'Out!' He commanded. They responded as quickly as they could, stumbling out of the car. Henry's legs were stiff and he struggled to stay upright. Bekka tried to hold him up, but with their arms tied, it was difficult. Zimmin put up with their stumbling for a while, then muttered 'to hell with it' and pressed the button on his communicator to set their hands free. Immediately, Bekka tucked herself under Henry's arm to give him support.

Grumbling to himself, Zimmin ushered the captives through a small door and into an underground tunnel. They walked along and down for a few hundred metres. The only light was Zimmin shining a light from his communicator to stop himself from stumbling. The rest had to do with what reflection there was from the smooth rock walls.

At the end of the long tunnel was an open wooden door. Zimmin pushed them through and locked the door behind them. They heard the slithering of his tail and his footsteps track back up the tunnel to the surface. The absolute blackness surrounded them. They were buried alive.

Chapter Forty-One

At first, Henry, Bekka, Vera and Davian stood in the dark in stunned silence. There was not the faintest light, and no sound penetrated into the cool cellar.

Davian came to life first. He petulantly kicked the door.

'Good idea,' said Henry. 'Let's see if we can get it open, or break it, or something. We've got to get out of here.'

'I've had enough of you and your ideas,' said Davian.

'What?' Henry involuntarily stepped backwards.

'You ruined it all. You three. You ruined it. Don't you understand?' Davian bashed the door with his fists, then leaned up against it.

'Ruined what?' Bekka asked.

'The whole plan. You've … oh whatever.' They heard him slide down to a sitting position.

'Does anyone have any light?' Henry asked.

'Yes, we all packed for a survival adventure, didn't we? I have the matches, Bekka has the kindling, Mum's packed food and water. Of course we don't have light.' Davian's frustration dripped off his sarcastic words.

'Look mate,' Henry was getting angry now. 'Just calm down, OK? Whatever your problem is, there's no need to take it out on us.'

'Yeah, what is your problem?' Bekka asked. 'We've all been kidnapped by the same people. They're the ones you should be angry at.'

'You have no idea, do you?'

Vera answered this time, and more calmly, though even she had an edge to her voice. 'You're right. We have no idea what you're talking about. How about we all sit and you can tell us.'

'I guess there's time,' Davian said. 'We have all the time in the world now. All of the rest of our lives.'

Henry reached out to find Bekka and the two of them sat together with their backs against one wall. He could hear, rather than see, Vera settle down too.

'OK Davian, tell us what is worrying you,' Vera said.

'Apart from the obvious,' Henry grumbled.

'There was a plan, right?' Davian said. 'A really good plan. I worked it out with Cat and Rose and Jones and everyone on the way here.'

'On the way here?' Henry asked, astonished. 'When? How?'

'Well, as you were having enough trouble with jumping and as Bekka is just a kid–'

'I'm not just a kid,' Bekka interrupted.

'– as this is so new to the two of you, we thought you had enough to deal with.'

'So you went behind our backs and hatched a plan?' Bekka was getting angry now.

'Look, we had to. The IGP made my release conditional on bringing down the gang.'

'They what? But you were acquitted. That they knew you'd had nothing to do with anything and that you were free. They told you.' Bekka slapped her hand on the cold floor.

'You believed that?' Davian sighed. 'I guess you were supposed to, and I guess Xedrog and Zimmin got taken in too. But that was the point. No, I was only freed on the understanding that I would come here and help set up a sting that would take the whole gang down.'

Henry shifted uncomfortably against the wall.

'Now you tell it like that, it does make a lot more sense.'

'What did you think I was doing?' Davian asked.

'Rejoining the gang, of course,' Henry said.

'What? Why would I do that?'

'Cat, she told that other cat …'

'Purrkins,' Henry said with a slight grin.

'Yes, him. She told him that you were rejoining the gang.'

'She had to back up what I was doing with her own rumour, otherwise the gang wouldn't have taken me on. She knew Perkins was bent. It was part of the plan.'

'But you were always with them. We never saw you.' Bekka was full of explanation. 'You wouldn't tell us what you were doing.'

'Yeah … well. We wanted to keep you out of it. Didn't want you getting hurt.'

'You didn't trust us. That's all.'

'And looks like I was wise not to. Look what you've done.' Davian's voice rose again in anger.

'What have we done? We had nothing to do with your sting. We were just –'

'We got you out of the way, we had you safely at that concert. And in just a few more minutes the police would have arrested all the gang members still on Karthur. Then Jones and me, with Rose's tech, we would have been on the ship, we would have stopped it from going to Earth, and notified the IGP. Tomorrow, Rose would have told you the whole thing, Cat would have won the court cases against Xedrog and Zimmin with all the evidence we'd collected, and we all could have gone to Earth. But you had to go and mess it up.'

'But we –'

'They were just looking out for me, Davian. Just trying to help me out. They could see that I was stuck, and they were just trying to help.' Vera's voice was conciliatory.

'You've got to know that breaking a bio-tracer is going to be noticed.'

'How? How are we supposed to know that?' Henry asked.

'You're the one playing with things you don't understand, then.'

Henry had no answer for that. No answer for any of it.

They didn't need to help out after all. They didn't need to do anything. If they'd just waited another night this whole 'adventure' would have been over. Now they were stuck in a cellar in the middle of the desert, just waiting to dry out and die. He could already feel his mouth getting dry.

They sat in silence, the full weight of the situation dawning on them.

'We can't just sit here,' Henry said after a while. 'There has to be something we can try. Davian, let's you and me see if we can get that door to budge.'

'Bekka, how about you and I feel our way around the walls. We have no idea how big this room is, or if there are shelves or anything that could be used to help us.' Vera's voice sounded warm and friendly. Calming, like a preschool teacher. Henry wondered what sort of self-restraint and care for others was needed to be able to sound that calm in this situation. But it had the required effect. Bekka's shaking settled as she listened, and Henry thought they'd all be better off if they got up and did something. Sitting in the dark and fighting with each other was not going to help anyone.

He and Davian investigated the door by feel. It felt solid. The handle did not turn, the hinges were on the other side, and they had no tools to work with anyway. Henry pushed and bashed. Davian threw himself at the door. But it was no use. The door was solid.

And it didn't take Vera and Bekka long to investigate the walls either. They were being held in an empty room cut into stone. Cold and dry.

'What do you think this was built for?' Henry asked as they all settled, dejected, on the floor.

'Maybe a wine cellar?'

'Veggie storage?'

'I think that they built it as a hide out. A place where they could go if the authorities found the oasis. It's supposed to just keep them for a couple of hours and then they'd go back to the surface.'

'But then, why the solid door? Why is there no food or water?'

Maybe they spun Davian a story about hiding, Henry thought, but this place was a prison. And he couldn't see how they were going to get out of it.

Look at the bright side, he told himself. At least they are leaving us alone. That Zimmin looked like he could be a vicious one, he wouldn't put it past him to torture them just for the fun of it. Or set the dog on them. But instead he'd just left them alone. Things could be worse.

He considered saying all that out loud, but he wasn't sure it would be helpful. The most helpful thing would be to sleep, just to leave the horrible thoughts behind for a while. There was no other way to pass the time.

The silence in the room was absolute. Everyone alone with their own thoughts.

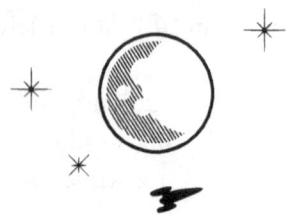

Chapter Forty-Two

Rose sat on the ground next to the Sambiss and buried her hands in his golden fur. She didn't know if she was trying to comfort him, or comfort herself. How could it have gone so wrong?

They both watched Julis make call after call. Eventually she put the communicator away.

'I have everywhere teams out looking for them. They search since we leave the ship site. But so far, there is nothing. We are leaning also on our informants and the people we arrested at the site, but no one so far tells where Zimmin would go.'

The Sambiss whined.

'Do you know where the headquarters are?' Rose asked. 'Maybe there's something there that will give us a clue.'

'Yes, I just ask my sergeant, he says they are pulling that place apart. If he finds something, he'll immediately tell me.'

'So we can't go there?' The Sambiss asked.

'No, we leave them alone. They are very good at this job. They will let me know.'

Rose sighed and shifted her bag to make it more comfortable on her shoulders. That gave her an idea and she opened the bag and started rooting through it while the Sambiss and Julis looked at her as if she had gone mad.

'Come on, come on,' she muttered to herself. Then, 'Ha! Here we go.'

She looked up at her two friends, a big smile on her face.

'I know how we can find them,' she said.

'What? How?'

'Find my phone,' said Rose.

The Sambiss wagged his tail, but Julis was still confused until Rose showed her the blinking red light on her mobile phone.

'This is where Bekka is. Or at least, it's where her phone is. If nothing else, it's going to give us a starting point.'

Julis stared at the phone and then at Rose.

'What do we wait for? Let's go.'

The Sambiss barked his agreement.

Julis put the coordinates of the flashing red light into her car's computer and Rose agreed to update the coordinates as they moved.

'If we had time, I'd link my phone and your car. But my phone technology is so far behind you. I mean, you try to stay up-to-date on Earth but between not wanting to stand out in the crowd and the lack of deliveries from civilisation, it's just a bit difficult.'

Rose felt so hopeful that she was willing to crack a joke. But then Julis put a call out for a couple of cars of backup and she realised again how serious this was. She was trying to find a friend, not just a lost phone. And there wasn't a big chance that the outcome would be good. The flashing red light didn't necessarily mean that Bekka was alive. It only meant that the phone was alive. And the phone might not even be with Bekka. Her mouth went dry at the thought.

But there was a sliver of hope. The red flashing light was a place to start. And it was more than they had before.

They followed the trail of the phone through the dark night, travelling over the Pelentra Forest and out into the desert wastelands. The car constantly crackled with communications from different police officers. Two cars full of officers were following them out to help with the search, and, hopefully, the rescue. And others were checking in, telling of the access to the main headquarters and the arrests of gang members all over the city. Police were raiding houses now, and warehouses throughout the planet. The clean up was intense and active.

Julis kept an eye on it all, but she didn't lose sight of the job in front of them. She regularly checked in with Rose and updated the position of the flashing light on the ship's computer.

And then, as the dry sands of the desert rolled out under them in every direction, Rose checked for a new position and found that the light had disappeared. She refreshed the screen. Nothing. She opened and closed the app. Still nothing. Then, she went so far as to turn the phone off and back on again.

The little jingle indicating the phone's restart drew the attention of Julis and the Sambiss.

'What's wrong?' The Sambiss asked.

'We've lost her,' Rose said, the lump in her throat making it hard for her to speak. 'She's gone.'

The Sambiss put his tail between his legs. Julis stared at the floor. Then she looked up at them both.

'Bekka is not gone,' she said. 'Just the light from her communicator is gone. Now, just wait a minute, let me see what I can see.'

Rose breathed again. She had put way too much emotion into that red blinking light. What was wrong with her? But where would they look now? The phone had been moving quite quickly through the desert. And that meant they were in their own flying car, not travelling on the ground. There wasn't even the trace of a scent for the Sambiss to follow.

Julis worked on the car's computer for a minute.

'There,' she said as a holographic map filled the interior of the car.

The Sambiss put his head to one side, then stood up so that he could see the top of the map. Rose also moved to the side in order to see more clearly.

'Now, we last saw her there. Just as we came into the sands.' A red dot formed on the map. 'And they have run away from all civilisation, so I think we need to look for a hideout in this horrible desert.'

'Who can live in a desert?' Rose asked.

'The Engedot like the heat in the day, though at night when it's cold they are pretty slow. But lizard boy, he will, I think, like this place here.'

Julis zoomed in. The desert sands rushed past Rose and the Sambiss. The dunes became larger. And then, there was some detail. Trees popped up, standing around a small pond of water. And next to the pond grew some buildings, as small as Lego blocks at first, but growing in definition until Rose could see just how tumble-down and ragged they were.

'How do you know that this is the place?' Rose asked.

'Well, I don't,' Julis replied. 'But the computer calculates it as the most likely to support life in this desert. So it stands as a good place to start.'

It all looked so life-like. Rose wished that they could just reach into the map and pull the captives out of it and into the car. But no, it was just a projection and the fight was ahead of them.

Rose looked from the map to the real desert unfolding outside the car. What if Bekka had been thrown out in this wasteland? What if she and her grandfather had been killed, and Rose had just been following an unaccompanied phone signal? What if the bad guys had found the phone and sent it off in another direction to throw everyone off?

There was so much that was unknown, but they had to go with what they had. And hope.

Chapter Forty-Three

As they approached the oasis, at a safe point, Julis slowed the car down to a crawl. Rose looked up from her intense study of the map.

'What's happening? We're going so slowly.'

'The slow car makes less noise,' Julis explained. 'And our backup must catch us.'

Surely Rose could see that they couldn't head into this situation without backup.

Rose nodded slowly, a frown on her face. She went back to studying the map.

Almost silently the car descended and they came to rest behind a large dune.

'The oasis is to the other side,' Julis said, her voice low as if Zimmin could hear them even out here.

'How far away is your backup?'

'It comes soon.'

Julis pointed to the map, drawing attention to two moving dots near the edge of the desert.

'OK,' said Rose and pulled the car door open.

'We should wait,' Julis whispered with some urgency.

'You can wait,' Rose said. 'I need to find my friends.' She stepped out into the sands before Julis could get hold of her arm.

'Me too,' said the Sambiss in a low growl and slipped out after her.

'Great,' Julis muttered as she hastily strapped on her blaster and followed them out of the car. 'We're just going to barge in and get ourselves caught.'

But in the end, she was impressed by the care that her guests took. The Sambiss crept silently ahead, nose to the ground, slinking low. Rose also walked slowly and silently, the sands hardly moving under her feet.

They climbed over the dune and slithered down the other face to see a row of palm trees that surrounded the oasis like a living wall. The old trees looked like they'd never been trimmed and the dry grey fronds drooping from the tops of the trees became large skirts around the trunks.

They were ideal for hiding behind and the intrepid rescuers stopped at the nearest palm and regrouped.

The Sambiss lifted his nose and thoroughly examined the air. His tail wagged slightly.

'No blood,' he grunted, and sniffed again. 'All were here. Two humans, and two arphaxad. One lizard man, one big Hunter.'

'When? When were they here?' Rose asked.

But the Sambiss shook his head. 'Faint smell. Not strong. In there I can tell you more.'

Rose nodded and shifted her weight to move. But this time Julis was able to hold her back.

'Wait,' she said. Rose tried to shake her off, but Julis became more urgent. 'Can we plan, just a little?'

Rose stared at her. Then she nodded.

'Let's first take out the Engedot and the Hunter. You point me in the direction. I am armed. Then we find your friends. I don't want to be guarding our backs always.'

Rose nodded again and they set out.

They could see a car on the other side of the pool of water. The Sambiss skirted the water and crept directly to the car. Then he looked through the gloom at Julis and Rose and nodded. He pointed his nose towards one of the ramshackle buildings and padded towards it, nose to the ground. The two others followed as silently as they could. Julis kept her hand on her blaster.

Suddenly a door opened and light streamed into the darkness. The air filled with the sound of barking and growling and a black shadow raced out of the light and jumped on the golden Sambiss.

The two dogs tumbled over and over each other in the sand. Julis whipped out her blaster and took careful aim.

'No! Don't hit ...' Rose reached out to Julis, but it was too late. She took the shot and the Hunter fell limp.

'Well done,' came a cool voice from the lighted doorway. 'That was quite a risk.'

Julis turned, blaster aimed towards the voice. And she found a blaster aimed directly at her.

'It's on stun,' she said. 'I could shoot twice if I had to.'

'That's interesting to know,' the cool voice replied conversationally. 'You might want to know that mine is set at a much higher setting.'

Yes, Julis knew. Zimmin's gun would be set to kill.

Why was he not shooting? She guessed that his eyes needed to get used to the dark. Or perhaps he was one of those who loved to monologue. She hoped so. Why had Rose been so determined to go ahead?

'So we are in a standoff,' she said. 'You would be deep in trouble for shooting a detective. Perhaps we can talk.'

Talking was what she wanted to do. Talking until the backup arrived. But she wasn't sure that mentioning the backup was a good idea. Maybe that would make him take the risk, shoot her, and run.

Then she saw something out of the corner of her eye. What was happening? She talked faster, louder. Keeping the lizard's attention on her.

'This is crazy already, capturing the humans. Where have you got them?'

'That is for me to know, and you hopefully not to find out. Who will miss a few –

Zimmin was cut short as Rose raced out of the shadows, and threw herself against him, bouncing off him and falling onto the hard sand. He didn't fall over, but still, he couldn't stop himself from looking away from Julis and towards this new distraction. Julis made the shot immediately, hitting him with a stun ray and dropping him to the ground.

Rose stood and brushed herself off.

'That's that,' she said. Then she looked over at the golden Sambiss and gave a little cry. She ran to him. 'Are you OK?,' she asked.

He had crept a little distance from the big black dog. There was a red patch on his shoulder, and another on his belly.

'OK,' he said in a shaky voice.

Rose shook her head and investigated the wounds. The Sambiss whined a little when she got to his shoulder, but the scratch on the belly didn't look too bad.

'Can you stand?' she asked.

The Sambiss got carefully to his feet. He limped a bit on his right leg, but, 'OK,' he said in a stronger voice. 'I'm OK.'

'Do you have first aid?' Rose asked Julis.

'Of course, in the car. I anyway need to go there and get handcuffs and a muzzle.'

She gave Rose her blaster.

'You look after these two.'

Rose looked at the two criminals lying, as if dead, on the ground.

'But … You shot them?'

'I've stunned them, that's all. It should last until I get back, but if not, you shoot them again.'

'Uh … OK,' Rose said in a shaky voice. She took the blaster gingerly and waved from one criminal to the other. The Sambiss pulled himself behind Rose and out of the range of the gun.

Julis laughed a little at that. Then she took off for the car. The stun would probably last at least until she got back, but she would be as quick as she could.

Before she had made it back to the palm trees, her communicator buzzed. It was the backup. Now she could breathe more easily.

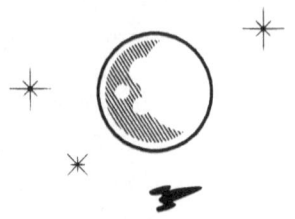

Chapter Forty-Four

The darkness in the underground cell was so complete that Henry had no idea how much time had passed. Sometimes he thought he heard noises from above, but he wasn't sure, and as every noise was frightening, he didn't want to draw attention to them. But then there came a noise they couldn't ignore.

'What was that?' Bekka asked.

Henry heard footsteps and snuffling in the tunnel beyond the door. Was he right about Zimmin after all? Had the big black Sambiss come to attack them?

His first instinct was to jump up and bar the door. He tried, but his body wouldn't move that fast. Davian got there before him.

They all held their breath, listening intently, but the sounds had disappeared.

'It's gone,' Davian said, his voice sounding shaky in the pitch blackness of their prison.

They listened to the silence for a few minutes.

Then there was no question. Everyone could hear running feet and shouting voices.

Now the four of them stood together, determined to face this new challenge, whatever it was.

The door opened with a crash and light filled the cell. Blinded, Henry struck out at whatever it was that was coming for them.

'Ouch! That hurt,' came a cry in return. A recognisable voice. It was Rose! And as Henry's eyes became accustomed to the light he could see their very own Sambiss, wagging his tail madly and licking everyone, Rose giving Bekka a hug, and a stranger, but a friendly one, standing in the doorway shaking Davian's hand.

They were safe.

* * *

Henry had never been so happy to see the sky. The early morning sun was rising and a few of Karthur's moons were still visible in the cloudless blue. The desert stretched around them grey and bleak in the early morning light. Now that they were safe, he could see the beauty in the rolling dunes. He could understand the attraction of even this small collection of buildings around the oasis. If you wanted to get away from everything, not to hide, but to be refreshed, this would be an excellent 'away from everything' place.

The seven of them stood in a small group next to the little oasis. Around them police were working industriously, checking out every building, dusting things down, investigating tunnels and pathways.

Julis was cleaning the Sambiss' wounds and binding him up. Henry was horrified at the thought of their golden friend going face-to-face with the big black brute. But the Sambiss kept reassuring them that he wasn't hurt as badly as it looked.

Julis had been introduced to the team, and Henry realised that he remembered her face from the original IGP ship. She'd been part of them all along. Sometime he was going to get a total explanation of this whole situation.

'It's so good to know you're all safe,' Rose said. 'We need to go back and let Cat know. She'll be so relieved.'

'And Jones,' said Davian. 'He'll want to know too.'

'Where is Jones?' asked Bekka.

Rose and Julis looked at each other in horror.

'He's on board the ship,' Rose said.

'With Cat?'

'No, not our ship. The transporter ship that Davian was supposed to board. The ship we were going to use as our evidence to bring the whole gang down.'

'The ship that's on its way to Earth,' Davian said. 'The one we were going to stop.'

'And Jones doesn't know how to use my technology and he doesn't have your backup.'

Henry stared at them.

'What are we going to do?' he asked.

Chapter Forty-Five

Jones held the bridge door notched slightly open and spied out the situation. He could see through the large bridge windows the beautiful blue planet Earth, stunning to look at, and very close to where they were now. He could see Xedrog, sitting, relaxed, in the captain's chair, looking very pleased with himself. There were others in the room too, but he couldn't see around the corners to figure out just how many, or what kinds of people they were.

He had to move now, or the whole planet would be at risk. There wasn't much he could do, stuck here without any allies, but he had to try. He took a step back and opened his bag to see what Rose had given him. But all the metallic technology was meant for disrupting communications or confusing navigation instruments; there was nothing there to help in this situation. Too much had changed. He'd have to do it his own way. And there was no time like the present.

He shoved the door open and barged into the centre of the control room.

'You're not going to do this!' he shouted at Xedrog.

Xedrog looked at him.

'Who are you?'

'I'm the person who is not going to let you or your gang go to Earth.'

'And how are you going to stop me?' he asked. 'The Earth is right here, right in my reach. And, look at you. You don't even have a blaster, do you?'

'No, but I have this,' Jones said, and launching himself at the console he put his walking stick to good use, smashing everything he could reach.

'Stop him!' Xedrog yelled.

The two henchmen jumped at Jones and, grabbing his arms, they pulled him away. But the damage had been done. Jones heard the motors powering down, and felt the ship's acceleration slow to a stop. The ship started to turn on its axis as it drifted helplessly through space.

'What have you done?' Xedrog screamed at him. 'We'll all die here! You've killed us all!'

'Well …. Good,' Jones said, trying to wrench his arms away from his captors. 'At least you won't be down there, messing that beautiful place up.' He nodded at Earth.

'What do you care? It's not even your home.'

'Oh I may not have been born there, but it's my home now. I'll do anything I can to protect it. And I just have.' Jones smiled with satisfaction.

'You're going to pay for that. In fact, you're going to pay, right now.' Xedrog pulled his blaster out of its holster and aimed it at Jones.

'Uh … Sir?' one of the henchmen interrupted. 'That might not be a good idea. That gun will blow the side out of this thing.'

'We're dying anyway,' Xedrog screamed, spittle flying out of his mouth. As he aimed at Jones, the henchmen let go and ran to the doorway to take cover. Jones pulled his bag off his back and flung it at Xedrog. Rose's carefully crafted (and quite heavy) technology hit Xedrog on the side of the head and he fell, unconscious. Jones snatched up the blaster and turned to deal with the henchmen. But they weren't going to stay in the room with the two crazy men. They ran, slamming the door behind them.

Jones laughed. This was brilliant. The most fun he'd had in ages.

Now what? Did he commandeer the ship? Lock this idiot up and take over? Free the crew?

Xedrog was right, of course. With no engines and no navigation, they were all going to die. There was no point in trying to do anything more.

But he'd done it. He'd stopped the ship and saved the Earth. That was all he could ask for.

However, the henchmen were probably going to find help to rescue their captain. So he decided to lock the door, just for safety's sake. It wouldn't hold them off for long, but it would be something.

He looked for something to tie Xedrog up with. He didn't want him coming to and trying for some hand-to-hand combat. Without the element of surprise, Jones wouldn't have much chance against Xedrog's brute strength. Eventually, he settled on some wires from the ruined console. He pulled and tugged until they came free and then made sure the still and silent Xedrog was bound securely hand and foot.

Then, after checking the door again, he turned to enjoy the view. It was all he had left to do.

The view of the Earth was beautiful. Unlike anything else in the universe. It wasn't a bad way to finish off his life, just staring at the view.

He felt the ship move, sideways this time. He stomach sank and his muscles tensed. Was there another console? Another way for the Vyynx crew to get this thing going? Would he have to fight some more?

Slowly the view from the window became obstructed by a dark shadow, and the Earth disappeared from sight. The ship stopped moving with an abrupt clang and a violent hissing sound filled the air.

Jones waited. There was nothing else to do. He held on to his walking stick and gripped the blaster tightly. He was prepared to die, but at the same time he wouldn't go down without a fight.

Suddenly, through the window came a bright light, making him blink and wince. Footsteps clanged through the corridor, coming straight for the bridge where Jones was waiting. He faced the door, blaster and stick at the ready.

Someone pushed at the door, but it didn't give. They struggled again. Jones waited, ready for action. Then a familiar voice met his ears.

'Hey Jones! Come on, let me in!'

'Sura!' He nearly dropped the blaster as he raced to open the door. 'What are you doing here?'

'Rescuing you,' she said with a cheeky grin. 'Though you took your time letting us know you were here.'

Behind Sura came a squadron of policemen. They took Xedrog, picking him up and dragging him out without ceremony. One of them also relieved Jones of the blaster he was holding.

He shook his hand.

'Boy am I glad to be rid of that. Weapons like that are just not my scene.'

'Looks like you did some damage though.' Sura checked the room out approvingly.

'Yeah, with this.' He showed her his walking stick. 'Nothing like a good bit of Tas Oak to help you out in a tight space. Oh, and Rose's tech came in handy too. For knocking Xedrog out.'

Sura laughed and the two of them slowly and carefully made their way out of the ship, avoiding the police scuffles with other members of the gang and the tight knots of first aiders that were treating the original crew members for cuts and bruises.

'How did you find out I was here?' he asked. 'I didn't have any way to let anyone know. And after I smashed up the console, I couldn't use the ship's gear either.'

'Rose told us,' Sura said. 'And Julis. She was quite insistent and our captain was incredibly happy to do what she asked. Even though we were halfway to another planet.'

'You were supposed to be waiting for us!'

'Well … our captain you know, he knows better. Until someone with higher rank burns his ear.'

They stepped out of the ship and into the hold.

'Come and have a drink and something to eat. Once these guys have got everything under control we'll take you all back to Karthur to face justice. We're on the home straight now.'

Chapter Forty-Six

Although Davian was at least a head taller than Julis, Henry thought that he somehow looked small standing next to her in the court room. His pale face was even paler. His eyes kept returning to rest on Vera, who was sitting between Henry and Bekka. Bekka was holding her hand and Henry murmuring, 'it will be alright,' at regular intervals.

This was it. Cat and Davian needed to convince the AI judge that Davian had done what was required. That he had set up the sting. That he had helped the IGP to find the gang members and make the arrests.

The problem was, of course, that he had been nowhere near the gang when the arrests were made. Unless you could prove beyond reasonable doubt that Zimmin was a member of the gang.

The AI was a hologram. As the court procedure began, at the time where a human court would be asked to stand for the arrival of the judge, the hologram just appeared, a little larger than life, at the front of the room. It was a man with pale skin and black hair. Just like Davian. The man looked so solid and real that Henry wanted to go up and touch him to find out if he actually was tangible, but this was a court and strict rules applied. The officials and guards dotted around the room were very real and they had very real weapons too, Julis had assured him. He stayed in his seat and kept trying to comfort Vera.

The first witness brought to the stand was Zimmin. Henry noticed, with concern, that the lizard-man didn't look nervous. He lounged at the stand, like he was leaning on a bar at a pub. All that was missing was the whiskey.

Cat began her examination.

'Are you a member of the gang known as the Vyynx?' she asked.

'I help them out from time to time,' Zimmin stated urbanely.

'Oh, I think it is more than that. You are one of the leaders of the gang, aren't you?'

'I don't know how you'd define that.'

'You set the objectives of the group and make them happen, you discipline members who are not obeying your commands.'

'You'll find no proof of that, I believe.'

'And when Davian offered you the chance to take your wares to a new planet, to Earth, you decided that this was a good objective.'

'You'll find that hard to prove too.'

'Your good friend Xedrog is, as I understand it, a joint leader of the gang with you. And he took your advice and captured a ship of pharmaceuticals with the intention of introducing them to humans on Earth. The IGP has the ship under our control as we speak.'

'I would not call Xedrog a good friend. He is more of a long-standing acquaintance. But anyway,' Zimmin waved that thought away as if it were no consequence, 'whatever he chooses to do has nothing to do with me. If he decides to go somewhere new, well, he is an adult. You would need to ask him.'

'Don't worry, we will.'

Cat tried this way and that. Asking Zimmin how he knew Davian. Asking what he spent his days doing – 'business' he replied. Zimmin had been clever. He had covered his tracks at every opportunity. His name was on no papers. His links to the gang were oblique. It was hard to prove anything solid.

Cat changed her tune.

'Could you explain to the court why you abducted four people: the two humans, Henry and Bekka, and Davian and his mother?'

Henry nodded his support. If she couldn't get him on the gang membership, at least she could prove the kidnapping.

'My intention was to rescue Davian's mother,' Zimmin said.

Henry sat upright, and Bekka gasped.

'I'm sorry? You intended to rescue Vera Jernoshef?'

'I had spent time with Davian when he was a child. I knew how important his mother was to him. You can't trust these humans, these aliens. We don't know them or anything about their home planet. So I gave Vera a bracelet so that I could make sure she was safe. That the humans wouldn't harm her or take her away with them.

'I was with Davian that night, and my communicator gave me the signal that Vera's bracelet had been tampered with. When I talked with Davian about it, he looked anxious. He obviously didn't want to worry me and he told me that he wasn't concerned, but I could see that he was deeply troubled. I took him with me to find his mother and make sure she was OK.'

Cat's tail flickered.

'Could you tell me why it was so necessary to take a hunter Sambiss, well known for his ferocity, with you if you were just checking that Vera was in good health?'

'Oh yes, well. Once the bracelet was taken off, we had no idea where these humans would take her. I wanted to find her as soon as possible so that the humans would have no opportunity to do her harm. What if they wanted to take her off-planet? We would have no chance of finding her then.'

'And then you kept all four of them locked in an underground bunker with no food or water?'

'For some reason, that I truly don't understand, Davian and his mother refused to leave the humans. I didn't want those humans to get away, not after the abduction of one of our own residents. So I thought I would keep them all safe overnight while I thought of what to do next.

'I didn't have a lot of time to plan this. I worked with what I had. I was thinking of how best to deal with the humans, whether to let them go back to Earth or to deliver them to the authorities, when I was so rudely interrupted by the IGP.'

The thing was, he spoke with such authority that even Henry had to agree that he had a valid point. Cat questioned him this way and that, but he stuck to his story. He said that he was sorry that he hadn't called the IGP straight away. He begged Julis for forgiveness. But that he was flustered. That he hadn't had to deal with humans before and he wasn't sure of the correct methods to use.

In the end, Cat let him go.

She asked for an adjournment and the request was granted. A polite murmur filled the room as those watching got up to stretch their legs and chat among themselves. Cat turned to a court official and asked a question. The official looked at his communicator and shook his head.

Then Cat made her way to where the team were sitting.

'How could he lie like that?' Bekka asked.

'It's OK,' Cat said soothingly. But she said nothing that was more encouraging than that, and Henry wondered how much this turn of events had thrown her plan.

'We obviously need to bring Xedrog onto the stand,' Cat said. 'But the ship hasn't arrived yet. Vera, are you able to come to the stand while we're waiting?'

Vera swallowed hard and nodded. Cat laid a paw on her hand comfortingly.

'I'll be as gentle as possible.'

Bekka squeezed Vera's hand and she stood to follow Cat when the court official pushed his way through the crowd back to Cat.

'They are here now,' he said.

'Excellent,' said Cat. 'Vera, you're off the hook. At least, you are for now. Let's try Xedrog first.'

The doors to the court opened and Sura and Jones walked in, Jones reluctantly leaving his gum tree branch with the officials at the door. Their friends crowded around them, hugging Sura, shaking Jones' hand and patting him on the back. It was like a meeting of friends that had been separated for years, not for less than a week. But oh so much had happened in that week. They would have a lot to catch up on.

Their shared snatches of stories were cut off as the officials called the court back to order, the holographic AI judge appeared again, and Cat called Xedrog for examination.

Xedrog slouched in the stand, looking a little worse for wear. The bruising on his head was visible through the healing gel that had been applied. He sagged untidily, holding on to the railing with one hand.

'Do you know the gang called the Vyynx?'

'I don't remember,' Xedrog mumbled.

'I find that a little strange. We know that you are, in fact, the leader of that gang.'

'I don't remember,' came the reply.

'Could you tell us what you were doing in the ship where you were found?'

'I don't know.' Xedrog stared at the ground.

Henry shifted in his seat. It looked like either Jones had given Xedrog a bad concussion, or, more likely, he had been told by his pal to 'not remember' or 'not know' anything. If they couldn't get him to answer even the simplest questions, how was Cat going to get anywhere?

'Oh well, if you can't remember that's OK,' Cat asserted. 'We have information from other places. I'm sure we can fill in the blanks. We've been talking to your friend, Zimmin. Or rather, I should say your acquaintance. He's told us all about your plans for the Vyynx and for the planet Earth.'

Xedrog mouthed the word 'acquaintance' with a look of puzzlement.

'He knows quite a bit about you. So if you can't remember, we'll go with what he says. I wouldn't trust him to give you a good report though. He says he isn't friends with you at all, really. That you're basically strangers. That he just drops in from time to time.'

'What? Hang on. Strangers? I've known him since we were kids. Since he first started paying me to stop the other kids from bashing him up. Paying me with the other kids' lunch money I recall.' Xedrog gave a half grin.

'Oh, so you are close then?'

'I'd say. He's the brains and I'm the brawn. That's what he says. What he's always said.'

'But this whole plan of going to Earth, we hear that was your plan. Going to a Class D planet and showing yourselves and so on. I mean, you know that's fully against the law. You coming up with that idea, that's a lot of years inside for you.'

'My plan? No that was never my plan. Like I said, Zimmin is the brains. He brought in that kid Davian and told me what we was going to do. It's always been his plan.'

'Well, I guess it's his word against yours then.'

'Trying to drop me in it, is he? I'm not having that. He might be the brains, but I have some brains of my own. I'm not taking the fall here.' Xedrog muttered.

'So let me get this straight,' Cat said pleasantly. 'Davian came to visit Zimmin, and they both told you of this great idea to go to Earth and sell your wares there? And you just agreed.'

'Yes, that's all. Not my idea.'

'But then you were the one on the ship in Earth's orbit. You alone, Xedrog. Neither Zimmin nor Davian were present. How can you explain that?'

'It all got a bit hairy when it all went down, and Davian's Mum, she took off, escaped. Took off her monitor and disappeared. Zimmin took Davian and a hunter Sambiss to go find her. We weren't letting her get away. She was our guarantee that Davian would stick with us and not turn us in.'

'Ah, I see. So Zimmin wasn't concerned for Vera's welfare?'

'Not likely. No, he was going to kill them at our hideout, remove the evidence and then join me. I mean, once we'd got to Earth, who needed Davian anyway? Once our ship was away. Her welfare?' Xedrog laughed his gurgling awful laugh. 'Nup. Not that.'

'And once again, it's a case of Zimmin's word against yours.'

'What? He told you different?'

Cat nodded. 'And you'll be carrying the can. We caught you in the ship, after all.'

'No. I can prove it was him. All of it. I'm not stupid. Check my communicator, it's got records of all of it. All our talks. All the times he lorded it over me. It's all there. You check it. His word against mine?' Xedrog grimaced. 'I knew he'd do this to me. It's there.'

It did not take long to do that. The contents of Xedrog's communicator were uploaded to the AI and parsed. The evidence was clear.

The AI made its verdict. Xedrog and Zimmin were found guilty of the many charges – murder, for starters, piracy, and the intention to invade a peaceful and undeveloped planet. And more importantly, Davian was finally and truly acquitted of any crime.

It was over, finally over. Xedrog and Zimmin were going away for good.

As the verdict fell, the team from Earth erupted into cheers. Some even said they saw a tear in Cat's eye. They hugged and danced. Davian picked his mother up and twirled her around.

When everyone had settled down, Henry put on his most mournful face.

'Now can we go home?' he asked.

The team burst into laughter.

'Yes,' said Cat. 'Now we can go home.'

'Are you coming?' Bekka asked Vera.

'Just try and stop me,' she said with a smile. 'Ready when you are.'

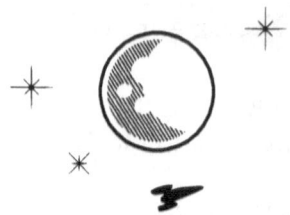

Chapter Forty-Seven

When he came to, Henry felt the now-familiar zero-gravity sensation. He checked first to make sure that Bekka was alright. She was floating near a window, taking in all the stars around her. She looked over to her grandfather and gave him a smile. She was fine, so Henry looked around at all his other friends. Davian and Vera were huddled together, talking nineteen to the dozen. Cat and the Sambiss were both asleep. Jones floated cross-legged in the back, reading a book. It was like a family reunion, like a relaxed four-day holiday where everyone is happy to do their own thing.

Sura had stayed on Karthur. She hadn't changed her mind. She had come to the ship to send them off, giving everyone (including Jones) a big hug and promising to stay in touch. She had waved a friendly farewell as they broke away from the docking station and flew into the sky and had kept waving until the ship had blinked out in the first jump on the way back to Earth.

Rose noticed that Henry was awake and brought him a bag of tea.

'It's becoming a routine thing, isn't it?' he said. 'One minute you think space travel is only for astronauts and Elon Musk, and the next you're jumping through the universe like a flea.'

Rose laughed. 'Sort of. I've never seen anyone who is still passing out by their fourth jump. Most people have got used to it by then.'

'I'm never going to get used to it,' said Henry. 'I really am too old for this.'

'It's alright Henry, we're nearly there now. Just give us a little while longer and then we'll get you home.'

'Home, to a proper cup of tea.' Henry took a suck at the bag and made a face.

'You know,' Rose said conversationally, 'I heard that some astronaut from Earth has come up with a way to have an open cup that works in space.'

'So I don't have to suck from a bag? There's another way to do this?'

'Yeah, but for some reason I didn't get the chance to fit out this ship with the very latest in technology for humans. We were in a hurry or something I remember.' Rose gave Henry a cheeky grin.

'I don't understand why Sura didn't want to come home with us. I thought maybe her desire to stay on the IGP ship was fake – you know, just part of your big plan.'

'No, she really was ready to go on her next adventure. We just used her a little to keep tabs on the IGP ship.'

'It was hard to say goodbye. And to Julis too, I guess. I didn't really get to know her. But it looked like that goodbye was hard for Cat.'

'Well, Julis and Cat go back a long way. At least this time they parted as good friends. You never know, Julis might find a way to bend the rules and come down to visit.'

They had decided to take the flight back at a gentle pace. Everyone had been a bit shaken up by the unexpected turn of their well-planned adventure. They didn't need to rush the ending, despite how desperate Henry was to see his home planet. So Rose and Henry chatted comfortably about the mechanics of space flight and Jones joined in now and then. Bekka pointed out a particularly beautiful constellation. Cat stretched occasionally, then curled up in the other direction and went back to sleep. The Sambiss twitched his leg, dreaming of chasing and catching who knows what? And Vera and Davian talked. They had a lot of catching up to do.

After a while, Henry remembered the book he had packed and settled down for a good read.

Eventually, after they'd all had a sleep and something to eat, it was time to finish the adventure and prepare to go back to Earth.

Henry felt like he could have powered the ship with the force of his yearning for home. He thought that by this stage even Bekka was looking forward to a bit of normal. But there was a little more of a wait to come.

Rose, Davian and Cat worked together, performing some serious calculations to make sure they would arrive at night, wouldn't hit the International Space Station, and wouldn't run into any aircraft or passing satellites on their way down. They didn't want to be noticed at all.

'Oh that's how that works,' said Davian at one point. 'I reckon that was the crucial bit I was missing and why I damaged the ship.'

'It's very hard to land on your first time, when there's no docking stations or anything. I was impressed that your ship was salvageable.'

'You did better than me,' said Cat. 'My ship was completely wrecked. I was lucky to get out alive.'

'But we'll do better this time, right?' Henry asked anxiously.

'Of course. We're taking our time and getting it right. We'll be fine,' Rose said quickly. Maybe a little too quickly.

Henry wasn't convinced. But Davian's mind had gone to other matters.

'Is there a better place to hide her once we land? I was in constant fear of her being found out there in the bush. My hiding place wasn't that unapproachable, and I didn't have anything to camouflage her with.'

'How about we put her down on my property, behind my house?'

'That will make it easier to carry the power source back,' said Jones with a laugh.

'As long as we all get back safely, that's all that matters.' Henry was becoming nervous with this talk of damaging ships. He had thought the trip was over when they turned the nose to home, but now he realised it wasn't going to be that simple.

'Don't worry,' Jones said. 'You're in safe hands. Rose has got this down.'

Henry realised that Bekka hadn't been part of this conversation at all. He turned to see what she was doing and found her deep in conversation with Vera.

'What are you talking about?' he asked.

'I'm telling her all about Earth,' said Bekka. 'We didn't get very far in our advertising before.'

'I want to know everything,' smiled Vera. 'Everything about my new home.'

'You don't even know if you'll like it yet,' said Jones.

'Oh I believe I will, it sounds wonderful.'

'I've only told you the good parts,' said Bekka. 'There are some bad parts too. There are jack jumpers – don't get bitten by a jack jumper, it stings. There are spiders, and snakes.'

'Not to mention the drop bears,' Jones said with a grin. The other companions groaned and Vera looked at him questioningly.

'I'll explain later,' he said.

'And then I'll explain again,' Davian interjected.

'The gravity is a bit heavier than Karthur,' said Rose. 'But not by much. It won't wear you out or anything.'

'I'll show you all the TV shows you should watch,' Bekka went on. 'They'll give you some history and culture so you'll fit in.'

'Oh yes, you'll find the technology incredibly backward,' said Rose. 'But it's quaint. You get used to it. And it doesn't hurt to be a bit rustic.'

Henry thought about how his home must look to these space travellers. They were quite right, the place was a bit rustic, when you compared it to ships that could jump through space, cars that could fly, and biometric tagging. He was so used to thinking himself better than the strangers who moved to Cygnet – more at home, knowing more about how the town worked, how the Earth worked for that matter. But now he realised that it was he who was on the back foot. How much could he learn from his fellow travellers? He could spend the rest of his life learning.

But it was better than that. They could spend the rest of their lives learning from each other. He could share his small amount of knowledge about his home, they could help him learn so much more about the universe. Life in Cygnet was going to be a lot more interesting.

***

In the dead of night, a caravan-sized ship winked into existence above the paddock behind Rose's blue weatherboard house and slowly settled down to land.

The door of the ship slid open and a golden retriever gambolled out, followed by a much more sedate fluffy white cat, and a group of what looked like human beings. But these were no ordinary Earth people.

***

Henry lifted his face to the cool breeze, smelt the eucalyptus on the air, and sighed deeply.

'Home,' he whispered. His tongue felt heavy in his mouth as he got used to gravity again. His legs dragged and he almost wished for the ability to float in zero G up to the house. But ...

'Home,' agreed Bekka.

Yes, there was no place like home.

Davian hugged Vera. 'Welcome to your new home,' he said. And she smiled a wobbly smile and blinked back her tears.

'I wonder what time it is?' asked Jones.

Rose laughed. 'I think it's time for a cup of tea. Why don't you all come inside and I'll put the kettle on.'

Henry had a lot of new knowledge to fit into his brain. A lot of experience to make sense of, as his life returned to normal. And a lot of things that he couldn't tell his daughter, his son-in-law, and most of his old friends. But he had a lot of new friends now, and he was much more willing to accept newcomers into the community – whether they were just from elsewhere on this planet, or from another planet entirely. He was looking forward to what his new life and his new perspective would bring.

But mostly he was looking forward to a nice, hot cup of tea.

The End

Thank you for reading. If you enjoyed this book, please leave a review at your favourite vendor website to help others find it.

Come over to rjamos.com to join my newsletter list and receive a free ebook.

Books by RJ Amos

Deadly Misconduct (Book 1 in the Deadly Miss series)
Deadly Misdirection (Book 2 in the Deadly Miss series)
Deadly Miscalculation (Book 3 in the Deadly Miss series)

Small Town Trouble
Challenge Accepted – A 30-day Short Story Project
The Universe is a Small Place

Find out more at rjamos.com

Acknowledgements

This book had been a three-year project that started with a 50,000 word draft written during NaNoWriMo in November 2019. Editing of that draft during 2020 made me realise that the trip to Karthur needed a lot more work and the second half of the book was written during 2021. The end of 2021 and all of 2022 have been spent polishing, giving it to people to read, then polishing some more. I could not have made it what it is without the help of so many people.

Firstly, I want to thank Moz, who is the most amazing accidental developmental editor. He has made the book so much better with his comments, like 'that wouldn't happen' and 'he wouldn't have said that' and 'make the new planet more different'. I'm also grateful for his physics knowledge that led me to believe that a double sun was more trouble than it was worth but that a planet without a tilt would be different enough.

Thank you to Caleb and Kerilyn who read the first draft and told me that yes, I could write science fiction.

Thank you Mum and Dad for your unwavering belief in and support of me. And for Friday conversations.

Thanks to Nicky who helped me to calm my 2020 anxiety enough to begin writing again.

Much thanks to Sheelagh for editing and to Jill and Jeannie for proofreading. Hopefully between us we have caught all the errors, both big and small.

Thank you Meng and Anna Lise for the gorgeous cover and the little extra details that make this book so beautiful.

Thank you to Stevie Davenport for her detailed first-hand information about Antarctica from her book *A Crack in the Ice*.

And most of all, thank you to God for the gift of creativity and the time to use it. May this be to Your glory.

Small Town Trouble

Chapter 1

The carefully curated alarm music on Mel's phone always sounded perfectly reasonable the night before but somehow modulated into shrieking birds by the next morning. She'd tried all the possible alarms but none made Monday mornings any more palatable. Maybe it was something about getting up while it was still dark.

She checked her phone for urgent messages or emails but apart from the looming meeting with Sharon there was nothing. And that was fine. The meeting with Sharon, the managing director, was enough by itself. A meeting with the big boss meant nothing but trouble.

'What sort of trouble though?' she asked herself for the fifty thousandth time that weekend. 'And what sort of boss drops that bomb on you just before you leave work on Friday?'

Clothes shrugged on, and hair tied back, Mel headed out for her morning jog. The sky was just beginning to lighten, but not by much. There was too much cloud cover to get even a hint of pink this morning, not that she could have seen it over the high-rise buildings. All the lights were against her too; she spent more time jogging on the spot waiting for lights to change than she did actually moving forward. And when she felt the first spit of rain on her face she gave it all up as a bad joke and headed back to the apartment for a long hot shower. If this was a foretelling of the week ahead she would need all the comfort a shower could give.

Mel worked at Thompson's, a medium-sized company that took produce from the farmers, packaged it, and delivered it throughout the country to the big supermarket chains. Thompson's was all about fruit and vegetables, fresh air and the country life, if you believed its advertising, but in reality the country had not been any part of Mel's working life. She worked in the Melbourne office. The office took up three floors of a skyscraper in the inner city. She was working her way up the ladder, and everyone in her working group knew it. She was on her way to be CEO, like her father, the owner of Thompson's. But days like this made her wonder just how long that was going to take, and just how much work she would need to put in.

It was definitely that kind of morning. The long hot shower was too long, as it turned out. One sniff of the milk carton showed her that she would need to stop at the café on the way to the station to get her life-giving coffee. And then she dashed down the subway stairs only to see the train pulling out just as she arrived on the platform. Why couldn't it have been two minutes late like it normally was?

Checking her phone again while she waited for the next train (that was, incidentally, running two minutes late), there was an email from Sharon to say that the meeting had been moved forward half an hour, giving her about five minutes from when she'd get off the train to be in her office, up to speed on everything, and ready to defend herself to the big boss. Whatever she was defending herself for.

But once in the train, she was grateful for the five minutes she'd had on the platform to gulp her coffee. It would have been impossible to drink it on the train, squashed as she was between a smelly armpit and a backpack that was holding something entirely made up of sharp corners.

The dash from the station to the office through the rain left her skirt splashed with mud from the traffic and she needn't have bothered with the precious minutes spent blowdrying her hair.

Altogether it wasn't an auspicious start to the week.

All things considered, it was something of a triumph to only be two minutes late knocking on Sharon's door for the meeting.

Mel always hated this office. It was probably because it reminded her so much of her father's. Big black desk, big picture windows overlooking the city, the feeling of impending doom as you walked through the door to get more bad news, the feeling of insignificance as you sat ill at ease in the straight-backed chair and wondered which of your failings was going to be painted in technicolour today.

'I was wondering when you'd show up,' said Sharon, gesturing to the chair in front of the desk. 'You're going to have to get a bit more punctual in your new position, I'm sure.'

New position? Maybe this wasn't a bad-news meeting after all. Mel sat with her head held high and back straight, and waited for some clarification.

'I've brought you here this morning to offer you a more managerial placement. Would you be interested?'

Managerial? That sounded ... hang on ... there had to be a catch.

'I'm interested,' Mel said cautiously, 'could I have more information?'

'Certainly.' Sharon crossed her legs and sat back to tell the story. 'As you know, the board has been concerned about our relationship with our primary producers. There have been issues, situations caused by the management being centralised and, shall we say, losing touch with the farmers. The issues are becoming more pronounced as we work to incorporate the changes that will lead to the farms being more energy efficient, and more environmentally friendly. There has been some resistance. The answer to that issue is to send managers out into the field, as it were.' Sharon paused so that Mel could acknowledge the pun with a weak smile. 'You are the first person chosen to fill this position. I am here to offer you a management position in Lillyford, working to integrate environmental footprint changes. Lillyford is a town close to several of our major farms and you would be the liaison between us here in the city, and the producers out there.'

'Lillyford! But that's ... that's in the middle of nowhere.' Mel blinked. She had worked hard to rise through the ranks of Thompson's. She had been sure that a promotion was just around the corner. She had big dreams of being CEO, if not of this place, then of somewhere similar. And now, Lillyford. A town she only knew existed because she had seen it on delivery orders and office paperwork. A tiny place, right in the middle of Tasmania. The state of Tasmania was a place she had never wanted to go to. Not even for holidays. She was a city girl. She had dreams of leaving Melbourne to go to New York or London. Not this, this was the wrong way. What had she done to be sent out to the country? This had to be a punishment for something. Sharon must want to get rid of her.

'In the middle of the farms, yes.' Sharon was unperturbed. She leafed through some papers on her desk and found a file. 'You would be looking after Hopwoods, Lingholm, Northfield …'

'What's this about, Sharon?' Mel forgot her professional attitude, put both fists on the desk and leaned forward. 'What have I done to be kicked out like this?'

Sharon looked Mel in the eye, 'Kicked out? This is a promotion to a managerial position.'

'Is there an increase in salary?'

Sharon looked at the desk again, 'Not as such, no. But I'm sure you'll find your expenses are less in a smaller town. And you have to appreciate we are investing in an office …'

'Kicked out.' Mel stood up. 'My whole career would be buried by this move. I'd lose my lease, I'd lose touch with what was happening here in the hub. No. No way.' And what would her father think of this? He owned Thompson's, and while he was completely hands-off when it came to Mel, preferring his daughter to work her way up with no special treatment, even he would be unhappy with this turn of affairs, she was sure. He wouldn't want her to be shut down like this.

Sharon leant back comfortably in her chair, easily meeting Mel's eyes.

'Melody, it doesn't matter what you think the reason is. The fact of the matter is that I am offering you this position in Lillyford. It is a position of some significance and responsibility. I think you'll find that Lillyford is a new challenge, a change that you need. Think it over, and get back to me.'

Mel grimaced at the use of her full name. That was another reason she didn't like to meet with Sharon.

'I don't need to think. You can offer this to someone else. Try Tom. I'm sure he'd take it. I'm not interested.'

Sharon frowned slightly and nodded, looking less sure than she had for the whole meeting. She half reached out her hand, but Mel was firm. She stood, nodded her goodbye to Sharon, and left the office. She'd been clear. There was nothing Sharon could offer her that would make her want that job.

She hoped it would be offered to Tom. It would get him out of the office. He was so slimy, that man. She wondered whether he was behind this, whether it was his aim to get her out of the way so that he could get the promotion she was working for. You really had to watch your back, didn't you?

Picking up her bag, Mel grabbed her friend Evie by the arm.

'Evie, we're going for coffee.'

'But ...' Evie gestured at her computer.

'No buts. I need coffee now, and I need you. I'll help you finish anything you're working on but we need to go now.'

'Alright, if that's the way it is.' Evie grabbed her bag and stood up in one smooth movement. 'I'm always up for a coffee.'

The girls made their way through the cubicle maze to the door and down the stairs. The look on Mel's face made their co-workers duck out of her way and then exchange significant glances as she passed. Once they got to the pavement Mel sped up even more.

'Mel, slow down.' Evie whinged. 'I can't keep up. I've got new shoes on and I'm going to break an ankle at this pace.'

'Oh, sorry, I didn't even realise I was going fast. I'm just so angry.'

She waited, arms crossed, unconsciously tapping her fingers. Evie strolled maddeningly slowly, eventually catching up to the impatient Mel.

'Do you like them?'

'What?'

'My shoes! Aren't they gorgeous? Found them in a bargain bin on Saturday on my way to get groceries. I couldn't resist.'

Mel looked at Evie. She really was a picture, from her blonde Marilyn Monroe bob through her cherry-red dress with white polka dots to the matching shoes with the two-inch heels. But Evie needed to know, especially today, there was more to life than shoes.

'They're very nice.' Mel's voice was flat. 'And you never can resist.'

'But these, they're so gorgeous.' Evie was a little pouty.

'Sorry Evie.' Mel started walking again but at a slower pace this time. 'I just have more important things on my mind right now.'

'More important than shoes?'

Mel laughed, 'Yes, there are a few more important things than shoes out there. I know you find that hard to believe but wait until I tell you this news.'

'Out with it then.'

'Not until I get a coffee. This is going to need some unpacking.'

The girls found their favourite booth at the back of their usual store, and ordered their coffees—flat white for Mel, mocha with two sugars for Evie. Mel prepared to tell her story. Evie was the office gossip, but she was also Mel's oldest friend, and the person who brightened her day. Evie's presence at the neighbouring desk was sometimes the only thing that got her into the office on a Monday morning.

'OK, here's the news. She wanted to transfer me.'

'A promotion?'

'Nope. A demotion if you ask me. She wanted me to work in Lillyford. Lillyford!'

'Lillyford? But that's in Tasmania. I mean, you'd have to move. You can't commute from here, you need to fly. Or worse, take the ferry.'

'Exactly. That's why I turned her down.' Mel took a refreshing sip of her coffee.

'Turned her down?' Evie was wide-eyed.

'It would be career suicide. I would lose my apartment. I would lose my place in the office. And who would have employed me with months or years lost working out in the middle of nowhere? Who would take me seriously?'

'Surely it wouldn't be that bad. You've always said that you could do a better job if you were given more control. Maybe you can use this opportunity to prove it.'

'More control? Over what? I want to manage the office here, not fields of cabbages. I said no. They can give it to Slimy Tom. Get him out of the office.'

'You've never liked him, have you?' Evie sat back in her seat and took a sip of her sweet drink.

Mel shook her head. 'He's never liked me. He's a horrible man.'

'But a bit dishy, you've got to admit that.' Evie looked at Mel slyly.

'Evie, you and men. I don't have to admit that. What's inside shows on the outside. He's a nasty piece of work.'

'He's never been a problem for me. You and he just got off on the wrong foot.'

Mel lifted her cup to her lips and thought about it.

'You could be right. But I'm pretty sure he's been reporting every one of my little slip-ups to Sharon. He's been trying to get promoted to my position for ages. I'm sure he'll be happy to take the job if it's given to him as a promotion. He'll probably wangle a pay rise too.'

Evie shook her head.

'There wasn't a pay rise?'

'Nope. Just an assurance that life would be cheaper there. Not convinced. But anyway, I've said no.'

The two girls chatted and Mel felt her blood pressure falling. Eventually she drained the last of her coffee. 'Thanks for the chat Evie. I guess now I've turned Sharon down I'm going to have to work doubly hard to get anywhere in this place. But I'm sure I've done the right thing.'

'Of course you have.'

'And hopefully I've heard the last of this. I can't believe that Sharon thought I'd even think about it.'

The girls pulled themselves out of the booth.

'But Mel, more importantly, don't you think these are the most gorgeous shoes you've ever seen? You didn't really look at them before. Look how strappy they are, and red, too!'

Mel laughed. She felt much better.

'Yes, Evie, they are the most gorgeous shoes I've ever seen. Happy?'

Mel and Evie headed back to work, Mel happy to put this day and all thoughts of Lillyford behind her.

* * *

Find out more at rjamos.com

* * *